Fo

A Texan Affair (Volume 3)

Redemption

"Some natural tears they dropped, but wiped them soon;
The world was all before them, where to choose
Their place of rest, and Providence their guide;
They, hand in hand, with wandering steps and slow,
Through Eden took their solitary way."

- John Milton, Paradise Lost

"We walk alone upon this Earth.
Companions, those that we call friends,
Appear not friends at all, but rivals to this spurious plot.
Bereft, heeding them not, we move from hence,
And hearken to another voice,
A guide who, softly speaking from within,
Reminds us whence we came
And what we owe to Providence."

- Unknown

Copyright © 2024 by Richard Joyce
All rights reserved.

ISBN: 9798869142719

REDEMPTION

A Texan Affair – Vol.3

Richard Joyce

PART 1
(A PERFECT LIFE)

CHAPTER 1

'Looking for Benevolence'

William was more than usually preoccupied that morning. As he made his way through the mist in the park, to be at his Grandfather's bedside, two quite trivial co-incidents, call them moral inconsistencies, refused to leave him alone. His grandfather had led a good enough life and was, it seemed, finally on the way out. He'd cashed in his cards, and was leaving it to others to sort out the arrangements for his departure (and for *'others'*, William included loving friends and relatives on earth and a Loving Father in Heaven). Surely Grandfather deserved a little tenderness from that direction. Couldn't he quietly have passed on, as in the due course of things; no trumpets blaring, no distractions, upon which his well-wishers might stumble? The old man had reached a ripe old age, had led a good enough life, had all his papers tied up and in order, was leaving behind no unfinished business, no scores to settle, just a gentle step across the threshold and a little sadness remaining for those left behind.

But this wasn't quite the case. What first was troubling William was the random location selected for his progenitor's probable departure. By complete coincidence, the name of the Hospital they were laying him in, right now, today, the *'Savoy Hospital'*, carried the very same essential prefix as the Season Ticket Holders' Stand at the local football club, namely the *'Savoy* Stand'. Yes, by supreme irony, (call it perhaps divine irony) it was the Stand where the old man himself had spent so many long and joyful hours watching the fortunes of his favourite side. He'd probably even be able to hear, from his dreary bed, the raucous cheers emanating from the happy crowd that very same afternoon. So what were the odds against that? A million to one? The hospital could have been named anything else: *The Hospital of our Sacred Mother, The Churchill Memorial, The Franklin D Roosevelt Military Hospice.* But no, The *'Savoy'*. That final terminus, from which Grandfather was most likely to depart on his last journey, bore within it a glaring insult to all those, like William, bold enough to believe in purposeful logic or even just plain dignity. What kind of a god would allow such a shameful coincidence? *'In the midst of Life, we are in Death'.* True, maybe, but, dear reader, isn't this carrying the saying a little far?

And, as if this weren't unusual enough, another chance factor, trivial coincidence, had also played its part in Grandfather's final story. The trigger that had rushed him to the 'Savoy' had been neither a loss of appetite nor a slow decline; quite the reverse in fact: a culinary favourite of his throughout his long life; a *lamb cutlet* (a morsel which Grandfather had greedily devoured on numerous previous occasions) chose to attack his abdomen and become a murder weapon, as it quite unexpectedly got stuck in his gut. A million to one again. Why, if he had to go, couldn't he have just caught a chill which turned into bronchitis and then pneumonia, and hey presto. Or tripped on a loose rug and tumbled downstairs. It could even have been an alternative food-stuff: a lettuce leaf or a piece of cabbage sticking to the corners of his gluey mouth and suffocating him. But a gentle *lamb cutlet*, of all improbabilities.

Enough. If our world were this random, William concluded, then God is either dead, indifferent, or a jester (theories that had already, in his twenty-five years, not passed unnoticed). And who needs a jester at the moment of ones parting, to remind you how close lie the borderlines between joyful life and mysterious death? *In the midst of life we are in death*, as the saying goes. Isn't the moment bitter enough already?

William Bellman, 25, on the cusp of full maturity, 5ft 11, wiry, strong, free spirit, had over the past few years come to cherish the *'credo'* of a benevolent God at work in a well-ordered, logical universe. He'd long since recognised Logic, Order, Consistency, and above all Benevolence to be the corner stones of any serious religion, a concept well-suited, to his own positive temperament.. William was indeed a young man more prone to smile than to scowl, and expected no tricks from the heavens.

What was troubling him though that morning was the apparent absence of logic, and certainly of design, surrounding Grandfather's imminent death. There has to be Purpose, he thought, as he stared into the patches of mist blocking his way; there has to be a plan; both in heaven and on earth. Otherwise anarchy. Doesn't Mozart, in every sublime musical phrase, clearly proclaim the need for design and logic? Doesn't a beautiful Constable *landscape* portray harmony between land and sea, sky and earth? Didn't Eisenhower have a plan when he sent his troops across the Channel to liberate Europe? Of course.

Okay. These impenetrable conundrums of Causality and Probability stubbornly refused to leave William as he strode through the mist. However, like most of us, whose mood is often determined by the weather, William began to emerge from his welter of despair as he reached the other side of the Park, and as the sun came out. With it, he began to realize that perhaps there could indeed be a pleasing chain of deliberate and logical strands determining his being on his way to the hospital at all that morning. Hard facts that belied coincidence, a miracle almost. How then? Well, first, his mother's insistence: '*go and pay your respects, because you never know when it might happen, and think how you'd regret it...*' uttered in her usual matter-of-fact manner, without ever suspecting this would *really* be Grandfather's D-Day. Secondly, they - that's he, his mother, his Grandfather, all those main actors in this particular drama - were, by nature anyway, a part of that mysterious union called '*kith and kin*'. Shouldn't it be natural then for that same flesh and blood to want to close ranks at this time? That went beyond co-incidence; the circumstances demanded it.

But most significant of all, lay the truth that William had actually grown steadily fond of the old man as the years had passed - a rare circumstance when you think of all those old cousins, uncles, aunts who are quite often discarded from a young man's thoughts as he approaches manhood, and whose death-bed he might well be absent from. This process of neglect had never come between William and his Grandfather because they shared a mysterious bond of enthusiasm for the fortunes of the local football club. Old and young alike, they were sportsmen to the core, united by the ties that bind all supporters of no matter what, and on those long Saturday walks to the game, through the ancient Park beside the Canal, a fellowship had been cemented that would endure. And (one is compelled to ask) are not enduring relationships, after all, really at the heart of the matter, the thing that makes us human and go to funerals at all? Yes, it was against all the odds really, an imponderable working of destiny, which had brought him to this point. Be fair, are we not blessedly guided?

He was also of course thinking, with a tinge of sadness, how much he owed to his Grandfather's obvious affection towards him. Had it not been Grandfather (he knew this from his mother) who'd paid his considerable school fees all those years? Had it also not been he, several years ago, who'd presented him with a miniature cricket-bat, inscribed with a message: *always keep a straight bat through life*, to mark the scoring of his first century in a school match? Had he and Grandfather not, on innumerable Saturdays, walked together, sat together, watched together, commiserated together and rejoiced together at the performance of their side, and, more significantly, had Grandfather not let it be known, quietly and consistently, through all those four or five turbulent teenage years, that he was on William's side, shared much of the same history and genes as William, and thus couldn't really help loving him either, a natural love which his grandson had grown to reciprocate?

From their initial shared enthusiasm, it had been but a small step for the relationship to develop its own momentum and for the Saturday event to become more than just sport but real living, a routine. As they finally escaped from the scrum and scramble at the North Exit, came an invitation to tea, at which the teenager, would watch his grandfather haul the raspberry jam and bread from the space he chose to call the 'pantry', and then, painstakingly, butter the face of the loaf and cut the flimsiest slices William had ever witnessed, after which he'd lift down from the hooks on the dresser those giant blue cups and saucers decorated with figures of young girls in pretty frocks cavorting at a picnic, laid them out one at a time on the table, checked his gold watch, set the whole paraphernalia on the table, after which perfectly-timed rigmarole, the tea in the pot would have already been standing for its statutory five minutes, and was ready to be released into the waiting cups. Never a drop spilt; that would be like spilling the Communion wine. What a work of art, what a masterpiece was this whole procedure, honed in the workshop of time. Looking back, it seemed to William he were witness to some mysterious ritual, as if the old man had forgotten altogether how to improvise.

His Grandfather was indeed a meticulous man. William often wondered on those afternoons if those genes would pass down the line and make him meticulous too Tea drunk, they'd sit together then, facing each other across the bare wooden table and lament for the fifth time that afternoon the shortcomings of their team and the individual players in it, until, glancing at his watch, and as if answering some secret summons, Grandfather would quietly get up and say, *'Would you like to go in now and see your grandmother?'* He'd nod in the direction of the hallway and they'd proceed quietly to the drawing room, where his grandmother invariably sat, on the low sofa, gazing at the clock on the mantel-piece noisily ticking away the hours. It was William's turn to play his part in this *danse macabre*.

'Darling boy, you never come and see your old grandma.'

She'd hug him silently, encircling his neck and clutching his head against her meager, powder-scented bosom, while he stooped motionless, hardly daring to return the hug, lest the powdered shape below him break into a pile of brittle bones.

'Well, I'm here now, Grandma.'

A slight hesitation, before, *à propos* of nothing really, *'Would you like to take the cloth, dear boy?'*

No more than a whispered query, and instinctively William looked around him. 'I can't see a cloth, Grandma. But where would you like me to take it? The kitchen?'

'Don't tease your old grandma.' She'd raise her arms for another stolen hug, while it dawned on William the 'cloth', *'take the cloth'*, was a reference to a career in the Church.. Hastily he'd reply, *'No, Grandma, I don't believe I'll become a priest. I'm going to be a professional footballer. I'm going to take the shorts and singlet.'*

She wouldn't hear of that; her old brain couldn't take it in. 'Such a nice profession. A profession for a gentleman.'

'Yes, but risky. You could break a leg. Career could be ruined.'

She'd notice the grin. 'You *will* tease your old grandma, won't you.' She'd try to steal another powdery hug. 'Darling boy.'

On the first occasion of that whole rigmarole his surprise had been genuine; the other ninety-nine times, he just played along, a joke to lighten the moment's mood, and perhaps not without a slight tinge of malice. After all, hadn't his life, until this date, been one long, joyful round of jokes? At people, with people, for people? So why not this time too? For nothing was sacred to William, and smiles and jokes seemed to work to his advantage. People liked him well enough. He need never worry about that, because instinctively he knew he'd been handed the most precious gift of survival: *'the ability to be liked'*. What more do you need to make your way in life?

And at last his grandfather was taking him gently by the arm. 'Come on; your grandmother needs to get her afternoon rest. I'll see you out.'

Released. And out into a September evening, scented with the pungent smell of bonfire smoke, a strange, soporific odor in that peculiar garden, which he never ever remembered smelling again in his lifetime.

William left the Park behind and was now in C road, the one adjacent to the turntables that got you into the ground. He imagined he could hear the good-humored roar of the crowd, see the mounted police on their shuffling horses, hear again the blaring dance-music floating from the stadium through fuzzy speakers. He felt the need to remind himself he wasn't an excited young boy on his way to his own football game. Yes, how things had changed in the interim of those few short years; a far cry now from the innocent days of raspberry jam and thinly cut slices. He was jobless, fatherless (but hadn't that always been so?), even his religion was an errant ship, a distant speck on a hazy horizon, and already his eager expectations of youth, those lofty goals he'd once set for himself, were shrinking fast.

Worse though, he was starting, just faintly, to call into question the wonderful relationship with the wonderful girl who'd held him so obsessed for many weeks. It wasn't that he was tiring of her, nor that she was tiring of him; quite the contrary. But he'd begun to discover that relationships with girls entail hidden agendas. Prices have to be paid. Nothing comes for free in the enchanting world of the emotions, and in the nicest possible way, Ingrid's concern for his current lack of drive and motivation was starting to become intrusive. Yes, Ingrid actually seemed more worried than he was about his current apathy. *'William, my love, don't - how you say? - moan. Just do something, Anything.'*

William was secretly starting to wonder if he could live up to it all. She was, to him, still lovely and he still loved her, but his brief, blind, thoughtless passion was already being replaced by that all-too-common phase when cold reason and hesitation begin, ever so slightly, to temper ardent heat. He'd more than once found himself falling back onto a phrase he'd come across in some fashionable Jewish text called *'Desiderata'*. *"Be kind to your body"*. Yes, that seemed to him increasingly an excellent phrase; it suited his temperament to a tee. He *was* kind to himself, didn't believe in overdoing things, while Ingrid, on the other hand, sailed through life like a self-respecting, hard-working swan, expecting nothing less from the people she'd invested in. She was neither kind to herself, nor was she kind to him. William often wondered these days why desirable girls like Ingrid apparently pursued an interior monologue whose undeclared aim was to invent, to summon up 'the perfect human', in much the same way as a car salesman might lavish praise upon his automobile product: *"Easy on fuel, good acceleration, five-year warranty, automatic gear change, ABS braking"*. Except that in this case, he, William, was the 'Hyperion'.

All that flattery Ingrid could lavish on him in the course of a day, those admiring glances, those little remarks, inserted to boost ones self-esteem. Hooked up with Ingrid was like being a Siamese twin: you were no longer just your own person. What nutrition you put into yourself had to feed her too. It was an awesome responsibility. Nevertheless, in rare moments of clarity, he still couldn't deny, she might just succeed in saving him from himself.

How polite she'd been that afternoon - it was a mere few weeks back, but didn't feel like it - when she'd met Grandfather herself, unexpectedly in fact, as he peered down from the top of the staircase. 'I see you're having a celebration,' he'd piped from the top of the stairs.

'Pity you couldn't have told me!' There was an edge of disgruntlement in his tone.

Ingrid had been well primed though. On her best behavior. 'I hear you paint, Mr. Riley. I'm Ingrid, a friend of William's.' She'd thrust out an elegant arm.

'Very pleased to meet you,' said the old man, as charming and polite as it had always paid him to be throughout his long career as a super-salesman.

'I'd love to see some of your work, sir.'

Who now was the greater charmer? The old man had been deeply flattered by this interest. 'I'd be pleased to show you, although I'm having a spot of bother with the clouds.'

Since the death of his wife, Grandfather had lived with them in the family house, and William's mother, Tessa, had conceived the brilliant plan of reviving the old man's interest in painting, something to occupy him through the long twilight days. She'd bought a paint-by-numbers kit along with an easel, a leisure innovation from '*Boots*', and now the old man only ever came down in order to eat his meals greedily and pass a few unnecessary comments on his daughter-in-law's house-keeping, or rather lack of it.

William remembered how, that late afternoon, he and Ingrid had followed the tiny figure up the stairs and into the large, dreary room - part of an earlier extension - where Grandpa spent most of his time, cut off from the rest of the house. A double-bed, a marble wash-basin, a gas-fire, an easel over by the window, all attempting in vain to offset the general drabness.

They crossed to look at the half-finished painting and watched as the old man attempted hesitantly a brush-stroke or two, obliterating the tiny black printed numbers that crawled like ants over the shiny paper.

'Never have been able to get clouds right.'

'The clouds look all right to me, Grandpa,' said William cautiously, and then, as if an afterthought, 'Whatever happened to those two oil paintings?'

'Which ones would they be, William?' His Grandfather's sharp eyes searched him, seeking to force an error from him.

'You know, the two on the wall at your old house. With the names on the back.'

His Grandfather had looked perplexed. Tired and perplexed. 'Can't say I remember any oil paintings with names on the back.'

It was a family mystery though, sort of folk-lore. The paintings supposedly, Gainsborough style, had been accomplished back in Grandfather's own youth and were to be passed down from generation to generation. But, like many family myths, the original truth had become shrouded in the mists of time. 'The ones that hung on the wall at your last home,' William prompted. 'When I used to visit, remember?'

Finally, as if clawing back an unwanted memory, 'Ah, those ones. Yes, I got those clouds fairly well right.'

Had he really known at that moment? William wondered. Or was he just play-acting? Ingrid was digging him in the ribs, clearly wanting to drag him away. 'Let's go. I think your Grandpa's tired.'

William knew better than to persist with his line of questioning. The old man had returned dispiritedly to the easel but, as he and Ingrid reached the downstairs floor, William couldn't resist remarking to her, 'God, what a wreck! What a waste of talent! Those paintings were good.'

He'd anticipated either confirmation or refutation from Ingrid, but instead got neither. The old man's former artistic pretensions, he realized, meant little to her, in spite of her best efforts. Nor did they really to him any longer. No more than just a loss. The part of his Grandfather that remained though, and that he loved, was still the part that cut thin slices of bread. No one could take the memory of that distant ritual away from either of them.

The hospital lay ahead now at the end of the road. William entered the subdued corridors. On the indicator board, he found 'GERIATRICS', and made his almost timid way to the third floor. "Geriatrics" was like "Calisthenics", he thought, names quite unsuitable for the activities they described. Why should someone choose such a heady word of Greek origin to describe the state of 'Being Old'? *To conceal perhaps, behind verbal jiggery-pokery, the appalling finality of that state,* was all he could come up with. There was no leaving from the place marked

"GERIATRICS". "*Abandon hope, all ye who enter here.*" William was not looking forward to this visit, hoping he'd quickly find a way out.

No one stood sentinel on the large, double-doors of the ward. He'd half expected at least a nurse, if not a spectral messenger from the grim boatman, '*Charon*'. So he wandered in alone. But how was he to recognize his kith and kin amid so much duplicated morbidity? He stood in front of a long ward with giant beds, each holding tiny figures scarcely denting their enormous cumulus pillows. In vain William wandered up and down, searching if only for a name, and was on the point of leaving, duty done, when he recognized his dear relative's sloping forehead and unmistakably protuberant, beaky nose. At least those features had endured the laying out. No clever concealing of a nose for the sake of uniformity.

Timidly he approached the bed of his progenitor, who, unseeing and almost enveloped in pillows, stared relentlessly at the ceiling, eyes fixed upon a spot beyond time. William leaned gently down towards the transfixed head, put his lips close to its ear, and whispered as calmly as he knew how, 'The team won again on Saturday, Grandpa. Beat Reading 2 – 1.'

But if the patient heard, he failed to register astonishment or delight. William redoubled his efforts. 'You remember 'Reading', Grandpa? How many times have you and I watched our team play Reading? The arch rival? Ten at least. It was always the one match you never could forecast. I don't mean 'you'; I mean either of us. Two towns so demographically and geographically similar. It must have been that which always made it such an exciting game.'

The résumé had equally little effect. Try again. 'Lofty Gregson apparently banged home the winner with five minutes to go'

No. Nothing. William turned away. It was useless. He might just as well not have come. And then he became aware of something light on his bare forearm, growing firmer and more painful by the second, until it transformed into the agonizing claws of a prize desert scorpion. A skeletal hand from the bed, clutching his forearm with desperate force. He turned, wincing. 'Stop it, Grandpa. You're hurting.'

But now a sound was rising from his progenitor's throat, a murmuring made almost unrecognizable, certainly unintelligible, by its rasping urgency. 'They took my money, my boy. If you were ever dear to me, avenge me. It was under my bed. But when I last looked, it had gone. And the documents with it. The documents: One, two, three, four, five, six, seven documents. Stewart and Archibald and Rosemary. Never could trust them. But *you*, I can trust. I know you're a good boy. Always were. You'll get it back for me, won't you? I'm going to be in need of it shortly. And don't forget the documents.'

William's Grandfather had almost hauled his fragile frame out from beneath the duvet, was almost standing on the bed, such was the urgency of this unexpected request. The outburst had triggered a low moan throughout the ward, as of people awaking grumblingly from sleep.

'But we don't know anybody called Archibald,' asserted William as urgently as he could muster. 'I don't know what you're talking about, Grandpa.'

The old man mumbled vigorously for a few moments and then shrank back again into the pillows. The moaning along the ward continued unabated though. William, shocked into inertia at first by the whole experience, was galvanized back into action by these sounds in unison, emanating, seemingly, from the Gates of Hell. Tenderly massaging his forearm, he hurried to the end of the ward, where he almost bumped into a staff nurse, presumably summoned by the low humming. She smiled briefly at William. 'Sounds like a beehive in there.' Then, regarding William more attentively, 'What's going on? Who are you?'

'I've been paying a visit to my grandfather.' William jerked his thumb over his shoulder. 'He's in the bed over there.'

'Name please.'

'Bellman. William Bellman.'

'We don't have anybody by the name of William Bellman in here,' said the nurse abruptly.

'No, that's *my* name. I've come to see my grandfather. His name's Riley. Eric Riley.'

'You don't have the same names?'

'No, I use my mother's name.'

She raised an eyebrow and consulted her notes. 'We have nobody by the name of Riley in here either, my dear. I think you'd better be going.'

'But my grandfather,' said William.

'We *had* a Riley,' said the nurse. 'But I'm afraid he passed on last Thursday.'

'Then who was that?' said William indicating back into the ward. 'He seemed in distress.'

'I'm sure I don't know, if I don't know what bed you're referring to.' William led the nurse back to the bed he'd fled from. 'Ah, Mr. Givens. That'll be Mr. Givens.' She approached the bed, gave a low whistle, felt under the covers for a moment, extracted a bony wrist, held it for a few seconds, and deftly pulled down the eyelids of the former Mr. Givens. 'I think you'd better accompany me, Mr. Bellman,' she said, looking into his pale face with a face almost as pale.

For someone who was, by nature, fond of fun and laughter, this whole particular *faux pas* didn't hold too much significance for William, After all, as the prophet says, '*God moves in mysterious ways his wonders to perform*', and so, beyond of course a tinge of sadness for his grandpa's parting, he quickly brushed the moment off. His grandfather had had the last laugh. Okay. The Deity didn't at least lack a sense of humour then. Just one more of Life's little practical jokes.

CHAPTER 2

*'In which William establishes his own Church
and discovers a Golden Egg'*

Humans are patently not a perfect species. They make mistakes. Groups of humans make group mistakes. Leaders of groups of humans make mistakes that are distorted at times into horrific and awe-inspiring errors. It's a law of nature and no amount of banter and clichés such as *'collective wisdom'* and *'in unity is strength'* will change it. Call it *'The Principle of the Many'*. Of course, it doesn't seem either fair or logical that we should be lumbered with this inconvenient trait, but it's unfortunately true. Another of life's practical jokes in fact.

What Grandma, (nor Grandpa, nor even his loving mother), never knew, about this stringy adolescent called William who'd been so fascinated by his Grandpa's bread slicing, was that this boy had recently, quite inadvertently and instinctively, stumbled on *'The Church of One'*, a Church devoid of any clumsy 'groups' at all. This of course explains why he was able to tell his Grandma with such certainty, that he *wasn't* going to 'take the cloth' - no, because, in fact, *'The Church of One'* contains no cloths, nor any other diversions and distractions that seem these days inevitably glued to the common Orthodox Faith: no Acolytes, Priests, Temples, Vestments, Robes, Hierarchies, Texts, Histories, Hymns, Icons, Relics, Prayer Books, Ecclesiastical Rules; no, there are only two simple, sacred tenets in *'The Church of One'*: (1) *commune directly with your Maker by original thought and prayer*, (2) *bear your conscience on your own back, and assume full responsibility for all your shortcomings*.

Wow! Bingo! Leaping lizards! Was ever, in the history of the world, an institution so simple and virgin pure? And it cannot but be certain that when God's own Son departed this wicked world and left behind Him instructions for the foundation of a 'Church on earth', His vision surely wasn't a church of mere bricks and mortar, but a living church, namely *'The Church of One'*.

Alas though, followers in those early days were scared; they were persecuted, and fed to brutish lions, and, for safety's sake (if not necessarily Truth's sake), they formed into confusing 'groups', and so, the humble voices of those brave disciples, martyrs, early Christians ceased to be heard amongst the clamour and conflicting demands of a million mindless followers, and yes, the ONE principle lost its way, to be superseded by a veritable 'Tower of Babel': strange tongues, strange beliefs, conflicting credos, all claiming to have met God, and all too numerous to be true. Yes, as the centuries drew on, the 'ONE principle' was smothered, and the *pure* Voice became tainted with half-truths and even downright lies. And so on and so on and so on.... Right down to this present day. Oh dear! What a fall was there! And if we are wise, honest, humble enough to draw conclusions from disasters, we must accept that the single most important mistake human kind ever made (or makes) in spiritual matters is to convert the '*One*' into the '*Many*': the many Clubs, Committees, Gatherings, Assemblies, Businesses, Firms and all such Groups that claim to manage our spiritual affairs, improve our lives, show us the true way. Beware, since even the very early Church, and all such Groups, are fatally flawed, will proliferate, will rise and fall, come and go, will be defeated and replaced by others, equally flawed. WE HAVE TO WORK ALONE....

Let's put it to the test. Does anyone really believe that a great work of Art generated by the creative spirit, Man's highest accomplishment, can be achieved by a Group? No, it cannot. Let's watch a couple of da Vinci's painter friends standing by the easel, as Leonardo struggles to finish one of his most famous works.

> *'I think you've got the wrong shade of brown for the lady's dress, Leonardo. Surely it's got to match her hair. Should be lighter....'*

> *'Darker, my dear Botticelli, darker not lighter. D'you want to extinguish the lady's features altogether?'*

'Listen, Angelo, you're just plain wrong, I think you're going colour blind in fact. Must be that cherub fresco you're working on in the Sistine. Too dark to see anything up there. Terrible light.'

'If I'd painted them lighter they'd have been invisible. Nothing to do with the light in the Sistine; it's just that **you** paint everything too light. For example, that Venus of yours looks like a ghost....'

'Sticks and stones, Angelo. How about we ask the artist here himself. Leonardo, what do you think?'

'I think bollocks to you both, and why don't you go get yourselves a plate of spaghetti, my treat. Mona and I'll finish this job alone thanks...'

Yes, *alone*. How wise da Vinci was. And if you're still not convinced, let's watch another little tableau Let's join the small group round the billiard table as Mozart labours to complete the final movement of Piano Concerto No.9, K271.

'You sure that C flat fits here, Herr Mozart?'

'It may not fit, Ludwig, but it's right. Believe me.'

'Sounds to my ear you need a C sharp, not a C flat.'

'Ja, Herr Beethoven, I have to be honest I think Wolfie's absolutely right, you know. He's already modulated down a 7th. The phrase is crying out for a flat. Are you sure you aren't going a bit deaf?'

'I'm sure of one thing, Herr Schubert, and that is, Wolfgang didn't invite you round to criticise; listen and learn from the Master. It's upstarts like you who...'

> *'Um Gottes Willen, meine Herren!* Give me a bit of peace. This last movement's already taken me quarter of an hour and it's got to be finished before Constanza gets back and asks me to put a shelf up in the kitchen.. Anyway, Ludwig, young Franz here may be right about the deafness. Didn't I hear you've got an appointment with an ear specialist? *Gott im Himmel, auf Wiedersehen!'*

Poor Beethoven. It's a wonder he struggled on alone with his failing health. But they of course were Titans in those days, in their lonely struggle with the tools of their trade. Yes, we can see, in the matter of artistic creation, even just two is too many, and three's a crowd. And, *um Gottes Willen*, if the principle holds good for Art, surely it must also apply to even more significant spiritual endeavours, such as Man's Communicating with his Maker: that most precious of all spiritual jewels. No groups, no pack-drill. And so it is….

But let's not forget, at the time of the strange events that set William on his path of initiation (which narrative I will shortly relate), the young lad had no inkling of this rationale that accounts for Man's sorry fall from grace, this '*Group'* obsession. A teenage boy's thoughts lie elsewhere. It was, on the contrary, simply with a naïve heart and a fair helping of common sense that William became the founder of ONE.

(Go back now, dear Reader, ten years in time and in William's life…)

****

CHAPTER 3

*"Remember now thy Creator in the days of thy
youth, while the evil days come not..."*

William, teenager, stomach full, inconspicuous among the other rowdy boys emerging from the dining-hall, waited in the windy divide that separated one half of the school's giant edifice from the other. He was expecting his mate (mate but not necessarily friend), whom we shall call T, and who was scheduled to emerge from the giant doors of the school chapel at any minute. Half an hour previously, T had approached William in the dining-hall with the hurried words: '*Willy, wait for me after dinner in the Divide; something I want to ask you,*' and had run off muttering under his breath (deliberately audible enough for his friend to hear) '*Got to tidy up the Vestiary again; two minutes notice; it's always the same...taking advantage... But don't forget to wait....*'

William had felt something slide gently under his heart as T had uttered what had sounded more like a command than a request. They were just mates after all, not friends; they owed each other no favours. He and T had, for two long years, stuck together through thick and thin, done the hard pubertal slog, wandered around the draughty passageways and confines of the school, arms linked inseparably round each other's shoulders. However, in recent days William had noticed a change; things weren't quite what they'd always been; T's behaviour was more erratic, more unpredictable; he'd dart off into little corners of the building when they were strolling together, and emerge 15 minutes later, a satisfied expression on his face, as if he'd just fulfilled one of the Ten Commandments. William was puzzled and unnerved, until it finally became apparent that his comrade was branching off, (*had already* 'branched off') into that most taboo of all areas for teenage boys, namely *Religion*. And worse too, it was possible his mate - one year older than William anyway and thus a year above him in the school hierarchy, was trying to drag *him* in too? Religion was for cissies.

That's not to say William was intolerant of religious institutions, or, like *Saul of Tarsus*, actively persecuted those who might demonstrate signs of interest. He was simply of the opinion religion was really for adults, not something that need concern him for a while longer. In fact, without ever admitting it to anyone, he secretly enjoyed much of the Chapel ritual: the organ, the joyful anthems of the choir at Evensong, the readings from the great Book, even some of the better sermons, which, on a cold January evening, could be quite amusing. But it was those sonorous and evocative words, scattered like a flock of birds in amongst the verses of the English Hymnal, that seriously thrilled him. "*In simple trust like theirs who heard, beside the Syrian Sea...*". An image, for example, as clear and pure to him as if he were standing in front of a giant oil canvas at the National Gallery. Where was this mysterious *Syrian Sea*? What fundamental truth lay behind this *simple trust*? So, emerging from Chapel each weekday morning, as he made his way into the chill Rutland mist and the stuffy classroom, he might take with him other images of warm and distant lands and the legendary deeds of those simple men who inhabited such places. At Evensong too, the choir would sometimes sing particularly stirring anthems, one especially that overpowered him: "*Be careful for nothing; but in everything, by prayer and supplication with thanksgiving, let your requests be made known unto God....*" The words, combined with the music, were stamped there without equivocation right into next morning, wrapped in such lyrical beauty that who could resist or fail to understand its gentle message? What's more, it often occurred to William that all these wondrous, sensual experiences had little relevance to the seemingly stark, message of Religion itself anyway, but concealed something else, some altogether different, profounder meaning, one which his own inadequate experience of life had not yet primed him to understand. Had his mate, T, sensed that 'something else' as well? William doubted it. Why else would he choose to dress up absurdly in a frock-like garment on Sunday mornings, and parade with base humility through the pantomime they called Communion? That whole paraphernalia was nothing less than an insult to the comradely defiance of their young years.

The shock of frizzy, unruly hair was the first thing William saw now, as T emerged from the giant doors of the Chapel. A larger than large head, followed by two glinting eyes, expressing all too well their contentment at the sight of William waiting there obediently for him. 'They held an unscheduled Communion service. No one told me.' The thinly-disguised frustration, the hurt, jerked from T, as he remembered how he'd been overlooked, and only hauled in at the last minute. 'I'd been planning to write that blessed essay.'

However, no further moaning spilled from T's lips. That was it. Who was he to hold it against his masters? His lot was always to go above and beyond the call of duty.

'What did you want to see me about, T? It's cold out here.'

William's frailty stood exposed for the pettiness it was, as T chose to ignore his friend's whingeing, choosing instead to allow a condescending smile to steal across his rugged face. 'It's hardly what you'd call cold, Willy. Anyway, let's get into the cloisters if you're so freezing.'

William was led helplessly to somewhere warmer and left standing for a moment, waiting for an answer to his query. Then T moved even closer to him than usual. 'They'd like you to be an acolyte, Will,' he whispered.

William's heart leaped into his mouth. Although he didn't know what an acolyte was, he'd a pretty good idea of what it might be. Something churchy.

He blurted out, 'What's an acolyte?'

'You know. What I do. In Chapel. Sundays. Surely you're not going to tell me you don't know what an acolyte is.' That was the trouble with T these days: his feigned patience and apparent long-suffering. He was tolerant though with everyone else except him..

'D'you mean a server?'

'Yes, a server. What else?' The deliberate hint of impatience flailed William as if it were a whip. 'Acolyte is the official name for those who serve at the Offertory.'

'Is it? I didn't know that.' William was stalling. 'And that's what *you* do?'

'That, among other things. Prepare the Offertory for the Communicant. It's a commitment, Willy.'

William summoned up all his strength. 'I'm not sure then.'

'Not sure of what?'

'Of what you just asked me to do.'

'Why not? It's a privilege to be asked, a joy to be wanted.'

'I'm busy at the moment,' was all William could manage.

'Busy with what?' T was now at his most humiliating, allowing his mate to realise he was letting slip a life-changing opportunity. 'If you take my advice, you'll at least think about it.'

At the end of the embarrassing pause that followed, William said, 'Who's '*they*', T?'

'What d'you mean?'

'You said: '*they*' would like me to be.... Don't you remember?'

"'They' is the Chaplain, the Headmaster, the other acolytes...how many more high-ups do you want?' T could no longer conceal his impatience. He was letting rip. 'God himself perhaps?'

William ignored the sarcasm. 'But why? Why me?'

'They've been observing you.'

There was sense of relief in William's reply. 'Oh yes, then it's probably just because they've seen me and you together often enough...' His voice trailed off as he realised his remark was absurd and that, true or not, it would make not the slightest difference to '*they's*' intentions.

'Many are called but few are chosen, you know.' T glanced now at his watch. 'Listen, I've gotta go. I can't stand and argue all night. I've got an essay to write.' As he headed off at a brisk pace, he called over his shoulder, 'It's not me who's asking you, anyway. It's the masters. Don't look a gift horse in the teeth.'

'*It's mouth, not teeth,*' William shouted back in a rare display of defiance, but T was already striding away down the cloister, leaving William to grapple alone with his inadequacies. At the end of the cloister, T stopped. 'I'll give you a night to think about it. Okay? I'll ask you once more tomorrow, and then I won't ask you ever again. Let me know what your decision is.'

'*No,*' William was thinking, as he watched his former mate disappear. '*No, I'm not going to be one of those goody-goodies who heap un-said derision upon themselves. No way.'* He knew T would be there next morning at breakfast, expecting an answer.

But he wasn't. Instead, the ultimatum came in a note scribbled on a scrap of paper as William was sitting down in his carrel for Prep that same evening. *"Meet after Prep tomorrow. Pincher's room. Don't be late."*

Pincher was the chaplain. They all called him that; nobody really knew why. William's agonising decision had been postponed then, not cancelled. But like a condemned man, he was ready to clutch at any straw, and this new initiative might yet offer reprieve, no matter what *'they'* got up to after Prep tomorrow in the chaplain's room. He'd go, head held high, reputation still fully intact as yet.

He did his best to avoid T next day, and, after Prep, made his way up the rickety wooden steps to the remote corner of the opposite wing of the school, where Pincher dwelt. From the little room came the sound of lively chatter. That couldn't just be the chaplain and T. It sounded like a roomful. William knocked and a piping voice called 'Enter'.

There were seven of them in all, crowded into the tiny box-room. Seated on the floor, two younger boys like himself, whom William recognised from their Sunday presence at the high altar, along with T and a larger boy, sprawled in one of the two armchairs, and on a high-backed chair that barely held his bulky frame, another boy from his own dorm, the very same sixth-former in fact who'd strangely come to sit on his bed two nights previously, without any apparent motive other than to chat in a monotonous whisper about boring things such as parents, family, his father's job, until William had mercifully nodded off.

'Ah, William. At last,' proclaimed Pincher 'We've all been waiting. Come and make yourself comfortable. There's a small space, I think, beside the other two down there. But then, you're only a slip of a thing, aren't you. I'm sure you'll find room.'

'Yes, sir,' was all William could think to utter by way of reply, puzzled by the Chaplain's turn of phrase: 'a slip of a thing', which hardly matched the circumstances; he had in fact surprised himself that term with the ever-increasing length of his legs and the gradual disappearance of his knobbly knees.

'We're all having coffee and biscuits,' the high-pitched voice announced, 'and discussing the reading in chapel last Sunday evening. I wonder, William, if you remember the reading. Would you like a biscuit, by the way?'

'No, sir.'

'Oh dear. They're very nice. Chocolate Digestives. I must say a growing boy like you needs all the sustenance he can get.' There were twitters of laughter from among the rest of the group.

'No, sir, I mean, *yes*, I'd like a biscuit, but *'no'*, I don't remember the chapel reading.'

The twitters burst into a full-blown guffaw.

'Ah. David, pass William a digestive will you. Well now, we certainly shouldn't be getting digestives mixed up with Ecclesiastes, should we?' There was a slight pause before Pincher continued, 'I must say, I think a growing boy needs all the *spiritual* sustenance he can get too, doesn't he? I know T here thinks so.' He indicated William's mate and continued, 'I'm sure everyone in this room would love to see you putting on a *spiritual* spurt to match the *physical* one you're so evidently managing.' He addressed his audience. 'Wouldn't you agree everyone?'

There were half-hearted nods from everyone in the room. In the pause that followed, William had an inspiration. 'Sir, what *was* the reading about in chapel?'

Pincher's eyes lit up. 'Ah, that's more like it, lad,. I'm glad to see you're taking an interest in matters more than just biscuits. Does anybody by chance remember the lesson?'

T remarked, 'I think it was from Ecclesiastes, sir.'

'Thank you, T. I think we've already established that.' Pincher produced an ingratiating smile. 'However, can anyone else throw more light on the subject?'

'Wasn't it something about 'evil days', sir?' It was the older boy slumped in the armchair.

'It was,' pronounced Pincher, 'it was indeed. David, I've had a good idea. Why don't you read us a couple of verses? To refresh all our memories.' David looked for a moment totally lost. 'There, take my bible.' Pincher handed him the small bible perched on his knees. 'Ecclesiastes Chapter 12 verse 1.'

David fumbled for a minute and then read out haltingly, *"Remember now thy Creator in the days of thy youth, while the evil days come not, nor the years draw nigh, when thou shalt say, I have no pleasure in them;"*

'Such a beautiful passage,' exclaimed Pincher. 'Thank you, David. And so beautifully read too. Remind me to put you in for the national Reading Prize later in term.' He sat back, Bible freshly perched on his knee. 'Now, I'm sure those few lines need no further explanation.' Silence followed, before Pincher added, with firm deliberation, '*Do they?*' Another pregnant silence while Pincher waited for a response that didn't come. He answered directly his own question, leaning carefully on each word: '*Don't – leave – things – too – late*. That is the message for this evening.' Still smiling graciously, he sat back in his chair, crossed his legs and switched his gaze back to William. 'Well now, William. As you may have already gathered, our small group meets here at about the same time each week for a little, shall we say, spiritual refreshment.' He leant into the final two words like a good conductor placing emphasis on some particularly important phrasing, and before dramatically concluding, 'We'd all be most pleased if you'd care to join us.'

William was not good at thinking quickly on his feet, but somewhere at the back of his mind he realized Pincher's suggestion was nothing less than T's proposal of the previous day dressed up in different clothing, and that he needed somehow to say 'no' politely.

'Um...I am very busy, Chaplain....History test...'

'We're all very busy in our own respective paths,' came the Chaplain's jovial reply.

An inspiration flipped into William's head from some unknown source. 'The orchestra's got a concert coming up and we have a rehearsal at this time every evening, sir.'

For just a brief moment, the expression of patient beneficence was wiped from Pincher's face, to be replaced with a look that can only be described as thinly malevolent, as if he'd found something in his coffee. 'How very disappointing; I'll have to see what I can arrange with the music master. I'm sure the orchestra can't be rehearsing seven days a week, non-stop.' The brief moment of his annoyance however had quickly passed, to be replaced by a gracious smile. 'We were all looking forward so much to your joining our group, weren't we boys?' Some eager grunts acknowledged the question. 'In fact, I was hoping to put to you another important proposal.' He paused. 'I'd be particularly pleased if you'd consider becoming an acolyte in Chapel. Like the rest of the boys here.' A beaming smile followed the suggestion. 'Sign up for the team, as they say.'

'Could I think about it, sir?'

'Of course you could. But don't take too long. Such golden opportunities come but once in a young man's life. It's a privilege, William, to be asked.'

William nodded gravely and replied, with as much earnest as he could muster, 'I'll think hard about it then, sir.'

The session mercifully came to a close with bonhomie and joviality, even relief, as the large body of boys jostled to find their way through the low doorway and down the rickety steps that led from the room. '*Good night, sir. Thank you very much*' was the general call in chorus, and Pincher, by the doorway himself as the boys struggled past, stood with head bowed, intoning, '*See you all next week, and may the Lord go with you.*' And William, from within the main crush, and as it came to his turn to pass close by the Chaplain, was certain he felt a slight pinch on his behind. It was all over in a second.

The burly boy, David, came the following two nights, sitting on William's bed after lights out, his large bum pressing the slim mattress down so that its sides disappeared annoyingly into the frame of the bed. His monotonous voice droned quietly on and on until William, feeling through the blankets the big boy's hand pressing on his knee, fell fast asleep.

Nothing happened for a week and William was starting to believe, with great relief, that this unexpected tidal wave had passed harmlessly over him, when the boy came again to his bedside, this time with a renewed sense of urgency in his mission. His hands were all over William's huddled shape under the blankets and he talked about the fun they enjoyed as acolytes, and the secret privileges that came with the job. William, half asleep, tried in vain to block out the monotonous monologue. 'You're missing out, William, if you don't join us in the Chapel group. You even get to drink some of the communion wine, lovely stuff, and hog some wafers. Pincher's pretty generous with the biscuits too at bible class.' William felt himself nodding off again, until the intruder's voice came out of the darkness with increased urgency and impatience. 'Look, William, it's bloody cold out here; why don't you come down to my bed and we can just get warm together. Come on.'

It *was* cold, he was right; the blankets weren't sufficient to keep out the icy wind from the open windows of the dorm. The boy stood up abruptly, his large shape looming now above William. 'Come on.'

William, over the months, had grown accustomed to obeying a voice, *any* voice, of command. He quietly got out of bed and padded across the floor-boards, towards the Senior's section, as if under some hypnotic spell. He slid under the boy's blankets, and for a while, lay inert, aware though of hesitant fumbling here and there. Despite his engrained response to authority, another voice on another level was racing in his sleepy head: '*Is this Sex? Is this what I watched at the cinema? The man and the girl? It must be...but it isn't; it's not the same. There's no girl.*' Combined with this hazy reasoning, there was a missing component: the sensation of excitement, which he always remembered feeling on those infrequent, illicit visits to the cinema. But here, with this sweaty, cumbersome individual beside him; he felt entirely unmoved emotionally. Yes, that was it. He arrived at it in a flash: Sex is a game for two; the other party in this clumsy rigmarole was lacking.

The larger boy's hand had grasped William's, and was compelling it downwards towards him. 'Come on, William,' he whispered. 'It's just a bit of fun.' And the next moment William, that naïve and indecisive teenager, saw, in a vivid pageant, his life and all that lay promised, threatened now at a meeting point somewhere beneath the duvet on his bed.

'What are you doing, David?'

'Come on. It's just a bit of fun. Everybody does it.'

That explanation sat starkly before William for a few indecisive seconds, before he jerked his whole frame up and out of the bed. 'Not me. I 'm not everybody. I don't want to. I'm going back to *my* bed. Okay?'

And, stepping silently over the polished floorboards, he returned to his own icy bed. No real, irreparable damage apparently done to that delicate mechanism which was his soul. He wrapped the covers tight round him, as though a talisman against further intrusions, and remained thinking disdainfully, *'How can it be fun?'* while his customary deep and peaceful sleep washed over him.

About two weeks later, T, whom he'd seen little of since the evening with Pincher, slid alongside him in one of the passageways. 'William, would you like to come down to the Crypt? We can pray together.'

'The Crypt?' (William was becoming adept at dodging difficult moments by repeating words or phrases). 'What is there to pray for?'

T couldn't resist a snapping response. 'Your stubbornness for one.'

And then, with the finality of a stone dropping into a pond, William suddenly felt, as with the other evening. no inclination to go anywhere at all with this demanding once- friend of his. Admittedly, for old time's sake, though, and for those days of innocence they'd spent together, he refused T's request kindly, and watched the boy stomp angrily out of his life. For sure, they'd meet as team-mates on triumphant games fields for two more years yet, but the fierce, shared intimacy of age 15 had ceased forever to exist.

However, the seed planted that day by T, the exhortation to *'go pray'*, didn't go away so easily, and germinated in William's mind, growing like the distant glimmer of a light that steers a vessel home to port, until some weeks later William went AWOL in a free period towards the end of that long 5th form year, and headed down to the dark and dusty Crypt beneath the Chapel, a place untrammelled through the ages either by heavy passage of footsteps or the rowdy spirits of youth,. And it was down there, in the murky darkness, that William laboriously founded the Church of ONE.

Strange how random events, no matter how apparently insignificant, can converge at one and the same moment on a person's spiritual development, on the process indeed of growing up. William, around about this same time, had received a communion present from a loving Godmother, a small book entitled *'The Life of Jesus'*, which included colourful and skilfully-drawn pictures showing Jesus in various well-known scenes from the New Testament. A tall, bearded man in middle-eastern robes, with long, well-groomed hair, a face more European than Arabic, an expression exuding endless compassion. As he lay idly on his bed during the hols, William had read the book from cover to cover, captivated by the pictures and this unusually homely version of such dramatic and earth-shattering events, which, until now, he'd only encountered in the 'Lessons' in Chapel.

Armed with this gift from his Godmother, the stories, the coloured depictions of Jesus in action, along with other random memories of stained-glass windows in churches, plus a recently-heard homily delivered in School Chapel: *"Ask, and it will be given unto you; seek, and you will find; knock, and it will be opened to you"*, William pushed the heavy door open and entered the Crypt on that dramatic morning.

Almost like a sleep-walker, he placed himself in a kneeling position at a wooden railing circumventing the altar on three sides, and fixed his gaze on a spot to his immediate left, the nearest corner of the rail. There, still vaguely mindful of the drawings in the book, and with as much fervor as his untrained mind could bring to bear, he attempted to summon the physical presence of the sacrificed Lord to a spot within two yards away.

Nothing happened. For a minute, he was distracted anyway by shouts from outside the crypt, as junior boys went running from one period to the next, until deep silence returned. He tried again. Nothing. Something was not right, and all at once he knew what it was: the place where he was kneeling, the rail, stood too exposed, was too prone to possible interruption and deflection of his thoughts. What if an acolyte, or a master wandered in and encountered this kneeling form directly in front of him in the gloom? The worrying possibility distracted William's concentration.

Down the unlit crypt stood a few rows of chairs leading, after a few feet, to the back wall and almost total obscurity. Back there, he'd be able to see without being seen; a far more effective place to achieve transubstantiation of the Lord. Seated now on the right-hand row, almost at the very back, he brought his full imagination at last to bear on those images in the book. With occasional mutterings of *Jesus Christ, Jesus Christ, Jesus Christ...* (not dissimilar to the intoning of monks), he fixed his eyes on the row of chairs across the narrow aisle, compelling his mind and body now to hold that template. Heavy, almost physical silence, filled the room. How long he sat there is impossible to tell. Was it two minutes, two hours, two days? But all at once, yes, the impossible happened: an ill-defined image had taken shape from the end of the row across the aisle. Standing or sitting? He couldn't tell, but the figure was watching him patiently. Had he dared, he could have reached out and touched it. No fear nor panic, but a moment's uncertainty now, as to what came next. Happily, all his endless training in chapel and church came to his aid: memories of solemn orations at Evensong or Eucharist, tossed up by the celebrant towards an invisible Deity. William already had a set of simple phrases in his memory bank which could serve immediately to initiate not a monologue but, rather, a *dialogue*, a face to face, with his Maker.

I come to thee, oh Lord..., Oh God, I am not worthy to receive... Lord Jesus, I ask that thou wilt.... He stopped there, repeated that last phrase: *Lord Jesus, I ask that thou wilt grant thy unworthy servant....* Yes, it was all about 'asking', he remembered. *"Ask, and it will be given unto you"*. That was why he was here in the first place, to ease his life a bit in this monolith school he'd found himself. And thus, stooping forward earnestly in his seat, William proceeded to list, in the direction of the silent 'presence', his requests, a string of minor and trivial demands, centering mainly upon himself, and finishing with a plea for the Lord to aid the school cricket side in the local derby on Saturday: '*Lord Jesus, help us beat D. College in the match next Saturday...*he repeated it, just to be sure, '*Lord Jesus, help us beat D. College...etc*'. And then, with some relief and a few whispered '*Thank you's'* he switched off, transmission terminated.

He was alone in the Crypt and outside he could hear the patter of running feet. He glanced at his watch; two hours had elapsed since his arrival there; it was as if, for an undetermined period, he'd passed into a warp where Time, as we know it, ceases to exist. He'd missed periods one, two, three, and it was break-time. In all likelihood someone would come in to tidy up, and he didn't want to be caught in there alone. He emerged into the blinding light and freshness of outside, and, as he swung the heavy oak door open, a few startled glances were cast from one or two boys in his direction, boys whom he knew, and who knew him. They went on their way however, leaving him to wonder first how he was going to explain away the time-warp to his disgruntled teachers, secondly how he would account, to would-be inquisitive comrades, for his presence in the crypt in the first place: *'I've just been having a conversation with someone who can DO ABSOLUTELY ANYTHING. ANYTHING AT ALL. EVEN THRASH D. COLLEGE.'* That wouldn't do. He decided in the end to remain silent; it wasn't their business anyway. Meanwhile he awaited the game the following Saturday with enormous anticipation.

They lost. D. College thrashed them, as they did most years. They batted first, made 190 for the loss of three wickets; William's side were bowled out for 123, William himself scoring just 3 runs.

Don't be disheartened. Try and try again. Another familiar homily from the pulpit came to his aid. Where would he be without the homilies? William was not someone to be easily deterred. As he sat dejectedly and alone in the cricket pavilion, watching the visiting team leave the field, triumph written across their faces, he was trying at the same time to understand why God, whose Son he'd, beyond all doubt, met now, hadn't answered his simple request. However, slowly it began to dawn on him that, as in horse-racing, if you wanted to make money, be a winner not a loser, you didn't stake all on one horse, you just put less on three horses. His request, he realized now shamefacedly, had been a win/lose situation, an all or nothing, an ultimatum, and you don't give God ultimatums. What, for example, if God hadn't wanted D. College to lose? Suppose there'd been someone cloistered in D. College earlier in the week who'd been asking for precisely the opposite result.

Bravely going out to shake the opposition skipper's hand, William had decided there and then he needed to hedge his bets, give God more wriggle room, ask perhaps for results that were less head-on and competitive, things that needed doing anyway, for the general good, things God couldn't *not* wish to perform for everyone.

William was back in the crypt Monday morning, period 3, to put his theories to the test. *But just suppose the template doesn't materialize!* A doubting thought crossed his mind as he sat down in the dark there. *But why shouldn't it materialize though? If you have a car-crash, you don't forget the next day. Memories like that remain implanted. Forever. Yes, if the Vision was there yesterday, it'll be there today. And tomorrow.*

William reasoned it out and jumped in feet first. *'Oh Lord, I thank thee for coming to me again; I pray thou wilt give me the strength and ability to get 100 out of 100 on my German spelling test this week'* (long shot, but not upsetting anyone else, so why not?). He repeated this request earnestly twice, before going on to the next request: *'I thank thee, Oh Lord, and I pray thou wilt grant our pupils here at the school this week a more generous, all-embracing attitude towards one another. And that includes me.'* (How could God refuse that?). Finally, to give the lie to requests that were ultimatums: *'Oh Lord, once more I thank thee; I ask thee to grant finally that a tile might dislodge from the chapel roof sometime in the next two days and land on Pincher as he's on his way to teach 5C Scripture.'* (William knew this would most likely fail, not because God could possibly like Pincher anymore than *he* did, but because the Almighty might well have other more sinister plans for Pincher).

He allowed almost a full week to go by as the days edged towards the near hysterical crescendo of 'end of term'. By then, Pincher was still alive, and the Chapel still intact; William had got 98/100 in the vocab test (a tad ambiguous, that result), but most remarkable of all, the Head, in Hall in the middle of the week, had proclaimed to the assembled school that term would end two days early owing to a German Measles epidemic spreading its way around. As the news sunk in, there wasn't a student in the place without a smile of pure joy on his face, as each hugged his comrade and made up with lifelong enemies. 'At least the Germans are good for something,' William overheard from one generally unpopular fifth-former, as they filed out of Hall.

Throughout the holidays that year, William continued his prayers in the isolation of his little bedroom. No one in the house knew what he was up to; he crept silently about, leaving his mother, Tessa, to wonder how he could spend an hour and a half of each precious morning languishing in his bed-room, instead of getting on with things. Was he reading, or studying, for those important exams which were looming?

She didn't want to disturb him but wished there was a man in the house, a husband, someone who could throw light on adolescent male behavior, and take action where necessary.

William was, of course, communing. Perched on the edge of the bed, he was fulfilling the ritual required of him by the Church of One and donning each day the 'amour of the Lord', like, say, those ancients of old, who called on their various gods to give them strength before battle. However, as we know, even Achilles was prone to frailties, and William too, it must be said, was not entirely immune, in his daily rituals, from the peremptory urges in the region of the groin,. which can assail a lusty, fit and healthy adolescent boy, near the turn of the twentieth century AD. A weak spot indeed. Although yielding from time to time to these bothersome 'frailties, William felt only a temporary sensation of guilt, and never allowed such lapses to drive a wedge between himself and his Maker. He was firm, fixed, and optimistic. The biblical notion of Sin - that startling tale in Genesis about a man, a woman and a serpent - had made few inroads into his consciousness, and so he continued to approach each new morning's encounter with his Maker in the naïve faith that God was on his side and not judgmental. A Golden Egg, in fact.

He returned focused to school and his new VI form duties in September, more than ready for the fray: In the corridor that first day, He bumped into T, who, with a sour and hostile nod, walked right past him. What did William care? To lose a friend (was he ever a friend?) and gain a far more influential One, why should he be worried? Time was now on his side too; the sixth-form academic programme was much more flexible, allowing abundant free periods in which he could still fulfill his morning spiritual obligations, perhaps even draw them out longer, until he would emerge blinking into the autumn sunlight, with the invincibility of Zeus.

They wasted no time in signing him up for the boxing team that October. The PE teacher was short of a light middleweight, someone dainty on his feet, and William had already, in previous terms, made his mark in the sporting arena, What's more, his legs, his lower thighs, his knobby knees, had mysteriously, throughout the summer, been transformed into muscular prototypes of a da Vinci life-drawing.

'Don't commit to a slugging match, William,' the earnest boxing coach repeatedly advised him in the gym, during training, and again now, as he leaned over the ropes to where William, pumping adrenalin, sat awaiting his first ever official contest against an unknown opponent. *'Keep your guard up, your chin in, and dance on your toes, not your heels.'* Wise admonitions, but dancing on his toes was already as inherent to William as to an African gazelle in lion territory. Strangely however, when the bell sounded for round 1, William showed no sign of getting off his stool at all, but sat, observing his scrawny opponent approach, flat-footed, ducking and weaving aimlessly across an empty canvas, and assuming an unconvincing air of defiance. Rightly so too, but he didn't realize he had the Lord to face. At still two yards distance, new leg muscles radiating sublime confidence, William sprang to his feet and fluttered across to the other side of the ring with all the certainty of a Cabbage-White butterfly scenting Buddleia; he feinted now a couple of times in front of the mystified fellow, before pumping a real-live jab direct into his unguarded face with all the force of a mechanical sledge-hammer. His terrified opponent dropped his guard and just stood there for as long as it took to receive a second such jab, and his 'corner' to decide their champion couldn't just be used indefinitely as an inert punch-bag, and decided to throw in the towel after no longer than 45 seconds. Frightened-face went off doubtless to hold hands quietly with his girl-friend beside a lake, vowing never to confront a founder of the Church of ONE again.

William, from then on, found time to develop his own pugilistic technique. Boxing held no terrors for him. He became a deadly weapon. In fact, word spread throughout the schoolboy boxing world that anyone would be unfortunate indeed to be matched against the *'Spirit'*, as he became called, since, in the ring, he seemed always to be invisible to his opponent, as counterpunches missed their target and met with thin air, until suddenly, Bang! Bang!, the *'Spirit'* became solid flesh and the sledge-hammer descended. The technique was blindingly simple. As in a Wild West saloon, the jittery *bandido* over at the Bar, mesmerized by the steely gaze of the Sheriff right opposite him, and startled momentarily by the snap of a pistol cocking somewhere across the room, drops his guard, lowers his gaze, and then, too late, looks up into the barrel of the Sheriff's revolver; just so, William, flicking with a fake left - the slightest of movements - provokes a moment of uncertainty in his opponent's mind, who unfolds a flurry of directionless jabs before realizing he's committed too early, and the 'sledge-hammer' is sliding inevitably towards the bridge of his nose. Bam! This simple maneuver (flick, withdraw, wait, bam!) is repeated successfully again and again (if the bout isn't already terminated in the interests of humanity), until the poor fellow's nose no longer resembles a nose, rather a misshapen piece of chewing-gum.

Don't commit is the watchword, just feint; dance around the outside of things, never get involved; these were the lessons our hero took from his boxing ritual. During one and a half years William never lost a bout, until that final one, when he himself was pummeled into oblivion by an opponent who took no notice of his flicking feints and just kept coming forward. It turned into a slugging match, during which the bell rang early and the lights went out for William, for good. He never boxed again. We are left to conclude his formidable opponent on that day was also a member of the Church of ONE.

However, besides that ignominious sporting defeat, William's final two years were marked with triumph and achievement; he strode through each day in the certain belief he could accomplish whatever the task. His precocious early brilliance in the sporting arena became brilliance in everything he undertook; he was a butterfly emerging from its chrysalis and taking wing. The distracted, vacant-looking, stringy, fifth-form boy (now grown tall, straight and lithe) had, in a matter of weeks been transformed into a young man of earnest resolve, and those self-indulgent adolescent days were just a memory.

More than often nowadays, he was to be found seated, silent and motionless, in the school library, grappling with vocab lists, or the subtle nuances of French Romantic Poetry, or else the baffling rules of German grammar, systematically laying bare their secrets until they no longer held any terrors for him. His grades shot up. He became undisputed champion of both Lower and then Upper Sixth German as the months rushed by, stamping his mark on the academic as well as the sporting world. The Church of One was working well for him.

Then, shortly before the end of his final year, two consecutive 'happenings' occurred, quite unrelated to his academic success, and of little particular interest to anyone other than himself, but deeply relevant to what one might call his 'spiritual development'. They marked a sign. One evening, following a cloudy, storm-threatening day, William emerged from the noisy chaos of the dining-hall and, quite unusually, headed off towards one of the grassy quadrangles that fringed the main buildings. He felt he needed to be alone, find a bit of time to himself. But as he stepped onto the grassy space he was stopped in his tracks by the vivid sunset blazing across the sky, and stood transfixed. He'd always loved sunsets, those deep profound colours and patterns weaving, it seemed, a desperate message for the weary world. This one in front of him now though was unique; a display of such magnificence that, as he stood spell-bound, he was already whispering involuntarily to himself the words that sprang into his mind at such moments:

> *"They, looking back, all the eastern side beheld*
> *of Paradise,*
> > *So late their happy seat,*
> > *Waved over by that flaming brand.... "*

They were lines from John Milton's *'Paradise Lost'*, but strangely inadequate on their own, an incomplete half of the picture. For a few seconds, he struggled to remember the whole phrase, failed, and acting on a whim, hurried across the grass to the conveniently adjacent School Library, and returned in no time with the relevant book in hand, and finger locked at the precise page.

> *"They, looking back, all the eastern side beheld*
> *of Paradise,*
> > *So late their happy seat,*
> > *Waved over by that flaming brand, the gate*
> > *With dreadful faces thronged*
> > *And fiery arms...*

Now it made sense; those two extra lines completed the desperate picture of Man's fall from grace in the Garden of Eden, chased by an angry God and forever barred, with the help of those fiery angels:

No hope of return. Doors locked, our Primal Parents left to fend for themselves.

William stood there for a moment in utter silence and disbelief at this cataclysmic message. *What was the crime? What misdemeanor so terrible as to deserve so harsh a punishment?* Even from childhood, William had never quite been able to accept this fanciful biblical tale and its unhappy ending. Neither the plot nor the characters seemed convincing: *Adam, Eve, a primal Snake, an Apple:* an extended metaphor presumably for the Sexual act: Covert deeds performed in the Garden by the Couple. *But surely, weren't these 'deeds' a supremely natural act anyway, and wasn't it God himself who'd designed our nature? Why was He so upset then, and how could so harmless an offence merit so harsh a punishment?*

His thoughts had reached an impasse. Had he overlooked something? Was it his own immaturity preventing him from grasping the whole picture? He hesitated, undecided ….But wait. This text in front of him, in black and white, was also not the *whole* picture, but a portion only, not a final statement. Rather against his habit, he thumbed eagerly through to the very end of the poem, and found the final lines of Milton's gigantic message.

> *Some natural tears they dropped, but wiped them soon,*
> *The world was all before them, where to choose*
> *their place of rest, and Providence their guide,*
> *They, hand in hand, with wandering steps and slow,*
> *Through Eden took their solitary way.*

This is a different context altogether. The verse has a quite different tone, and an optimistic twist in the message. The couple aren't dead, haven't become extinct in the fire. They survive, they're penitent and sad as they set out on their journey; it's a parting and aren't partings nearly always sad? Perhaps God Himself (*dropping natural tears*) was sad too.

It didn't take William a moment to recall his own experiences that first day in the Crypt. The God he'd encountered then, (still encounters each succeeding day), was this same gentle God, a God of relationships, not blame, the God indeed of his Church of One.

Could it have been just sheer coincidence that William's attention was distracted by something else that evening, something nearer to hand and even more compelling, as he consigned his recent salutary thoughts to a lack of experience? One of the school masters was passing nearby on the driveway ahead, not twenty yards away, and leading, by his side, his younger daughter, Lucy, un-confessed sweetheart of many a boy on campus, 15 years' old or so, a nymph that came and went in the school vicinity as rarely as a roe-deer. They were heading home from a visit somewhere probably. William's eyes were drawn now involuntarily and compellingly away from the already dwindling sunset, towards the pretty girl, almost woman, who, half hidden by her father, was peeping out at *him* too. He just *knew* she was. There can be no mistake. Hers was no more than a fleeting glance, the kind of timid, curious stare a fawn might give when caught grazing in the corner of a field. *Farouche,* the French call it. A female glance, instinctive even at such a young age, a glance that expressed interest, even longing, camouflaged in an array of indifference.

William already knew that glance, had encountered it before in other girls, and realized, with apprehensive certainty, that, yes, he would be unable to resist Lucy, or another like her, if she passed his way in another situation, in a bolder, less sheltered place perhaps; he would have to surrender himself one day to whoever it might be, with as single-minded fervour as to everything else he found significant. No half-hearted dalliance. She was just too enticing, too beautiful.

Before him, in the shape of the cheeky girl, behaving like a boy inside the puzzling body of a woman, stood portrayed for him at last, beneath the canopy of that fading sunset, the great dichotomy in human life: the fierce, endless confrontations of mind and body that assail the young male emerging from puberty. Sex, in a word, Passion, Love. Yes, it's called '*Love*', a word which, in the vernacular, is tossed around and sung about in cheap ditties. 'Love', that complicated emotion, which, with apparent ease, accounts for a major part of the world's corruption and devastation and is the answer to the riddle of Eden. William knew some day for sure it would assail him too, and he'd just have to cope with it.

A Man, a Woman, a Serpent, a Tree, an Apple, Disobedience, Original Sin, for which our Ancient Parents were cast out, while we, condemned forever to repeat on Earth the same destructive act of defiance. Breathtakingly, each moment we teeter, unknowingly on the edge of disaster before tumbling in.

He couldn't stop looking at this girl opposite him.... *He, Lucy, Lust, Knowledge....* Puzzled, he tried unsuccessfully to pair the list up again, and found one item missing from the original list: that mysterious *'apple'*, which Eve handed to Adam? *What did that stand for then?* For a moment he was lost, until the answer slid easily alongside him. *"He saw that it was very **good**"* (more or less *God's own words, according to 'Genesis').*

Yes, for '**good**' read *'beautiful'* ; that elusive 'apple' must represent *Beauty,* that endless fatal attraction, which, in whatever form it comes, blinds us all and deprives us of our sanity and reason.

The scales fell from Adam's eyes that evening, as the final glimmer disappeared from the sky, and Lucy went on her way. He'd bitten into the Apple, and found her beautiful.

'Don't apples go moldy though?'
'Yes, indeed, they do.'
'And how might the Church of One avoid this whole conflict?'
'It can't. Just keep praying. That's all. You'll muddle through.'

CHAPTER 4

'In which William reluctantly leaves Eden and, with Providence his guide, ventures out into a challenging world.'

William's mother, Tessa, who found it hard to bear the possibility of her only son venturing off to the hazardous far corners of the globe on a 'gap year', arranged for him instead to work within a few miles from home, at a Prep school on the outskirts of London.

He quickly endeared himself to his paymasters, an uninspiring middle-aged couple, who saw in him someone they could rely on and pay little. An ideal formula for them in fact, particularly since they, after long years of hum-drum classroom work and coping with the infantile behaviour of young boys, were clearly losing their own enthusiasm for the job. They'd found, in William, a potential ally, who might bring to bear all those pedagogic virtues they themselves were in the gradual process of relinquishing.

William lost no time making himself needed, indispensible in fact to the school and its apathetic bosses. This was all too easy for him; the busy world raced by outside, while he passed his days immured in this pleasant little enclave of academia. Why should he worry? His meals were cooked for him, his phone calls paid for, his accommodation in the school buildings taken care of (and cleaned!), and his sole responsibility outside the classroom was an evening's duty in the dormitories.

Despite the slim pay, he put his heart and soul and imagination into his teaching. This was in his nature anyway, and besides, after a day or two of assessing his charges in the classroom he quickly realised it was in his best interests too; to keep on top of them somehow. *'Self-satisfied little embryos, prisoners in the womb of ignorance'* was the phrase he found best summed them up, and which, mistakenly, he let slip to the class one particularly frustrating day early in the week.

'*Se-er*, what's an 'embryo'?'

'Look it up for prep. Discover it yourself.'

'Sir, *we're* not 'self-satisfied'.'

'I'm glad to hear it. There's certainly nothing to be satisfied about.'

(Class smart-arse) '*Se-er*, (an almost unbearable whine accompanied anything this particular pupil said). *Se-er*, I emerged from the womb almost exactly nine years ago, so my mother says ....No, I tell a lie, it was nine years this coming Friday.'

'Congratulations, and happy birthday!'

'So, you see, I can't be a 'prisoner'.'

'You exchanged one jail for another, that's all.'

'*Se-er*...' (Not so much a whine this time, but a begrudging surrender to his teacher's superior wit).

Yes, William quickly discovered that was the key to it; these spoiled kids needed challenging and outsmarting, because underneath lay anarchy and riot. In fact each morning, William crossed the small courtyard from his digs to the classroom, reminding himself of this important pedagogic axiom: *Challenge and control* . K*eep pitching the material a short step above what they thought they knew.*

It worked for William. He tried at first to develop some kind of a pattern to the lessons - Geography, History, English, Arithmetic. Got appropriate text books for the core subjects, and quite soon realized Sanderson, his Boss, at that first meeting had been cynically right: the pupils knew nothing, planned nothing, cared nothing.

He abandoned a schedule, but taught them what little he knew of everything. And when Geography, History, English, Arithmetic, began to tire, he delved into literature, read poems and stories, allotted play parts, strayed far from any syllabus. And as the days went on it became clear the kids were strangely settling down, listening to him, behaving themselves, taking home things that he'd said. It was an awesome responsibility, one that he was actually enjoying though.. Just so long as you didn't fail them, kept your slate clean, remained honest, didn't cover up, then each day they picked a little piece of you to take home that evening, refreshed. '*Mu-um*, Sir said Mr. Sanderson must have fought in the War. That's why he looks so funny.'

'Oh dear, my darling boy, you mustn't be so rude about people.'

'But, Mr. Bellman ...'

'So you said, dear. I heard. Which War was that then?'

'I think it was the War of the Roses. We got this bit to do for Prep: *Now is the winter of our discontent*....I think he wrote that.'

'Sound awfully challenging, Darling. *Who* did you say wrote it?'

'Mr. Bellman.'

'Really? Well I hope you're also practising your tables.'

'Yes, Mum, we do a bit of that. Boring.'

For William, Everything just came down to the word '*challenge*'. So, to keep ahead and while away the hours, he picked poems, bits of poems, left them with a conundrum within the poem, let them unravel it. '*Jonathan Swift*, boys. Famous poet some two hundred years ago.'

'*Se-er*, why's it always hundreds of years ago?.

'We have a lot to learn from the past.'

'They didn't even have running water from taps.'

'Who needs taps when you can drink from a stream. Listen.'

'Is this one of those poems we...

'Yes, listen. Prize for anyone who can unravel this.' (William knew full well even his betters in the school would have difficulty coping with this one.)

> *There was a time,*
> *'Ere ever man was born to rob their honey-pots,*
> *That bees were fully endowed with reason,*
> *And only lost it by ordering so their lives*
> *As to dispense with it.*

He read slowly out-loud to them, and as he came to the end, was confronted with puzzled faces, and indignation, that their teacher should cheat, should choose to read to them in a foreign language, knowing they didn't speak it. William read it again, handed out a worksheet. 'Okay. No explanation, Boys. Prep tonight: *High marks for anyone who can interpret the meaning of those lines. Paraphrase it.*'

'What does 'Paraphrase' mean, Sir?'

'Put in your own words, on paper, what you think is the meaning of that poem.

'Easy!'

(Smartarse class swat): '*Se-er*, it's *not* easy, *is* it?'

'No. Class dismissed. See some of you on the games-field. Don't lose those papers.'

Next morning, they came back to the poem. 'Okay, so what was it all about? Get your paraphrases out.'

'Sir, even my Mum couldn't make any sense of it.'

'Perhaps she doesn't like honey.'

General laughter.

'Sir, what does 'endowed' mean?'

'So you haven't done your part of the bargain eh, Snooks?'

'We... I mean *I* ... couldn't work out what 'endowed' meant.

'There's always a dictionary. Got a dictionary at home?'

'Yes, Sir.'

'It means 'equipped', Snooks ...'gifted'. Something, I'm afraid, you, at your particular stage of evolution, aren't.'

Laughter.

'That doesn't make sense either, Sir. Why do you keep talking in a foreign language?'

A hand raised.

'Yes, Smith?'

'Sir, is it this?' Consulting paper: '*There's these bees, and they keep finding someone's stolen their honey.*'

'Half right, Smith. At least you put in the work. Read out exactly what it says on your paper.'

'I just have, Sir.'

'Anyone else care to contribute?' No volunteers. 'Okay, let's move on, do something else. I don't know where to begin about this poem. Perhaps we'll work on it another time. Say in five years.'

'Sir, you won't be teaching us in five years.'

'How do you know? Could be ten the way you're going.'

'Sir, Sir, Sir...' One particularly annoying embryo, raising his hand up and down in the air as if pretending to lift weights. Desperate though to be included for once.

Daring to stake all.

'Yes, Jones? What is it?'

'Sir, my Dad's a practicing chemist. He said they used to call Chemists '*Dispensing* Chemists.' Is that what it means?'

'Is that what *what* means?'

'The word at the end of the poem.'

'Yes, Jones, it *is*....'

Impossible to believe the look on Jones's Face. Pure joy. 'I knew my Dad would get it right!'

'And *no*, Jones, it *isn't*. But mostly, *no,* I'm afraid.'

'*Se-er...*' (the whine, as the kid slumps back into his chair).

Sustained silence from class in general.

'Okay. Don't worry. Let's get on with marking these sums.'

They continued with the arithmetic for five minutes before slowly, silently, deliberately, peremptorily the class swat raised his hand. 'Sir.'

'Yes, Whiltshire?'

'You know that poem?'

'The one we decided ten minutes ago was too difficult?'

'Yes, Sir.... Could I have a go?'

'Make it short then.'

'Well, Sir, I guessed, you see, it was as though the words in the poem had a different meaning from what the dictionary says.'

'They very often do.... But go on. You're on the right track.'

'Well, Sir, for instance, 'dispense' probably doesn't mean to 'hand out' - like the chemist - but to 'get rid of something.'

There's utter silence in the class. *What is it about 'truth and being right' that makes everyone in a room really listen, spellbound? Is it because it so often doesn't happen?*

'Go on, Wiltshire. You're correct so far.'

'Thought so, Sir. And another word: 'Ere', it's a different spelling from the *air* we breathe. I looked it up; it's old-fashioned for '*before'*.

'You're cracking it, So what did you write?'

'Shall I read it?'

'Yes, read it.'

The spell-bound silence continues as the rest realize they're in the presence of genius and are about to learn something that will change their lives. Meanwhile, Wiltshire is reading out: '*At some time long ago, even before humans came into the world, a race of super-intelligent bees were in charge (like ruled things), until they became too clever for their own good and stopped being intelligent at all, and were replaced by ordinary bees.'*

Wiltshire smiles sheepishly, as if he hadn't just performed a miracle, done the 4-minute mile, set foot on the moon, while the rest of the class sits still, so silent you could hear a pin drop.

'Your own work?'

'Yes, Sir. Promise.'

'I'll arrange for you to see the Headmaster. Get a pat on the back.'

'Thank you, Sir.' He grimaces.

'Sir?' Snooks, breaking the silence.

'Yes, Snooks?'

'What about the honey?'

'A side-line really, but right, it's about bees, so obviously honey. Well done, Snooks. Brilliant! Your Dad was right too. Let's get on now with marking sums.' (The bell rings outside). 'Okay, we'll finish marking tomorrow. But wait, Prep. Yes, I've had a good idea. Prep tonight: finish the Maths exercise, get hold of Wiltshire's paraphrase, and figure out *what point the poet's making about the human race in general*. Anyone else fancy a pat on the back from the Head?'

'*Se-er.*' (a giant, universal whine as the class pack up their things and start to leave).

'Oh yes, I nearly forgot. Also find out who wrote the verse which begins: *"Now is the Winter of our discontent"*.... Write that down, before you leave the classroom. Use the encyclopedias you don't have at home.

'*Se-er!*'

William felt that, if not the boys, at least *he* had edged a little closer in his general understanding that day. He decided not to set the boys any more such conundrums for a long, long time, but in future concentrated on more mundane aspects of learning. However his instinct told him simply that unless *homo sapiens* can comprehend the mysteries and subtleties of its own language, it will, like the bees, be condemned to extinction and replaced by some other more creative race. And what's more, just like the boys perhaps, he'd discovered, something remarkable, something vital, from that little exercise;

something he didn't know before. That is that Words are the vital cog that give us humans the edge. And beware, all demagogues, who lose sight of that message.

Wiltshire's version next day, about the 'Winter of discontent etc...', was just as insightful as the one about the 'bees'; the rest of the class were nowhere near. For President then! Such an unlikely personage would hopefully qualify in time for the Church of ONE too. For sure, William certainly wished he'd been as clever as Wiltshire at that young age.

A stroke! It must be a stroke. At mid-term, William was invited up into the Sanderson's residence - a flat above the school on the third floor - where they lived in splendid isolation, allowing Sanderson to keep a vigilant eye on the chaos beneath. It was a dreary place though, and as he sat in the armchair opposite Mr. and Mrs. Sanderson, and responding as best he could to the small-talk taking place seemingly a long way off, it came to him in a flash of guilt and regret that Mr. Sanderson clearly possessed an 's unfortunate disfigurement (the lower side of his face dropped noticeably) which might just have been caused by a stroke. He'd heard indistinctly about things like that. Paralysis on one side or another.

'Darling, would you get Mr. Bellman another Sherry please.' She leaves. 'Well, Mr. Bellman, I hear good reports about you. You appear to have established a good rapport with them. No riots yet.' He attempted a smile which changed into a sneering grimace. 'Ah, here's your Sherry. I've also heard reports from some of our parents.' He paused 'Challenging' seems the word of the moment. Don't take offense now, Mr. Bellman; it's a compliment, not a criticism. We like to challenge out boys, don't we Darling.' He attempted a half turn in the direction of his wife. 'We're both so grateful for the way you've settled in, You might seriously think about Prep School teaching once you've completed your university studies.' He gave his wife an endearing look. 'Aren't we, Darling?

'Aren't we what?'

His wife, who must once have been a looker in her younger days - debutante perhaps - had said not a word until now, and there was a slight edge to her voice as she turned towards her husband. 'What do you mean by *'aren't we'* Dear?'

'I meant, *aren't we grateful.*'

Mrs. Sanderson merely nodded. There was a sense of desolation, despair, on her face - as also on her husband's - as they both now sat back, and almost officially handed duties and responsibilities over to this energetic young man, and bowed out of tasks they were both too tired and dispirited to do. *Where had it all gone?* said the look.

'Well, keep up the good work,' exclaimed Sanderson as he ushered William out of the flat and attempted something else that one does on occasions such as this but which was also beyond him now, a smile.

Meanwhile William was overcome with a sense of remorse about his failure to have spotted the stroke sooner. He should have had the wit to see what was staring him in the face. Not only had he amused himself at his boss's expense, he'd also amused the boys. Should have kept his mouth firmly shut.

He went circumspectly on his way, a salutary lesson learned, but glad the ordeal of the 'flat at the top of the building' was now behind him. Permanently, he hoped.

CHAPTER 5

"In which William discovers a kind of father and something of himself."

William had established a casual friendship with a colleague at the school, Collingwood by name. He taught at a slightly higher age-level, boys of 11 to 13, old enough to be cunning as well as mischievous, and William had often passed W's classroom window to be met by the sounds of chaos. No learning going on there, just disruption, commotion and despair; at any moment, he expected Collingwood to come flying through the window, or out the door, crammed tidily into a waste-paper basket. Collingwood was a nice enough fellow, just in the wrong job; that was all.

In the long Autumn evenings of that hum-drum term, the two friends would occasionally drive together into the City in the evenings in Wallingford's new car, he nervously at the wheel (courtesy of his recent Provisional Driver's License), while William, similarly apprehensive, sat in the passenger seat, in the role of 'qualified adult.'

As they navigated the confusing heart of Trafalgar Square one evening, William broached his friend cautiously on the matter of his classes, his job at the school. He'd often wondered what had prompted his mild-natured colleague to choose a job so apparently alien to his obvious nature and accomplishments. It was quite evident he possessed no latent aggression at all, a characteristic vital to any would-be Prep-school teacher, nor did he seem to have that kind of eccentric brilliance (in map-reading, or chess, or tiddly-winks), which can often appeal to mischievous ten-year-olds. Puzzled, William looked amicably across at his silent friend, hands loosely on the wheel, and exuding the same wishy-washy incompetence with which he attempted to control his classes. 'Those boys give you a tough time, don't they, Wally.'

'Damned blighters,' Collingwood swerved to avoid a serial tailgater.

'Why didn't you give Secondary a try? More your level, wouldn't you say? More serious.'

Collingwood didn't seem troubled by the implied criticism, largely because he was too busy avoiding annihilation at the hands of a large Skoda gliding past. He just muttered, as William slammed his foot hard down on another non-existent brake in the passenger seat. 'Why would it be any different in a Secondary school?'

'Older kids. More respect for learning, for reading, for knowledge.'

'I don't read. I don't even like reading. Except the Mail on Sunday morning.'

William suggested it might be his eyesight needed fixing.

'I had innumerable tests; my parents were forever dragging me into the Optician's No, there's nothing wrong with my specs.' He paused to avoid a motorbike, two feet away from his left inside wheel. 'I read 'Geography' at University, that's the trouble. My preferred specialty. I love wading through rivers. Not much scope for that in teaching, is there? Not much scope anywhere in fact. Maybe I'll quit and join the Met Office. I'd be good at that.'

It was a longish speech for Collingwood, and was also the moment the car hit them. Not more than a glancing blow but enough to place a dent in one of the wings on the passenger side. William distinctly remembered one facet of the calamity; it was somehow locked in his memory: *the on-coming light had turned red several seconds before they'd reached it*, and Collingwood, for his part, had neglected the signal altogether and just carried right on through. 'What's that idiot doing?' He expressed his dismay in the usual lackadaisical manner, and slammed on the brakes directly in the middle of the busy intersection at Whitehall.

William wasted no time being polite. 'Wally, it was *your* fault; *you* crossed a red light.

'Huh! Well I hope you won't say that, if it comes to court,' shouted Collingwood with a surprising display of aggression and spirit.

No one had been hurt; just Collingwood's pride and a graze to his car. It could have been much worse. The tailgater pulled over of course and asserted, in a language known presumably only to him, 'You little dumb-arse shit-face. I trust you got f...... insurance.' He then went on to confirm vociferously what William had just stated and was all too ready to confirm. 'It was *your* bloody fault, mate!'.

They exchanged the usual phone numbers and insurance details, and for the rest of the evening Collingwood said very little, smarting from the damage to his car and his dignity. William secretly wondered whether each day was like that for his friend, a series of unavoidable failures. In truth, he found, to his surprise, that innately he had little sympathy for Collingwood anyway, and his general incompetence: the man had choice; he should use it to pick the right job and take taxis. They reached home with no further incidents, and that seemed to be the end of the matter.

The months went by. William adapted to his sheltered but productive life in the same way a medieval monk might watch the seasons pass and the years glide gently by. He saw little of Collingwood and assumed the matter of the car had been sorted. He got on with his simple life at the school, took advantage of nearby London and its sporting facilities, played football on Saturdays, came back to the school after the match, lay on his bed and listened to Brahms or Beethoven.

He rarely visited his mother, even though W… was a simple drive away. She lived alone in that big house, quite self-reliant apparently, and, besides, in all honesty, William - as he had with Collingwood - felt little sympathy with his Mum's situation; it was *her* life, the one she'd chosen, and, in truth, he enjoyed his own independence too much to allow his mother to impinge upon it. He had as yet absolutely no experience of that emotion called compassion, nor, certainly, had he encountered 'Love'. Just occasionally he thought too of the enigma of his absent father (about whom he knew nothing), and wondered what emotional cataclysm must have occurred to drive his parents so irreparably apart. When and how and why? His mother never once raised the subject. Perhaps, he wondered, he didn't have a father, so complete was the secrecy surrounding his provenance.

One weekend however in late winter, he found a note left for him in the school's office asking him to ring his mother in W…. He rang that evening from a phone box and as the dial tone rang six, seven times, he found himself half hoping she wouldn't pick up. But she did.

'Hello'. The clear voice (slight twang of American) he recognized so well came down the line, followed by the common English pattern of response, a slow and deliberate repetition of the number just dialed. He broke in on her laborious recital.

'Mother, it's me, William. I got your message.'

'Darling. How lovely to hear from you.' A slight hesitation, as if she wasn't quite sure how to set the tone with this son she so rarely heard from. 'I hope I'm not intruding. I know how busy you must be.'

'Is everything all right, Mother?

'Of course it is. Why shouldn't it be?' A hint of irritation in her voice that she should be a cause for concern to anyone. Even to her own son. Tessa had always fiercely guarded her own independence too.

'Well you don't often leave messages.'

'You can hardly be called a star yourself when it comes to communicating, William, my Love.

'Well I'm communicating now, Mum.'

'Yes you are, and I'm so happy to hear from you. What've you been doing? Anything exciting?'

William knew his mother must have a specific motive for contacting him, was almost glad in fact that was so. It wasn't like her to beat around the bush; she'd get round to it sooner or later. Meanwhile he knew he'd have to play along with the kind of telephone small-talk he himself found so difficult.

'Not particularly exciting, but, yes, I'm playing in the school orchestra. Can't remember if I told you. We're putting on '*The Creation*'. 'Haydn', you know.' He sensed the hesitation at the other end, his mother rather desperately bewailing the gaps in her education.

Wishing to spare her embarrassment, he attempted to briefly explain. 'The music's beautiful, even if the words are a bit far-fetched, a bit simplistic. But the music makes up for it. Nobody really listens to the words. Unless there's a 7th day Adventist in the audience. Anyway, it doesn't matter; let's face it, Haydn was a musician not a poet, and simple, pretty librettos are nice to hang your music on anyway. Mozart did it all the time. You could set Mozart's Requiem to "*Bah, bah Black Sheep...*"; it would still have the same impact. '

'You sound so knowledgeable, William.'

'It's obvious, if you listen.'

'Maybe I could come. When's it on?'

'End of the school year. Early July.'

'That sounds like the end of the century. Hope we'll see you before then.' They were still making small-talk, and William waited patiently for the real reason, the hidden motive behind the phone-call. She, like him, needed motives. 'By the way, I've taken the liberty of opening a letter addressed to you.'

'Oh!'

'It looked so official. I thought it might be important. Didn't want it to go astray in the post.' William didn't break his silence, waited for his mother to explain. 'Have you been in an accident, darling?'

'What kind of an accident? No.'

'Well, the letter's either from the police or from an insurance company. I'm not exactly sure which. Perhaps I should just send it on. It says you were a witness or something.'

William had already guessed what it was. 'Look mother, it's nothing. Don't worry. And don't send it on. Perhaps I'll come over one Saturday and you can just give it to me.' He paused, thinking ahead. 'I'm not actually playing next Saturday. Not picked.' He tried not to let his voice sound as disgusted as he felt at his omission from the team. 'Are you free next weekend?'

'Of course. That'd be lovely. And as it happens, your aunt Elizabeth's over from America for a brief stay, and you know how much you like her.'

'Okay. And don't worry about the letter; I know what it is. It's nothing. I'll get to you on Saturday morning. How's that?'

'I'll kill the fatted calf.'

'Don't go overboard, Mother. I'm hardly the prodigal son. Wish I were.'

She gave a little laugh and rang off, probably deliberately, anticipating another diatribe from her hectic son on 'team selection'.

Collingwood. That driving incident. That's what it must be. Yes, he *had* been a witness, but it all seemed so long ago. And Collingwood's fault too. Would the insurance people really want to hear that? Depends which side they were representing. He put it out of his mind and thought about his mother instead. Living in that big house. Much too big for her needs. Watching out selflessly for Grandpa. Taking herself off to work, week in, week out, never showing signs of changing her habits, locked stubbornly into a life of duty. The most stubborn person on earth. He felt he should take the opportunity of this coming visit to raise such matters.

The house's ponderous, pre-war facade stood set-back from the road behind a high privet-hedge, which concealed it - isolated it even - from prying eyes, and spoke of a more opulent age when people could afford to vacate the busy town, in search of privacy, space and a more rural setting. Neatly-planted cherry trees lined the wide avenues in this part of town, and even the tops of stately oaks and elms could be glimpsed beyond the houses. Discreet, well-manicured gardens lay hidden at the back, immaculate lawns and paved paths running up to dainty goldfish-ponds and colorful rockeries.

This was the place where William had grown up, had viewed the house for many years through the rosy spectacles of youth, and as he drove up the wide avenue and parked the car in the driveway that morning, for just one moment he experienced the old schoolboy sense of joy at coming home and school holidays, before fiercely shoving such childish reminiscences back where they belonged: firmly in the past. His old life, he knew, stood poised now on a fulcrum, and there was no longer room for nostalgia. The 'spectacles' were coming off, and he compelled himself at that moment to see the house as it really was: *a utilitarian dwelling lacking 'soul'*. He rang the bell and waited for his mother to open the heavy front door, mildly aware how time was moving on, how there might shortly come a moment when things he'd always taken for granted - the house and his mother alone in it - would have to change, as he wrestled with his own elusive plans for an uncertain future. .

She came to the door. William hugged her, more to please her than himself. 'Are you all right, Mum? You look well. You know, the more I see this house, the more I think you should find something smaller. It's too big for you.'

Her still young face, for once radiant with the prospect of seeing her only son for the first time in months, assumed a startled, almost hurt expression. 'William, darling, that's all I need on a Saturday morning. Are you an estate agent or something?'

Her gibe stung him, and she instantly regretted making it. They stood for a moment, eyeing each other, both inevitably searching mutual signs of change. William said, 'I'm sorry, mother, but we have to be realistic.'

'Maybe so, but you don't need to take on your man-of-the-house attitude quite so soon. I've managed, you know, without a man for coming on twenty years. I'm still capable of looking after myself. Anyway, don't stand there; we can talk about all these things later. Come and meet Aunt Elizabeth.'

William entered the dark hallway, already peeved he didn't have his mother all to himself that weekend. 'Mother, I didn't mean to bully you; I just meant you could maybe downsize a bit. Move to the seaside. You know how much you like the sea.'

As she led the way into the small kitchen at the back, Tessa said, 'It's just a minor matter of the grandparents'

'They're not your responsibility. You know that; we've been through this lots of times.'

'Your grandmother's getting frailer by the day. Somebody's got to look after her.'

'Yes, but why should it be you?'

His Aunt Elizabeth was getting up from the kitchen table as they entered, and Tessa whispered urgently, 'Later, William', while William notched up yet another example of his mother avoiding talking seriously about anything. She said, 'Come and meet Aunt Elizabeth.'

'My, William! How you've grown. How are you?'

That broad American twang. William loved it. His mother had a trace of it too, not so strong though, eroded by the many years she'd spent in England. William glanced now from one sister to the other; they were so alike in looks as well: the dark curly hair graying frighteningly, the warm brown eyes, the wide mouth; they could have been twins. And back in Connecticut, there was yet another younger sister, and a brother too, a whole clan of Bellman's, whom, of course, he'd never met.

His aunt was coming forward to hug him, while William shot out a protective hand to avoid the inevitable embrace. He'd never been fond of the rituals of informal greeting. His aunt however, grinning still, grabbed the outstretched hand and shook it warmly. 'We're very formal, aren't we, William?' she said smiling, and they stood for a moment holding palms, uncertain who'd be the first to let go. 'Still, I suppose you're the man of the house now, earning your own crust. Got to look after your mother.' She shot a look at her younger sister. 'He's so good-looking, Tessa. My sole nephew, in spite of all my millions of siblings. You're so lucky..'

There was no mistaking the sincerity in Elizabeth's greeting. William had always been fond of this lady who looked so like his mother. He said, 'You'd better get going yourself soon, Aunt Elizabeth. *Tempus Fugit.*

'William, really!' Tessa interrupted,. 'What *are* you thinking?'

Elizabeth however remained unperturbed. 'You never know, William. And anyway it's 'Lizzie' please, not 'Aunt Elizabeth'. You know that. We don't stand on ceremony here.'

William glanced at Tessa. 'We don't stand on ceremony, Mother. You see?'

Elizabeth smiled. 'She knows that well enough, believe me, William. But tell me,

how is *your* love life, these days?'

'Negative, I'm afraid' replied William hurriedly.

'What? A good-looking guy like you?'

'Maybe, if that's what you think.' He grinned. 'But teaching, you know, it leaves no time for dalliance unfortunately.'

Elizabeth laughed. 'You know, Tess, your son's got a surprising way with words; it must be 'all this *teaching*'. She mimicked William's expression.

'I know,' said Tessa. 'I just can't keep up.'

'Tell me though, seriously, William, how do you like teaching?'

'It's okay.'

'Rather non-committal. You're a dark horse. Is this job permanent?'

'Just a gap year,' said Tessa promptly. 'One year, or two maybe. I don't know if William's decided yet.

They both looked at William, who said firmly, 'I'm not staying on at the school, no.' He was adamant.

'Have you got other plans then?' asked Elizabeth.

'Not yet. I just know I won't be staying at H... next year.' As neither sister said anything, he added, 'I'm moving on.'

'Where?' asked his mother abruptly. And then, to her sister, 'William never confides anything to me. He's like one of those clams you pries off rocks on the beach.'

They all laughed at the image; William with less enthusiasm than the others. Tessa added, 'The beach my son's so keen on sending me to.'

'Which beach is that?' asked her sister.

'Oh, don't worry, Lizzie. It's just an in-joke. When I'm tired out, he means. A retirement home by the sea.'

William jumped in. 'You're not getting any younger, Mother.'

'There he goes again,' said Tessa. 'Bossing me.'

And Elizabeth remarked, 'Well Tessa, it's right, in a way. Maybe you *do* need bossing. And it's nice to see your son taking an interest in his Mum.'

A brief silence, before Tessa replied, 'Perhaps.' She glanced at her son. 'Looking after me, yes, maybe. However, he doesn't seem very clear what he's going to do with his *own* life.'

William made no answer, and Tessa prompted kindly, 'Aren't you, William?'

'Maybe not, Elizabeth. 'But I think I know what I'm *not* going to do, namely Teaching.'

Elizabeth remarked discreetly, 'Yes, gap years. Difficult to know what to do. I was the same, I remember. Finished up selling hamburgers to doped-up groupies at pop festivals. What did you do, Tess? I've forgotten.'

Tessa hesitated a second. 'I was over here in England. Remember?' She paused, seeming embarrassed. 'And then came that lark of ours, that dreadful year, chasing murderous crooks round Texas.' Under her breath, she added, 'That *dreadful* year.'

Elizabeth seemed almost embarrassed too, and William, filling the moment's silence, said, 'Mother, it can't have been *that* dreadful!'

Tessa ignored his interruption. 'And then, after that disaster, William was born.' She looked at her son. 'Thank goodness!'

'Who's the clam now Mother? I know nothing about your past. Perhaps someday I should.'

'Yes, good idea,' said Elizabeth hurriedly. 'Your mother has quite a chequered career, you know.'

'Not *that* chequered, Lizzie. You make me sound like a terrorist'

'I wasn't imputing anything, Tess. I promise, But shouldn't William know a bit about your past, your growing up, our family?'

They sat there silently, seeming to want to steer clear of that subject, until Elizabeth broke the ice. 'I've had a brain-wave, Tessa. I've got the perfect thing for William's second year. Send him to Hillcrest.'

A sudden silence followed, as if for everyone, something new and strange had entered the room. A stone dropping into a silent pool.'

'Is that that high-school you went to in America, Mother?'

'Yes.'

William sat pondering the idea for a moment, and Tessa said, 'Yes, Liz, I suppose it's theoretically possible. As a last resort. We'd need to think quite hard about it.'

'They've got a whole new administration running the place now I've heard, Tess, if that's what you're worried about. No ghostly memories.'

William said, 'Sounds more like a horror film, Mother,'

Elizabeth laughed. 'Who knows? William could even bump into his father out there. That would be ironic.'

Tessa was taken aback, less than ready to reply, and annoyed with her sister for raising the subject. The two of them sat silently now, absorbing the full significance of Elizabeth's remark and shrinking back from its consequences

Tessa finally broke the spell. 'No, I think that's courting fate Let's leave those skeletons securely locked in the cupboard, Sis, and, anyway, for sure Adam will be long gone from there anyway.'

William remarked peevishly, sarcastically almost, 'Ah, *that* mystery. Don't forget, Mother, I happen to know who that particular 'skeleton' is. And I don't need to be sheltered from this subject.'

Liz, however, bluntly pursued the subject, regardless of Tessa's objection. 'How do you know, Tess? He might have got his old job back. It's not beyond the bounds of possibility.'

For a few seconds, Tessa remained silent and then softly, but adamantly, replied, 'I *do* know, that's all. I know Adam too well.'

The two sisters fell silent, both wondering if they may have gone too far. At last, William broke the silence, still in that same accusative tone of voice. 'Mother, I'm sure you have the best intentions, but don't you think it's a bit offensive hearing you both organizing my future life, and discussing a father I never knew?'

'William's right, Sis,' said Elizabeth looking across the table at her sister. She turned now to William. 'Real sorry, Will; we got carried away. They were exciting times for all of us, you see.'

'Maybe, but my life, I think, is excluded from them. Can we change the subject? Didn't you mention in your message there was a letter for me, by the way?'

'Ah, the letter; yes, of course,' said Tessa, relieved at this abrupt change of subject and yet clearly still unnerved how close the two of them had come to raising a subject she'd for so long avoided. 'I almost forgot the letter. Let me go and get it.'

'Look you two, said Elizabeth, getting up from the table. 'I've got to go to the shops. I think I'll pop out and leave you to get on with the nitty-gritty. I'll only be in the way. What's this letter, Will? A secret admirer? A ghost from the past? Sounds real exciting.'

'I think, Aunt, it's a letter from an insurance company, asking me to bear witness to an accident I wasn't involved in.'

'Oh dear,' said Elizabeth casting a concerned glance at her sister. 'Not so exciting then.'

'William was just a passenger,' said Tessa hurriedly.

'Well, Will, if you'll allow the wise voice of experience from your senior aunt, I advise you to play stumm, say nothing which could incriminate you.'

'That's right,' agreed Tessa, 'don't admit to anything. That's the way these things work nowadays. So many accidents. Let the insurance companies fight it out.'

'Sounds a funny way of carrying on,' said William. 'If the thing happened, then it happened. Anyway, let's have a look at the letter.'

Elizabeth left forthwith to do her shopping, and Tessa to find the letter. She came back two minutes later, handed it to him. 'Sorry I opened it, but it's always best not to be caught off guard. I think they're suggesting someone comes this very day.'

'What? On a Saturday?'

'Maybe the sooner the better. Get it over and done with.'

William opened the letter. He read briefly and turned back to his mother. 'You're right, the bloke's coming at 2 pm.' He glanced at his watch. 'In an hour and a half's time.' He checked the letter again. ' *"... unless we hear from you meanwhile to the contrary"*. Mother, did you reply to this?'

'No.'

'Then…'

Tessa didn't let him finish. 'Darling, just say nothing. Aunt Elizabeth's right; I remember now your grandfather always says "if you're a witness, act stupid".' William merely nodded, and she added, 'Well, we've time for lunch. I bet you're hungry.'

She busied around in the kitchen, while William sat in the little adjoining kitchen, looking blankly at the letter. After several minutes, he called through, 'Is that really what Grandfather says?'

'Yes, Darling. He spent his lifetime sitting in cars. Probably involved in numerous things like this.'

'What did Grandpa do exactly?'

'Commercial traveler, I think they called it in those days. Drove all round delivering food to shops.'

There was a pause before William asked, 'Did he have any potential for painting, Mother?'

'Funny question. I suppose he might have done in his early days. Why do you ask?'

'There are some pictures he always talks about. Oil paintings. On his living-room wall. Whenever I used to go down there. D'you know anything about those?'

Tessa hesitated, thinking. 'Can't say I do. All I do know is that your Grandfather made a lot of money in the firm.'

William sensed the matter of the paintings was being shut firmly once again. A family secret, he supposed. No one would ever come clean about the paintings. He called, 'Come to you maybe one day, Mother?'

'What, the money or the pictures?'

'The money, I mean.'

'Maybe. That would be nice.'

William didn't reply for a minute or two, wondering silently about the wide discrepancy between skillfully using oils like Rembrandt, and selling food to retail outlets. Then he asked, 'How is he, by the way?'

'He's fine, William. Fit as a fiddle. It's your Grandma I'm worried about. I think She's on the way out.'

'What will Grandfather do when...'; he corrected himself, '*if* she goes?'

'*When* rather than if, William.'

'Just a figure of speech.'

'You and your figures of speech.'

'It's what I do, Mother.'

'What? Make up figures of speech?'

'Well, not exactly, but I'm a word person, didn't you know? I deal in words.'

'No, I didn't. But then you rarely tell me anything about what goes on in your head. A word person then.' She repeated the sonorous phrase: 'how wonderful. A *word-smith.*' Isn't that the correct term?'

'I'm not sure, Mother.'.

What do 'word persons' do exactly?'

'Find words easy. Express themselves well in all facets of the language.'

'There you go again. What are 'facets'?'

'Aspects, subjects, areas. Look, I'm just good with language, that's all. I seem to understand it instinctively. Other people obviously struggle with it.' He thought for a moment and then added, 'I think I could talk the hind leg off a donkey.'

They both laughed happily and Tessa said. 'How nice, darling.'

'Not so nice for this loss adjustor who's coming though,' continued William, still smiling. 'Talk *his* hind leg off too.'

Tessa just couldn't resist saying quietly, 'You must get it from your father.' And as she spoke, she realized, with some distress she'd just broken again a vow of long-standing, namely never to refer to William's father in front of William; while at the same time knowing full-well he was bound to want to hear someday.

'Do I, Mother?' he asked. 'Was he good with words then?'

'Yes, and theatre.' She tried to palm it off, appear unconcerned.

They fell silent again and Tessa believed she'd covered the moment up, before William said, 'Mother, why do you never talk about my father? Surely I'm old enough now to know about him.' Tessa made no reply, and he added, 'I'm old enough to vote and kill for my country; surely that's old enough.'

She pretended she hadn't heard, got up from the table, went on preparing the meal, until William said solemnly, 'I'm no longer a kid, Mum.'

'I agree, William, but I'd still rather not talk about him just now. You see, although you may find it hard to understand, for me it's like digging something nasty up after it's been buried for ages.'

'Was he that bad?'

'No, I don't mean that. Of course. But it's hard for me.'

'You can't keep that sort of thing locked away forever. D'you realize that?'

'Don't pester me now please,' exclaimed Tessa. I'll tell you when I think the time's right.'

'William muttered, 'It *is* right. That's what I'm saying.'

Meanwhile, Tessa went on transporting lunch dishes between the kitchen and the breakfast room, mouth tightly shut and a determined expression on her face. 'Well?' asked William finally after a few minutes.

Tessa felt the ground slip at last from beneath her feet, knew she'd have to yield sooner or later. She let out a hurried breath, which might have passed for a sigh. 'Okay, but not now.'

'*Why* not now?' William insisted angrily.

'William, you must trust me. I've promised to tell you, and I will; I know you have a right; I've known for a long time.' She sat down, put her hand on his. 'But let's get this insurance business over and done with first. It won't be easy and I can't have that coming in between.'

William muttered, 'There's always a 'but', and Tessa continued, 'I'm afraid two 'buts' actually; I simply refuse to go into it all if Aunt Elizabeth's here. She's bound to throw in all sorts of unreal stuff. I just know it. She knew your father too, you know.'

William could contain his frustration no longer. 'Mother, please don't call her Aunt Elizabeth. Just plain 'Elizabeth' will do. I'm not a baby; you've just said so. Elizabeth won't mind what I call her.'

'All these requests, William. You're altering my life before my very eyes.'

'It's called growing up, Mum.'

'Yes, I suppose so.'

They ate lunch largely in silence, Tessa secretly dreading the arrival of the insurance man, who was bound to tie her naïve son in knots, and dreading, too, the moment she'd have to disinter the secrets of William's birth and his father's strange disappearance all those years ago In the hope of deflecting her son from thoughts about his father, and at the same time desperate to dispel the silence that had fallen between them, she said, towards the end of their lunch, 'So what's all this 'good with language' business, William? Tell me more about 'word persons'. Wouldn't they actually be called word-smiths?'

William couldn't resist taking the bait. 'Word-smith, word person, what's the difference? It's simply something I've discovered this year at H, Mother. There are people who understand language and people who just don't understand it at all, and probably never will. People, that is, in high-up positions sometimes. They get by, but can't really cope.'

'Isn't that a bit of a sweeping statement?' was all Tessa could think of to say. 'Who, for example?'

'I knew you wouldn't understand. That's why I never talk about it to you. It's not something you can talk about really.'

'Try, William,' Tessa insisted. 'I think you've got a point. But who're you referring to? Me? Am *I*, for example, one of those people who can't cope?

'I don't know. I think actually you love language more than most.'

'That's a relief. So *who* then?'

'Look, there's this colleague at the school, the one who had the accident, the one for whom I'm apparently meant to be covering up and lying for.'

'William, really!'

'It's true, Mother. But leave that for the moment; let's stick to what we're discussing. Well, this bloke told me he doesn't read anything; never. And he's meant to be a teacher. What can he possibly teach? Without a grasp of his own language?'

'Mathematics perhaps?'

'Okay. But even a Maths teacher has to *explain* things to people, communicate his subject.' Tessa, in spite of herself and disturbing thoughts about Adam, found herself being drawn into this strange and novel argument, felt herself genuinely intrigued by her son's youthful enthusiasm. William continued, 'You see, my theory is that the language is *per se* more important really than the subject matter. If Collingwood - that's my friend's name - happens to be good with figures, and wants to send rockets to the moon, that's fine. But he shouldn't be *teaching* that stuff. He can't. I think he may actually be dyslexic.'

'Can *you*?'

'Can I what?'

'Explain things to people.'

'Yes, with ease.'

'Are you a good teacher then?'

'I suppose I am. I'm one of the lucky ones.'

'Why 'lucky', William?'

William looked at her intently. 'There's nothing more important, Mother. In this world.'

'Than what? You're losing me. Teaching?'

'Yes, perhaps. But it's not just teaching; there are other things.' He looked hard for a moment at her. 'Understanding your own language is a gateway to so many other things.'

Tessa waited but there was another lengthy silence, which she finally broke. 'Gateway to what?'

'I don't know. Everything, poetry, music, relationships, there's no end to the possibilities, and the marvelous thing is they're all linked, if you have the language. That is, if you're not upside down and back to front with your own language. And I'm not.'

Tessa instinctively knew now what was coming, dreaded it really, and said it for him. 'Do you want to be a writer then?' She paused a moment and added with a smile, 'Or as second-best, a politician perhaps?'

William threw his hands in the air. 'A politician! They don't use language, they manipulate it badly for their own ends. There's a big difference. Using language is a journey of discovery, not a means to an end. You discover things.' He stopped, thought a bit, continued dramatically, 'All the great poets and musicians are on a journey into themselves.' Tessa nodded because she knew her son had hit the mark. And she was thinking: *And one so young. Only a few years back he was sitting on my knee...* William continued, 'Aren't we meant to do what we're good at, Mother? What's that bit in the bible about using your....'

The front doorbell rang and William was cut off in mid-sentence. Tessa opened the front door to the loss adjuster.

'Good afternoon. Is this right for Mrs. Bellman?' The smart young man, balding slightly, pasted what might have passed for a smile onto what was otherwise an earnest expression of business-like efficiency.

'Yes, I'm Mrs. Bellman. Come in. You're here to talk to my son, I believe.' She wondered how her son, the 'writer', might deal with this humourless emissary from the world of finance, and the black bag of subtle tricks he was grasping tightly in his left hand. 'Come into the living-room. You won't be disturbed there. I'll tell my son you've arrived.' She went back into the dining-room. 'William, it's that man from the insurance. Remember, don't commit yourself, *don't* admit to anything.'

'Leave it, Mother. I know how to deal with this.' He made his way to the living-room, wondering where any supposed difficulty could possibly lie. It was straightforward, a fact was a fact, wrap it in whatever ambiguous guise you liked. What's to be gained from turning fact into fiction, from concealing some things and inventing others? Just confusion, that's all.

'Hello.' The loss adjustor made no attempt to shake his hand, just stood in front of the fire-place and fiddled with some documents he'd placed on the low table.

'Shall we sit down?' William prompted.

'No thank you, this won't take long. I don't want to occupy too much of your time on a Saturday.' William nodded. They stood facing each other. After a few moments, and having adjusted his papers, the man said, 'I have to ask you some important questions relating to an accident. Just a formality. Are you Mr. William Bellman, resident at this, your permanent address...'? He sought momentarily for the address, '...Ah yes, 64 the...'

William finished it for him, '64 Terrace Drive. Yes. And no.'

The man looked at him enquiringly.. 'Yes, *and* no?'

'Yes, I am Mr. Bellman, but no, I'm not resident at this address.'

He checked his notes again. 'It says here you live with your mother at....'

William interrupted politely again, 'Well maybe, but I'm not actually living at 64 Terrace Drive permanently. This is my mother's address; I visit occasionally.'

'Do you have another address then?'

'Yes, but it's certainly not permanent. Only very temporary, in fact.'

The adjustor couldn't conceal a hint of impatience. 'I see. Can you let me have that address?'

'I could if I knew it. It's a small room in a school, which I will shortly be vacating. The room, that is, not the school.'

'You are vacating the school shortly then?'

'I'm not vacating the school. I'm vacating the room; I'm leaving the school. Sorry to be so pedantic, but I thought you'd want to get everything correct.'

The adjustor ran his hands carefully through what remained of his hair. 'I think, for the purposes of the record, that we take your mother's address here at W…as being the most permanent address we have.'

'William said, 'I suppose, yes; it all depends on how permanent you mean by 'permanent'. My mother could sell tomorrow for instance, and then neither of us would have a 'permanent' address.'

'Mr. Bellman, I take your point entirely. But it is Saturday and I think we should move on.'

'Ah, there's more, is there?'

'A little more, yes.' He referred to his notes again. 'I have to ask you a few short questions relating to an accident, a car accident, that my client was involved in some months ago.'

'Months. Was it so long? How time flies by.' As the man patiently nodded, William added, 'Well, I suppose you get hundreds of accidents. Please forgive the pun, but the *wheels* of justice move very slowly, don't they?'

'Well we do have a lot to deal with. Now, Mr. Bellman, moving on; I want to make it very clear that your answers to these questions are absolutely true to the best of your knowledge. That's all that matters, and no one can then accuse you of implicating yourself.'

'Golly. Am I already implicated by default then?'

'I can't of course answer that question, but as I said, so long as your answers are....'

'...True.' William completed his statement for him. 'Gosh, truth is such a complicated business. Was it Jesus, or perhaps Shakespeare, who said: *"What is Truth?"*?'

'I'm not well read enough, I'm afraid, Mr. Bellman.'

'No. But anyway, to the matter. The questions, please.'

'Yes, of course.'

He fumbled with his papers and, meanwhile, William sat down in one of the armchairs and indicated another. 'I think we've probably dealt with the difficult stuff and can relax a little.'

The adjustor didn't respond, but took his papers over and sat down. 'Do you know a Mr. Collingwood?'

'Yes.'

'Is he a friend?'

'Yes.'

'How long have you known him?'

'Uhh...two months...*at the time of the incident*, eight months *now*.'

The adjustor noted down the reply and William said, 'No, wait a moment, it was seven months, not eight.'

The adjustor nodded but allowed the detail to pass. 'Mr. Bellman, I want you to think hard before you answer this question. Were you, on the evening of the 15th October last, accompanying Mr. Collingwood as a passenger in his car?' There came no reply. The adjustor coughed and said, 'Mr. Bellman?' Still no reply as William appeared to be sinking ever deeper into his armchair. 'Mr. Bellman., did you hear....'

'Yes.'

'Ah, good.' He went to write down on the form.

'Yes, I *did* hear, and *no*, I can't be sure.' The adjustor eyed him skeptically. 'I was thinking hard, you see, as you suggested, and I just can't be sure of that precise date. It was a long time ago.'

'Then shall we say 'there or thereabouts'.

'That's fine by me, so long as I'm not incriminating myself.'

'No, I don't think there's any chance of that. Now, where were we? Ah yes, the learner driver….'

William, at this point, leant forward abruptly in the armchair. 'Mr. Loss Adjuster, can I stop you just there. I'm unable to understand why, in the space of half an hour, we've made so little progress in what seems a very straightforward affair. You see, the matter's blindingly simple. Why this lengthy prevarication?' He paused, as the adjustor, seemingly at a loss to know how to proceed following this quite irregular intervention, tried unsuccessfully to interrupt, placed the wad of papers back into his briefcase and took them out again, while William continued, 'Sorry, sir. Am I losing you?' Still no answer, and he went on, 'May I suggest then we do this process by narrative rather than Q & A. That will speed the procedure up. I'll tell you exactly what occurred, you listen and enter the details, perhaps at a later date. It will also lead to less ambiguity. You can interrupt of course at any time.'

The adjustor was now leaning forward too. 'If that's all right with you, then I'm happy to proceed that way. No matter how irregular it might be.'

'Irregular it may be, but true,' said William. 'You see 'time's getting on and I have shortly a very important dialogue to have with my mother. That is, before Aunt Elizabeth returns.'

'Fine. I 'm so sorry to be keeping you.' The adjustor seemed almost relieved to cooperate in this new initiative. 'Then, over to you, shall we say?' He accompanied the remark with a kind of conspiratorial smile.

'Right, some time in the middle of last October, I accompanied my colleague, Mr. A. Collingwood, in his car on a trip into central London from H…. As a driver with a temporary license, he was legally at the wheel, while I was accompanying him as a driver with full license. At what must have been about 6.30 pm, we were passing through Trafalgar Square and heading in the direction of the Mall. There were a lot of rather difficult traffic lights and there was also a considerable amount of traffic, and I noticed my colleague appeared slightly nervous.'

The adjustor stopped William there. 'We don't want value judgments, Mr. Bellman. They're not admissible. Your own personal opinion doesn't really count.'

'Okay, facts and facts alone. Put the personal opinions in or leave them out as you think fit. I don't really mind. So, Mr. Collingwood was *nervous*, and we were approaching quite quickly a crossroads where traffic coming from Whitehall meets traffic entering The Mall. A light at this point controls both sets of traffic. Unfortunately…' he paused, 'No, 'unfortunately' is bound to be a value judgment. What's unfortunate for some is fortunate for others, isn't it?' The adjustor nodded agreement and William continued, 'Omit 'unfortunately'… Mr. Collingwood did not notice this light at all, and crossed it just after it had turned from yellow to red.'

The adjustor interrupted. 'Are you sure you mean that? That sequence?'

'Yes. It's a fact. Is it also a value judgment?'

'Well that's open to a fine interpretation.'

'It's certainly a fact. I noted it distinctly at the time.'

The adjustor wrote briefly in his notes. He then looked up. 'Have you perhaps anything further to add? Any extenuating circumstances?'

'Something perhaps like, "Mr. Collingwood was fast asleep at the wheel at the moment of impact" do you mean?'

'Well, not quite so drastic.'

'Mr. Adjustor, what may be extenuating to one party will be, I assume, the opposite to the other party. I've just related what happened. Can I leave you to do the extenuations?'

The adjustor reached for his briefcase. 'Well then, that seems to be that. You're right; it's refreshing to come so quickly to the heart of the matter.' He stood up and really did smile this time. 'I need detain you no longer, Mr. Bellman. You've been most cooperative.'

William accompanied him to the door. 'Will I be hearing from you later?'

'I don't think so. Your statement probably concludes the whole matter in fact.' He smiled again, 'I'll leave you to the tender mercies of Aunt Elizabeth.'

William rejoined his mother in the back room. There was an expectant expression in her eyes; it said '*Has he coped*?' She said, 'Well?'

William simply nodded and then said, 'Mother, I think I'm going to have to go.'

She looked up in surprise. 'Go? Already? I thought you were at least staying the night.'

'No, mother, I mean go…leave… travel abroad perhaps.'

She tried to make light of what she'd just heard. 'Why? Was the interview in there really that bad? Are they coming after you or something?'

'No, Mother, it's not the interview; that's sorted. I just told the bloke what happened. A letter could have done just as well.' Tessa sat there looking at her son, unsure whether to laugh or cry. William continued, 'You see, I have to go. For myself. Remember what we were talking about before that bloke arrived? About what I should do this coming year? Well, I was working through it during the interview, and I've reached a conclusion: Where I am now, at the school, is just too stifling. And too cosy. I have to get out and see the world. Maybe write something. But you can't just write in a vacuum.'

Tessa felt a fissure gently pries itself open in her heart. Was the loneliness then to start all over again? Since that dreadful day twenty years before, when she'd received the letter from Adam, William, her beloved tiny son at the time, had been her anchor, her purpose really for existing. Nor was she even a person who could accept loneliness easily. It had been hard for her. She herself had been raised in a tight family unit, sisters, a brother, a purposeful mother chivvying her along. Trying to stay calm, she now said, 'Where might you go then?'

'Maybe America. Maybe Europe. Somewhere where I can be myself. There's nothing more important. I can't let things stand in my way.

And deep down Tessa knew it had to be. 'You will come back though?'

'I'll always come back, Mother.'

She murmured then, involuntarily, 'Your father's son, I knew it.'

William looked hard at her. 'What was that, Mum?'

She had now no choice but to repeat, 'I said, your father's son.'

They both stared at each other for a moment, before William said softly, 'Tell me Mother. You promised.'

She closed her eyes tightly, as if envisaging the moment she'd opened that terrible letter from Adam so long ago outside the post office in Bridgeport and read its contents so unbelievingly. 'Your father wrote to me, William, to tell me he wasn't coming back.'

William stared at her. 'And was that really so bad? It happens to people all the time.'

'He knew I was pregnant. That I was going to have you. I'd told him. But he didn't care.'

William was answering brutally, as if with his head only, not his heart. While each reply drove daggers into Tessa. 'Again, it's not uncommon, Mother.'

'He gave no reason. I don't believe he even had a reason. We'd had no falling out.'

William hesitated before asking 'Were you in love with him?'

She was silent for a moment, and then said, 'Desperately. But I don't believe he was in love with me.'

William said bluntly, almost challengingly, as if that statement concluded the matter, 'Well then.'

Angrily, Tessa said, 'But I was having his child. He left me no address. No means of contact even.' She stopped for a moment, and then added, '"*we cannot meet again*", those were his words. They're engraved in my heart.' She glared at William. 'That's not so common, is it?' There was vehemence in her voice.

William shook his head. 'But why? What were his motives then?'

Tessa was still angry. She could never *not* be angry when she thought of that moment. 'Wouldn't we like to know? Sure, in his letter he invented a whole bunch of reasons; the reasons of a self-indulgent egocentric. Let me think.' She lapsed into silence, then said, 'Yes, I remember how he put it: *"I'm different. I feel I am reborn."* How nice.'

William nodded, attempted in some way to mitigate the sarcasm in his mother's voice. 'Nice? What do you mean?'

'What I mean is, how nice and how easy it must be for someone to re-invent themselves, just walk away.'

'Yes, but *why* did he do that?'

'Listen, William, your father, Adam, had been involved in some very dangerous things.' She paused, watching her son's reaction carefully. 'We both were. Me too. We were together then. We could have both been killed.'

'What dangerous things?'

'We went after someone. It was impetuous. We were young, thought it would be easy, an adventure.' William waited, amazed, hardly able to believe the fairy-tale he was hearing. 'We shouldn't have got involved in the first place. I think your father got carried away.'

'Was this a near-death experience you're talking about?'

Tessa looked hard at her son. 'It could have been. It became one. We others pulled back in time luckily.' Nodding she added, simply unable to paint the complete picture for her son, 'Your father was very badly hurt.' A silence descended on them, William trying to come to terms with what he'd heard, Tessa desperately trying to regain her composure, push the matter back into the recesses where it had sat for so long. Finally, gently shaking her head, she said very deliberately, 'Your father was not an easy man, William. I believe what we'd done together, that whole venture, unlocked something in him, gave him a way out of a deep dissatisfaction somewhere inside him. I couldn't understand it at the time, and I still don't really.' She shook her head again. 'He was not a happy man. I often think our 'adventure' gave him the opportunity to re-invent his life.'

'Is that good or bad, Mother? Are you trying to excuse him now?'

She shook her head vehemently. 'No. It's just what happened.' She sank her head and seemed nearly in tears but finally managed to say, 'At least that's what he seemed to say in the letter. "*A fresh start.*" I suppose I wasn't enough for him.'

She stopped, tears running down her cheeks. William said, 'Where is the letter? Can I see it?'

'I threw it away. It got lost somewhere along the line. I don't know where it is. It's not important now.'

'It's very important,' William exclaimed. 'But, ah well...'. He reached a hand out to his mother's cheek. 'You're crying...Don't cry. You've got *me*.'

Her hand brushed his face. 'I know; that's what keeps me going.'

Enough had been said. They were both exhausted. They sat looking at each other for what seemed ages. At last, Tessa said, 'William, this writing you talk about. You have to be careful. Writing can be dangerous too.'

'How? How on earth?'

'Well I tried it once myself. Tried to complete the story, explain if just to myself what had happened.' She smiled. 'I even fantasized an ending. Perhaps make it more palatable, I suppose. I'm not sure it did me any good though.'

The resignation had appeared in her voice again. William said, 'It doesn't have to be like that. Writing is good. I'm going to find that letter. Find out what happened. I'm going to find my father. Believe me.'

There was such adamancy in his voice that Tessa was alarmed. 'I knew I shouldn't have told you.'

'Mother, I have to know who tried to kill him, and who saved him.'

Tessa said quietly, 'We two got out, just in time. I've told you. But I think it's unlikely you will ever find your father again. You see, he's a rolling stone, always was, and this experience gave him the chance to start again. Perhaps with a new identity even,.' She mustered all the sarcasm she could, 'To be "*reborn*" as he put it.'

'So my father walks the earth with a false identity?'

'Possibly. He's illegal.' She paused and then added, 'Another good reason for his not coming back.'

'So you don't know what he does.'

'Of course I don't. I don't know anything about him. Except the letter said his new life would give him a chance to write; yes, write for his '*own generation*', as he put it. What do you think he could find to say to this '*new*' generation?'

William shook his head. 'I wonder if I'm like him.'

'You're not like him at all, William, actually.'

'You said I was. Remember? Before we started on all this. I must be.' There was a long pause before he said, almost as a question, 'The writing, you mean?'

Tessa nodded. 'Yes. Perhaps.'

'I wonder if he did write anything.'

For just a moment his mother seemed taken aback, confused. Then she said, 'He did. He had a vivid imagination; that I can tell you. He was quicksilver, more actor though than writer.'

She seemed drained. William, after a long silence, said, 'You love him still, don't you? Despite what he did.'

'Maybe.'

'*I* wouldn't.'

'You have to forgive in the end, William. It's the only way.'

'I know, but I just don't believe I could.'

Tessa said, 'And now you're leaving too.'

'I have no choice.'

She half smiled. 'We're back where we started then. But William, I won't stop you. You must go; together we must think of somewhere sensible. And now that you know about your father, in a strange way, I feel a great weight off my shoulders.'

It was over. William returned the following morning to the leafy London suburb of H..., where the great trees were starting to bloom, and as he drove, he tried to fashion a living person out of the brief description he already had of this new-discovered father, this quicksilver man, who'd metaphorically died and come back to life.

And thoughts about his father engendered thoughts too about his grandfather. The paintings. Did his mother know more than she pretended? Had it been the old man too - as well as his own father - who'd led the bohemian life ('*egocentric indulgence*' she'd called it), until abruptly he'd been summoned back to toe the line, raise a son, provide? If so, there probably hadn't been that much difference after all between his praiseworthy grandfather and his apparently profligate father? Except the divergent routes they'd each chosen for themselves. And what of himself? Was this self-same wayward gene now rising from the ashes to confront him too?

However, he wouldn't allow himself to be deflected for long by these abstract concerns. Life was for the moment, and he had decisions to make. To find himself and to take care of his mother. Those final weeks of June were almost painfully beautiful at H...: the scent of the flowers, the birdsongs, the long summer evenings, the great elms hanging heavy under the weight of their leaves, the smell of fresh-cut grass and the voices out on the cricket square far into the evening. He allowed himself to relish this short-lived paradise and forget about the imminence of his potential journeys.

In his little room that first night back, he pictured, indulgently, another young man of an altogether earlier century, sitting in the same twilight, writing lines that would shake literature. *'Oft methinks how rich 'twould be to die, to cease upon the midnight with no pain.'* That poet had in fact *been* 'dying', desperately fulfilling his own visions. William had no desire to die - his life stood enticingly before him - but he longed to be able to pen lines like this literary hero, and often idly wondered if he, too, would hear the nightingale at dead of night in these self-same woods Keats had heard it. *"Thou wast not born for death, immortal bird"*.

Meanwhile, two days after they'd all met together, Elizabeth had flown back to Connecticut.'

'Did you say 'artistic' or 'autistic', Sis?'

They were sitting having breakfast together in the airport terminal and Tessa spelled out the little word that had come to disturb her dreams the previous night. 'Autistic. A...U.'

Elizabeth had thought about it for a moment or two. 'Maybe, a little. He's very serious, isn't he? Almost disconcertingly so. He doesn't laugh like you and me. But he's a lovely boy, Tess. I love him.' She walked through the departure gate leaving Tessa hoping 'love' meant 'like', in an 'aunty' sort of way. She wondered too how long it might be before she saw her sister and her family again. So much for her to do, with Grandfather not getting any younger by the day.

William took part in Hayden's *'Creation'* on the final two evenings of term, performed to a packed audience in the ancient school hall at H. In the second desk of the cellos, he found himself scarcely daring to touch bow to strings, as the hushed opening bars of that great work summon the brooding silence, the uncanny darkness, the unnatural stillness of a world devoid of life, or a God. He was astonished by how easily chords, harmonies, could summon up in the imagination so accurate a tableau as this and could paint so vivid a picture; it was music straying again into the world of Art.

The music soared into the Major key - the key reserved by composers for joy, gladness, exuberance, jubilation - and, in one giant, sustained chord, the listener gazes spellbound on God's works: "*let there be light, and there was light*". At that moment, the nineteen-year-old boy knew he too had gazed, for one short second, on that same Paradise.

One further notable event happened to this young, mildly autistic visionary and poet-in-waiting, during his time at H...: he performed his own first miracle.

On the last Sunday evening of term, he and Collingwood marshaled their young charges on the pavement, crocodile formation, towards the school swimming-pool, situated up on the hill in the hub of Main-School. It was a rare treat, a tradition, in this sweltering weather, and as the term reached a climax, for both boys and staff alike of Junior School to sneak a visit to the pool, set in the heart of those scenic ancient buildings, and to relax for an hour or two. There was a buzz of excitement that evening among the boys, staff and wives, scattered around the pool or wallowing in the clear water. A scene of simple pleasure.

Afternoon turned to evening, and most of the bathers began drifting off towards their various duties, or in response to the chilling air; however, a few parties still lingered on, and among them the Head of the Junior School, his wife, and William too, who'd handed over to Collingwood the responsibility for walking the young boys back down the hill. The pool and surrounds were fairly empty.

William's boss, S, a genial, middle-aged man, was by now paddling inexpertly in the empty pool, accompanied by the gentle chatter and occasional shouts and whoops of those remaining pool-side. William, raising his head from the book occasionally and glancing at his boss, assumed S was making the most of the recent departure of the boys, and enjoying the privacy of a lone swim. As it turned out, such privacy could have come at a very heavy price indeed. Whatever the reasons for this solitary swim, S was now drifting gently around in the empty water, occasionally gripping the side of the pool, and joining less and less in the general banter, almost to the point where he'd been forgotten. William too had pushed his deck-chair one notch down and returned to his book. Only very slowly did the plaintive, high-pitched and rather urgent cry intrude upon his reading. At last he looked up and saw S wallowing in the dead centre of the mass of water, reaching out flimsy arms, as if to take a grip on empty air, head dipping disturbingly once or twice beneath the surface. It was for perhaps no longer than three quarters of a minute before William emerged from his enthralling book and realized that his boss was indeed drowning, and that no one else pool-side, seemed aware at all. Hurling his book away, our hero dived in, shorts and shirt and all, and swam with rapid strokes towards the Headmaster.

A drowning man is not governed by calm reason; flailing arms and empty shouts contrive to increase the panic and sabotage any efforts of the rescuer. William had had no lessons in life-saving, but somewhere in his memory he'd heard it said you take the unfortunate person firmly under the chin and, in that way, propel him steadily towards safety. Hold the head up at all costs. Such a procedure seemed total common sense anyway. He was a strong swimmer and had little difficulty supporting S, while calmly issuing instructions to the wriggling mass he was supporting. It seemed to him all the more strange he was gripping the body of a man who, at normal times, would have been issuing instructions to *him*; how dramatically now, and in the most unexpected way, the roles had been reversed as he steered the illustrious man to safety and eager outstretched hands. Death, the great leveler.

William left H... forever two days later, and, as was customary, went to pay his respects to his boss and bid him goodbye. As the two shook hands, S gave him a broad if slightly sheepish smile. 'Perhaps that little misadventure in the pool the other day need go no further, Mr. Bellman. We wouldn't really want my lamentable swimming skills known in the wider community, don't you think?'

William looked at him steadily for a few seconds, puzzled by the absence of any sort of gratitude. 'Of course not, sir. Mum's the word; you can rely on me.'

'I know I can, and all the best in your future endeavours.'

Throughout his life, William never once mentioned the incident to anyone, even his best friends. He'd given his word.

PART 2
(A FAR FROM PERFECT LIFE)

CHAPTER 6

"In which ADAM RILEY returns to old haunts"

Adam Riley, alias Sol Smith, had always instinctively understood space and spaces; he possessed that all too rare gift of spatial awareness. As he dumped his suitcase that afternoon beside the trunk of one of the old chestnut trees lining the school drive-way and ran off to join a rowdy kick-about on a nearby patch of grass, although quite unaware of it himself, that vital gift of his quickly became all too apparent to his nine-year-old teammates. Was he Nat Lofthouse or Stanley Matthews, or God? He was certainly an ace, the kind of bloke you had to have in your side. They cast covert but admiring glances at him as he placed slide-rule passes again and again to the feet of colleagues and, like lightning, spotted infallibly those invisible little lanes that randomly open up and come and go upon a football-field, those avenues in constant flux, all too familiar to chess players. Space lay at the heart of them all, because space can be filled at any moment by a team-mate, and the opposition's defences split by a well-aimed pass. Great generals know the principle, Formula 1 drivers know it, Entrepreneurs know it, Ballet dancers know it. It's not something that can be learned, it's a gift, and that afternoon Adam's fellow-players could only wonder how this mysterious conjuror had discovered a secret that seemed almost as important as splitting the atom.

What's good for games is good for life-skills too. You notice those *non-spatials* for instance as they stand forlornly at the edge of the highway, surrounded by recovery vans and flashing police cars, while you yourself coast past them on the way to catch the flight they're going to miss. You watch them every day too on the busy high street, reversing into angles they'll never make, while their back wheel lands on the kerb and there front end protrudes at 45 degrees.

Even on the putting green, amongst those wise veterans of sport, the secret undulations that lie between ball and hole may well leave the uninitiated mystified as their putt veers wildly to the right or left, to the accompaniment of excited shouts of indignation and self-pity. They have no sense of space, and golf has caught up with them.

So, twelve years later now, and once more setting foot on the sandy soils of Hillcrest's football fields, he smiled as he remembered how he'd attempted to explain to that original team of his, years ago, the idea of *space*. 'A football's not a magnet, boys. You've got to keep moving. Away from the ball preferably.'

'You've got to get it first, Coach.'

'No, you get it *if* you move away from the ball.' They'd failed to understand, and he'd tried another tack, a rather desperate one. 'Look, imagine a soccer field's a giant chessboard. Anyone play chess?' A few affirmative murmurs from the group. 'Good, well, a chessboard has a lot of different pieces, doesn't it? So also does a soccer field. The pieces are you. But the pieces don't all move in the same direction, nor at the same time.' He'd waited a second or two, hoping for a light of understanding in anyone's eyes, saw none. 'You see, guys, the pieces are all interactive, dependent on each other; where one piece moves affects all the others.'

'Still can't see what that's got to do with soccer, Coach.'

'What I'm trying to explain is that you can't stand still on a soccer field, even if you *haven't* got the ball. If you stand still, you surrender the initiative, they'll attack you. In chess, and in football too, that's fatal. You lose. And, if some of you are thinking of joining the military service, then it's fatal in war as well.'

'We haven't got a war on right now, Coach.'

'You will have when you meet 'Dallas Royals' in the State play-offs.'

A few despairing chuckles, and someone bold enough to voice that despair. 'We won't be standing still, Coach, we'll be running; in the opposite direction.'

When the chuckles had died down, Adam replied, 'Precisely. That's what I'm trying to show you. You stand still in life, you'll be losers.'

Blank silence, until *'Wise-ass With the Voice'* said, 'Can't we get on with the practice, Coach.'

And Adam realised he'd gone too far; War and Life were well beyond their experience and not helpful. 'Okay, Life's something you'll learn later. Let's stick to chess. Bishop, Rook, Pawns etc, if you keep on the move, attack from different directions, sooner or later things'll open up, you'll get the opposition's King in check-mate.'

'You mean, score a goal, Coach?'

'That's right!' exclaimed Adam with delight. 'Well done, that Pawn there.'

Adam, the new-Adam, really *had* believed what he was preaching. Keeping on the move was what he did best; it was his own mantra. And the mantra suited his talents well, a personality which responded to the idea of a world in constant flux. When, in that fateful September of 1967, he'd awoken on the couch in the little house beside the lake in West Texas, he'd taken a new name and new identity, and with only two other people in the world aware he hadn't died, he'd set off, determined to lead his life as if on a chessboard, seizing opportunities, never being tied down, moving from job to job, the bane of all hopeful bosses, those self-satisfied proponents of restraint and restriction. Yes, he'd grown to hate bosses; they stood in his way. He was the Scarlett Pimpernel of the 20th century: *they sought him here, they sought him there...* but they couldn't find him anywhere: he'd already moved on.

From the little lake-house, he'd moved first north, up to his old hunting grounds of western Canada, where he'd taught school again for a while, moved on, and, for a time, callously sold encyclopaedias to down-trodden families that neither needed them nor could afford them. Sick of that, he'd moved back to the UK, his native land, on a false passport and with money he still had access to in the US. There, not always teaching, he was driven on by the belief that around the next corner would come Nirvana, a state of contentment for his restless soul. However, as the years passed, he'd noticed himself again and again slipping into complacent mediocrity, while, over his shoulder, he always saw others richer, more fulfilled, more successful than himself.

For all his supposed bravado, Adam hadn't been, nor was now, a happy man. The hope of Nirvana had faded, and, like a horse afflicted with lice or ticks, each day had become a permanent irritation. Disillusion had set in, and, with that, the certain knowledge he hadn't ever got over Mary, and knew now he never would. Whatever he did, he would have to bear the memory of her with him. What's more, he was becoming increasingly worried about his own security, outside the law and under a false identity. *At any moment, might not the authorities come knocking at his door? Best to keep on the move then.*

Worst of all though was his endless obsession with the mysterious circumstances surrounding his 'release from death' on that dramatic day in September 1967. *Who had released him, left him lying drugged on a bed, helpless and at the mercy of someone else, a stranger, and deprived of his own freedom? Why and how had it ever come about?* To be sure, he was free now to come and go, make his own choices; but freedom received at the hands of another is not freedom at all; just another form of bondage. He needed to go back, track down this ghost that haunted him and had deprived him utterly of memory. This remorseless state of inertia, all these lonely days; perhaps no one would ever know *quite* how lonely.

At last, he'd come to the decision to leave this nomad existence in Canada and 'Old Europe', and to return to those haunts at 'Hillcrest' itself. Texas, where he'd started out so long ago. He determined to look bravely into the teeth of those violent events that had struck him down, and perhaps re-find a sort of peace, and even restore his broken memory.

It would not be easy; would the school for instance even be there, intact? And if indeed it *had* arisen from the ashes, could he ever risk being recognised as a major participant in those dreadful events of '67? He knew he could only regain access to Hillcrest under yet again a new identity.

At that very moment, now, he sat, binoculars slung around his neck, watching intently, hopefully unnoticed from the security of his car, as the little school up on the hill went about its daily business. There was clearly movement of people. Each passing day of his unofficial watch convinced him that the school had not just been neglected, left to decay in the wake of the calamity, but reinstated, almost certainly under new management. Periodically during the day, he took up vantage points, at about half a mile distance, moving with the passage of the sun from place to place, to avoid windscreen glare, which might catch the attention of a casual observer at the school. Daily he kept up this solitary vigil, homing in with the binoculars on the occupants, intent on wresting precise details of them, their manner, their timetable, even their features, as evidence of a school with a completely clean slate, no remnants of the former 'Hillcrest'.

Throughout three long weeks, he mapped the movements of the occupants, so as to know, at any given time of the day or evening, where and when they might or might not be, until finally he felt ready to make a move and start a new life. No room for slip-ups. They'd known and buried him in '67 as Adam Riley; now he was to be Sol Smith: same man, same face, new name. He had to be sure no one from that era remained. Just one person would be enough to expose him. He would only have one chance.

As the sun dipped behind the flat prairie that evening, he stepped from the car, clambered over the school boundary fence and walked boldly across the playing fields towards the brightly-lit building to his right. It used to be the dining-hall, a much-loved area for food and fun and relaxation. Was it still the same? He checked his watch again. 6pm, supper. And on Wednesday evenings, a special supper when the boarders and staff too, dressed up in their finery. As he looked now into the Hall, he experienced an involuntary thrill to notice they'd retained the old custom of formal dinner - for him a first sign that this establishment seemed indeed to be one which promised a custom-led community, one which honoured tradition, and which he might one day, with luck, become a part of again.

Although Sol knew he had little to fear of recognition from the student body itself, which would inevitably have altered over several years, the staff at the top of the tables, and the possible Headmaster, were a different matter; some may well have stayed around throughout these years of absence, and be able still to recognise him and give him away, by an impromptu greeting: *'Adam! Can it really be you?'* He scanned the features of each intently until he felt confident: There was no one in that dining-hall he knew, or might know him.

The following morning, Saturday, he presented himself at Reception.

'I was just passing through on my way up to Oklahoma; thought I'd drop in, have a look at the school. I've heard so much about it.'

'Well, that's mighty nice, Mr...'

He shot out a hand. 'Sol, Mr. Sol Smith.'

'Mr. Smith. Gee, I just love your accent. You must be from England.'

'Correct, although I know this part of America quite well; I've travelled a lot in the Southern States.'

'Well, sure is nice to see you, Mr. Smith. We'd be delighted to give you a little tour. Mr. Doublejoy - that's our Principal - is away this weekend but he'd really enjoy showing you round the school. How long will you be staying in these parts. Perhaps next Monday? Mr. Doublejoy'll be back then.'

'Monday afternoon would suit me just fine. I'll look forward to that.'

'Say 2 p.m. Mr. Doublejoy'll be here in Reception to greet you. Could I tell him by the way how you came to hear of Hillcrest?'

'You bet. I'm doing a Masters in American Literature at Washington State right now. On and off that is; sometimes more 'off' than on, I'd say. Anyway, I bumped into a few of your former students up there recently. Lovely people. Can't remember names of course; hopeless with names; the scourge of middle age. Let's see, perhaps, if it'd help to give Mr. Doublejoy a bit of background about my movements, you'd like to tell him I'm on my way to Oklahoma to visit some of the dustbowl locations that feature in 'The Grapes of Wrath'. See Sallisaw with my own eyes, so to speak.'

'That's real nice, Mr. Smith. Can't say I know the town myself. I have to confess to being a bit of a stop-at-home. We Texans don't tend to get out and about as much as we should.'

'Why should you? Such a lovely state yourself. *'God's own country'* I believe is the saying.'

'Sure is. And I think Mr. Doublejoy'll be delighted to meet you. He teaches a few classes of English here himself. Matter of fact,. I've got a feeling you'll have a lot in common'

'Fascinating...uh, what should I call you? Mrs...'

'Sally. Just call me plain old Sally.'

'Thanks then, Sally, and I'll see you 2 o'clock prompt next Monday.'

The two of them parted company, leaving Sol armed with enough information about the Principal to enable him to concoct a suitable story about his life so far. Why should he worry anyway? He grew up in England and had spent the last few years back in England. His credentials were excellent even if his CV was largely fiction.

'Seems like you've dropped in as if heaven-sent, Sol. (First name basis almost from the word go; but hadn't that always been the way at Hillcrest?). We're losing our Head of English for this coming term. Family problems. I was wondering how I was going to fill the position. I'm of course tied up with admin; otherwise I'd have filled it myself. If you could plug the gap, I'd be more than pleased; you'd be a veritable *deus ex machina.*'

Mr. Owen Doublejoy, Principal at Hillcrest, had cursorily checked out Adam's CV and seized upon the opportunity to extricate himself from an imminent staffing problem by going out on a limb with this rather well-qualified academic from the Old Country. Adam couldn't believe his good fortune. The two of them had subsequently set off on a tour of the attractive campus (one which Adam already knew only too well).

'D'you think perhaps, Adam,' Doublejoy had continued, 'you could fill the gap this term; see how you like the place, and then we could talk again in August to assess if you'd be interested in a more permanent position. You know, I never seem to be sure, from one year to the next, who'll be here on the faculty and who won't. Things are like that over here; very fluid.'

As Doublejoy continued, describing the details of the job he was offering, discussing extra-curricular possibilities, live-in duties, particular skills he might be able to offer the students, Adam was all the while spotting spaces, looking out for flexibility. It seemed ideal on the face of it; Doublejoy was portraying an outfit perfectly in sync with his own opportunistic lifestyle: nothing rigid, a spontaneity not dissimilar to the old Hillcrest he remembered: a space where one could breathe. Had he fallen on his feet?

Back in the Head's luxurious study, Doublejoy had taken another glance at Adam's false CV. 'I see you've had quite a few jobs outside of teaching. It's something we like in our faculty at Hillcrest. Mature, tried and tested teachers with not too narrow perspectives.'

Adam had sipped his bitter coffee and leaned back in his swivel chair. 'Yes, but I believe I'm about ready to come back to teaching, Owen. You know how the saying goes: *'Those who can, teach; those who can't, line their own pockets.* Well, I think I'm about ready to stop lining my pockets and join the academic fraternity again.'

They'd both laughed long and loud at Adam's concise résumé. It was clear to Adam, this potentially new boss had a sense of humour too and was far removed from the fusty, self-satisfied managers he'd grown used to in London.

Leaning abruptly forward now in his chair and assuming something bordering on a business-like tone, Doublejoy said, 'Look, I'd like to make a suggestion. We're on vacation now; term starts at the end of April. If you could start in three weeks, we can see how it goes from there.' Adam pretended to be taken by surprise, made a show of hesitating, and Doublejoy added, 'Of course, we could offer you a bed here for tonight, if you'd like to look around a bit more, and take your time. Where are you currently staying?'

'The Holiday Inn down the road.'

'Fine. You could consider my proposal overnight and we could meet up again in the morning. Say 10 o'clock.'

'That suits. I'm currently taking a break from my Masters anyway, a sort of sabbatical. And if things didn't work out, I could always take my studies up again in the Fall.'

'Look, don't decide right now. Give me your decision in the morning.'

Adam however had already decided. He'd long forgotten, on his journeys, that wonderful informality of the old Hillcrest. It was all flooding back to him now though. The matter was concluded.

Adam awoke early next morning with heart lighter than for years. They'd given him an apartment with wide oblong windows overlooking the school lake, which had been converted from the small muddied pond he remembered from earlier days. Now ducks floated on the rippling lake and rowing-boats waited beside a jetty almost hidden in the reeds. The sun had just come up and he hauled himself from his bed and took another stroll around the campus. His stride was light. All the old buildings sprang at him, each bearing its own special memory. A gentle spring breeze caressed him as he wandered down the hill to what had been the new girls' dorm. Bricks, once shiny new, were now mellow and fading. Reminders everywhere, almost sometimes too poignant, of things done and achieved: the amphitheatre, the swimming pool, the soccer field, the busy noisy dining-hall, the classroom blocks sprang at him from all sides. This, right now where he stood, was the very path he'd chaperoned Mary down the hill that night after a play rehearsal, when the sudden excited bark of coyotes had so vividly reminded them of the magical unreality of where they found themselves together. Could he perhaps have the chance to live it all over again? It was like re-entering Paradise. Not merely the beauty of the place; no, it was more. These sensations, combining together, couldn't really be expressed in words. Words were inadequate to describe them; it was love really. It was an almost overpowering sense of hope and happiness, which for years now he hadn't known and had even avoided. It was the sensation he'd felt, when he used to creep down to Mary's room at dead of night, certain she would receive him. Adam met Doublejoy at 10 a.m. and gave him his formal decision, and left, promising to be back again in time for the summer term.

'We'll have a bachelor apartment ready for you. Perhaps the same as you had last night.'

They shook hands formally and Adam went off to collect his luggage from the motel. No need to return to DC. That was a fabrication he'd given the Receptionist. He already had his sole earthly possessions with him. Nor did he head off towards Oklahoma, but instead took the road to Abilene, en route for a place called Possum

Kingdom, a hidey-hole of former days.

****

CHAPTER 7

"How William wrestles in the throes of Education, and is initiated into the enchanting perils of the fairer sex"

"How greatly this candidate, with his all-round prowess in so many activities, will add to the extra-curricular life of the College,"

With the aid of his high school, proclaiming boldly on his behalf, William obtained a place at the prestigious university of C..., where he was to continue the linguistic studies he'd commenced with such success at high school. Entry to the hallowed halls had also been made possible by a generous financial grant from his paternal grandfather.

William, plunging enthusiastically into his studies in those first few months, found himself delving into the intimate thoughts, ideas, passions of no more than just a few heralded foreign writers, masters of their trade, literary giants of their age. *But why so few works*? In the silence of his room, he wondered why he was required to focus so fixedly on a mere one or two authors? Shouldn't he just pick up another book at the local bookshop and widen his scope, until his knowledge of German literature of the 17th and 18th century would be as broad as the sea itself?

The first few months hurried by, and he was still wondering why the syllabus seemed so limited; week upon week had passed, and still, like detectives with magnifying glasses, he and his fellow students were required to bury themselves in just one or two selected texts, take them apart, put them together again, and present each week verbatim to their fellow students a critical 'Paper'. He dreaded this written requirement, couldn't get it right, the words not flowing, sitting nervously at his desk, when it would have been all too simple just to write off his thoughts in one glorious generalisation: *not bad, but not as good as the one we read last week.*

Worse still, there appeared to be no help at hand, and even less advice. No wonder disillusion started to set in, and William gazed with hatred and disgust at the well-thumbed little book on his desk. Indeed, *small'* (not large), seemed the mark of not only his chosen faculty but his chosen university as well. Didn't the very name, *University*, boast a *'universal'* education? For the first time in his life, he was looking failure in the face.

He had a personal tutorial each Tuesday with his French tutor, a young lady who listened to his essays calmly, correcting him here and there and never appearing to intrude upon or question his overall abilities. It was almost more than he could bear to admit to this sweet young lady his belief that he was failing. 'Am I perhaps on the wrong course and not suited to the study of literature? I can read the text all right, but critical essay-writing is *so* difficult.'

She however merely smiled back and kindly shook her head. 'Don't worry, you're doing well; it'll come.' She offered no explanation as to *how* it might come, leaving William to believe she must be a conjuror, who, with the wave of a wand, would put a basketful of words at his feet and put him out of his misery, Either that, or just plain not interested in his plight at all

The tutorial continued on its way (they were discussing a quite gripping novel by Francois Mauriac) and William began to think she'd forgotten altogether about their earlier discussion, until, quite suddenly and unprompted, she put her Mauriac gently down on the desk. 'What do you want to be, William?' Long Pause. 'Do you want to be a writer?' There was just one person and one person only (his mother). who knew about his secret ambitions. Quite how this pleasant young lady also knew, William could only guess. However, she left him no time to wonder, but continued, 'What do you want to write about?' It seemed a reasonable enough question, but William didn't know. He just shook his head, as the faintest of smiles brushed across his tutor's face and she let slip, and she leaned back on the chaise longue, letting slip an enigmatic *'yes'*, and added, Shall we get on with your essay? Why don't you read that final paragraph and let's see what specifics we can draw from the text.'

In sa trice, she seemed to have completely forgotten about his writing ambitions, and William started to read out his paragraph, thinking it was unlikely he was going to receive any more advice. William got halfway through reading his lamentable essay, when, out of the blue, and as if addressing someone else in the room, she raised a hand and remarked, 'I suppose if you want to be a writer, you've got to have something to write about.' She was nodding her head now. 'You know, *I* tried writing myself actually, and decided it wasn't for me.'

'Why not?' William asked urgently.

. 'Oh, I imagine, Mr Bellman, I was just too content with my life, too wrapped up in myself Too self-satisfied. You've got to be driven.'

To William's relief, the relaxed smile appeared again as she reached for a large volume nearby on the shelf and thumbed through a few pages. 'Ah, here it is. Yes. I expect you'll recognise this: *Die Kunst ist lang, das Leben kurz.*' and closed the book again. 'Wrong language, but I suspect that's one of your set texts in German, isn't it?'

'It is,'. William replied, 'It's *Faust*, I think.'

'Correct.' She thought for a moment. 'I forget the saying in the French, however, of course in the English it's: "*Art is long and life is short.*"' She replaced the book carefully. 'All too short, I'm afraid.'.

'Pardon, *what* is?'

She smiled again. 'Life. Life's too short, Mr Bellman. Too much to cram in.'

William acknowledged with a grin, while she continued, 'You know, I've always believed since then there has to be some element of suffering if you want to be a writer.' William looked at her in surprise while she continued, 'Call it a feeling of discontent.'

William laughed openly. 'I'd better go back and tell my girl-friend it's all over between us.'

'No, don't do that!' She hesitated, and nodded then her head as she continued, 'But I think suffering and experience are the key to good writing.'

It was time for the end of the tutorial and she made movements to pack papers together. As William made a move too, she gave him a final smile. 'You'll be alright, Mr Bellman. Don't forget, *Die Kunst ist lang!* Go out and see the world. See how other people live. It takes simply years to learn how to write. Suffer a bit too. We'll give you here the nuts and bolts; experience will do the rest. See you next week. Keep working on the Mauriac.'

William didn't easily forget that advice, so freely given. He particularly puzzled over her notion of *suffering*, and occasionally found himself wondering about his so-called Father, who apparently wanted to be a writer. Was *he* suffering too. To judge from his Mother, Tessa, and her sister, Elizabeth, he seemed to have had his fair share of suffering. *Near death, back from the dead.* It was really more than he wanted to cope with though. Enough of that whole fairy-tale. Hadn't he already wasted too much time?

And then, quite unexpectedly, as the final two weeks of his second year at C… drew to a close, came a letter from a school-friend proposing a roughly-patched-together trip in the vacation to a distant corner of the British Empire, untrammelled as yet by the tentative footsteps of tourists or inquisitive students alike. A wholly new experience awaited him. After a modicum of thought, he packed his cricket bat back into its bag together with all his idle summer plans, and agreed - naively it must be said - to this precarious journey into unknown territory.

For six long weeks the two friends trudged, often aimlessly, never peacefully, always anxiously, through the grime and dirt and disease of an alien world, where beggars pursued you step by step, stridently claiming a coin and then another and then another until your heart hardened as you realised with dismay that no amount of coins would be enough to satisfy the awful needs of the entire impoverished nation. Assailed each moment by disturbing sights and sounds and memories of a world a million miles remote from their own cloistered, privileged existence, the two of them clung like driftwood to the familiarity of each other, as the only refuge from a tide that threatened to overwhelm them both. They fled this madness at the end of six weeks, not looking back and suffering, both physically and mentally, in fear of what might be following behind. Separating finally, they returned, each to his own calm and sheltered home; in the words of the poet, '*sadder and wiser men*'

What had happened though? What remarkable metamorphosis had occurred? As William stood that day on the pavement opposite the gates to his college, he felt a lightness in his head despite the burden of exams that awaited him in just a few months. He visited the libraries, read feverishly what others had written about the works in his current assignments, and at last began to realise it wasn't *his* opinions his tutors sought, but instead, what learnéd critics, down the years, had noted, and how their ideas had been phrased. His marks went up, week by week, and daily he gave thanks to that advice he'd received from his lady French tutor: *don't be too self-possessed.*

William's Finals required a lot of writing, a lot of words, but, immune from the usual silent hysteria that pervades most exam rooms, William latched onto a couple of key questions and, once writing, he didn't stop, as he embellished the kernel of his answer with tasteful flowery circumlocution, until he'd fashioned two essays which combined both substance and style enough to impress even the sternest of examiners. He was still frantically scribbling his neat summing up as the administrator proclaimed *'time'*.

He knew he'd pulled it off. He walked out of the Hall, certain that all those hours of reading and commentaries and dictionary work, and chaotic lectures and tutorials had paid off, and that he'd made the grade; ready at last to move from the safety of the familiar, to the harsh uncertainties of new people and places.

*****

{**Hamburg 1991**) It was a sweet and harmonious entry he had into the world of adults. The '*German Assistantship*', for which he'd applied in 1990, took him to London and an official interview at the 'British Council'.

'Why are you seeking this Assistantship, Mr. Bellman?'
'I'm keen to continue to improve my language and see a bit of the country whose language I'm learning'.
'From your record, you seem an all-rounded sort of fellow... adequate degree... responsibility...' The Board had looked at each other and nodded. William felt confident and at the top of his game, and a few weeks later received a letter accepting him on the programme and, in addition, placing him in charge of the group that would assemble at

Victoria Station, and be whisked away on an 'initiation' weekend at *'Königswinter am Rhein'*. This little resort town stands at that point where the river Rhine makes its fabled bend, below Koblenz. It's Germany at its most beguiling, the epitome of the German idyll, the Teutonic myth, in which medieval castles perch atop craggy rocks, and peer precipitously into the mysterious depths below, where mermaids sport among the eddies, and lure unwary sailors to their watery deaths Yes, 'The British Council' had chosen its spot well. William, finally released from the endless constraints of his arduous studies, was already sniffing a sense of glorious liberty ahead, and wasted no time in succumbing to the spell of this magic place; the shackles were dropping away, like a butterfly emerging from its chrysalis, the kind of liberation that occurs perhaps once only in a person's life.

Besides the organised morning lectures and the idle afternoon at the sunlit pool, where the young men and women silently sucked in each other's physicality, there had been arranged, in the late afternoon and early evening of the final day, an outing down the famous river. As he and most of the other students sat beneath the boat's canopy, talking, laughing, and swilling beer, there can have been very few who didn't slip gradually into that place where reserve yields to relaxed intimacy. William had already, at University, experienced casual intimacy with women, the sort of indulgence that is little more than just experimentation and passes in the night with no trace of obligation. Within this fairy-tale setting though, the attraction he was experiencing, from two particularly pretty, vivacious and uninhibited girls right opposite him, contained a new, more dangerous element altogether, which one could only call 'Enchantment'. His feelings were wholly new and unsettling. He just couldn't withdraw his gaze from them, nor they from him, as if all three were bound by invisible cords. William offered little resistance to this sweet spell, but let himself sink gently into the thrall of these pretty 'Rhine Maidens', abandoning himself and his authority with the same reckless folly as those pitiful sailors of old. Who should care if the boat be shattered on the rocks? Let it be engulfed by the deep waters and bear its passengers with it. *"For one moment's bliss, I renounce all thoughts of heaven."* William's recent studies of *Doctor Faustus* and his entanglement with the Devil reminded him all too well of the dangers that lie in wait for the unwary in this magical land. Doctor Faust's moments of madness, surrendering as he did to the tight little pocket of desire that assailed him, were to become to William, as well as to Faustus, all too familiar in the ensuing months. *Did the entire land lie then beneath this spell?*

The boat drew into dock at last, as the sun dipped, and he found himself with an unforeseen dilemma: which of the two ladies should he chose to prolong the magic? Susan, slight and trim, forever smiling and excited? Vanessa, plumper, smaller, but with deep, smouldering brown eyes? He couldn't make up his mind, wanted to sample both.

It was Vanessa he finished up with, almost by default; Susan had perhaps sensed his indecision and opted out, pleading other arrangements for the evening. Vanessa and he continued on to her small bedroom, where they quickly finished up in each other's arms. They both had much of one another to explore. and it wasn't until late into the night that they abandoned their passion and William, casting off his desire, wandered frustrated to his own room. What, he wondered, still deep beneath her spell as he drifted into sleep, could he possibly have to offer in exchange to this Beauty, endowed as she was with such evident enticements. The intricacies of Sex eluded him entirely, and he'd discovered, in this little encounter with Vanessa, how completely unfamiliar he was with women and their apparent desires. He felt his own inadequacy like a bullet in the heart. It would be yet another long, hard lesson to be learned. Step by step, he supposed, like every other hard lesson he'd experienced.

But not for now. Next morning, still trailing traces of witchcraft, he put last night's experiences behind him, said goodbye to the warmth of *Konigswinter*, and caught the train for Hamburg, his designated place of work for the forthcoming months, a northern city, supposedly covered in ice and snow for one half of the year, cold and inhospitable too in its manners. In spite of this however, and still bearing thoughts of his amorous experiences beside the Rhine, he contented himself with the belief that a major city like Hamburg was cosmopolitan enough to provide opportunity to experiment further in those exciting arenas he'd so recently discovered. He had no wish to let his new-found amorous delights slip into neglect.

Whether, though, because of his sundry enchantments on the Rhine, or perhaps the sense of exuberance and liberation one feels in a foreign land, William's libido had secretly and silently blossomed during those few days, leaving him in a state of heightened sexual tension. It's a quite natural process, a chemical change, a hormonal shift, common to all red-blooded young males of the species (females too perhaps, who knows?) at one time or another; however, as a result of this hidden metamorphosis, William's life would, once more, never be the same again: a biological mechanism had been set in motion that would temporarily quite overwhelm him. In general, the common effect of this process of change, this sudden increase of sexuality, although rarely dangerous, might leave the victim disconcerted, puzzled, and, for sure, helplessly obsessed with girls, women, the female, all of which explains why William, on the train for Hamburg that day, was, right this minute, eyeing intently a fellow-passenger, a sultry Fräulein, tall and of northern stock, who'd just got on the train and was now sitting directly opposite him, crossing her long legs back and forth to reveal the tops of her stockings, even in fact parts of her underwear. William could scarcely deal with this new situation, given the circumstances. His immediate thoughts were to somehow get the girl as quickly as possible into the public toilet along the corridor and there, satisfy his immediate needs (and hers perhaps too). But how, without his being caught in the act and escorted off the train by the German police. The matter required much more delicate handling, but he didn't know exactly what; nothing in his experience had prepared him for a dilemma like this.

    The Beauty, who'd been gazing nonchalantly out of the window for several minutes, as if indifferent to the whole event, had now turned back from the window and was casting covert looks directly at him, challengingly, almost defiantly. The only other occupant of the carriage was an elderly man reading a newspaper and wrapt in his own affairs, leaving William to assume this new move of hers could only be on his behalf. In addition to this sweet torture, the train seemed to be slowing, jolting a bit, and it would be no more than a moment before the gentle rocking of the train would bring those lovely knees into joyful contact with William's own. And so it was, and William's pulse quickened and heart missed a beat. Something had to be done. Were he Clint Eastwood or Charles Bronson he would stand no nonsense but whisk her out into the corridor, where he might arrange a later assignment, or fall in love and she in him. In a less dramatic movie, who knows, he might simply have found an attractive partner to share the drab wintry.days of Hamburg. That sort of ending of course is all right on celluloid, but William knew in his heart he was simply not like those cinematographic heroes; it wasn't a relationship he was after anyway, chasing some floozy all over town; no, he had work to do, he was on a mission (to where he didn't quite know yet) too vital to just chuck away on a movie-star. William for a moment was finding a welter of reasons to excuse his blatant inaction. At the end of his tether, he wondered if perhaps the gentle route might extricate him from his difficulties: to reach across, place his hand on the lower part of her thigh, simultaneously whispering *'You're very pretty.'* Okay, it might work, but that manoeuvre, to pull it off, needed years of practice and precision timing. Wouldn't she merely take fright at the clumsy approach, and start screaming.

William's courage was by now already failing. Nothing had prepared him for this situation. The whole adventure was almost more than he could bear. *What if she slapped his face? What if she burst into tears? Might she not drop a lawsuit on him twenty years from now?* But, on the other hand, the voice within persisted. *Why dally? Act quickly, decisively.* "Fortune favours the brave."

By chance, the girl herself put him out of his misery. That moment when their knees did actually collide was the moment when she looked up, smiled, stood up, getting ready to leave the compartment as the train began slowing down. William had already chosen anyway to resort to his Option 3: pretend he wasn't there, and to allow the whole drama to slip into indecision, kidding himself that it was hard, perhaps impossible, to believe his motives and hers could ever so wondrously coincide.

Thus, with these scrambled thoughts, he stepped off the train at Hamburg *Hauptbahnhof*, and watched the tall girl stride off down the platform, altogether unaware apparently of his presence, while the world inside his head screamed: "*Oh, unhappy he who feels desire, yet cannot sense desire in other*s."

******

CHAPTER 8

"In which Adam, at 'Possum Kingdom', West Texas, prepares to start his Diary, while his son begins a new life in Hamburg."

"Dearest Tessa, I woke to the sound of wind and lapping water - that sound you and I remember so well - waves against the hull of a boat. Slap...slap. I was on soft bedding, in a lake-house on the shore of Possum Kingdom...."

In this very room where he now sat, on the self-same couch, with a view across the wide stretch of lake, Adam read once more his copy of the vital opening three lines of that letter he'd sent to Tessa, and which had lain untouched, secreted in this little house, for so many years. It had been the watershed, that letter, the first contact with her, since he'd been struck down and taken for dead at Hillcrest in '67; however, between that desperate moment and now, his memory still lamentably failed him: how had it come about? Who had placed him there, and why? Had he been saved? And, if so, from what? It was all still a void.

He glanced around. Little or nothing seemed to have changed inside; all was as if, for seven years, the little lake-house had slept, remained unoccupied, even unvisited; an ideal place perhaps, he wondered, to come and write, to rid himself on paper of the emotions, the sadness, the despair, the hopes he'd carried within him over these past few years of restless wandering. They say writing, or talking, can ease pain and longing and bring release, perhaps even restore memory. Maybe, with time and care, words might complete the jig-saw and lend him some peace. Wasn't he a writer anyway? Yes, but it had been a long time since he'd written anything of substance or kept a diary. Gone were those heady days at Hillcrest in the 60s (Bill, 'Hamlet', the thrill of Mary, the Assassination), all of which he'd documented so precisely.

He took a long look again at the inside of the lake-house, and went to sit in the spring sunshine on the dock, where the *'water laps against the hulls of the boat ....'* The enormous panorama of the Lake, the warm wind, the sun, the sounds of the waves, gradually lulled him; he felt contentment spreading over him. He would linger for a while in this uninhabited house, and take the consequences if someone turned up. And, most important of all, in these glorious surroundings, his memory might begin the process of restoration. If not here, then where at all?

There were small and large power-boats - not many - out on the water, momentarily endowing their owners with a glimpse of glorious freedom and fulfilment. He could do that too; he'd always hankered after such a type of boat, gliding across the water, linking you with one secretive island after the other, giving you the chance to switch off the engine and sit rocking, as the water and the current takes you where it will. Providentially, there was just such a boat here, at the end of the dock in fact, perhaps belonging to the mysterious owner of the shack. Whoever he or she might be, they wouldn't miss it today even if they might miss it tomorrow. No harm done. Adam walked to the end of the dock. The boat was certainly sea-worthy. But the key? Perhaps - most unlikely - there was no need for a key. Give it a try. The large engine was in place, dangling its propeller into the water. And a cord and handle protruding at the top of the casing. He took hold of it and pulled. There was slight resistance and a low snarl down in the water. He tugged again and this time, with a definitive purr, the motor sprang gently into life. Adam went to the front of the boat, pushed the gear forward and the boat moved slowly out into the water.

He was free, in one of the most beautiful, scarcely inhabited places on Earth. He determined there and then that at each break from his duties at Hillcrest, he would take the opportunity to drift around this great stretch of water, exploring the little coves and beaches and headlands, acquainting himself with this mysterious place. If the owner of the lake-house returned, perhaps he'd recognise him, and then he would either kill him - he was up to it - or more likely, make apologies, tie up the boat again and hire himself a room nearby, and another boot. For the first time in years, excitement was stirring in his heart at the thought that in these few weeks, before he was due to take up his job at Hillcrest, he might at last recover himself and some of the spontaneous joy he used to feel for life, find once more a true, honest identity, and perhaps even settle down.

He let the spring sunshine sink into his pores as the boat drifted around the edges of the great lake. This was the place he would make his own. His secret place. Where, also, he would come, alone, to write his sad testament of so many years of wandering, and find a place to store his work, safe and hidden from prying eyes. He thought hard about it; he knew there were little nooks and crannies, behind cupboards, at the back of drawers, where his writings would lie undiscovered, ready and waiting to be retrieved on each subsequent return.

Adam tied the boat up at the dock, went inside, and opened his lap-top. He started to write ….

CHAPTER 9

"In which Adam's son makes some interesting friends and discovers the joys of life in the big city."

The journey came to an end. William watched the statuesque form of the girl glide down the platform and disappear into the crowd. An opportunity lost. Regret. An abject failure looked him in the face once again, this time in what - he was becoming aware - is a very difficult art He followed her down the platform, consoling himself with the thought that his imminent life on the loose in Hamburg might offer opportunities similar to the one at which he'd so abjectly failed, and the chance to atone for this disaster.

It was not to be however. Although not dangerous *per se*, it's clear William's now maturing body, combined with the usual intensity he brought to bear on every new challenge, left him very vulnerable to the lure of the fleshpots, those salubrious localities, tucked away in the back-streets, awash with senseless chatter, and peopled by restless, superficial folk, who, like water flies, flit upon the surface of things, claiming great projects and achieving none. No, William was more a *'Hamlet'* than an *'Osric'*, unsuited to such a superficial *milieu*. He was, in essence, a pure Academic, naïve to the world and all its distortions, and therefore desperately, at this moment, in need of a guardian angel.

Whether by chance or design, (or by practical joke) his Guardian awaited him at the end of the long station platform, in the form of a disgruntled mentor: Herr Dnieper, a tall, sombre German who'd lost the art of smiling, had he ever had it. They crossed the busy road together, for the most part silently, and caught the tram heading out of town in (to William's surprise) an easterly direction, William had quickly gained the impression that this gangly man, with his stinted movements and almost inaudible voice, had been damaged somewhere, somehow, perhaps on the Eastern Front (he was the right age for that disaster), where of course he would have gained a horror of war, and hatred for all those who attempted to wage it against the Fatherland, and, in particularly, young Englishmen, who he might have felt were responsible for the whole fiasco in the first place. William had begun to feel distinctly uncomfortable in the presence of this surly, silent man, and, as a sort of relief from this brooding mask confronting him, he allowed his mind to stray back for a moment to the lovely, leggy girl and their strange chance encounter on the train. Was she a virgin? Was she perhaps a young prostitute? Whatever her circumstances, he concluded, they were better by far than those of this sorry fellow opposite him on the tram. And, in spite of the empty outcome to his and the girl's encounter, William's instinct told him it had been a good encounter; he felt glad he'd met her and certainly wished her well, because she was beautiful, a purveyor of beauty, and *young*, and how can the world and its remorseless timetables begrudge a few precious moments of indulgence? Besides, when did young people ever flourish by following too closely the dictates of their elders?

The tram continued remorselessly east out of the city. The endless drab post-war apartment-monoliths of the inner suburbs, had now almost imperceptibly given way to an ugly outer suburb - once probably a peaceful medieval village on the outskirts of this large Hanseatic port - where ugly stores on either side of the street vied with each other to be even more garish and unattractive.

Finally the tram did a half loop and came to a juddering halt. The end-station. They'd arrived, and Dnieper made a jerky, lurching movement, bringing William abruptly from his reverie. 'I've personally arranged, Herr Bellman, for you to be lodging with the grandparents of one of our pupils. You'll of course be glad to be away from the distractions of the city.'

William winced inwardly. It was a prepared speech in halting English, while William sat wondering how this boring fellow could have the effrontery to judge where and with whom he chose to live?

They descended from the tram and William waited to be led off to meet the grandparents, but even this turned out to be a false alarm.

'From here we take the bus,' intoned Herr Dnieper and William's heart sank once more. This ugly concourse then was not in fact their destination. Dnieper checked his watch impatiently as, five minutes later, a bus trundled in to take them on their journey to the '*Eastern Front*'. Dnieper glanced at his watch and grumbled, 'One minute late. *Alles fällt zusammen* (everything's going to the dogs*).*

With lightning speed, William checked his own watch. Dead on time, *this* bus was dead on time. Dnieper had got it wrong. The country didn't appear to be going to the dogs at all, but was working with almost full Germanic efficiency. William knew Dnieper was clearly wrong, and the full realisation hit him that this old man, this veteran of combat, who'd staked his life on winning, would never be content again, even with perfection, as his country struggled to get back on its feet. He simply had his own agenda.

The bus trundled out into the wide-open, level countryside of Schleswig-Holstein, leaving the city behind altogether; what had been shabby buildings now became the countryside: farm tracks, tilled earth, and clusters of cottages dotted here and there among the endless fields..

'We get off at this stop.' Herr Dnieper stood up, his head almost touching the ceiling of the bus, and alighted clumsily onto a gravel path. William followed, doubting the rural wasteland that met his eyes would ever qualify for city status. It was beyond that. For whatever mysterious reason, Herr Dnieper seemed to have taken on himself to save this new young English teacher from the sins and lure of the inner City, while failing to realise that more than half the world now lived in big cities like this, and managed to survive without being turned into *pillars of salt*? What right had he anyway to impose his rigid views on others? William had finally concluded this strange, lanky man, now shuffling ahead of him, was either remembering the sins of his own youth, or had simply lost his mind somewhere out in the frozen horrors of the 'Eastern Front'.

Down the desolate farm-track lay a small settlement of tiny houses, a cluster whose isolation one might glimpse from the highway in disbelief, as one hurried past on the *Autobahn*. How, William was asking himself if he could ever be happy here. Where was the silvery laughter of young girls, to chase away the gloom?

'We must go down the lane.' Dnieper plodded off, avoiding as best he could the large watery pot-holes, leaving William to drag his suitcase in pursuit. A quarter of a mile further on stood the first of the four cottages.

'*Hier sind wir*. You may find Herr und Frau Muller slightly old, Herr Bellman, but they are good, honest folk, and will look after you well. Come!' William unscrambled this short pre-rehearsed introduction, while Dnieper twisted his face into what seemed a faint smile, and abruptly launched into a longer, more complicated directive. 'Your duties in the school start on Monday at 8.00 am. You take the bus and again the *Strassenbahn*,(tram) and alight at *Haltestelle* '*Fernkirche*'. You walk through the park to the North of the high-road, where you will - how you say? - *come upon* our Grammar School.' He leant on the English phrase, as if to emphasize his depth of knowledge in the language. 'This journey will take you forty-seven minutes. Buses leave for the city from the end of the track here at 6 hours every morning. *Alles klar, Herr Bellman? Komm!* Dnieper knocked loudly on the door, leaving William still wrestling with Dnieper's phrase '6 hours'. *Does that mean 'six hour intervals' or what?* Until joyfully he realised this unlikeable pedant was confusing *Stunden* ('hours') and *Uhr* ('o'clock'). He'd meant to say the latter. An elementary error, putting paid to Dnieper's infallibility.

They were an old, vigorous couple,. hardy immigrants of former days and wartime, originally from Pomerania - a country in those cold, inhospitable lands by the Baltic - which had changed hands frequently in the upheavals of war, until finally becoming a part of Poland. Although they never once mentioned their endurance, William somehow sensed it was etched upon their faces.

Herr Muller was a man in the vigorous first flush of old age. Life, thought William, had little more to hurl at this old peasant, nothing perhaps besides a simple and honourable death, maybe tomorrow, maybe in twenty years from now. He was essentially ageless. The weathered skin, the gnarled hands, the wily smile, the way he rubbed his eyes in the evening if you met him in the hallway, muttering *'uh... **huh**, uh... **huh***', as in a Greek chorus, all this proclaimed, the popular image of a medieval serf. As the days passed, William was to learn he was a builder and had designed and built this present house with the money they'd salvaged when fleeing the advance of the Russians in '45. But beyond that, their secrets, their hardships, were never discussed; they'd assumed a new existence, remote from their origins, and all day long the old man plodded from house to garden to garage, performing vital duties with rigid, but positive fingers, pausing every now and then to remove the cap and scratch his scalp. His presence melted into the land as if they were one and the same; on just one occasion only, was William to discover the awful fragility that lurks even beneath such bastions of solidity.

If the old man was benign, the old lady, Frau Muller, was saintly. It was she who, each morning before daybreak, rose to prepare her things in the cold kitchen, stoked the boiler, put the pot on the stove, accomplished her chores, and, as the clock edged towards 6.30, trudged up the wooden stairs and knocked on William's door. '*Herr Bellman, Herr Bellman, es its schon Zeit,*' (it's time), and minutes later, poking her head round, she passed in the kettle of boiling water he would need to carry down to the freezing bathroom and prepare himself for the day. Then, without fail, she'd meet him in the hallway. '*Kalt ist es!*' (It's cold), she'd cackle, and, like a wraith, would silently disappear into the kitchen. Thus, the morning ritual, and every evening, as time went by, and when William returned late from the city on the last bus, and crept through the front door: she was there, materialising from thin air, stooped and weary, muttering to herself, '*So spät, so spät, Herr Bellman*' (so late), as though it fell to her alone to spare William the horrors of fatigue. '*Kaffee? Kaffee?*' There was renewed hope and forgiveness in her voice, as she hit upon the remedy for all ills: *Kaffee*, always *Kaffee*, and on occasions, shoved unobtrusively through the doorway, some rich cakes, or a slice of *Butterbrot* with sausage. Yes, this surrogate mother grew daily into her role; She thrived on the young man's dependency.

How could William up and go from this place, despite his yearnings for a taste of the big wide world? It had been his intention to rent a room down in the city centre, but as the days turned to weeks, he felt drawn into a fragile, intimacy with the old couple, impossible to disturb or neglect. it would have broken unspoken rules which lay far beyond his understanding. Perhaps there would be other ways of adapting to his isolation.

At Possum Kingdom, 1974 ...ENTRY FROM ADAM'S DIARY

Glimpsed unexpectedly from the highway as I cruised by, awakening sparks of memory that had their origin in childhood: a unique little 1930s-style house, quaint, set in amongst a row of stark new-builds... gables, beams, bay-windows, a pretty porch... a complete anomaly really in this day and age, powerful enough however to awaken in me vivid, childhood memories, as if they were clouds parting on a windy day to let in the sunshine.

Parents, brothers, sisters, friends, people long gone and passed away, who once were the rock and the pillars, holding up that comely little house. The games we played, the sense of immortality which, day in day out, accompanied us along our way, an existence beyond happiness. Where in heaven's name did those people, those moments, vanish to? In vain I struggle to arrest this shadow, this nostalgic image of home, which, all too soon I know will disappear. I sit watching the fleeting moment like a faithful dog that waits at the gate for the return of those it loves, those little ones it's set itself to guard, but whose departure has left just emptiness behind. The dog waits on at the gate, its heart filled with a sadness it will never comprehend. And look! As for me, observe how just a mere pin-prick of words on paper have unlocked these jewels of the past, and brought tears to the eyes of one whose memory has long since been scoured away. How many other dim memories lie dormant, waiting to be discovered by the pen? Mary, for instance. Might I unlock her enigmatic secrets too? Relive them? Stupid bitch! They say women are devoid of certain cogs. clearly, any inkling of Perfection quite eludes them, distracted as they are by all their ad-libbing and improvisation and cobbling and patching things together; the concept of Perfection flies right past, missing the mark altogether. Didn't Mary, with her preconceived notion of the perfect courtship, hopelessly fail to understand how perfect was the thing she already possessed? ...But wait; had I not best avoid that route? Hasn't Mary now no place in my recollections; she's long-gone, and vindictive outbursts will certainly help for nothing.... But if it must be Mary, then clear and cool-headed; let the facts speak for themselves .... I confess, I'm hopelessly undecided.... I need to set the record straight, to tell it how it was, but this short, muddled, indulgence of the pen here, true though it might be, is but random, and not fulfilling any purpose. Have I even lost that precious art of writing, which was always my salvation...?

Adam, frustrated, disturbed, replaced his pen on the desk, glanced out at the Lake and started to pace, up and down, like a caged animal, back and forth, talking to himself from time to time. hoping physical activity might jog a sluggish memory. He looked around. The copy of the letter he'd sent to Tessa sat open on the desk. *Yes, it started with her of course, with Tessa. and finishes with me, here on this very couch...* He sat down and typed a few words... stood up abruptly, casting the letter on the floor... *No, it didn't start with her, it all started with Mary and that visit to Elk Lake... Those are the boundaries; those are the events I must record and not stray beyond.*

There ensued a long silence in the room, Adam deep in thought and mumbling quietly to himself: *And am I just recording, like a humble diarist, events that transpired? This writing of mine is to be no diary, no mundane journal, no daily account of what I've done and what I haven't, and where I've wandered these past years. Would that not be foolish in the first degree? Myself, on the run, exposing to the world (and to the Law) my, destinations, whereabouts...* A further long pause ensued. He glanced down again at the letter. *Yes, did I not, in that letter, promise Tessa that I renounced a domestic life,... adopt loneliness, in the name of Creativity... to unfold on paper to the world, as and when, my innermost thoughts ...That was the life I chose; then I must be true to Tessa, true to my word, true to myself....*

He rested his head on the desk for many minutes, before looking out at the silent lake, as if he could suck inspiration from the placid water. His thoughts were reaching a culmination, a crux....*This writing is in search of a better name; my notes, a day to day account of trivial matters, will simply not be enough; I reach for something more telling; my writings from henceforth will unfold my innermost thoughts and feelings, my loves, my frustrations, my hatreds, all bound up in one collection; I will remain free...and give to the world my* **Reflections'**.

"*Reflections*", yes, the right term, and let me see, maybe something more (there have been moments, you see, when I shrink at what I've done, and what I have to write). *'Then let it be* **Reflections and Confessions.**

Still uncertain, he stopped pacing. *Reflections on what though?... When I reconsider the contents of what this diary must contain, then why not let it be, at every point on the compass,* **Reflections on a tragedy**? *Are there not already enough tragedies in this desolate world for there to be yet one more? Then let there be one more, and leave the reader to choose...earthquakes, murders, broken love affairs (don't I already know that all too well?) Yes, "Reflections and Confessions on a Tragedy"...How does that sound?...* He hesitated a moment, and then came to a decision: **",Reflections and Confessions on a Tragedy": from the pen of 'Sol' the Solitary".**

CHAPTER 10

*"In which William ventures out into the city,
and encounters a lonely friend."*

While Adam, in some tiny corner of the world 5000 miles away from the son he'd never known, was struggling to start his Diary, William himself had been wrestling to make the most of the domestic isolation imposed upon him, and bend it to his advantage.

As September turned to October and thickened into winter, he established a routine. The temperature had already dropped below zero, and stayed there. He woke each morning to find patterns of ice inside the window pane; he would descend to the freezing bathroom, take the *Kaffee* from Frau Muller, dress hurriedly, as, at the door, the old couple would click their tongues, and Herr Muller would make a display of tapping the barometer, before putting on a theatrical act of sympathy, and asking himself if there'd ever been cold like this. William meanwhile was venturing out, stumbling blindly between the icy ruts towards the bus-stop, glancing with a sense of near panic at the luminous dials of his watch, as he observed the head-lamps of the bus approaching with its usual Teutonic precision

However, strangely enough, as the days went by in this routine, William had grown quite accustomed to the silent, huddled, animal warmth inside that bus, and developed a sense of intimacy with his fellow passengers, those who had little chance themselves of complaining about the cold, nor any hope of altering their heavy lot; those huddled Germans on their way to a mundane job, and who couldn't afford the leisure of complaining about the weather.

His daily programme at the school was light and made few demands, and so, by the middle of the day, he could seize his moment to catch the tram into the city, where he wandered the streets until lunch-time, thrilled, and with a sense of almost disbelief, that these were the very people, the very places, he'd read about and studied for three or more years, the real Germany, now coming to life before his eyes, the country of Doctor Faustus, of trams, of Beckenbauer, of Hansel and Gretel, of witches and fairy stories, not to forget the very people who for the last few years his own country had been locked in a life and death struggle – it was all new to him.

Politically, Germany was only just waking up from the iron grip of Communism and, in the West, (he shouldn't forget), the people were metaphorically still shaking their heads, and trying to dismiss from memory the living nightmare that had been the war and Hitler for five long years; they resembled someone who wakes from a fearful dream, doesn't know where he is.

It couldn't escape his notice there was a new lodger in the little house at *Oststeinbeck*. Heavy footsteps echoed, at the end of each working day, on the bare wooden staircase, and, passing William's door, reverberated on up to a room directly above William's, a dingy roof-garret in William's imagination. For a while into September, William paid little attention to the footsteps; then one evening, by chance, the two lodgers met face to face on the stairs. 'Gerhardt Stauffer' was a young man, perhaps mid-twenties, blond, straight hair, high cheekbones, a trace of the wolf perhaps in his expression, but with a lightness and modesty in his eyes which contrasted strongly with the usual steely arrogance of the 'natives' of Hamburg. The two men nodded to each other, and as Herr Stauffer passed on his way up, he mustered a fatigued smile and murmured, as if about to expire, '*Arbeit, Arbeit.*' (*work*). William wondered *what* work, while assuming, from the weariness in this man's eyes, an occupation far more demanding than his own leisurely existence.

They passed more frequently on the stairs that month, exchanging grunts and nods, while the young German would push back a wisp of unruly blond hair and murmur the inevitable '*Arbeit.*' Language difficulties had at first prevented them from attempting all but the most basic form of communication, but as the days went by, they attempted to exchange a hasty, punctuated conversation together. One evening, Gerhardt even ventured uninvited into William's room, strolled around and fiddled with his radio, looking for a clearer signal, while uttering jabbing, unrecognisable comments in both languages.

Then, one night, meeting on the stairs, Gerhardt, instead of his usual sigh, barked out two brash commands, '*Komm! Komm!*', like the report from the mouth of a machine gun, summoning William to follow him upstairs into a cramped, tiny garret, suitable for little more than a dwarf. William had often imagined this tiny space overhead, and hadn't been misguided A narrow bed tucked into the corner by a skylight and looking out onto the cart-track and barren fields beyond. A small table in the centre of the room, covered by a plastic cloth. A single upright chair, a pungent paraffin burner, filling the space, besides warmth, with the acrid, stench of fuel. A basic chest of drawers. No decoration of any kind on the walls. The room was bare, and would measure half of William's, which in itself was small. For Gerhardt to get in and out of bed, he'd need to incline his head to avoid a sharply-angled ceiling. A simple lamp on the table struggled, even in day-time, to cast a dismal light.

Gerhardt hesitantly motioned his guest over to the solitary chair, while he perched himself on the edge of the bed, uttering the kind of animal grunts William had already grown used to on the staircase encounters. Unwilling however to impose on his new-found colleague, William remained where he was, and silently took a closer look around the garret: note-paper, envelopes on the table, clothes strewn on the bed, shaving instruments, a small transistor radio on a shelf, beyond that, a complete absence of books, or reading material which might allow him a form of contact with the outside world.

Gerhardt at last seemed to lose his nervousness. He offered William a cigarette, took one himself, and from his jacket pocket, pulled out a lighter along with a passport-size photograph of a young woman smiling happily against a back-ground of garden and rolling hills beyond. 'Girl-friend,' he said, eagerly indicating the little picture, and thrusting it over to William.

William, quite unsure how to respond, gave the photo a cursory glance. 'Very pretty. Here, in Hamburg?'

'Dresden.' The reply was instant and accompanied by a warm grin, as if that word explained everything. 'Dresden.' He repeated the name, and William looked down at the photo once more. 'Very nice. She's very nice.'

'*Meine Verlobte.*'

William guessed at the word. 'Your fiancée?'

'Ja, fiancée.' An even more enthusiastic grin. Then, catching William quite off guard, 'You have picture too?'

William had no such picture. He was far from that. Girl-friends? He had none, as such. He'd dabbled, that was all. How though was he to explain the whole context of his own solitary existence the integral differences dividing him from Gerhardt Stauffer? In the short silence that followed, he juggled his options: '*No, I'm afraid she died recently.*' or '*Sorry, I'm in between girls at the moment.*' or '*It fell out of my wallet on the U-Bahn yesterday*'. At all costs, he felt he needed to avoid saying '*I don't have a girl-friend.*' Seconds passed, until he jumped decisively from his chair. 'Wait, *Warte*', and hurried down the staircase to his room. There was in fact a recent photo downstairs in his wallet, a Polaroid of Susan, sitting daintily at the swimming pool in *Königswinter*. She'd handed it to him as a keepsake on the spur of the moment that final day. '*Did she qualify as a 'girl-friend? Almost certainly not.*' He found it now and retraced his steps, clutching the glossy, square piece of paper, and handed it over to Gerhardt, not unaware of his own duplicity.

'Verlobte?' muttered the German politely.

.'No', William smiled back at him. 'No. Just a friend.'

Gerhardt's expression registered disappointment. A friend (eine Freundin) ,of course, could probably mean a variety of things, but, clearly, in Gerhardt's world, it didn't mean that special someone whose picture you kept in your breast pocket. William realised his little subterfuge had fallen flat despite his efforts.

'How you say? Very nice.' Gerhardt handed the photo back politely and with some hesitation.

William, changing the subject altogether, said, '*Dresden*, that's a long way. Do you ever go back there? To visit perhaps? Does *she* ever come here?'

Gerhardt responded with a short laugh, as if the question were absurd, and he started to rub his finger and thumb together '*Nein. Kosten.*'

'Don't you ever see her then?' William was not just being polite; he was genuinely puzzled.

'Perhaps some day.' He looked hard at William before adding 'DDR. Very bad. Very bad.'

William already knew it had been suicidal to try and get out of East Germany. He was left wondering if this fellow had made a daring rush for it sometime in the past, promising to return to her. Perhaps he was a spy though. He certainly didn't look or behave like one. Perhaps the two young lovers had resignedly gone their separate ways Perhaps they'd just stopped loving each other. Or worse still, maybe they'd been driven apart by the politics. He didn't know the answers to these questions and Gerhardt would be unlikely to provide them either, as he seemed devoid of any imagination.

William felt impelled to get off the subject as smoothly as he could. 'You come from there, Gerhardt. You *can* go back, can't you?'

Gerhardt seemed not to have understood. 'Yes, Dresden. No go back.'

'Maybe your girl-friend will come here, will join you someday?'

Gerhardt paused and then just said, 'Maybe.'

Did this 'maybe' more likely mean 'never'? 'What then do you do here, Gerhardt?'

The German ran his hand through his mass of wavy, fair hair. '*Arbeit. Arbeit.*' repeated William mechanically.

'*When* do you work then? Nights?'

'Ja.'

That was it. William could see, from the glazed look in Gerhardt's eyes and a certain restlessness, that their informal meeting was unfortunately at an end. William of course was in search of a friend, someone perhaps to share the lonely evenings down in the city, go somewhere together at weekends, meet for lunch in the giant student canteen he'd discovered a few weeks back. However the more he thought about it, the more unlikely it seemed this strange fellow from Dresden would be the friend he sought. Their background, their culture, their language, even their daily schedules were unlikely to coincide, but, that was not all: something indefinable about what they essentially were, by nature, their education, their aspirations, found them both too far apart to reconcile any differences. William got up abruptly, bade his friend good night and went downstairs.

CHAPTER 11

*"In which William finds a rowdy gang of
friends and settles in to his new life."*

The Mensa.

As he was idling away an hour or two in the Dammtor area of the city, William had stumbled one lunch-time quite by chance, on the enormous student canteen known as the Mensa, It was an event which would change his life unalterably. He was standing watching a throng of chattering students heading past, in the opposite direction to his, and feeling hungry, he decided to follow. The Mensa was, he quickly realised, one of the vital hubs of the University, the place students converge on when they feel hungry and their brains addled by lectures and hard work. They congregated there to eat primarily, but also to talk, argue, and shout.

Although not 'officially' a full-time student, William convinced himself that gate-crashing an evening class on 17th century English literature twice a week surely qualified him for the right to be counted a 'student', and thus to obtain a subsidised meal along with the rest of the students of Hamburg. He summoned up the courage to stand in line and obtain a pass. It worked: he looked the part and the small amount of Euros he handed over, obtained for him - no questions asked - a sustaining lunch each day for the coming months, in the company of a seething turmoil of academia: Bean Soup, Pea Soup, mashed potato, yoghurt, whatever was on the menu.

For a week or two he ate his lunch alone, and watched the students stride past with their laden trays and a confident air, as if they knew exactly which table they were heading for, because they did it each day. One particular table, he noticed, seemed especially lively, as if its occupants were more keen on talking than gulping down yoghurts in order to get to an appointment or a lecture on time. They seemed, to William, to be meeting with all the deliberation of conspirators, delighting in their illicit talk of gunpowder plots, a group bonded to each other by desperate secrets. Standing out among this group, William noticed each day a bearded Greek, who shouted loudly, aggressively, in defence of his own provocative arguments, two sturdy young Germans, more listeners than talkers, a tall, garrulous man, who liked the sound of his own voice and took issue with almost everything that was proposed, in a fluent but accented German, and who went by the name of 'Macintosh', shortened frequently to 'Mack'. William puzzled about the identity of this Mack, because although his German was immaculate, he occasionally broke into an equally fluent English, but infallibly with an American twang. Last of all, a tall, slim girl, haughty and aloof - at first appearance anyway - who appeared each day alone with a tray and steered herself inevitably towards this gang of rowdy inmates, settling herself calmly, like an incongruous orchid in the midst of thorny weeds. As the days passed and this routine seemed fixed, William wondered if perhaps this beautiful girl's apparent aloofness was less a sign of her character than an adopted impression that she strove to convey within this company of vociferous males. At any rate, whatever the case, he consigned this Beauty to his lustful list where, during the long, empty tedious afternoons, when he might summon her to his day-dreams, along with Susan and Vanessa from Königswinter, as an antidote to the violent hormones that were assailing him ceaselessly in his lonely room at *Oststeinbeck*

For a while, William sat in the Mensa each day at an adjacent table listening and being no doubt an object of observation and curiosity himself, until, after a few weeks, he summoned up the courage to place his full tray down at an empty seat on a corner of the *'international'* table, and to ask if anyone would mind his joining them. His own perfect English accent clearly stood out like a beacon, and must have worked in his favour as a passport for his presence there, because there followed a brief silence before the Greek, Georges Papaloizos, said gruffly, from the bottom of the table, 'You've as much right to that chair as everyone else in this Hall,' and, as a few other voices joined in, some evidently laughing at their friend's bluntness, Georges added, 'Isn't this after all a democratic world we live in?'

That memorable afternoon, William, still remembering his student years at C..., slipped significantly and with ease into this tight, but cosmopolitan little group that so prided itself on free speech, and yet usually finished most lunch-times in complete disarray, as one or other of its members pushed the boundaries of argument too far, and intruded on someone else's beliefs. By chance, that very afternoon the puzzling and sensitive matter of Catholicism, with all its inherent virtues, vices, and contradictions, had been chewed over, following a hasty description by one of the group on an article describing the Pope's current tumultuous visit to Central America. Contraception, Abortion, even Transubstantiation had been tossed frivolously in the air, championed, denigrated, exposed as endemically corrupt, right up to the moment when the tall Beauty, Ingrid, with particular reference to the first two topics, proposed that someone (a woman preferably) should have the guts to bring a legal action against the Pope for interfering in matters which surely must solely concern women.

'Ingrid,' remarked Georges, the stocky Greek, 'I agree with your indignant female views on Abortion, even Contraception - you've every right to them - but women these days unfortunately push the boundaries so far on almost every issue, that we males are becoming redundant.' Ingrid was about to protest when Georges concluded, 'You know me, Ingrid, you know me well; at least admit I try to keep things in balance.'

This final statement received such cries of derision and uproarious laughter from the others at the table (who seemed to know Georges better than he knew himself), that even Georges shrunk back into his corner, speechless for once. He rallied though, seconds later, and his voice, laced with sarcasm, said 'Okay, Abortion maybe, but what about Transubstantiation? Might not the women want to claim that prickly one for their own too, and any other irrelevant issues as well?'

Mack, the tall English-American, retorted abruptly, 'Ask Ingrid herself then, Georges.'

'I am. Who do you think I'm looking at right now?' Ingrid remained silent, a trace of a smile appearing on her face, as Georges continued, 'Ingrid, this matter of transubstantiation, do you think women might shortly claim their own wafer all to themselves?'

'I never said I did, did I Georges? said Ingrid disdainfully. '*You* said it.'

Georges however was not to be gain-said entirely. 'I'm only referring my question to you because you're the only female here who can possibly answer it. I'm proposing maybe a special communion wafer cut maybe in a curvaceous shape, and easier to swallow in their more delicate anatomy; perhaps also with even greater magical components than the original?'

More derisive laughter, while Ingrid smiled enigmatically, like the Mona Lisa, and said ,'That's ridiculous Georges, and you know it.'

William, who'd sat silently throughout this somewhat ridiculous exchange, had come to the conclusion that, after many days of wandering alone in this big city, he'd at last arrived in the right place, among this high-spirited exuberance of youth. Into the silence that had followed Macintosh's sarcastic irreverence, his clear-spoken English dropped like a polished stone into a murky well. 'Without wishing to offend any devout Catholics here present, I'd propose the entire Catholic Church could be placed in the dock, not merely for infringing women's rights, but. for Fraud.'

'Why's that?' asked one of the sturdy Germans, grinning. 'I don't understand. What means '*fraud*', and what means '*placed in the dock*'?

'Prosecuted,' exclaimed Mackintosh, '*verfolgt*'.

'Ah, I understand. And '*fraud*' ?'

Mack left the question unanswered, and William said, 'Fraud is the act of pretending to be someone or something you're actually not.'

'Interesting,' said the young German. So, what do they pretend then?'

'They pretend to be the one true church. That cannot possibly be true, you see. All around us, there are other religious organisations claiming the same thing. They can't all be right. And most likely none of them are.' This provocative comment, from this total stranger, was received with a longer than usual silence, and William took the opportunity of driving home his inflammatory remark. 'With what evidence do the Catholics claim such a thing? They've bamboozled the people for centuries.'

Ingrid uttered a silvery laugh, while Günter - the German - said predictably, 'What means 'bamboozled'?

'Tricked,' said Mackintosh.

'Ah, led by the nose; *ich verstehe* (I understand).' Günter looked around the table and then directly at William. 'Well, we seem to have a Pastor in our midst, *nicht*?.' And since no one seemed anxious to answer this sarcastic proposition, the tall German added, 'Or is this perhaps a second-coming of Luther?'

There were a few smug laughs before William replied, 'I'm certainly closer to Martin Luther than I am to the Pope, that's for sure. But I'm not a pastor, no. I'm not a member of any church actually, except my own.' The rest of the table remained predictably silent, following this unusual statement, and William added 'I suppose you could say I'm a reluctant Protestant.'

'What means 'reluctant'?

Ingrid said quickly and impatiently, '*widerwillig*, Günter.' She glanced at William. 'Isn't that right? Someone who *doesn't* wish to be? Is my English correct?'

'Ah, we have an Englander in our midst!' exclaimed Günter, while William looked across at Ingrid. 'I think so, yes.' He turned back and eyed Günter. 'I'm not Martin Luther; I'm William, from England.' A moment went by and he added, 'I have a lot of respect for Luther though and what he believed in. I also think he was very courageous. What often surprises me is he lived so long.'

'Why?' asked Günter abruptly,' expressing probably the surprise of most around the silent table.

'Why what?'

'Why are you surprised he lived so long?'

'Well, didn't the Catholic Church do nasty things to people in those days if they didn't believe what they were told to believe? Am I right?'

Silence round the table, before Georges, the Greek, down the end, mumbled, 'They *still* do.'.

'*What* do they do, Georges?' shouted Mack scornfully 'Torture you?'.

'Yes! Mentally.'

'Ah! Günter exclaimed. You mean the Inquisition, ja?' And almost simultaneously Mack, laughing wildly from his corner of the table, shouted at Georges, 'I suppose the Inquisition is alive and well, Georges; eh? Right now.' He paused. 'Probably *needs* to be, with heretics like you around.'

Georges's response was quick and angry. 'You know that's ridiculous, Mack. It doesn't do to take a subject like this lightly Torture can never be justified. Haven't you ever heard of human rights?

'Thought you'd get on to that sooner or later,' replied Mack. 'We all know about you and your precious *freedoms*. The pure Greek air you breathe. However, right now I believe we're talking about the Catholic Church and their whole grand charade. In the here and now, not back among the Ancients, where you seem to exist. Why don't you listen for once?'

The arguments, as well as incoherent, appeared to be leading to a squabble between the Greek and Mack. William meanwhile had been sitting quietly, wondering when Georges and Mack would come to blows. But surprisingly, Georges had now retreated into his shell like a reluctant snail, acting as if no one but he understood or even mattered. 'I'm telling you, our freedoms are *still* being eroded. Just more subtly that's all.' He shuffled impatiently in his seat, as if ready to get up and walk out.

Mack looked across at William. 'Don't worry about Georges here. He'll sulk for a few minutes, and probably leave. Let's get back on track. What were you saying about the Catholics? It's interesting, I think and I agree. Tell us, what's your problem with the Church?'

William, by now, had in fact no wish to prolong the argument, but found it hard to resist Mack's gentle persuasion. 'The same as Martin Luther's really. Corruption. They're not what they claim to be.'

'Give us an example. What's this about 'fraud' you were talking about?'

'It's transparent, Mack. They're no more than a business selling a product that's not authentic. Their whole edifice has been based on a lie.'

'What means edifice? asked Günter predictably.'

Ingrid said hurriedly, 'Structure. *Struktur*, Günter,' and she glanced again at William for confirmation.

William nodded. 'Yes, that's a good word; or system perhaps.' He stopped, smiling. 'I've forgotten where I was?'

'You were talking about fraud and corruption,' said Mack, a hint of impatience in his voice now. 'And Günter, for hell's sake, give Luth here a chance, and stop interrupting.'

'Ah yes, said William; I remember.' He continued, choosing his words carefully. 'The fraud element is not just for now; it's always been there; from the start. The Catholic Church invented an entire system supposedly to meet people's spiritual needs, but that system simply wasn't based on truth. It made the Church very rich though. Wouldn't you call that fraud?'

'Yeah, I would,' replied Mack. 'That's fraud alright. If your facts are right.' Mack looked intently at William, seeking perhaps a flaw in his argument. 'Tell us again what the facts are.'

Although this discussion had originated around the table alone, it had by now attracted several listeners drawn from other tables in the Hall.

William didn't flinch in his reply, regardless of his larger audience. 'It's the whole system. Their very existence. They claim to be the one true church. That's ridiculous. They invented it; for their own purposes. There is no *one* true Church….. God is not in a church. He's in us. Each of us.'

William, as he went on , seemed to be expressing thoughts that had lain dormant in him for years. His words were coming not from him but from somewhere else. This final remark was followed by such an abrupt silence that it seemed as if the entire Mensa had been hushed. Günter broke the silence. 'Quick somebody, go and get the Inquisition; the pastor here needs torturing. He's blaspheming.'

And Ingrid, from the corner, where she was sitting quietly, said. 'That's not even funny, Günter,'

'Why?' said Günter. D'you agree with Luth here then?'

Straight-faced, Ingrid replied, 'I agree with some of the things, yes.' She turned to William. 'You said you were a reluctant Protestant. Why 'reluctant'? Isn't Martin Luther good enough?'

'I think he was very good. A good teacher. An innovator. He brought religion closer to the people.' Ingrid nodded, and he added 'But that's only halfway.'

Ingrid looked puzzled 'I don't understand.

'He brought the Bible back, gave the world a whole new template. But I believe there's more to religion than just the Bible.'

Ingrid sat there, shaking her head. 'We're taught the Bible has all the answers. What more is there?'

William didn't reply immediately. His voice now had sunk to scarcely audible, and he felt a mysterious fatigue overtaking him, as if a car battery were running out. Finally he replied to Ingrid. 'What more is there? God Himself, I suppose you could say. Isn't that what religion is: the pursuit of God? Not the pursuit of a book. God has to be at the heart of any religion. Not books and words.' William slumped back in his chair, drained of energy. As if in sympathy, the listeners round the table waited quietly for him to continue; however, it fell at last to the tall American to break the spell. 'Okay, guys. Let's just suppose Luther only went halfway; what's the other half? What are we poor flock supposed to do meanwhile.'

William's abrupt reply caught everyone by surprise He said softly, 'DIY, Mack.'

Mack could hardly believe what he'd heard. There can't have been many who even understood this very English phrase. He called sarcastically across the table. 'DIY, Günter. 'Do It Yourself.' He mimicked Günter's voice. 'Ingrid, tell us how you say *'Do It Yourself?'* After a few seconds, Ingrid, replied impatiently, 'We say in German *'selber machen'*.

Gunther sat back, repeating *'selber machen'* over and over, while Ingrid continued, 'But don't ask me what William means by it here. Ask him.'

William answered for her. 'You don't need an intermediary to communicate with your Maker. You have to *selber machen*. Why should we leave it all to a Church or a priest to intercede for us?'

Mack asked the question everyone wanted to. 'Is that your own solution, Luth?'

William took a moment to reply, running his hand slowly across his brow. 'I try. Yes. Years ago I certainly did *selber machen*. But I've lapsed.'

'So, tell me, *how* do *you* communicate with *your* Maker?'

'Clear and simple, Mack. You keep in touch, that's all. On a permanent basis. It's the essence of any relationship: daughter, wife, girl-friend, anyone you like. You don't get someone else to do the talking for you. That's right, isn't it?'

Mack replied drily, 'Maybe. But I can *see* them; they're visible; that's the difference. You won't catch me talking to something I can't even see. They'd haul me off to an asylum.'

'You just have to find your own secret spot to do your communicating. That's all. Lots of people already do it. It's called prayer, Mack. People do it all the time. And it's convenient too. You can choose your own spot.' Mack searched vainly for a reply, and William continued. 'Or would you rather revert to the old days: gods on Mount Olympus? Like the Ancients?'

Mack grinned. 'At least they were visible'

William shook his head. 'The human race has tried it; it never worked. And then we moved on to 'kings', remember?; wielding supreme power, making all the decisions. Nebuchadnezzar and all that.' Mack didn't offer any reply, and William continued. 'Just think of the mess the rulers have made down through the ages. The corruption. The bribery. The indecision. The wars. Yes, invisibility's the only answer, believe me. God can be at more than one place at the same time then. He's always listening and available.'

'In that case, count me out, Wilhelm. I like your story, but I don't like your solution. If I have a problem, I prefer to go to the courts.'

Günter interrupted with a laugh, alleviating slightly the tension. 'It's the lawyer speaking. I thought the pragmatic lawyer would appear soon.'

'He's a lawyer is he?' said William smiling. 'Are you a lawyer, Mack?'

'I might be,' answered Mack sullenly.

With a wide grin on his face, William said, 'Well, to quote: *it's easier for a camel to go through the eye of a needle than for a lawyer to enter the Kingdom etc etc*'.'

'Luther's actually quoting Jesus Christ at me now,' said Mack grinning in spite of himself. 'Is this another second coming?' An uproar of laughter followed this remark, while other tables in the vicinity looked enquiringly across. Mack added loudly, 'Look, I don't think this nonsense has anything to do with lawyers. It's quite simple; the fact that God's invisible shows he doesn't exist. Not that he's in hiding. Isn't that a more likely theory? He's on our wish-list.'

'Mack,' said William, 'what we're talking about in plain language is called 'prayer'. Nothing out of the ordinary. People talk to God all the time. Silently perhaps. Especially in distress. Can you deny that?'

'Well, if I've got a problem, I'm not going to go off and talk to the sea about it. I'll go to the courts. What's the matter with that?'

"The matter *is* that a judge can be fallible too. He can even be corrupt. For years societies have put their trust in courts and judges and kings. And for years decent people go on being treated like criminals, put in prison....'

'And sometimes getting off scot free, too. Don't forget that. I hope one day you don't find yourself in a difficult law-suit.'

William nodded. 'Me too.'

'How the hell's an invisible god going to help when your wife's just walked out and taken the kids and everything in the house with her?'

William shrugged. 'I don't know. It's difficult. But things work out over time if you're honest with yourself.'

'I prefer to let a judge decide.' Mack sat there stubbornly.

It was at this critical moment, Georges, who'd become locked in silence, shuffled in his chair, stood up abruptly, and walked out of the Mensa on his short, stocky legs. People round the table watched him go.

Mack said to William, 'Don't worry about Georges. He's an atheist anyway. Probably can't stand this religious talk.'

But William was glancing at his watch. 'I think I've got to go too. Sorry, I'm late for a Lecture. Thanks for allowing me to join your table.' He offered no other reason for his precipitous departure, grabbed his briefcase and headed for the door. As he reached the exit, he shouted back, 'Mack, 'join the Church of One.'

'What the hell's that? This guy's crazy.'

.Loud laughter followed and Günter shouted, 'Have a great day, Luth'..

What was it compelling William to leave so suddenly? A strange urgency, coupled with an unaccustomed surge of energy, had deprived him of any will of his own. Trancelike, he made his way towards the house at *Oststeinbeck*

Back at the table, they watched William disappear, some with a sense of disappointment. This strange newcomer had held the table for almost an hour, argued about unsettling questions of religion, which had contained a bold directness that couldn't be dismissed.

Ingrid broke the tense silence. 'I love his accent. It's better than yours, Mackintosh. More *English* English. Less American whine.'

'Could that be, d'you think, because I grew up in America? And I believe, by the way, the term is 'drawl', or 'twang', not *'whine"* replied Mack with as much sarcasm as he could muster. It was already clear to everyone Mack was himself in thrall to Ingrid's stern beauty, and consequently sensitive to any comment she might pass his way.

'It could indeed,' agreed Ingrid

And Mackintosh added, 'Well there's no accounting for women's tastes, anyway.'

Someone else exclaimed, 'It's not the accent she loves; it's the person.'

*****

William seemed to fly back to the little house in *Oststeinbeck* for reasons quite inexplicable to him at that moment. He just knew instinctively his presence was urgently needed back there, but didn't know why.

Strangely, when he walked in, mid-afternoon, the little house seemed deserted. Neither the old lady with her cluck, clucking and head-nodding nor the old man, who habitually spent his day shuffling from room to garage and back, neither of them was there to greet him in the hall, nor Gerhardt, who anyway William wouldn't expect to see at that time of day. The house was wrapped in silence

He dropped his briefcase and coat upstairs in his room and came softly down again, still uncertain what could have impelled him back to the house. He gently opened the little kitchen door and looked inside. Herr Muller was sitting stock-still on the other side of the wide wooden kitchen table, cap resting in front of him, gazing emptily at the door

Mildly surprised, and wondering if he'd interrupted a perfectly normal part of the old man's routine, William greeted him with as natural an air as he could muster. 'Ah, Herr Müller!'

The old man didn't move a muscle; just continued to stare intently ahead of him, like a cat fixed on its prey.

'*Is he looking at me or through me and past me?*' The thought flitted through William's mind, to be replaced instantly by the certainty of what actually was occurring there. *There's something distinctly not right here. Those eyes aren't alive like a cat's, no. they're devoid of life altogether.* Instinct took over, as William sat down as calmly as he could opposite Herr Muller, and smiled at him.

He needed to be sure. 'I'm sorry to disturb you Herr Muller...' No, he stopped mid-stream, certain now he was not talking to a functioning mind. His eyes remained totally unresponsive. The old man had moved not a muscle in his face.

William tried again. 'Herr Muller, I'm....'

Again, no recognition, and William at last put a name to the predicament: *He's had a stroke!*

This realisation had of course all happened in a moment. Simultaneously, while trying to stay rational, he had to considered his options. Alone in a remote, icy corner of nowhere, he knew he would have little access to help. And where was bustling Frau Müller for heaven's sake? She never went out, she never visited, to the best of his knowledge. Certainly not on her own. Use a phone perhaps? He couldn't remember ever seeing either of the old couple using one, and besides, where should he ring and how could he explain precisely what had occurred. William realised his only option was to deal with the situation himself. He placed his chair directly opposite the sick man and, barely more than a couple of feet away, and mustering all his mental strength, he met Herr Muller's steely gaze with one of his own.

For how long did they sit there? William felt his strength draining away, as he attempted to transfer his own sound mind across to the dead one confronting him. Minutes ticked by, and with traces of blood now trickling from his nose, William thought he heard a click at the front door, and in a few seconds Frau Muller was there by his side, clucking.

'*Ach, Herr Bellman, mein Mann spinnt dir doch eine von seinen Geschichten, nicht?*' (Dear oh dear, Mr. Bellman, has my husband been telling you one of his fairy stories?).

. William, blood running from his nose, glanced at Frau Muller, and headed towards the door.

'*Mein Gott, Sie bluten, Herr Bellman!*' (you're bleeding).

Still fumbling in his pocket for a handkerchief, William caught, from the corner of his eye, a glimpse of Herr Muller placing a cap firmly on his head, rubbing his eyes and preparing to go about his daily business, as if nothing were more normal than that

. '*Gott im Himmel, meine Lottchen. Ich schlief' weisst du?*' (For heaven's sake. Lotte, I must have fallen sleep).

William recovered slowly that day from this ordeal, still unable to comprehend what he'd done. Drained of all energy, he lay on his bed, overcome with exhaustion, while his hormones, like solar particles bombarding a dead planet, induced a procession of desirable females - Susan, Vanessa, the Girl on the train (and now, Ingrid), all kinds of phantom beauties - swimming across his vision. He was experiencing what he'd come to call '*Hormonal Acceleration*'. How was he to cope with these insubstantial shapes, sent from he knew not where? Desperate, he endured temptation almost beyond endurance.

At last, aware he was lost if he did nothing, he resorted to the only remedy he knew, summoned up s giant effort, leapt from the bed, changed into skimpy shorts and singlet, went out onto the stony track beyond the house, and, lungs pumping, ran and ran along the track as it disappeared into the barren fields beyond. He lost track of time; for hours that afternoon he pounded the hard earth and the icy fields, until, mud-bespattered, he appeared once more at the door of the house as dusk was settling on the land.

Frau Muller, shaking her head and clucking like a chicken, muttered, '*Kaffee, Herr Bellman...Ach!*'.

Throughout what remained of that long winter, as the weeks crawled past, he wrestled frantically in his little room with physical sensations quite new to him. His life had changed perspective, why and how he couldn't say, and, ignorantly, he ran and ran against the gripping cold, attempting to suppress and outpace his own demons.

He needed someone. We cannot be alone. His experiences that winter had jerked him from complacency; and he knew now, beyond doubt, that life, our lives, is not some pleasant sojourn in an easy land, but a life and death struggle from which we emerge winners or losers.

As he pounded the icy track that afternoon, another thought occurred to him, a thought which literally took his breath away: *Supposing* - he could barely bring himself to pursue the idea - *just supposing that giant pageant in the sky, that historical cataclysm, called 'Paradise Lost', along with all its moral and religious significance for the human race, what if it never actually happened at all, but was little more than a figment of a writer's imagination, the pictorial fancy of some Hebrew scribe, and was, at best, merely an allegory for Human Kind's unending personal struggle with its own sexuality. Could it be then that Paradise Lost, far from being just some historical event, happens **now**, in present time, over and over again? To each and every one of us, as we wrestle hourly with urges often too strong to be resisted? Wouldn't that interpretation make more sense of the scarcely believable biblical tale of 'Adam and Eve'?*

He stopped pounding the ground for a moment and gazed into the icy waste beyond, rehearsing over and over those dire sensations that had visited him a while back in his silent room and which had sent him out there in desperation, to flee his own sexual temptations... *If God lies indeed within us, then daily we must face our own Heaven and Hell.* ..William scarcely dared to pursue the logic of this thought. Just think of the implications: *We, and not some stern father-figure who metes out punishment for misdemeanours and promises Salvation if we toe the line, what if it's **we** who are responsible for our own actions, **we** who are the creators of our own Heaven and Hell. Redemption lies in us, every minute of the day.*

He jogged off again towards the tiny, distant house, and a line from a poem by *Goethe* flicked into his head. '*Und so lang du das nicht hast, dieses Stirb und Werde*' ,('And if you don't experience this Dying and Becoming'). What is meant then by this '**Dying**' and '**Becoming**'? Strange concepts indeed, which he'd never really understood until now, but now all too true and clear in meaning: *We*

Die, *and then **Become**, in a never-ending cycle, the human lot on Earth, the Enlightenment's rational interpretation of Sin and Redemption.*

Stirb und **Werde.** These two distinct polarities stood hand in hand plainly before William now, looming above those all too comfortable concepts he'd once held: the old irresponsible, leisurely life of books, music, ideas. Far from it: You die, and then you are reborn each waking minute. Perfection is forever unattainable and we alone must answer for our successive failures; it's we who are responsible for our lives. Not anyone else. Nor can justice be meted out in some comfortable courthouse; it's in our own hearts that the truth lies.. Yes, Human 'Law' becomes superfluous, while sly lawyers sit forever on the sidelines, unemployed.

What a picture! And all other alternatives to this vision are laughable.

"Did you, the accused, or did you not, enter the premises of Couple A and B and murder them in their beds, with intent to steal the money stashed beneath their mattress?"

"Yes, your Honour." (The unshaven malefactor looks down at his feet, then up again, shame-facedly, at his Judge). *"Yes, I did."*

No condemnation necessary; the malefactor's already sentenced himself. He's entered a state of '**Stirb**', a state in which he must suffer and rebuild, wait patiently, until his deed is lost from memory, fades into forgetfulness and is no longer a part of his life, as inch by inch he regains the state of '**Werde**'. No need for prisons then, nor the degradation of communal punishments. The criminal's already imprisoned himself, denied himself the simplest of life's pleasures, as he struggles upwards for retribution.

Just consider the alternatives to this Eden: A complacent world that turns its back on truth, and goes its own way, preferring betrayal, addiction, abuse, calamitous relationships, that whole catalogue of duplicity in which men break their oaths, while ladies seek annulments; where pornography peeks unchallenged from every corner, and lawyers, unnoticed, rule the world.

No, that way is laughable. It can never be a fitting substitute for a world where people simply tell the truth, where daily we Fall from Grace, but where, mercifully, the door stands ever open to hope, and, inch by inch, we clamber towards that paradise portrayed so imaginatively by the honest scribe?

———

(At Possum Kingdom) ENTRY FROM ADAM'S DIARY

REFLECTIONS and **CONFESSIONS**

London – the 'Garret' (profile of an artist)

On his journeys, Adam found his way finally to his native home, London, in May 1968, cautious and under a new identity, and by luck discovered a small apartment in the heart of the city which he called the 'Garret', a place to hang out in and not attract too much interest. Despite the distant, inevitable hum of city traffic, it was silent and remote, a writer's idyll. Small rent, a secret little place at the summit of a three-storey block, which passed unnoticed by the thousands who hurried by each day in pursuit of their business. He was two people now. Henceforth he'd be in two places simultaneously: Possum Kingdom in actual time, while within his memory and imagination, the 'Garret'.

As I write this, I see all the harsh irony, the anger that bursts to the surface with every sentence. And I am ashamed. However, I think I've been through the worst and am undergoing, as Shakespeare puts it, a sea-change. I notice in my heart now and again uncertain signs of a silver lining, the rising perhaps of a new dawn, and realise how very bad, how suicidal, must have been those days that I've lived through, and about which I write now, in the hope of expurgating the stain of sadness they left in their wake. I look now for joy each day that passes; I scarcely dare to believe the signs of happier thoughts and a lightness I've not experienced during two years of aimless wandering.

Reader, please bear with me. I'm not alone in this desolation. There have been others, I know, who have borne worse, far worse, sufferings not of their making but engendered by the injustice that humanity delights in handing out to its inhabitants. I'm thinking in particular of a writer from the early sixties, an author from Russia who made quite a stir when his small book came out. Banished to Siberia during the purges, he wrote a successful diary of each day of horror in those frozen wastes. He was called Aleksandr Solzhenitsyn, and the book appeared as 'One Day in the Life of Ivan Denosovich'. It was a best-seller, went viral overnight. It's a great read, highly to be recommended. Well, I believe that by writing out the wretchedness of his experience, he could explain it to himself and literally expurgate it, as I'm attempting to do. So let me model my writing on this similar 'first-person' style Solzhenitsyn adopted, so as to give my account an authentic ring: I'll call it **'One day in the life of Adam Riley'.**

….I descend one floor of the narrow stair-well. It's Monday morning; I'm off to work. My first ever *'real'* job. You see, for once in my life, I'm not going off to try to impart my most intimate thoughts, morals, beliefs, unique skills, my *soul* in fact, to someone else, to someone (by definition), who doesn't know how to value my sacrifice anyway. No, I've done with that sort of prostitution. That was my old life; this is my new. I will no longer squander my talents. They're unique. (Interestingly, Beethoven went through this crisis too, tried teaching, being short of cash. He quickly realised though his own precious creativity was impaired.. And thank goodness for that;; can one imagine a world bereft of those three final sonatas? Along, of course, with everything else. With humility, I, like Beethoven, am reigning in on that sort of compromise; it's my *time* I sell now, not my soul.

At work I'm what they call an AO. That's my official title. AO. Administrative Officer. Dull, bitty, incomplete kind of work. I already know it's not for me (I feel it in my water) but thankfully it's not too arduous and leaves my brain with enough battery in the evenings to hone my own verbal skills and wait for my moment. Short stories. No money in it (unless you happen to get sent to Siberia, like Solzhenitsyn. Or go swimming with sharks, or clamber up rock-faces without a rope, play for England in whatever the trivial sport, all in all, get your face on the screen or in the newspapers, and become a celebrity. You get published then.. People love danger, violence, hardship, suffering, so long as it's not happening to them. Gratuitous danger. We're all drawn towards horror and death; someone else's though.

For the time being I'm exempt from all that; I've got to put in the hard, lonely graft first, and don't seriously hope to receive the call to the Publisher's office at any moment; rather, I'm passing my days in what you might call a self-inflicted Purgatory, by definition an interim state, a state of impermanent preparation. In general, it requires one toes the line; each morning I dutifully don a smart suit, trip out to help someone else accomplish *their* dream. I'm masquerading as an AO (Administrative Officer), in an office-block not far from here, a bus-ride away. I keep alive the hope that red-letter day will come for me; and Purgatory will become Paradise; you never know Then I'll break out, risk all, and metamorphose.

A part of my purgatorial torment involves incongruous thoughts of Mary, of course. Thoughts of her and the good times come bobbing in and out, to distract me.. However, for the record, it's been a whole year since that female nemesis of mine last appeared on the sky-line, making in-roads into my psyche. I've warded her off. I'm starting to sense I'm pulling away from her. Inch by precious inch. Despite occasional, lapses; like this morning, when memories of her came flooding in from nowhere at all, on the bus to be specific, as I gazed out the window from the top deck Is it perhaps that we're living in close physical proximity? Walking the same London pavements? No, it's not completely gone away, but like the Spartans at Thermopylae, she *shall not pass*. I'll discard her altogether, I swear it. I sit precariously atop a gigantic wave, paddling for my life to ride the it before it rides me. Not a moment to blink. Just do my 9 to 5, keep my head down, and wait for my moment. How do you balance that dichotomy? It makes me nervous leading two lives, watching and waiting.

On the first-floor landing I nearly bump into Roger, who's the only tenant on the block with an adjoining bathroom, as against our *en suite* units, no matter how tawdry they may be. It's a distinct disadvantage for Roger and his lady friends when they're caught scurrying across the communal staircase in their bathrobes. He's recently erected bamboo curtains to replace the door, and you can see he's painted the interior a lurid mauve, supposedly to give it up-market flavour and impress the girls. I can't see why he bothers..

Anyway, this very morning I pass him as he emerges from among the strands of bamboo together with his latest protégée, who slips past, wearing one of Roger's robes and little else. I wonder if she knows her boy-friend's got a bath-room fetish..

'Don't think I've seen that one before, Roger,' I whisper as he speeds past me..

'My new flatmate,' he replies smugly.

'I mean the bath-robe, Roger.'

He gives me an indecipherable look, and disappears into the privacy of his flat, waiting no doubt for the moment he can catch me off my guard too.

I take the number 30 along The Marylebone Road to Portman tube station. On the way, on the bus, I gaze mournfully at the pretty girls. So many of them, so many tons of pretty girls, London is ridiculously full of them, each one of them a threat, as they glide carelessly along the pavement exuding nonchalance, exercising some strange power over me. What do they think about? Do they think about anything? Do they have actual thoughts? For that matter, do they have actual feelings? I don't know, so I ask the question: Do pretty young women have physical sensations, like we do, those surges of desire that keep you up at night, that boiler down in the belly refusing to go out? Do they experience any of that? Do vaginas really count for nothing in the great female sexual scale of things? Or, do the young females of workaday London simply drift, make themselves up, look as pretty as they can, while all the while they're waiting, antennae up, for something to happen, someone to make it happen, a male, a hero to drag them off willy-nilly into another universe? Even then though they must make a decision. Oh, where are those more orderly days, the times of Jane Austen for instance, when pretty girls weren't asked to cope with decisions, but to pick obediently their parents' choice, a man of standing, esteemed within his circle, secure in his career, with property to add to his already abundant purse. How though, in these modern garish times of ours, where fairy-tales are made to leap from every corner proclaiming a fragile thing called 'love', subtly reminding those maidens that 'feelings' are *all* that count, and that if you just hang on, Mr. Right will materialise, come knocking on the door. Well, he won't. Don't be deceived; Mr. Right's a fairy-tale too; it's all down to instinct and timing; that's all that counts.

I get off the bus, switch off my fantasies, my frustration; my anger, which, I notice, are still alive and well, and enter my place of work. The office block's a 5-minute walk from the tube station, secreted in an unmemorable back-street, which was once the vigorous hive of one of Victorian London's infamous cotton sweatshops. The sweatshops have vanished of course, however you still see a lot of girls in pretty cotton dresses round the sandwich bars, but, after several weeks at the 'Bureau' (where I spend many hours of boredom and am paid a pittance), I'm starting to believe the sweatshops just migrated further on down the street.

However, to paint my initial journey to work more vividly, let's go back to that first day, to describe what I've got myself into. Day 1 - so long ago, it seems almost lost in time. The programme that day was of course a little bit different: once off the bus, I find my way to the impressive and expansive foyer of No.67, the headquarters of the whole show. On the large wall I notice a photograph of that national emblem, Prince Philip, meeting staff members. A girl appears. Brisk, efficient. Pretty . Prince Philip's secretary perhaps?. 'Let me take you over, Mr. Riley.'

I give her an interrogatory smile. 'Over?'

'To 167'. She smiles too, then adds, 67 is HO, 167 is FE.' While I try and unravel this puzzle and, simultaneously, admire the elegant way this cool secretary walks, she says, 'You won't be working in the main building for at least two years, if ever.'

I'm supposed to understand that, but don't, nevertheless feel a bit deflated by her downbeat tone. I follow her like a stray lamb that's realised it's best to trail after the flock. We cross two streets and enter the dingy office block, which, as explained earlier, is secreted within the hub of London's contemporary fashion world.

HO, I've already worked out, stands for Head Office, so I ask the girl, 'What's FE?'

She smiles again, politely, almost compassionately, 'FE, Further Education. Didn't they tell you that at interview?'

'No.' My attention's distracted by the loud clanging of metal. The elevator in 176 is one of those ancient types with hand-operated iron gates, which sound right now as if they're, tumbling, on some unwary passer-by. These lifts, it turns out, are operated all day by a mealy-mouthed cockney named Albert. He looks like he did service in World War 1 and behaves like he's never forgotten he saved the nation.

'How's Albert today?' asks my pretty escort, as we ascend in the direction of floor 4.

'All the better for seeing you, my Dear.'

Albert scarcely moves his lips when he speaks, nor does he smile or look at you. His stare seems fixed not on the gates, the blank wall behind them, the floors sliding past as we ascend, but focussed on a strip of land in Eastern France that goes by the name of *Somme*. Weeks, months later, I idly worked out that Albert, in his lift, probably completes, in the course of a morning, the same mileage, up and down, as the distance from Marble Arch to St. Albans. In one week, at that rate, he'd be approaching Birmingham, and in one year, Los Angeles. He's not plump though, not overweight; he's remarkably wiry, probably as thin as when he came out of the trenches all those years ago. Astonishing. What a generation!

'Going anywhere this year, Albert?' my desirable guide enquires.

'Nowhere you'd know, my Darling.'

It sounds like a rehearsed dialogue. I assume Albert will be staying at home somewhere near Peckham during his two weeks' entitled leave, looking after his bed-ridden mother, drinking sherry, taking the odd day-trip to Brighton on the Brighton Belle.

He seems quite at home with my glamorous receptionist; I suppose if you complete a trip with the same passenger between London and Birmingham on a regular basis each week a kind of informal bond is established. However, Albert reserves for me a wary stare, and solemn silence.

The lift comes to a grinding halt. Floor 3, and Albert swings the gate open neatly with a yellow duster wrapped around both the iron gate-handle and his wrist. I make to step out but Albert's grating voice stops me in my tracks. 'Your floor, Sir,' and the tall, grey-suited, silent other-passenger, alights without a word or a nod in Albert's direction.

'Miserable sod!' says Albert under his breath to my guide. 'Pardon my French.' And the lift is once more coasting upwards again.

This eminent-looking man who's just alighted is actually Head of Washington's Publishing Group it turns out, headquarters on the 3rd floor of 167. Mr. Washington's apparently making one of his infrequent visits, and left the chauffeur waiting outside with the Rolls. 'His wife's usually alongside,' Albert informs us. 'She's as bad as 'e is. Has a dog as small as your fist, Mexican breed or something. I'd as soon stand on it, I tell yer.'

Digesting this vital piece of information, we reach floor 4. Stepping out, I read in bold letters on a brass doorplate the official Company name, which I'm afraid I can't reveal because of the laws of libel. Inside the door, a tall, wiry man is hurrying out of the urinal, fumbling with his flies.

'Ah, Mr. Pekoe,' cries the receptionist. 'This is Mr. Riley, the new AO.'

'Well, Mr. Riley!' A wild grin suffuses Pekoe's face, and he comes at me, arm outstretched, zipper half undone. It's a storm, a tornado. I prepare to dodge out of the way. 'Welcome to E Branch. We've been expecting you. Come and meet Jack.'

I nod goodbye tactfully to the pretty receptionist (never know when she might come in useful) and follow Pekoe down a corridor. Tucked in the corner of the modest square room and flanked by two desks and a large grey filing cabinet sits Jack Foreman. Another desk, opposite him, is vacant; waiting presumably for me.

'Jack, this is Mr. Riley, the new AO for Group 1. Show him the ropes.'

Pekoe leaves as suddenly as he's come. I don't see him again for three days. Next to Foreman, a plain-looking girl called, I learn, Anne Gubbins is perched on a low chair with a note-pad on her knee. They're not actually working though; Anne, it turns out, is actually Branch Information Officer (BIO), with an office across the passage. When she speaks, it comes out as a whine, like bad bathroom plumbing, and at the exact moment that Pekoe ushers me in, she's hell-bent on flattering Jack's head off., while Jack, immune apparently to the flattering, seems to have anticipated my arrival, as he nonchalantly pretends to listen to Anne, and, at the same time, chucks a batch of papers onto the large desk opposite his. He allows the BIO girl to finish her whine before addressing me.

'You'd better check those diagrams for errors against the originals.'

I look at the papers. In fact, I look at them for 15 minutes without being able to make any impression on their meaning. All this, while Foreman leans back, balancing his chair on the back two legs, while Anne, seated by now, on the corner of his desk, occasionally allows her bulbous knees to scrape against his, as they continue their nauseating rendezvous. They quip endlessly, vying with each other for who can get the final quip in, like one of those mating manoeuvres you see on TV's Wildlife series.. It's mating in fact, that Anne has in mind; Foreman, however hasn't (he's cosily married), and is just using Anne as a kind of mental pencil-sharpener, to pass the time.

I shift my gaze to the bundle of papers. They include what are certainly diagrams: triangular, rectangular, in all different sizes, some merely on tracing paper, which I suppose are the originals. Foreman at last gets in the final quip and sends Anne packing with a pat on her broad, mournful arse. She's electrified with pleasure, squawks like one of those cockatoos they have on the Wildlife programmes and flies off giggling. Foreman however sighs wearily and returns his chair to its four legs. The reason I already know he's a genius is that he remains infinitely cool and in control, no matter what the pressure. I am to see this even more clearly as time goes by. In the course of any given day, Foreman devises new forms, despatches memos, draws graphs, like a machine. Girls rush in and have orgasms watching him in action; but Foreman is unaware. Nothing disturbs his greater aura.

'So, how d'you like your first hour at the Bureau?' Hands behind his head and smiling sardonically, the genius addresses me for the first time since my arrival.

'What exactly am I meant to be checking with these diagrams?'

'Oh, don't worry about them; let me have them back.'

'What sort of work do we do here, Jack?' I ask in desperation.

'Decide the fate of millions of innocent little Technicians,' he replies, the grin never leaving his face. 'You'll soon pick it up; it's too complicated to try and tell you. Just keep a low profile, and don't let these girls get you down.' (It's a prophetic warning from the Master). 'Look,' he continues, handing me now a scrap of paper. 'Here's a set of numbers. Down in the bottom of this building there's a basement full of old exam scripts tied up in batches. I want the batches of scripts that match up against those numbers. Don't be longer than half an hour. There'll possibly be someone down there to help you.' As he's handing out these instructions, there's been a more than usual sardonic smile on his face, which I can't quite account for.

It takes me half an hour to find my way down to the subterranean cavern they call the basement. It reeks of dust and parchment. It's deserted. *What is a 'script' anyway?* A script is the name for an examination answer-book; it's what the technicians write their answers on. *How am I supposed to know that?* I'm not. I'll just have to 'pick it up', as the Master has implied. I return after an hour and a half with three heavy bundles of scripts, each tied round with coarse string. Two further batches, I hadn't been able to locate. In all my future time at this nameless Bureau, I shall never be called upon to perform a more laborious or unnecessary task than that search in the cellar. Was it maybe a hoax, a prank, at my expense?

'Hello,' says Foreman. 'Where've you been all this time?'

There's another female in there, hovering by the filing cabinet. She has a friendly face, and also asks me how I'm enjoying my first day at the Bureau. It's clear from her expression she expects the answer 'no'. She exchanges a few friendly quips with Foreman, who behaves this time with less condescension than with Anne Gubbins, and leaves. She must be higher in the pecking order.

'I couldn't find two of the batches,' I say.

'Batches of what?' asks Foreman.

'The Batches you asked me to get from the basement.'

'Oh, those! Doesn't matter. Looks like we won't need them anyway. Chandler's going to pass all the candidates *en masse*. Looks like I'm going to have to have a word with Charlie Chandler. He's stepping out of line. FETCO's not going to like it.' Foreman lapses into a most unusual silence while I stand there, waiting, wondering if he's actually speaking the same language I use. His last four sentences have left me struggling. They're impossible to decipher. *Perhaps I should ask who 'Chandler' is.* 'Put them over there in the corner,' Foreman concludes, and temporarily I'm relieved from this mental 'See-saw'.

And it's at this juncture, just as I'm laying the batches of scripts in the corner, that a good-looking girl, who has one of those vaguely voracious, predatory expressions you sometimes encounter on young, clever women, enters our office together with a friend. The two of them stand there for a second or two, facing Jack rather than me, until the friend says, 'Go on, Maureen. Show them,' and at that moment I have conclusive proof of Foreman's genius. The girl, Maureen, the man-eating one, hoists her skirt and petticoat all the way, to reveal her stocking-tops and knickers beneath. 'Look!'

Jack, unmoved, continues scribbling on the pad in front of him, bent over it, jotting, doodling, like an artist touching up what he did the night before (he's busy drafting a new form for internal office use, I learn later).

'Jack FOREman!' It's a shout. 'Look! It's my leaving present.'

Jack at last looks up and says, in a dead-pan voice, 'The petticoat, Maureen, or the knickers?'

Maureen flushes, a shade more than she's doing already. 'The petticoat, you great big cumbersome boor!'

Unmoved, Foreman says, 'Is that B-O-O-R or B-O-R-E, or even B-O-A-R?'

A slight hesitation. 'All three!'

'Very nice, my sweet,' says Foreman and resumes his jotting.

This man, I tell you, is ready to take over the world!

Maureen continues, 'D'you like it? It's from the typing pool.' She does a twirl, holding the dress high.

'As I've said, very nice, (he doesn't bother to look up again), but you'd better go and show the typing pool then, or you'll have Mr. Riley here with the hot flushes.' *The control of the man is astonishing. How does he know my heart is pounding inside its narrow casement?* 'Have you met our new AO by the way?'

Maureen doesn't know now whether to lower her skirt and shake my hand, or whether to try to shake it with the skirt still up. She decides to lower it.

'It's very nice,' I stammer.

'Thanks,' she says. 'That's more than I can get out of that callous pond-life, Foreman.' Foreman doesn't look up but grins down onto the page. 'Bye, Jack. You'll miss me when I'm gone, you know. Nice to have met you Mr. Uuhhh....'

Foreman has the last quip. 'Sure I'll miss you. You're a good sport, Maureen.'

The two girls depart noisily.

'Some girl,' I say. 'Does this happen every day of the week?'

'Almost every.'

'How did you know I had the hot flushes, Jack? You're right, but how did you guess?'

'You're the type.' Foreman grins. 'You've got Public School written all over you. I don't suppose you had your first sex until you were twenty-three.'

'With a *girl*, you're right.' (I'm doing the quipping now, I realise; it's surprisingly easy to catch on to amidst this office banter).

'Well,' replies Foreman, 'I take the *other* persuasion for granted.' He produces a sigh for reasons I don't fully understand. And in walks Simon Swan.

Tall and slim, jet-black hair (dyed, no doubt), immaculately clothed in a City shirt, grey worsted suit, sober knitted tie, an air of the sensitive, mature Academic.

Foreman says, with only the slightest hint of deference, 'Here's another one who didn't know his arse from his tit till he was twenty-three.'

Simon Swan is up the next rung of the ladder at the Bureau, and Foreman's immediate boss. Mine too. He's Head of Group 1, E Branch. He says ingenuously, 'Oh, who's that?'

Foreman dodges the question. 'Maureen Durban's just been putting on a show '

'What kind of a show?'

'She's been revealing her undies.' He glances across his desk at me. 'By the way, Simon, have you met your new underling? This is Adam Riley. Still in a state of shock, I think.'

Swan shakes my hand and gives a welcoming smile. 'Jack been initiating you into the Bureau, I see.'

'Maureen, more like,' says Foreman. 'Doing your job for you, Simon.'

'Maureen Durban,' echoes Swan, nodding nonchalantly and with little apparent interest. He glances at his watch. 'Is anyone going over?'

'Lunch!' shouts Foreman, swinging his chair forward onto four legs, slapping his hands on the desk, and rising from his seat. (I'm surprised by how big Foreman is).

We all head first for the Urinal, where Foreman tells Swan about Maureen Durban's recent exploits.

'Tramps!' exclaims Swan, and gives his 'dick' an extra careful shake.

Foreman smiles conspiratorially. 'Mr. Swan doesn't have a very high opinion of the female employees in the Bureau.'.

'There's not a single one of them with any style,' says Swan, carefully now massaging his soft hands in the basin. Style, it becomes apparent, is important for Swan; he's one of those young Executive sorts who go to Mahler concerts at the Festival Hall and play tennis at the Camden Hill Club. He's in the process of buying property around Camden Hill.

'Come on, Simon, says Foreman, zipping himself up. 'You know you're hung up on those publishing women.'

The coincidence is that Swan once worked for Washington's Publishing Group, whose boss I saw earlier climbing out at the 3rd Floor. Why Swan moved from the Publishing world, where his genteel air must have made him ideally suited, and came to the Bureau, where he's a fish out of water, will perhaps never be known. Rumour has it though, Pekoe enticed him to the Bureau on the promise of *better prospects and better girls. 'Be your own boss. Simon. Larger typing pool too. More choice.'* And that's not the last of the 'coincidences': Pekoe, by chance, served as a lieutenant in Gibraltar with Swan - National Service colleagues. Interestingly too, Pekoe's current boss at the Bureau, a Mrs. Hod, was formerly a highly-paid exec with Debenhams, and guess where Pekoe was employed for a spell after National Service, yes, Debenhams! Such though is the Bureau's hierarchical structure. Old Boy's network. And, to crown it all, complete the circle, it appears likely Swan's and Washington's umbilical chord was never completely severed either, working as he does just one floor above his old firm, leaving open the eventuality that were the Bureau suddenly to go belly up, Swan would just slide one floor down, to retrieve his old job. But that's the way it seems to work with '*Business 'Executives*': they scuttle like rats back and forth from one sinking ship to another.

I'm thinking, where does that leave me? Am I '*executive* 'material now? One thing's for sure, my new suit nowhere near fits me like Swan's - I wear it uneasily. I'm already starting to feel like a duck out of water among these strange people, and I've only been here a couple of hours or so.

Swan hauls his hands finally from the luke-warm water and dries them on a clean patch of the pull-down towel. 'There's not a girl in this Bureau who remotely compares.'

'You should never have left, Simon. Why *did* you get out, by the way? I never did find out.'

'It's a long story, Jack.'

'Can't have been for the money anyway. Ah well, we all make mistakes.'

On the way to the elevator, a neat little black secretary hurries past.

'That one, Simon?' asks Foreman enquiringly, with an upbeat at the end of the phrase.

'Rita?' replies Swan, tasting the name delicately on his palate. She's got a little style, but she's common as dirt. The Bureau attracts the wrong sort of woman. Not necessarily individually, but *en masse*.'

We reach the lift. Albert has by now covered seven miles on his laborious journey, the distance between Marble Arch and Edgware.

'How's Albert?' asks Foreman.

'As well as could be expected, Mr. Foreman.' Albert evidently doffs the proverbial cap to Foreman. He doesn't know quite what to make of him and errs on the safe side.

'Going anywhere this year?'

'On what?'

'On the National Express of course, Albert.'

I'm tempted to add: '*On the LA Freeway, Albert*', but I refrain. I don't feel Albert likes me, and is wondering whether they'd repulsed the Hun for nothing.

'It's all right for some, Mr. Foreman,' says Albert swinging open the gate.

The Bureau's grandiose subsidised refectory is at the top of 67. Most of the Bureau's staff and hierarchy eat their lunch here. They all stroll in and take their place in the serving queue, tall men, a bit like Swan, but lacking his suave sophistication. They all seem to have titles too, grandiose labels denoting their role in the Bureau, and are referred to by the label rather than their actual name. It's quite common. You're lining up for instance with your tray of food, when the door opens and Jack might say, 'Ah, here comes FETCO.' It can be baffling, and your first instinct is to try to unravel the puzzle. **FETCO**, Further Education and Technology Coordinating Officer. The acronyms roll off Foreman's tongue. There's Head of E branch (**HE**), Head of Advanced Technology (**HAT**). Director of Graphics (**DOG**). Head of Institutional Management (**HIM**). Coordinating Officer For Further Education Examinations (**COFFEE**).' He reels them off proprietarily, as if all these important figures somehow belong to him. 'Ah, here comes (**SMART**) Section Manager for African Regional Trade. He points to an insignificant-looking, bespectacled figure, and checks his watch. 'Yes, dead on time. Never misses. And I guarantee he'll be closely followed by **COPULATE**.' We wait tensely for the owner of *this* label, and at last the canteen door swings open. 'Ah, here she is. Right on schedule.' (Foreman appreciates punctuality, it's clear).

'That's a good one, Jack,' I comment. 'What's her acronym stand for?'

'Coordinating Officer for Personnel, Leave and Trainee Education, of course.'

He know them all. He seems wedded to this bizarre *modus* of communication. It's a game to him.

Can I ever lower myself to this institutionalised rubbish?

Yes. As we stand in line (Foreman, myself, and Anne bringing up the rear), I experience a moment of inspiration. 'Jack, how about: Section **H**ead of **I**nstitutional **T**echnology, Has the Bureau got one of them?'

Foreman forces a begrudging smile, and, as the acronym hits home, Anne Gubbins spews a jet of water in my direction from the glass she's been sipping from,.

'Watch it, Anne,' remarks Foreman. 'Best behaviour in the canteen, remember?' He gives her the obligatory pat on the backside and adds, 'At least our new AO has a sense of humour.' For some reason, Anne Gubbins finds this hilarious.

It becomes slowly clear to me where this acronym business originates. All these labelled individuals, in another time and place, worked for the former Colonial Civil Service. They governed and administered territories in Africa and India. Acronyms were one of their tricks for keeping a tight hold on the natives. Baffle them with mysterious non-words, as if they were James Bond. Once the colonies were sold off, back they all flocked, these men, to the home country, where the Bureau awaited them with open arms. *'Come and join us. And bring your pensions with you. And your acronyms.'*

My reflections are interrupted abruptly by Foreman. 'You're the new member, Adam. Why don't you go ahead in the queue. Seems like we've got the two usual offerings today. Steak Pie and Toad.' (SPAT). I carry my Toad to an empty table by a window with interesting views onto the Euston Road Underpass, and am joined by Swan, Foreman, and Anne.

'Simon Swan and Jack Foreman! My two favourite men in the Bureau!' cries a shrill voice. This is Rosemary, who works in Exams Div (ED), and thus only gets to see her 'favourites' at lunch time. 'Can I sit with you handsome brutes?'

Swan moves over robotically, and without saying anything. It's as if he's persuaded himself Rosemary's not sitting next to him at all, but is a kind of mirage. It's left to Foreman to keep up pretences. 'Rosemary darling. This is Adam Riley, our new AO in E. Say hello to him nicely.'

Rosemary eyes me up and down. 'Well, hello! It's soon going to be difficult to know who's the most fanciable man at the Bureau,'

'Flattery will get you everywhere, Rosemary,' quips Foreman.

'I mean it, my Dear. The men in E Branch just get handsomer and handsomer. Simon love, are you taking me to the Mahler tonight?'

Simon pretends not to hear, and Foreman says, 'Simon's off women today, Rosemary. He's calling them all 'Tramps'.

'Who's 'Tramps', Simon?' asks Rosemary with manicured indignation. 'Tell me. This instant!' Rosemary herself has glasses perched on her nose and seems to be edging resignedly and gracefully into spinsterhood, so it's a daring challenge. Swan meanwhile inspects his Toad more closely, while Rosemary gives up. 'He's certainly off me *all* the time.'

'That's because you throw yourself at him, Rosemary,' says Foreman.

'What else can I do when I'm in love with the beastly man?'

'So are half the girls in the Bureau. The competition's too stiff, Rosemary.'

Rosemary turns again to Swan. 'Is that right, Simon? You off women today?' Simon just grins up from his plate, and Rosemary adds, 'See? He's not even talking to me. D'you know, I think it might be possible to die from unrequited love.'

'Try playing hard to get,' suggests Foreman.

'That never works; it just become *impossible* to get.'

Rosemary's still talking about her love for Swan, as Foreman, twenty minutes later, hauls himself to his feet and heads for the door. 'Exams wait for neither beast nor boy.'

Swan and I follow him.

'Jack, what exactly is it we do here at the Bureau?' I'm attempting at last to come to grips with reality, as we scurry madly across to 167. The question's been bothering me since I came up in the lift with Albert this morning.

'D'you mean they never told you at interview?' Predictably, Foreman shouts this defiant challenge at the top of his voice as we swing back into our little office.

'Not really; just mentioned something about exams. Said the Bureau sets Examinations.' Lunch is over, and I'm trying hard to keep the conversation at a sensible level.

And at last we're ensconced alone, face to face, confronting each other across a large desk. Foreman says, 'We process technology examinations for over half the apprentices in the country. We're an Examinations Board.'

I try to appear impressed. 'That's a lot of exams.' I pause for a moment as the logic of the situation catches up with me. 'If it's so many, why don't they just hand some of the exams over to the teachers?' Caught off guard, Foreman doesn't reply immediately, so I add, 'Where I've ever taught, the teachers set the exams themselves. They know the subject matter and also know their students, what they can and can't do, and should or shouldn't know. What's wrong with that?'

Foreman pauses for a moment to let this totally novel idea sink in. 'Nothing, except it's obviously unsecure and open to the worst forms of corruption.'

'Corruption by who?'

'The teachers, of course.'

'If they're teachers, they wouldn't *be* corrupt.'

Foreman drops his voice slightly, in order to lend maximum force to his biting, sardonic reply. 'That's the most naïve statement since Snow White said to the Witch "What a lovely red apple". Where've you been living for the past few years, Adam? The North Pole? Or should I say perhaps the Garden of Eden?' He sits there on two chair legs, complacently grinning as ever 'Come to think of it though, it's not surprising they hired you; the Bureau has a reputation for recruiting naivety. If they tell you too much, they know you won't sign up.'

I ignore the slight. 'You've got to trust someone somewhere, sometime, Jack.'

'No you don't.' He answers somewhat defensively, as if suddenly seeing the spectre of his own job at risk. 'This is important stuff, Adam. Writing national exams is important stuff. It's got to be fair.' He reverts to a grin and continues, 'Or at least it's got to be *seen* to be fair. Young kids' lives are at stake.'

This is the longest string of sentences I've heard Jack Foreman utter in the three quarters of a day I've been in his company. He really believes this stuff. However, *I* don't. I come from a 'teacher' background. I know too well the lengths dedicated people will go to be 'fair' to their charges. Break their backs doing it. The odds of a dead piece of wood appearing within, say, a sample of fifty healthy teachers are enormous. Perhaps Foreman's never been in front of a class, or, alternatively, believes everyone in the world is identical to the gang of vacuous and - dare I say it - corrupt buffoons he's currently sharing the workplace with.

I attempt to reply. 'You're talking about 'fair', Jack. And okay, I realise it's got to be fair. But *is* it? The bigger the operation, the more complicated it gets, and the greater the room for error, for mistakes to be made.'

'Foreman places his finger over his mouth. That intolerable grin has appeared on his face again. 'Don't let the powers that be down the corridor hear that word 'mistakes.' It worries them.'

I shake my head in disbelief. 'That's precisely what I'm talking about. Big isn't necessarily good is what I'm trying to say.'

The tea-lady appears and nicely and kindly and politely hands each of us a delicious cup of tea and a bun (compliments of the Bureau). She leaves, and I say, 'See what I mean, Jack?' For once, Jack doesn't, and shakes his large head. I continue, 'That tea-lady has just performed a simple task to perfection. She didn't need a whole host of walking Acronyms to help give us a nice cup of tea.'

He still doesn't quite get my drift, and replies, 'Why not?'

'The Acronyms swim to the top, if they're not there already, and become complacent and incompetent. Probably corrupt too. That's why not.'

Following a slight hesitation, Jack and the Grin look at me from across the desk. 'I can see we've got a rebel in our midst.' (To be fair to his sense of justice, it seems there's a hint of admiration in his rebuke.) 'Do you realise how many careful stages are involved in the production of just one exam paper here?'

'No, but I know you're going to tell me.'

'Probably about twenty, if not more. Twenty stages.' There's a pause while I wait for him to list them and he waits for me to say 'wow!' 'Stage 1, a meeting to pick an examiner. Stage 2, a phone-call, from you, to officially nominate that examiner, stage 3, the examiner writes the paper, stage 4, a moderating committee meeting is set up to discuss the draft paper, stage 5, back to the examiner for re-writes....'

It goes on and on. I get the picture. Foreman reaches stage 15 as the tea-lady mercifully interrupts, to collect the cups. What he's been trying to make me understand is that I'm a cog, a small cog, within a giant wheel. All of which is locked inside a Process. And I already know, beyond doubt, that I don't want to be part of a process; I don't want to spend my life being a cog in a wheel either. No matter *where*. It seems I'm on the side of like my humble teacher friends, who strive to be perfect in a world that's governed by imperfection.

Jack knows he won't get through the whole list this afternoon. He's even managed to bore himself. He chucks a few scripts at me and says, 'You'd better start by seeing what mistakes of syntax you can find in these. You'll be doing this job mainly for the rest of your life or until the government decides to withdraw funding. Whichever is first.'

And the remainder of the afternoon drags on in a silent armistice, until 5 o'clock, when Foreman springs to life and announces he's off. 'Never give the Bureau the satisfaction of knowing you're working on unpaid time.' He heads for the door and then turns with an afterthought. 'Put those files carefully away in the filing-cabinet before you leave. What, among other things, the Bureau can't forgive is untidiness. Do a bad job, they might give you another chance. Be untidy, you'll be out. See you tomorrow.'

The door closes and I'm left thinking that at least I know now what I have to do to get out of this place.

I sit on the bus heading home, down the Euston Road, leading into the Marylebone Road. Two of the busiest streets in London. It's rush-hour. Inert, on my lap, are two exam papers; I want to just check this evening how many 'syntactical errors' I can find. But right now they're not occupying my thoughts.

I'm puzzled and troubled by a strange ambivalence. I can't make up my mind. who these people are I've spent the day with. Who speak in absurd tongues and appear happy to pass their lives as cogs in a wheel? Just who are they? They're not me. But who exactly *are* they? What motivates them? Would one voluntarily spend ones days struggling in from Bishops Stortford on a commuter train, as the years race by? For a meagre pay-rise and a chance someday to wear one of those cherished acronym labels?

It's not me; I know it. I haven't the patience, I'm not tidy enough, and that stuffy prison of an office fills me with dread. I might just as well wear handcuffs and restrainers. You know, despite his bluster, I get the feeling Jack Foreman has faced the same ambivalence I'm feeling now. I can't put my finger on it.

Meanwhile, a Day in the Life of Adam Riley draws to a close. I can't decide which one of us suffered most, me or Ivan.

CHAPTER 12

"In which William encounters an old German legend and puts at risk his own immortal soul."

Finally, seemingly months later, the cold grip of winter began to give way to a slow thaw and, with the onset of Spring and all its wondrous buds and blossoms, William's anxieties began to disperse. Daily he felt stronger and more hopeful. Plans, which throughout the winter had been ephemeral only, and had come to nothing, grew now into firm projects: he would go down to see Susan in the Palatinate; perhaps that way temporarily rid himself of the unending stream of enticing female visions that plagued him so; he would buy a motor cycle (to avoid that desperate bus-ride each morning); he would experiment a little with life, unimpeded by rigid timetables and other people's claims on him. He had some hard thinking to do.

Providentially, as if to spur him on towards fulfilling these positive decisions, William's self-effacing flatmate, Gerhard, quite by chance one Saturday morning in early March, led determinedly all four occupants of their little house at *Oststeinbeck* - himself, William, and the old couple - outside into the yard to admire his shiny, new, yellow 'Trabant', standing proudly on the gravel..

As they all walked towards the shiny new car, the old lady, Frau Muller, couldn't resist a stinging remark beneath her breath (deliberately within William's hearing though): '*Na, Herr Bellman... Die Arbeit.*' (work, Herr Bellman, how about that!). This mild rebuke, as they all gazed astonished at the shiny German economic miracle in front of them, was followed by another equally sensitive comment to the effect that William had been '*burning his candle at both ends*'. Meanwhile Gerhardt had happily lowered himself into the driving seat and was beckoning William to follow. As he climbed into the little car, trying to ignore the old lady's comments, he asked, 'Is it *yours*, Gerhardt?'.

Gerhardt's face lit up with the joy of ownership. '*Ja, mein. Komm!*' He reached a proprietary arm out through the window, waving at the old couple standing perplexed on the gravel. '*Wilhelm, Komm! Fahren wir.*' (Let's drive!)

William meanwhile was forcinged himself to think positively and practically about Susan in the Palatinate. 'Gerhardt, do you ever take a holiday?'

Gerhardt was firing up the engine. 'A holiday? No, Hamburg good for me....'

'Yes...but perhaps get away for a bit....We could drive together to....'

Gerhardt was already backing out and turning the car round. Shaking his head, he said, 'Na, maybe. But the money....'

'We could drive in your car perhaps and meet your girlfriend from the '*other side*'.'

Gerhardt shook his head reluctantly. 'The money, Wilhelm...'.

William momentarily lost patience. 'Life is more than just *Arbeit*. What do you do with your money anyway? You're always working....'

'I save. We must work and we must save.' There was a hint of smugness in his tone and manner, as he pronounced his credo. '*Arbeit, Herr Wilhelm.*' He waved a saucy finger at William, precluding any further talk about a holiday.

'Work for what? Save for what?'

'For a car, of course.' A big smug smile lit up his face. '*Komm.*' He drove carefully past the old couple and out onto the road. William had, up till that moment, avoided looking at Frau Muller, but as he wound down the window he heard her remark, whether to herself or to him he wasn't sure. '*Arbeit ist besser als laufen, nicht...?*" (work is better than running, yes?).

Indignantly, and unable to contain himself any longer, William generated his silent response. '*Yes*, my *dear lady, yes, but you, in your latter years, aren't party, in the heat of the afternoon, to strings of beautiful female apparitions in well-nigh transparent garb, passing by your bedside and vainly offering tantalising relief to your tortured body. What, my dear old lady, is there left for us 'thinkers' to do but run? Or succumb, and perish? For sure, cavorting in a shiny tin can on wheels will most likely provide merely temporary relief to Gerhardt anyway.'*

Next day, determined, William swallowed his frustrations and splurged part of his own hard-earned money on a motor-bike at a second-hand garage in *Billstedt*. The machine was certainly not in reach of the Palatinate and Susan, but as he perched proudly atop the long leather seat, grasped the handlebars for grim death, and spluttered down into the city among the fumes and jostling traffic; he too, like Gerhardt, experienced the brief joy of ownership. He padlocked his new bike against a wall and set off on his usual walk into the city centre, circumventing the *Binnenalster*, that miraculous little inland Lake, redolent this time of year with the alluring scent of lime trees. On that particularly bright morning William was spell-bound for a moment by how the effect of the water lapping gently against the shoreline combined so harmoniously with the jagged contours of the city a mile or so off; it stood out like in a painting, a veritable work of art in itself. He wondered how the City's architects could have integrated the Ugly and the Beautiful with such precision, into one perfect whole. By design or by chance? His thoughts meandered as he drifted into sleep, now prone on the Spring grass; this combination of opposites, ugly and beautiful, that he was observing across the lake was not unlike those perfect German symphonies, Beethoven, Mozart, and the rest, as they invariably encompassed within each work similar stark contrasts and opposing emotions, symphony after symphony. Eyes closed, he meditated on this apparent strange duality within the German temperament.

He nodded off, stretched out on the grass, fatigued by his earlier difficulties that morning with the Trabant, not to mention his brief, vicious spate of envy occasioned by the old lady. However, he awoke several minutes later, refreshed and still contemplating this mysterious duality he'd discovered, black and white, joy and sadness, love and hate, good and evil, a whole string of opposites everywhere, inherent not just in music but all works of art, and in people too, and life itself. Not without irony, he realised those remorseless sexual urges of his were probably part too of that same creative pattern which humans strive for, and were indeed most likely what generated those glorious works of Mozart in the first place. Was it perhaps true then that humankind cannot experience the Heights without the Depths, the Rational without the Irrational, Reason without Madness?. In that case then, beware, for such dichotomies must be dangerous, and are not be toyed with.

With these heavy thoughts swirling back and forth, he found himself heading now in the direction of the Mensa and the raucous cut and thrust of students like himself, who might distract him from such brooding thoughts.

But no, he'd remembered suddenly an enigmatic line in German literature, in 'Faust' no less, one of his favourites: *'Zwei Seelen wohnen, ach, in meiner Brust'*. (Alas. two separate spirits occupy my soul). Yes, this little snippet must surely have some bearing on the dual nature of existence: *'zwei Seelen...'* (two souls). Here was this strange divergence yet again: *two souls within one breast...*

William was entering the City, at that little corner where the Lake gives way to the markets and the rush of busy traffic. For a moment he stood and watched the eager shoppers coming and going, out of the Baker's and into the little *Supermarkt*, their earnest eyes fixed on the trivial little business of shopping. How innocently and naïvely humans can often behave, quite unaware of the hellish depths that lie, untapped, down in their souls. *'Zwei Seelen....'* Yes, 'Doctor Faustus' again, that German fable, hidden deep in the German psyche, the story of the ageing professor, grown weary of struggling to understand the meaning of life, who sells his soul to the Devil in exchange for a second chance at life, the promise of youth and carnal delights.

The 'Herr Doktor', like a young fox, blinking blithely in the Spring sunlight, hormones on fire, ventures out at last into this exciting world, little realising living's not that easy, there may be a price to pay, there are bound to be repercussions. Barely over the threshold of the house, he notices a sweet peasant girl, pursues her, becomes infatuated, falls in love, breaks her heart, and his own too. *Gretchen* becomes pregnant and, overwhelmed with shame, does away with her child, which, in the eyes of the Law means death. Faust must watch the girl dragged off to execution. Is this then not Hell enough for him? How far must one fall in this perpetual game of checks and balances?

Faust learns the hard way that it's not for us poor humans to overreach ourselves, to aim too high in blind enthusiasm... we are bound to fail. Life can never be the paradise Faust seeks.

Unaccountably, untypically too, William that morning, buoyed up by the exuberance of his new-found understanding, and finding himself down in the sleazy harbour quarter of the city, dropped his guard and took precisely that very same flippant path as did his hero, Faust. He enlisted that same evening a reluctant Gerhardt to accompany him to the infamous place the Germans call '*die Reeperbahn*'. 'Just for a bit of fun, Gerhardt.'

'Ja,' exclaimed his friend, with an enigmatic smile. '*Die Reeperbahn*', that is no place for us, but for sailors.'

He was right. The *Reeperbahn* lay within the heart of the Hamburg harbour, a simple street, well-lit, where ladies of the night sit in majestic state of undress and offer comfort to the weary, aching sailors who come in.

'Why not, Gerhardt?' asked William. 'It's not just for sailors. I'd like to see it. People talk about it. Anyone can go there. It's a tourist attraction.'

Once more Gerhardt offered his enigmatic smile and an excuse. 'I do not like these ladies; they have no - his English failed him for a moment - '*Sein' (reality)*.'

'How do you mean, '*Sein*', Gerhardt?

Gerhardt for a second appeared lost for a reply. Then he said hurriedly, 'They have *Schein* (appearance), not *Sein*. I do not know the English.'

But William picked it up. 'Ah, '*Schein und Sein*', yes, I know the expression. Let me think...'*Schein und Sein*' 'Apperence and Reality'... Ah, I've got it.' He looked at Gerhardt triumphantly. 'You mean 'substance', Gerhardt. That's what you mean, isn't it? The women have no 'substance'.' He paused and then said, 'You're right too. They don't. But that's not what the Reeperbahn's for, is it? Not what we're looking for either.' Gerhardt still seemed undecided, mumbling 'substance, substance', until William added, 'Don't worry, you can get a coffee and leave me to the tender mercies of the women. I know what I'm doing.'

Gerhardt had still showed signs of hesitation, (perhaps anxious for his friend), so William said finally, 'Come on, I'd love a lift anyway in your new sports car.'

That evening, as they drove towards *St Pauli*, William felt increasingly stimulated by the thought of what they might find on the *Herbertstrasse*. He was puzzled by how buoyant he felt now, in contrast to the self-doubt that had assailed him earlier at the lake-side.

'Where we park, William?' William's errant thoughts were interrupted by Gerhardt's indecision.

'Anywhere, Gerhardt. Here's good enough; we can walk to the *Herbertstrasse* from here.'

Following the distant glare of artificial light and the crowds of jostling men, the two of them were drawn slowly towards this most unnatural of places. They wandered for a while, among the crowds, catching tantalising glimpses of human 'dolls', arrayed in windows like fairies on a Christmas tree. Gerhardt was starting to display signs of distress and discomfort, even embarrassment, uttering from time to time animal-like grunts, until William wished he'd never asked his naïve friend to come in the first place.

For just seconds only, the compelling aroma wafting from a coffee house overcame the other sweet delights that beckoned outside on the street. 'Let's get a coffee, Gerhardt. I can see your heart's not in this.'

Gerhardt grunted a bit more and then said, 'Kaffee, ja.'

They were both swept inside, along with others, and for just those few brief moments, while Gerhardt went off to get the coffee, leaving William perched on a little stool, matters stood precariously in the balance. William was already experiencing an unaccustomed nervous excitement, stimulated by the general noise, the smells, the lights, the persuasive power of numbers, that whole mass of seething humanity, gathered in one spot at one time, and with one shared intent, and all blatantly confronted by displays of overt sexuality.

Gerhardt came back from the counter empty-handed; he'd not brought enough money to pay for the coffees. William, reaching impatiently into his pocket, handed Gerhardt his thick wallet,. 'There's cash inside the wallet,' he said. 'Don't spend it all. Bring me the change.'

While Gerhardt returned to the counter uttering incoherent grunts, William sat on, starting to confront the thought that if he didn't do soon what he'd come there to do, he'd lose the will to do it. He'd at the same time spotted a young woman leaning against the door frame, neither inside the coffee house nor out, unaccompanied, provocatively dressed, quite incongruous among the milling crowd of men. It took him no longer than a second to judge what her mission was, and at that precise instant, she glanced up and caught his eye. That sudden movement, combined with this unexpected eye-contact, acted as a spur, and he found himself already heading across the crowded room, offering the woman just the faintest of nods as he moved into the street without looking back. He knew she would be following; it couldn't be otherwise. He was involuntarily swept across the road towards the brilliant lights, and only then, finally, did he turn his head. She was nowhere to be seen.

Perplexed and angry, William was sleep-walking now in the same direction as all the other males, goaded on by *their* appetites, making for those lighted little cubicles and the undressed ladies within them. He passed one, stopped, surveyed the scene for a minute or two: a young woman reclining on a shabby couch, reminding him all too well of the 'girl' on the train, and a cinema clip of a younger Marlene Dietrich. He stood now on the very brink, poised to dive in. But still he hesitated. It was not all about just plain sex. There was another element, he knew that for sure; it was just downright Curiosity that had brought him to this place as well. Didn't he, like Faustus, owe it to himself to see it through? Didn't he, after all, lay claims to being a writer? Wasn't experience valuable to him then? But over and above all his various reasoning lay one over-riding and quite unexpected feeling: the tempting urge to disobey. Yes, to bend for once the rules and see for himself what the apple tasted like... why not just give it a try? Why not just topple over the forbidden parapet, and see what's on the other side?

Such was his almost paralytic hesitation, he found himself moving on, glancing idly in other windows, descending now towards where the street begins to slope down to the harbour, the water, the ships, yes, and the sailors, hardened by custom, who come up to seize their rough pleasure. He hurried back now, retraced his steps, hoping she'd not already gone. Marlene was still there, the self-same one, in the window, and the lights, the blaring music came at him, blocking out more sober thought. He stood now for a full minute, a swimmer on the edge of a pool. He gave the nod to the woman at last. She must have moved and stood up, but he didn't recall it, and found himself in a drab, dimly-lit room somewhere above the street, the girl hurriedly removing outer garments, giving vent to a few monosyllabic orders in her language, '*Willst du dich ausziehen?*' (D'you want to get undressed?) and then retreating to a large unmade bed and propping herself against an array of puffy pillows. He though, over on the other side of the room, was breaking into an unnerving sweat, and any thoughts of desire were already being strangled beneath a blanket of anxiety as he experienced the first signs of an uncontrollable trembling throughout his frame.

,'*Setzt das Geld auf dem Tisch, Liebchen*'. (Put the money on the table). She called from the bedside, and repeated, more peremptory this time, '*Ja, das Geld!*'

A whole new wave of anxiety flooded through William, as he suddenly remembered Gerhardt. *What the hell! He must be wondering where the hell I am.*

He placed his hand in his pocket. '*Wieviel?*' 'How much? How much do you want?' His pocket was unusually empty, so he let his hand explore the back pocket, as another wave of panic started to descend. *Pick-pocketed. I've been robbed!* Still no sign of money. He tried the jacket on the back of the chair. No. *Where the hell's my money then!* He knew now beyond all certainty that Gerhardt had his wallet. In the coffee house. The game was up. '*Um Gotteswillen. ich hab kein Geld.*' (Heaven's sake, I haven't got any money),

He waited for the guards. However, instead of the guards came a flood of overwhelming relief. Did he really want to go through the whole procedure anyway with this impudent woman looking less and less like Marlene by the second? In this sleazy room? Reason was intervening. He would take the consequences; he was sure he didn't really desire at all this messy female flesh over by the bed. *I'm saved*! *On a pure technicality.*

The girl on the bed wore an expression of annoyance '*Kein Geld, kein Spass. Na?*' (No money, no fun, yeah?)

'I'm sorry. *Es tut mir Leid.* A mistake.'

He face fell. 'Okay. You must go!'

She must have pushed a button somewhere, because two men appeared in the room. Two sturdy Germans with no-nonsense expressions on their faces

'I'm sorry,' William repeated. 'It's a mistake.'

They ushered him out, not roughly but firmly. They were by the door to the street, the crowds still out there. They had him by both arms, one on either side, and were propelling him onto the street, his jacket following him through the air.

A host of faces watched him for a moment, some grinning, others astonished, and he made his way quickly from the windows. *Is this the right direction for the coffee house?* Humiliation coursed through his mind. Then anger. *F... Gerhardt!* He reached the coffee house and Gerhardt of course was nowhere to be seen. His immediate dilemma hit him like a bucket of cold water, obliterating all thoughts of his recent demise. *No Gerhardt, no car, no money, 10 miles back to Osteinbeck in the cold night air to his digs.* Rational mind took over under stress. He walked in what he believed to be the right direction for where they'd parked. *Down the hill, heading away from the bright lights. Was it two streets or three? About five minutes' walk. Very little chance of finding Gerhardt's tin-pot of a Trabant anywhere.*

And out of nowhere, in the darkness, loomed the unmistakably tinny shape of a Trabant, same colour as Gerhardt's, bright yellow, and indeed a human form inside (*was that a person?*) hunched in the front seat. His mind was playing tricks, then giving way to shock, astonishment, joy, all emotions tangled up in this happy conclusion to the evening's frightening dream.

He knocked on the window of the car and Gerhardt jerked in his seat, and wound down the window. 'Ah, you back. I waiting.' A pause followed and then, 'You have fun?'

'Gerhardt, I had no money.'

'*Ach Ja.*' He climbs out of the car, reaching into his back-pocket. 'Your...how you say...wallet.' He hands him the black leather wallet. 'I keep it for you. I spend all the money.' His face spread into an unaccustomed grin. *He has a sense of humour then.*

No explanations. No questions. No *post mortems*. They drive in silence towards *Oststeinbeck*, Gerhardt gripping the wheel and focussing on the road ahead. He doesn't drive with the same ease and indifference as William always did. And meanwhile, William is wrestling with the evening's events - the significance, the possibilities, the potential disaster, the providence - from which is slowly emerging in his mind, a colossal sense of relief, of gratitude at the unexpected outcome to it all. Which, at last, formulates into a short, almost mundane collection of words that encapsulate the entire, nerve-shattering experience: at a particularly long set of traffic-lights; both of them find themselves glancing at each other and William spontaneously allowing this pithy culmination of his thoughts to spill out into the silent car: 'Wow, another one of life's little practical jokes.'

Gerhardt grunts and drives on.

(At Possum Kingdom) ENTRY FROM ADAM'S DIARY

REFLECTIONS and **CONFESSIONS**
London – the 'Garret' (profile of an artist)

'How did it all go wrong? Or did it all go wrong at all? Is this perhaps just the norm? Look, there must be millions of lonely guys like me out there wondering how they've offended the female sex, and wondering too what on earth they personally are going to do about it. In search of a female, *any* female, desperation inscribed indelibly on their foreheads. You see them outside bars, discos, dating agencies (can't see myself frequenting any of those venues, no matter how desperate). Okay, in London there's, say, 10 million people, so 5 million females, and then narrow it down to 2 and half million desirable ones. That's still a lot; so how come it's so difficult to make a breakthrough? Girls want a fun time, that's why, and preferably not with a psychologically disturbed odd-ball. Deep down they're conventional. Little time for deep thought.

Why then don't I just take a few leaves out of Beesley's book downstairs? Full of charming swagger and just enough charisma to make his victim believe he's not a total mental retard. Well, if you really want to know, it's because I despise the bloke. I've still got a bit of pride and I can't stand the way he's always on the verge of trying to muscle in on some of the no-hope girls I occasionally bring back to the flat. He just can't let go. Not for a minute can he permit the thought someone else might actually be enjoying what he regards as his sole inalienable rights. Greedy, miserly bastard.

I'm late for work. I've been at the Bureau at least four weeks now. Long enough to realize how much I despise the place. The other day I went to a retirement ceremony in Exams Div (EX). A little man with drooping moustache and indomitable blue eyes (the kind of eyes that please the Director General (DG)), and who's been at the Bureau forty five years. It's kind of a record. As a leaving gift, HEX presented him with an alarm clock - to wake him up when he no longer needed to. Perhaps it was intended as a joke.

    I take bus No.30 as usual along Euston Road. Number.30s are due to arrive on the quarter hour, but I've noticed they always come on the half hour, together in twos, so one is full and one entirely empty. It's a dodge. Every rush-hour, one bus-man gets a 'free' ticket. I'm tempted to report it.

    Albert's waiting in the lift and completes his first mile of the day as he ferries me up, and, as I enter the corridor of E Branch, 15 minutes late on account of the buses, Pekoe nearly bumps into me, hurrying out of the Toilets and adjusting his flies on the run.

    'Morning, John.'

    He glances at his watch, to make a point, and hurries on, but turns back at the end of the corridor. 'Oh, by the way, I'd like to have a chat with you. Shall we say - he looks again at his watch - 9.45?'

    Dismissal? Could I be so lucky?

    'Sit down, sit down,' says Pekoe as I enter his office at precisely 9.45. We have the usual preamble, complaining about Public Transport etc, until he says, 'Well!', places both hands behind his head, leans far back in his chair, and asks.. 'Do you like us?' I glance around nervously, not quite sure who he's referring to. 'Because,' he continues, '*we* like *you.*'

    After some reflection, I finally get the point. 'Well, I like you too,' I say, aware it sounds funny.

'Good,' says Pekoe promptly, lurching forward in his chair until his nose is within three inches of mine. 'I hoped you'd say that because you're the sort of person it's worth investing money in, to train.'

'However,' I go on, 'I'm not sure the job is really me.'

'When I say 'train', Pekoe now continues, disregarding my remark entirely, 'do you have any idea of the sort of sum we're talking about to train an AO?' I shake my head. 'What would you say if I told you 2, 000 pounds. You cost us 2, 000 pounds before you even walk in the door.'

'I'd say *Whew*!'

He disregards that remark too. 'So we can't afford to make any mistakes in our selection process, you understand.'

I nod. 'What kind of training do you mean exactly? Has the training already begun?'

'On the job training. Best kind of training there is. Learn the job by doing it. Trial and error. So long as there aren't too many errors,' he smiles.

'The trouble is,' I say, 'I don't see how I can ever do the sort of work Mr. Foreman does.'

He nods sagely. 'Jack Foreman's good, but he's not the best. Forget Foreman. The question you have to consider - and I mean here and now - is: Are you with us or against us?'

I give Pekoe a solid silent minute before replying, 'With you'.

'Well, good luck,' says Pekoe, standing up and holding out a flabby hand. 'You've made the right decision. Welcome aboard.'

What else could I have said? They'd caught me off guard.

Jack's already in the office. He's sitting at his desk with his crash-helmet on, studying some computer print-out. Jack Foreman weaves his way in from Chiswick every morning on a motor scooter. He's too afraid to learn to drive a car. How he survived seven years as a Colonial Officer (CO) in East Africa without a driving license is anyone's guess.

'Hello, my old fruit,' he says. 'Made a commitment for thirty years, have you? By the way, Mrs. Hod wants to see your exam results. Print-out's on the desk.'

'I haven't done an exam.'

A smile flits across Foreman's wide mouth. 'These are the mid-autumn retakes.' He gives me a weary look.

I know, by the way, where Mrs. Hod's office is. Down the corridor, on the corner. She has a wide perspective of London from her desk.

'Don't keep her waiting,' says Jack.

I grab a pile of letters on my desk. *First Veronica, second Mrs. Hod.*

Veronica's the secretary in the typing pool specifically assigned to me and Foreman. I wander into the Pool with my pile of handwritten letters. She's varnishing her nails. 'Let me have them in forty minutes, Veronica,' I say tight-lipped (I already know it's the only way to get anything out of her).

Across the way, the little black typist, Rita, pretends to type while watching out of the corner of her eye my confrontation with Veronica. In fact all those other girls are watching too. Do they desire me? If so, I wonder why. I'm just a jumped-up guy in a suit that doesn't fit, and who doesn't know what he's doing anyway. Must be the confrontation. Everyone likes a good drama.

Get yourself another girl. A remark from my past swims tantalizingly across my mind, like a salmon slipping across the TV screen. It was spoken by the mother of a girl I used to know. Mary actually. She must have known her daughter very well. All those compounded years of experience and wisdom.

'Got it, Veronica?' I look her in the eye and she looks me in the eye and nods moodily. 'What's the matter, Veronica? Having a bad day or something? Nail varnish not drying?'

Some of the other girls laugh. Veronica looks down at the pile of letters. I leave.

Work at this time of the year in the Bureau consists apparently of examination assessments. Results, to put it another way. After looking at the print-out, we, the AOs, take our recommendations for who's to pass and who isn't down the long corridor to COFET (Coordinating Officer for Further Education and Training), that's Mrs. Hod, who makes the ultimate decisions. It's a big job. In most cases, interestingly enough, she rejects our recommendations and sends us back to re-assess. Which in real terms, let's face it, means fiddling

Redemption

with the pass mark (not piecemeal, but whole-meal). Lowering the overall pass mark, so that ten thousand more candidates will slip through. Or vice versa. Mrs. Hod's maxim is as follows: 'I'd rather see twelve candidates walking around Piccadilly Circus with Certificates they didn't deserve than one candidate without a Certificate he/she *did* deserve. Lower the pass mark accordingly. I feel like a kid caught with his hand in the honey-jar.

Mrs. Hod sits behind her large desk as I enter. She doesn't recognize me even though we cross four times per day in the corridor. She gazes at my print-out. While evidently trying to remember my name. Finally gets it.

'Are you sure the pass mark should be this high, Adam?'

I've done my homework. 'It *was* last year, Mrs. Hod.'

'That's neither here nor there. Perhaps the examiners were stricter this year. Who *are* your examiners, Adam?'

(If I tell her she won't know them). 'In this subject, Mrs. Hod?' I stall.

'Yes'

'Mr. Grey and Mr. Paget.'

'Paget. I don't know Paget. Grey, of course, I know. Is he really *still* examining?

(She hasn't fired him, so of course he is. Examiners work for the Bureau until they drop dead over a script. Even then, they go on getting summoned to Committee lunches for a few months). He's a bit strict, isn't he, Adam?' She looks at me for confirmation.

'He examined the course last year, Mrs. Hod.'

'As I've said, if we take that line of argument, there's no knowing where we'll end up.'

'Isn't is possible the students might just have been a worst bunch this year?'

'Everything's possible. It's possible the exam was a lot more difficult. Who are we to judge? *We're the Examination Body, Mrs. Hod, that's all!*. Lower the pass mark, Adam. There are so many variables in this game. I'd rather see ten candidates walking around Piccadilly Circus with Certificates....'

I look her straight in the eyes, feigning interest. Back in the office, I fiddle the print-out until the same number pass as last year, while all the while wondering if it wouldn't be a whole lot simpler if you left it to an honest teacher who knows his pupils inside out etc etc. The pass mark stands now at 37 as against 44.

At this point, Veronica enters the office and hurls a bunch of letters at me... (they actually, between her hand and my face, take off and finally slide across my desk). She stomps out without a word. Foreman smiles sardonically. I leave the letters and return to Mrs. Hod for a signature.

'What was the pass mark last year, Adam?'

'44'.

She signs. Then the phone rings on her desk, just as I'm hearing once more about Piccadilly Circus. It's Savage, in Personnel (P), I can tell.

'He's no longer in control,' I hear Mrs. Hod mutter. 'If he goes on like this, he'll jeopardize the whole Bureau.'

Then she repeats "yes" fifteen or so times before becoming aware I'm still there. She places a hand across the mouthpiece and pushes the signed print-out across the desk. 'Thank you, Adam.'

Now I head direct down the corridor to the typing Pool, where I fire Veronica on the spot. 'You've just lost your job,' I tell her..

Her face falls. I continue by informing her I will personally see Pekoe and supervise her dismissal. Why this should worry her, I can't say, but ten minutes later she grovels into the office to beg forgiveness. Which I give her.

'Read the riot act in there, did you, Adam my Boy?' asks Jack.

I nod.

'Good old Public School training coming out.'

'Perhaps I should see a psychiatrist about all my educational hang-ups, Jack,' I remark with all the irony I can muster 'D'you think it might help?'

';No one ever suffered any harm from psychoanalysis,' replies Foreman.

'Had some yourself, Jack?'

Jack, by reply, gives me the kind of look suggesting: *Wouldn't anyone require the services of a psychiatrist working in a place like this?* He gets an Oscar for his performance.

At this point, I return to the typing pool. In there is Swan, talking to Vivienne - according to him, the *only* girl to come anywhere near a 'Publishing' girl.

Veronica looks down in confusion at the sight of me. Rita looks up. I pass Veronica, I pass Swan and Vivienne, I advance to Rita's desk. Rita has an Afro, and beneath it, a puckish face. Her long finger nails stand out blood-red against the typewriter keys. I've already fallen in love with those nails.

'Busy, Rita?'

'So, so.'

'It's lunch hour.'

'Don't get a lunch hour, do I?' she says aggressively.

'Why's that?'

'Mr. Swan's always giving me letters, isn't he?'

'Don't you eat lunch at all, Rita?'

'Sometimes.' She turns her head and looks out of the window. Her neck reminds me of a reed pipe, her lips the unfurled petals of a rose.

'Like to keep your figure trim, eh? She shrugs. Her shoulders remind me of those symmetrical diagrams in Maths books. 'Where do you live, Rita?'

'Wood Green.'

'Wood Green, eh? North London. Get the bus in, do you?'

'Tube.'

'Ah huh. Let me see now, that would be...Piccadilly Line. (I snap it back at her with an air of finality).

'That's right.'

'Get your things together, Rita. We'll go for a walk.'

And I picked Rita up. It was that easy. Where did I get my crazy confidence from? I think it was on account of my frustration with Mrs. Hod and my annoyance with Veronica. Plus, Swan's added presence in the typing pool. And anger can sometimes make me forget my inhibitions. *Get yourself another girl.* Those unbidden lines traverse my vision once more. The lady was almost certainly right. Particularly if things fell into place this easily. Sixteen pairs of eyes follow Rita and me out of the typing pool and to our consummation.

'D'you like it at the Bureau, Rita?'

She shrugs again. Her waist reminds me of a wasp. We're walking now along the Marylebone Road. Afro hairdos are in vogue, I notice; almost all the black girls have one. I get a surge of electricity as I glance at Rita's.

'Were you born in England, Rita?'

'Ethiopia.'

'East Africa,' I toss back without hesitation. 'D'you like England?'

She shrugs. Her thighs remind me of the curve of an hour-glass. When I was a young boy, really young, there was an old travel book in my father's bookcase. I think it was called *'Travel in Distant Lands'*, and it had beautiful black etchings of native scenes, *'White hunter shooting buck on the mountains'*, *'Initiation into the tribe'* etc. One picture I used to return to again and again, showed a 'native' girl tied to a stake on the seashore. The tide of course was coming in, and she was bound to die. What struck me was this Nubile seemed resigned to her fate; I supposed she'd transgressed some tribal law or done something wrong; and it even occurred to me she was being offered up to make the crops grow. Certainly something unfair. But the main attraction wasn't the right or wrongs of it but the fact she had very little on. She was virtually naked. Later, of course, I got wise and thumbed through my Dad's pile of subscriptions to National Geographic Magazine and even went looking for the occasional nude on BBC documentaries; but none of those alternatives ever succeeded in putting the scene into so delicate a context: a naked female sacrificial victim. Could I now, as I walk up the Euston Road, be revisiting my childhood sexual fantasizing? My very own sacrificial victim?

Roger Beesley is also 'entertaining' at his flat. I can hear Tony Bennett on full volume. I shan't forget to mention this to the psychiatrist (if I ever feel the need for one): the sheer pace Beesley sets, combined with the tooth and nail sexual rat-race that living in a city like London inflicts upon the male bachelor; they're disturbing, nerve-jangling. Yes, I can hear myself right now: "*Doctor, it's not just Beesley. Have you any idea of the need a young male has to 'score' in a place like this? Just to keep in the race! Maintain self-respect. I have cousins, step-brothers, uncles, with a twenty lap lead on me already. All of them more than ready to insist on comparing notes, swap anecdotes, even right in the middle of a squash game or something.*"

Inside of three minutes, Beesley pops into my living-room, where it's me, this time, 'entertaining'. He must have sniffed Rita. She's on the couch and Beesley's undressing her slowly. WITH HIS EYES.

He makes small talk for five of my precious minutes, the kind of vacuous intercourse that's placed him at the top of the league table.

'Beesley, old Boy, didn't you say you had an appointment with a bathroom consultant this lunch hour?'

He gets my warning message finally, and slinks out the door.

Rita's calves, as she heads for the bedroom, remind me of the tall, straight masts of a ship in port. 'Rita, let's make love.'

She shrugs. 'Mr. Riley, I didn't know you were like this.' She pops a piece of gum in her mouth.

I'm not, Rita, really I'm not. Circumstances mould me into this; It's Beesley's peevish meddling under my very nose; it's society twisting me into a shape I scarcely recognize. This is not me at all. I'm just an AO

Rita fakes some feeble mental resistance; it's all part of the game really. After a bit, she relaxes, waiting for me. She's peeling off her afro, yes, removing the hair on her head; and all at once I remember what always used to puzzle me, even disturb me about that etching back in my Father's study: it was that the young girl seemed devoid of hair. All other attributes, yes, but shaven on top.

I panic. Despite Rita's charming component parts (the waspy waist, the reedy neck etc), I realize that what's happening now, twelve inches before my eyes, certainly *isn't* an attribute at all. *I don't want to share my bed with a bald-headed female.* Not my fault, not Rita's. But there it is. Moreover, worst of all, I realize I'm experiencing what is known in the bachelor trade as 'erectile dysfunction'.

I rush to the bathroom, leaving this '*stranger from a Distant Land*' alone in my bed, wearing nothing except that resigned expression she'd worn so many years before on the palm-ringed beach.

For heaven's sake, is this real, or is it a dream? Will I wake up in a minute and realize I've been fantasizing? Hell, I scarcely even *know* this stenographer from Wood Green.

I search for love but don't know what it is. I'm confused. I used to know, but don't any longer. It's such a tiny word too - LOVE - so loaded however with great import. That little monosyllable, throughout human history, has launched religions, ignited wars, inspired blockbuster movies, emboldened the participators of *crimes passionnelles,* and, in antiquity, *"launched a thousand ships"*.

Would I recognize that four-letter word if it came my way again? I hope so. I knew I loved Mary the moment I saw her gliding across the airport terminal towards me. And I kind of knew I was only messing with Rita when I chatted her in the typing pool.

So where has that tiny monosyllable vanished to in my life? It's complicated. I should never have let Mary go in the first place. But I'm learning. I'm pretty sure now you don't just love component parts, but the whole. And also that that 'whole' can take one second, a couple of years, or an eternity. There are no short-cuts, but you have to do your best to get the timing right. Between men and women there's a timing imbalance. The thunderclap rarely happens instantaneously to both parties. That time, with Mary, it was me who made a silent commitment there and then, on the spot. No prevarication. She didn't. She took a bit of time, chewed it over. Why can't we just meet in the middle sometimes?

So, girls, please try not to prevaricate, and please, can't you just refrain from expecting us to perform circus tricks? Decide on the hoof. Take a leap in the dark. We both have a lot to lose. And win.

As for Rita, she's a pretty girl; I wish her well. I'll see her again in the typing pool, make a point of politely acknowledging her. We both learned a lesson, I suppose

CHAPTER 13

*"In which William makes friends with an existentialist
artist and meets someone who knew his father"*

Although, throughout his university years, William had tended to neglect his daily source of strength and inspiration, he'd always known the foundations of his Church of One were sturdy enough not to crack on account of his absence; the God he envisaged was as wide as the sea and would wait patiently for his return.

He'd reached the end of his contract by October, but decided to stay on in Hamburg until Christmas, continuing the roaming existence he found so hard to relinquish. He'd already been more than a little overwhelmed by the beauty of the falling leaves in October along the wide avenues he bestrode each day, but more than that, if truth be known, he was even more overwhelmed by the presence of Ingrid, the tall, graceful girl he saw each day in the Mensa, gliding, tray in hand, like a swan on the *Alster*, regal, distant, untouchable. That he might come to know her better, that he might come to understand what, if anything, could unlock the heart of such a lovely creature, or whether such creatures could ever be induced to fall in love at all.

'Ah, Ingrid. Yes, don't worry about Ingrid; you'd think she was a goddess, but she's not.' Mackintosh was immediately dismissive when William casually mentioned her. 'She's the same as all of us; cool exteriors, inner turmoil.'

William waited and wondered. How did Mack seem to know so much about her anyway? And so, as summer slipped almost imperceptibly into dripping autumn, his visits to the Mensa continued unabated, increased even, prompted by this added incentive.

One particular October afternoon there'd already been upwards of a thousand students coming and going through that vast Hall, entering and exiting in one continuous, turbulent stream. To the casual observer of Teutonic customs, which William had become, this whole methodical feeding process was nothing short of a miracle; he compared it to one of those familiar chess-games he'd observed in the park on his way to school, watching stubby old men as they hauled giant pieces, as large as themselves, across a chequered concrete slab, one by one slowly disappearing as they grew tired of the game, leaving just a faithful few behind to protect their 'King'. Such too was the gradual emptying of the Mensa that day, as the usual faces sat on, arguing, discussing, shouting if necessary, unaware of the covert glances they were attracting from the cleaning women, whose job it was to sanitise the place with cloths and mops and fluids, in preparation for the next onslaught.

Georges Papaloizos, the Greek, for example, holding forth interminably on his favourite topic, 'Freedom'. Freedom from working restrictions, from conventions, from moral obligations, from just about everything. The rest of the group of students, trained, in the disciplines of dialectic, tolerated Georges' ranting much like a despot might tolerate a trained leopard, and at first remained condescendingly patient, simply because that's what Georges was, a young Greek, who, on the face of it, possessed in his veins precious Socratic blood, a legacy from down the line of the western world through hundreds of years.

That particular afternoon, Georges held the floor. 'They won't make me work. Not against my will. They're drones.'

Not surprisingly, a few moments elapsed before Macintosh, the tall American, who could be equally dogmatic, took up the challenge. 'Work's an essential aspect of any civilised society, you bloody fool.'

'It's not work *per se* I'm against,' shot back Georges, ignoring the insult to his person. 'It's *organised* work.' He paused, to let that sink in. 'Organised *labour*. Let's put it that way. Society destroying all that's best about itself through its own exertions.' Once again, Georges hesitated, sensing he wasn't carrying his audience with him. 'Okay. It's difficult, I realise.' Silence ensued, prompting Georges to try again. 'It's not unlike the image of the.pelican then.' He glanced around the table, paused a second. 'Anyone heard of the mythical pelican, tearing its own entrails out to feed its young?'

Red rag to a bull. There was a flutter of laughter before Mackintosh said airily, 'Another one of those inevitable Greek fairy stories.' He turned to look hard at Georges. 'What in hell's name has a large bird with a giant beak got to do with society's organisation of labour in the final years of the 2nd millennium AD? I swear you're crazy Papaloizos.'

'It's the perfect simile; that's what,' Georges answered, unabashed.

Someone else added, more politely in the ensuing silence, 'Georges, I'm afraid, *en masse*, we don't understand.'

'Nor are we interested,' said another.

Georges waited a moment before replying. 'That's because you're ignorant. E*n masse*.

And amidst the outcry that followed, it was Jürgen who chose to add, almost apologetically and scarcely audibly to those further down the table, 'By the way, this is boring talk. Did anyone hear about Kurt Weiler?'

At that point, just before 4.00, Kurt Weiler, most people's friend and a frequent member of the group, was mentioned, but the question was lost in the common endeavour to put paid to Papaloizos, whose arguments would inevitably lead - everyone knew it - to nebulous wild-card: 'Freedom'.

'What you're so ardently denigrating, Georges, (it was Mackintosh again) is neither work, nor the pressures of it, nor even bloody pelicans, and certainly not freedom. It's progress.'

'If progress means the mindless regimentation we've got nowadays, then you're right.'

'Progress means complexity and organisation, my dear friend.'

'Then you can keep it. I have no time for complexities. Let others worry about complexities; I deal in principles. Life's more simple than we think, you see'

'*Broad* principles, I suppose you mean, Georges,' Mack said mockingly. 'Principles, divorced - as yours usually are - , from reality are little use to man nor beast.'.

Jürgen's voice chimed in again now, this time with more urgency. 'He killed himself. He's dead.'

Georges either never heard Jürgen or chose to ignore what he'd heard. He continued to maintain his argument. 'Principle and reality are always bad bed-fellows, Mack. But that was always your problem, wasn't it? I prefer to leave the details to unprincipled lawyers like you to sort out.' A triumphant smile crossed his face and he sat back as if there was nothing further to discuss.

And in the short space of silence that followed, it was left to the quiet female voice of Ingrid to ask, '*Who* did, Jürgen? Who killed himself?'

'As I said... Kurt. They discovered his body in his room. On the end of a rope.'

Jürgen, now holding the floor, let the grim details emerge, chattered on about how he'd tried to ring Kurt, on an entirely different pretext, had been forwarded to another number, who'd wanted to know who he was, so he'd hung up and phoned Weiler's home, his parents. 'A bit disconcerting asking to speak to a dead man....'

This stark, final remark dropped like a shard of ice onto the already chilled and silent table. No room for debate now. These facts were not open for discussion, but a reality which each individual had to come to terms with alone, with the knowledge that their unfortunate friend, by a quirk of fate, could well have been any single one of them.

Jürgen followed up his explanation. 'I gathered from his parents, Kurt had run into problems with his girl-friend. A bust up.'

So that was it, and William, recalling his recent exploits up on the Reeperbahn with Gerhardt, experienced a sharp blow under the heart, and tasted sourness at the back of his mouth, He couldn't be quite certain, but hadn't that been Kurt Weiler he'd noticed, that very same evening, standing alone and gazing intently into one of the brightly-lit windows on the strip? And if this were so, then where might it leave his naïve friend, Gerhardt, whom he'd dragged so reluctantly and irresponsibly to the place, and whose mentality and circumstances might not be so far removed from those of Kurt's.

Georges' blunt interruption cut into the silence. 'Then that explains it, doesn't it?. Happens time and time again. Difficult to live inside ones skin, especially when there's a sexual relationship involved.'

This intervention came so out of the blue, and was so tasteless, no one for a few moments could think of a reply. It was Mackintosh who finally broke the dismayed silence. 'I've always thought you were a callous bastard; Papaloizos; now I'm sure. It's a friend we're talking about, not some metaphysical nicety, some bland principle.'

Georges remained undeterred in the face of this attack. 'You're right. It's not metaphysics; it's plain facts.' He eyed them all for a moment. 'Don't look so horrified. This isn't the first time someone's killed themselves for love. *'Romeo'*, for instance? And how about young *'Werther'*? You've all read those sad books. Literature's full of similar examples; authors just love the theme. It's commonplace.'

'Except that this is a friend, Papaloizos. I've always thought you were crazy.' Georges made no reply. Just glared at Mack, who went on, 'Of course we've read those sentimental books. But we're not talking about fiction now. This is an actual friend.'

'As you said. And so? What's the difference, for hell's sake?' Georges was starting to show signs of impatience too, his recent unruffled calm starting to crack beneath Mack's relentless scorn, and perhaps himself, too, feeling the strain of the unsettling message they'd all just received. 'I liked Kurt, but what good's that to him now? It's the causes we have to consider. And the causes are always the same. It doesn't take a genius to work out why our friend killed himself.'

Such self-confidence, such certainty, left Mack with bated breath. He simply asked the question everyone wanted to ask. 'So *why* then, Papaloizos? Enlighten us.'

Georges remained silent for a second, as if searching for the precise words to frame the matter. Then he said quietly, 'Guilt. Guilt tipped him over the edge. It's invariably the same. He couldn't live with his guilt.'

The simple, unexpected utterance, the stark word 'guilt', seemed to have taken the floor away beneath Mack's feet. 'Guilt For what, for heaven's sake?'

Georges hesitated again. There was a pained expression on his face, as if he didn't expect to be understood. 'Guilt is our consciousness. It's our response to life. The thoughts in our head.' He paused and then said with finality, 'It's the human condition.'

'Yours, Georges, not mine.'

Jürgen, the lawyer, intervened, for once ahead of Mack. 'Mack, let's keep this rational, shall we? Before we lose sight of our purpose altogether.' He turned to the Greek. 'Georges, it's clear nowadays, law and medical science both affirm the balance of mind of someone who commits suicide is invariably disturbed, and the victim ceases to be responsible for his or her actions.'

'True, maybe. But what is it that so disturbs the victim in the first place? Before the critical point?'

'Could be many factors,' replied Jürgen. 'You surely must understand that.'.

'It's guilt that disturbs the mind, said Georges. 'Listen, we all have a choice. We are free agents. We are always responsible for what we do. Every sane one of us. If we're not, then who is?' There was silence now round the table. They seemed to be hearing a different Georges, while William was secretly wondering whether he himself had experienced an after-shock of guilt that night. *If not him, then possibly Gerhardt. Certainly Faustus, as he watched Gretchen go to the gallows.* 'Look, I'm not referring to individual cases,' continued Georges. I'm referring to the human condition. The human race as a whole. We are vessels crammed with posthumous guilt, believe me. Guilt spilling over into our lives. We don't know why. We don't know where this sensation comes from. It's just there, in us. We are born with it. We inherit it.'

And Ingrid interrupted quietly, 'You mean right and wrong?'

Georges leapt on the question eagerly, like a cat that's too long been playing with a mouse. 'Yes, I mean the knowledge of right and wrong. Sin. Biblical 'Good' and 'Evil'. That which is fed to us from childhood in the Bible. We feel accountable for our rights and wrongs; and the knowledge eats us up.'

'Accountable to who then?' asked Ingrid.

Georges momentarily eyed his watch and hoisted himself out of his chair. 'Afraid I'm late, Ingrid. I've got to go. But therein lies the question. The irony is, we're not accountable in fact to anyone. Guilt is like God. It doesn't exist. We invent it. If we fail to understand that, then we're all enslaved.' He glanced at the cleaners approaching the table. "I think somebody wants us out of here.'

He set off across the hall, short, stocky legs working to and fro like a well-oiled machine, shoulders hunched into his black donkey-jacket. He was already by the door when he turned and shouted at the top of his voice, 'And don't forget Nietzsche's immortal words: *Alles ist erlaubt* (everything is permissible).

It took Mackintosh a few seconds to compose himself. At last he addressed the whole group. 'He's an odd mixture, that latter-day Socrates. He harbours more contradictions in his head than we, or he, care to admit. One minute he's insisting on rights and wrongs, the next he's saying there are no rights and wrongs.'

The encroaching pack of cleaners closed remorselessly in on the table.

They walked together - William, Georges, Mackintosh, Ingrid - in the chill evening air down towards Dammtor Station. The dead leaves crunched underfoot, and the sun was filmy behind the rail tracks. They were silent, locked in themselves, unwilling to break the magic, each, for a moment, immersed in the splendour of the Autumn evening, but aware too of the advancing black wave of office workers streaming up the hill towards them from the station. It was a few days after the dramatic announcement in the Mensa about the death of Kurt Weiler, and they were still struggling to come to terms with the tragedy, to put their world to rights again.

Georges finally broke the silence. 'See what I mean?'

'*What* do you mean, Georges?' Mack was ever quick to take up a verbal challenge.

'Look at them; the robots. Don't they seem like robots to you? No, they're not *like* robots, they *are* robots.' No one answered, and Georges continued, 'D'you want to be one of them?'

'I suppose, Georges, you're going to say our alternative to this robotic march of progress is '*Freedom*'. Yes?' The sarcasm wasn't lost on anyone.

'Oh, please don't get on to that.' Ingrid's gentle, piping voice broke in on the sparring. 'Look at the sunset. Isn't that freedom enough for the time being?'

'Ingrid, please!' Georges had a soft spot for the girl, drew back from putting her down. 'No, it isn't enough. You've all got to decide; you know that.'

They'd reached the Lombard Bridge, flooded with its race of cars, and all of them drew instinctively to a hurried halt in front of the traffic, and stood absorbing this other miracle of progress, this wide, curving sweep of concrete bending its away across the Alster, daring you to follow.

'And you, I suppose,' said Mack, unable to let the matter drop, '*don't* have to decide on your future.'

'Sure I do. I *have* decided. Don't you remember? I opted out. Became an artist.'

'Oh yes, you did, didn't you? That was a fortunate alternative for those lucky enough to have talent. But, Georges, we can't *all* be artists....'

Georges left him no time to finish as he took the leap, like a swimmer poised on the edge of a pool, and strode out across the bridge, short legs working like pistons. 'I'm not '*all*', Mack,' he shouted back. 'I'm *me*.' He dodged a car and shouted again, 'Anyone coming? We're at the parting of the ways here. Come back to my place, see some paintings, have a coffee.'

Ingrid, already heading off in a different direction, raised her voice too against the din of cars, 'Thanks, Georges. Another time; I've got a lecture at the Uni.'

'I'll join you, Ingrid' called Mack. 'You're going my way. I'm heading for the *Teestube* (tea-house). See if there's anybody there I can't beat at chess.' He caught up with her and they both disappeared into the traffic.

William watched them go, regretting yet another opportunity missed to coax Ingrid alone into the intimacy of a cafe. Glancing hurriedly over his shoulder, the departing image of the girl, tall, stately, sexy, remained with him as he caught up with Georges halfway along the Bridge. *Does Georges ever wait for anyone or anything? Can he really be so self-sufficient and absorbed? The Artist's temperament perhaps*? Taking another quick look at the seething throng of people and cars ahead of him, he realised how this mass of the city, this alien panoply dedicated to the god, mammon, filled him with such dread, reminding him of all his own uncertainties and frailty. The fact that this 'artist' ahead of him, Papaloizos, apparently felt no such apprehensions seemed all the more remarkable.

He caught up at last with Georges, who seemed uncannily to have read his thoughts. 'You know why? You know why I don't feel overpowered? Because I save all my insecurities for the canvas. That's why.'

They drew away from the bridge, walked on towards the Opera House, Georges now muttering, '*Kurt was neurotic, you know.*'

William found it difficult to hear him against the din of traffic. '*Who* was?'

'That poor chap, Kurt Weiler. He had no outlets, I guarantee it. And then got entangled with a woman. It's fatal.' William waited for the explanation which would surely follow. It was often a waste of breath interrupting Georges in full flow. 'And then, let's guess, she went absent for a while, that burning heart of his life, for whatever the reason, and in her absence Kurt sallied off to the whorehouse one evening to alleviate his loneliness.' Georges stopped and looked hard at William. 'He was a sensitive guy, you know.'

'How do you know all this, Georges? How d'you know he did that?'

'I don't, but I assume.'

'And, what would you have done in that same scenario? Snuck off to your canvases, I suppose.'

Georges took a moment to reply, and then said, 'It *did* happen to me. And you know what I did? I didn't wait around. I wrote our entire relationship off, there and then, and with all my force, I burned the woman out of my life, cauterised her, exorcised her.' He paused, perhaps imagining it all over again, and allowed a gentle, unusual smile to drift across his face. 'Better than letting things drift. You see, I don't believe in *best friend*s'. Certainly not with the opposite sex anyway.' William let the remark pass by him, unwilling to embark on that difficult topic, and Georges concluded, 'In the words of your famous Charles Dickens, it's *humbug*. I don't believe in befriending my former lover. We're all just too nice to each other these days.'

It was a *cri de coeur*; William knew it by the note in Georges' voice. He replied, 'A bit of a generalisation, Georges.'

But Georges was not to be gainsaid. 'Everyone's the same, believe me. We all react in the same way.' He peered over the parapet. 'All those people down there coming home from work, they're all the same. All neurotic in the final analysis; like Weiler.' He quickened his step 'Anyway, come on.'

Night had come. The sunset had faded from the sky. Lights were blinking along the road and in the office-blocks. They made their way across the dark, gutter-like stretch of water linking the the *Binnenalster* with the city's heart, and came finally to Georges' place.

It wasn't the first time William had visited this chic apartment on the *Rothenbaum Chaussee*. That first occasion, he'd quickly realised Georges wasn't someone who just pretends to creativity, but is indeed a working painter, a practising artist, with portraits and canvasses surrounding his studio, propped against walls and spilling into his living-space. However, his creations, far from resembling the measured grandeur of classical times or the lustre and magnificence of the Renaissance, seemed dedicated to the concept of ugliness, a display which seemed a glorification of 20th century discord: Incomplete landscapes, grotesque animal shapes, figures of humans with bulbous growths and abnormalities, all lay sprawled across floors, suspended carelessly from walls and even abandoned in his living-space in itself, each defying reason, logic or beauty, so that the apartment resembled less a temple of the Fine Arts, but rather a madman's interpretation of *Dante's 'Inferno'*, reminding one of that grim inscription above the portico of *Hades:* "ABANDON HOPE ALL YE WHO ENTER HERE".

As they stepped now into the apartment, William found it hard to forget Georges' very recent enigmatic response to Mack's taunting out on the Lombard Bridge: *'Didn't you know? I opted out. I became an artist.'*. But how could this 'vision of Hell' confronting him keep Georges sane and shelter him from life's emptiness? Could these surreal fantasies really be a talisman against the heartbreak of losing, say, someone like Ingrid, or, for that matter, be a sturdy defence against the degrading temptations of the *Reeperbahn?* There seemed, he felt, a vital cog missing in his whole chain of logic. How could such ugliness compete with the ever-present allure of either beauty or lust? He cast another glance at the painter, hunched in his jacket, self-contained, so apparently defiant, and self-contained, and in a moment's instinctive leap it came to him, he realised the identity of the missing cog, the key to Georges' strength: It lay not in those twisted end-products, but rather in the simple creative act itself, the brave assertion of ones own existence. Yes, the mere act of 'doing' justified the end-product, and gave purpose to Georges' life, buoyed him up, protected him. William understood now why Georges seemed always to be flying, as if he had wings.

The artist handed him a small Greek coffee and broke in on his thoughts. 'By the way, à propos of 'neurotic' back there, Ingrid's a beautiful girl, you know. And an exception.' William waited for the point. 'But she's dangerous. You *do* know that, don't you?'

I hardly know Ingrid at all.'

'Well, be careful. She'll ingest you. Like a boa constrictor. Without even knowing she's doing it. Men walk on a knife-edge in love affairs; I know all too well, believe me. Men are especially susceptible; they become entangled. Women though make straight for the goal.' William didn't know how to reply to this patronising remark and lacked the experience to understand it. Georges continued, 'Strange, but for example, you don't often find women hanging from house beams. They seem to have other ways of dealing with their guilt, hold it together more. Self-harming, have you heard of that?'

William felt himself being dragged into deep water as Georges pursued a train of thought quite outside his own experience. He replied blatantly, 'Yes, I've heard of self-harming.'

'It's a woman's way of dealing with pain But it's just a temporary escape; and involves other people, you see, shifts the guilt onto someone else.' He took a swig of his coffee, finishing it in one swallow. 'We artists are loners, we live inside ourselves. We don't need others.'

This too bold assertion dragged from William the inevitable response. 'What about love then, Georges? Isn't love meant to be the supreme act of needing someone?'

Georges brushed it off. 'Haven't we already dealt with love? Too precarious. 'I don't believe in love. It's just a state of mind. It's not real. I've been there, remember?'

'But Georges, a woman would never believe it's not real? They're the opposite.'

'I don't know what any woman would ever believe. I'm not a woman. I haven't got intuitive powers.' He relapsed, as was not uncommon with Georges, into a moody silence, and they both sat there, as if up a *cul-de-sac,* while William was left wondering idly if his companion was re-living some moment in the past when he *had* believed in love?

At last Georges emerged from his meditation, and with the trace of a rare smile on his lips, said, 'Listen, my friend. Woman has the soul of a child, the body of an angel, and the cunning of a fox. Men love the first two, and hate the third. It's an old Greek saying, and something my mother always used to tell me.' He laughed open-heartedly at his wit.

'You must have had a beautiful mother, Georges.'

'Yes, she was called Helen.'

'Was your father called Paris?'

'No, Menelaus.'

This flippant exchange had the effect of releasing the tension between them, and. William's eyes strayed again over the pencilled figures arrayed on the floor, as he wondered if it was the very absence of love that had engendered in Georges' imagination such malformed creatures?

Georges noticed him gazing. 'How d'you like them?'

'Yes, I like them,' he lied, 'but I don't understand them.'

A flicker of disappointment crossed Georges' face, hurriedly replaced by that dogged frown. 'The world's moved on, William. The world of Art with it.'

'From where to where?'

In response to this blunt question, Georges indicated a particularly formidable sketch nearby on the wall (the head of a conga eel about to sink its teeth into a lady's arm). 'From beauty to ugliness. Beauty died, you see, my friend. The Madonna, the landscapes, the gorgeous cherubs, all have been slowly obliterated and replaced by ugliness. I realise, of course, you were expecting Beauty from me. Sunset over a city perhaps? I *could* have done that. But it just wasn't in me.' He shook his head. 'I had the skill, but not the heart.'

'So where then did it die? When did this obliteration of Beauty occur? And why? What caused it?' William found himself growing impatient, but, at the same time, intrigued, recognising what Georges was trying to say. How often had he stood in museums and art galleries and asked himself, *Why all this ugliness?*

'I can't of course put a precise date on it, but summer of 1914 might be a ball-park figure.' Georges nodded solemnly. 'Yes, the heart went out of the world then, as we started slaughtering each other.'

William understood the message but found it absurdly over-stated. 'The First World War wasn't the only war in human history, Georges. There've been other wars and mass killings since time immemorial; and, in the wake of each separate slaughter, the shoots of Beauty have always sprung up. Mankind has never lost heart. How come was it at this particularly specific moment?'

Georges, for just once, admitted uncertainty, and. shook his head. 'Yes, this time it managed to eat into human consciousness and remain there. Some maintain God died with it, or at very least withdrew in disgust and left us to fend for ourselves.' This final remark came right out of the blue, and Georges continued, 'I personally subscribe to that belief. Have you heard of *Nietzsche*?' William nodded and Georges continued, 'Then you'll know "*Also sprach Zarathustra*" (Thus spoke Zarathustra), the work in which he utters that dramatic statement "*Gott ist tot*".'

This bland remark hit an unexpectedly sensitive spot in William 'Outrageous statement, you know, Georges.'

'You may think so. But that belief is held by not just a few writers. From the turn of the century, right on up until now. *Kierkegaard*, *Heidegger*, *Kafka*, *Sartre*. There's a whole range of them out there. Existentialist philosophers and novelists.'

William's knowledge of these writers was slim He knew the names but little of the substance. He sat now silently for a moment expelling air forcefully between his lips, in a speechless gesture of disbelief and rejection. He'd already grown used to the Greek's sweeping statements and now found it difficult to resist the thought that possibly *Nietzsche* fell into the same category. Such sweeping gestures of despair seemed so alien to everything he lived by. 'So where's the proof of all this, Georges?'

'Just look around you. Here!' Georges indicated his own ugly images in front of them, 'And, of course, in the collections of the majority of modern art works wherever you look. Starting from Picasso perhaps. None of them make sense. They're all distortions.' He paused for a moment. 'We artists don't have the luxury of picking and choosing. We have to represent reality; it's our duty. And I for one am true to it. Reality is no longer Beautiful.'

'It *is*, Georges. You perhaps just don't happen to see it. What you're maintaining is shocking. What if you're making a mistake?'

'I'm not making a mistake. I accept it, that's all. You apparently don't.'

A strained silence took hold of them; this provocative argument had turned personal and started to engulf their brief but growing friendship. Finally Georges broke the silence. 'Listen, William, this is not personal; we have to look bravely, honestly, with clear-sightedness, at the world confronting us today.' He eyed William steadily and then got up from his chair, leaving William wondering if his own visit was coming to an abrupt end. But Georges called from the neighbouring room. 'Let me show you something.' He returned a minute later carrying a landscape in oil, figures reclining on the grass, men fully clothed, ladies wearing nothing. 'Forget God for a minute.' He indicated the painting he was holding. 'This is Beauty, an 18th century interpretation of it. Not my own work I hasten to add. And yes, it *is* beautiful; but it's beauty without reality. It's illusory beauty.' The words came spilling out, as if he'd given this lecture time and again, knew it by heart. 'Where do you think those artists of the past, the one who painted this picture for example, and all those other massive painters of the Renaissance, and not to forget musicians either, drew their inspiration from?'

'Tell me.'

'The job of an artist, a *kept* artist of those times, was to glorify his Maker in his works, to praise God, to redefine beauty again and again.' The painting Georges was holding could have been mistaken for a replica of the Sistine roof. Nymphs, cherubs, podgy babes stood out in brilliant colour. 'Look at this painting. It's to the glory of god. It's an attempt by the artist to define God and his works. Reproduce God even. He wanted to do this, and he was employed to do it.'

'So why not go on doing that, where did it all go wrong?'

Georges took a moment to reply. 'Well, it was cheating really, wasn't it?. Phoney. You've got to remember; half the time the artist was not his own person; he was working for his paymaster. A little bird in a gilded cage. Chirping to please his master.'

'Was there anything wrong with that?'

'On the face of it, no. But the artist didn't need to struggle. To search for meaning, to strive for truth. There was no depth; and in fact the work said nothing.'

William couldn't believe what he was hearing. This brazen dismissal of what most art lovers held for magnificent. He replied, 'It said a whole lot to those that received it. Bach and his church masses. All those Renaissance masterworks. The Sistine Chapel.'

Georges interrupted him hurriedly. 'All right, there were of course the odd exceptions, the honest brokers, with deeply held faith; but most are fake. That's all I can say.'

William allowed a smile to cross his face. 'So you admit then there was once a God that you could sing the praises of?'

They sat looking at each other, as if across a gulf, until Georges said, 'Then it all began to change.'

'What a shame is all I can say.'

Georges ignored the remark. 'Midway through the last century. Industrialisation. The depravations of human nature. Mobility, Poverty. Access to communication if you like, the world became a darker place. And then that Wars. They put paid to Beauty altogether, and God died.'

He sat back, complacently satisfied with his performance, while William couldn't help thinking there was a flaw somewhere in Georges' logic. That final remark touched a sensitive spot. 'How can God be dead, Georges? God is *in* us. An idea planted in each one of us. It's *us* who are God. A part of God at any rate. We're fashioned in God's image. God cannot be dead until the last human creature on earth lies dead.'

There ensued a hush between them, as Georges sat on and on, devoid of any response.

William continued, 'Those existentialists need to redefine their ideas. Re-inventing God is laughable. You can't kill something that's un-killable. You can't kill an idea. It just transforms itself into something perhaps worse.

Georges sat locked in his seat, listening intently. At last, he sat abruptly forward in his chair, nodding affirmatively. 'How do you know so much, William?'

William grinned. 'They don't call me 'Luth' for nothing.'

They sat staring at each other in silence, and Georges finally closed his eyes until they became slits, just a thin line visible - squinting almost – and slowly turning into a radiant, deferential smile lighting up his stubborn face. 'Okay, forget everything I said. about God being dead and all that. I probably lost my way. But just remember this.' He paused. 'The flip-side, the advantage of God being dead is that we're all free. No controls.'

'That's an absurd concept,' William blurted out.

Georges was insistent. 'Yes, at liberty to do what we like. No restrictions on our actions.'

'It's impossible. The freedom you're asserting is impossible. God is inside each of us. There's no freedom from that.' Georges was shaking his head vigorously, but William continued. 'I've heard you say it yourself. We have to answer for our actions. We're responsible for them. There's guilt in all of us. That's not gone away. I've heard you say those very words.'

Georges smiled again. 'Perhaps.' But at least we won't have God to answer to. That permanent state of unease you're referring to may or may not remain, but our actions themselves will no longer be judged. Believe me, we can do whatever we like. *Alles ist erlaubt.*'

'Not true!'

'Are you a churlish priest perhaps?'

William looked hard at his friend, and then said enigmatically, 'No, I'm not a priest. Well I *am* a priest, Georges, but in my own church.'

Georges said, 'I don't understand, my friend. However, rest assured, we're on our own. God isn't with us. You can almost feel the loneliness.' He indicated his drawings. 'That's what my work attests to: Solitude.'.

They were still arguing when they left the apartment, walking hurriedly across town towards the *Neuer Wall,* where presumably they'd find Mackintosh still immersed in a chess-game. Perhaps also in the company of Ingrid, a possibility William both hoped and apprehended.

'Look, William.' Georges' voice emerged abruptly from the small gap between the two tightly-wedged lapels of his donkey jacket. 'I don't fully understand your beliefs, but I'm going to tell you something, something which might at least clarify mine.'

He was right; William had, earlier in the evening, been careful to confine his own arguments with his friend to mere interesting abstractions, and at that moment was concentrating on where they were going now, rather than where they'd come from. Not Georges however. He was like a dog with a bone, unwilling to relinquish his treasure until he'd stripped every ounce of meat from it.

As he struggled to make himself heard against the incessant roar of the traffic, Georges barked out the word, 'Okay', usually the prelude for a rant. But it wasn't a rant; it was a question. 'Have you heard of Existentialism?'

This dramatic utterance caught William off guard, and he could think of nothing better to reply than 'Yes, vaguely. Has this anything to do with what we were talking about earlier, Georges?'

'Everything to do with it.'

Desperately trying to keep warm in the piercing wind, and preoccupied still with the memory of Ingrid hurrying away with Mack earlier in the evening, William found this resurrected topic rather irksome, and actually difficult to pin-point precisely what they *had* been talking about; he seized now upon the most memorable catch-phrase. 'You mean the death of God?'

'Yes, in a nutshell. You could define it as that if you like.' Georges paused briefly, like a seasoned lecturer marshalling his thoughts prior to delivering the key to his speech. 'In the year 1942, some twenty-five years after what we may assume to be God's withdrawal from human affairs, and in the middle of yet another deadly war, a simple, unassuming novel finally puts its finger on the amazing truth of mankind's predicament.'

Even Ingrid and the piercing cold couldn't prevent William from blurting out the obvious question. 'What earth-shattering novel was that then?'

'A Frenchman. *Albert Camus*. And a novel called *'L'Etranger'* Heard of it?'

'I think I may have read it. Or some of it,' said William. 'But it passed me by.'

'It passed a lot of people by. Until it went viral. The world, you see, wasn't used to heroes they didn't like.'

William recalled briefly a phrase that had always puzzled him. 'D'you mean 'anti-hero'?'

'Yes, Some people choose to call it that.' Georges dismissed the expression with disdain. '*Anti-hero*' doesn't do justice at all to this particular main character, nor, as a matter of fact, does '*l'Etranger*' (the Stranger) do justice to the themes in the book'

'So Georges, what would you give for the title?'

Georges paused for a moment. 'Mersault's no Stranger; 'He's an '*Outsider*' A much more subtle translation.'

William said, 'And I presume Mersault's this special hero, or rather, '*outsider*'.

'Yes. Consider this: for the first time in literary history comes a main character actually at odds with the world and with people's general idea of a hero; someone in fact you love to hate. It shook the literary world.'

Georges paused, leaving William dubious, and in some doubt as to how to reply 'Isn't there perhaps another word for Mersault's condition? A medical term?' William struggled to remember.

'What?'

'Oh, yes. I remember, Autism.'

Georges strode on, not even deigning to reply, while William attempted to explain 'Someone so wrapped up in themselves they hardly notice the outside world.'.

'Whatever you like to call it,' shouted Georges against the din of traffic.'Although I don't believe there's anything medical about it. It's a state of mind.'

They'd reached their destination, the *Neuer Wall*, a long, straight slab of road dissecting North and South of the city, and renowned for its busy traffic. Georges, rapt in his thoughts, was showing no sign of slowing his pace and strode out into the traffic..

William reached out and grabbed his arm. 'I think we're here, Georges.'

Georges stopped abruptly on the verge and looked around like a startled sleep-walker. 'Ach, the *Neuer Wall*! I hate this street. It's too busy; out of keeping with the rest of the City. It's utilitarian. Runs in a straight line from A to B.'

'I thought most city roads did that.'

'Ja, but it has no style.'

'I didn't know you were a city planner, Georges. Besides, I thought you admired ugliness for what it is.'

Georges cast William a defensive glance. 'You mock me, my friend. Ah well, you're probably right. Where were we?'

'Where *are* we, you mean, Georges? I think we've reached our destination'

They were standing outside the *Teestube* (tea-room), secretly glad to hurry into its warmth. The *Teestube*, chic and modern, a coffee house that had recently sprung up on the cultural map, pandered to the young of the city, to well brought-up Germans who wiled away their hours inside its dark interior against a background of subdued lighting and piped 'Mozart'. The young clientele sipped tea, eyed each other's good looks in the darkness, and occasionally got up to stuff Euros in the cigarette machines in search of *Rothandler* or *Peter Stuyvesant*. There was never any bother in the '*Teestube*', and revolutionary writings by people such as Albert Camus were scarcely more than a ripple on the surface of their complacency. To William, it seemed an odd venue for the likes of Georges and Mack to frequent.

Mack, however, enjoyed playing chess there, and, to William's relief, was minus Ingrid; he caught sight of him in a smoky corner, saying goodbye to a tall, well-dressed young German (presumably his recent opponent), and idly setting up the chess-board for another game. He was chess crazy.

He looked up as they approached. 'Ah, Georges, William! What a relief. That guy's the only person I ever lose to at chess. I need one win at least this evening or I won't sleep properly.' He eyed them both. 'Anyone feel like a game?'

William hated being beaten by Mack at chess; he considered him a self-inflated addict of the game, a player who made more of his victories than his abilities really deserved. He hesitated anyway now, for, as they approached Mack's table, he became aware of the silky sounds of Mozart's Piano concerto No.22, drifting gently through the audio-system; it was a treat he didn't want to miss. He slumped into an armchair, by way of an excuse. 'No thanks, Mack. I need to warm up. It's cold out there.'

Did Mack or Georges, he wondered, ever take time to listen to the unpretentious musical beauty that was caressing his ears at that instant? Probably not: the music was perhaps too old-fashioned for Mack's ears, and besides, so far as Georges was concerned, Mozart had preceded 'God's death' by a matter of a century and a half, had composed at a time when Beauty had been still quite fashionable, and the clashing ugliness of modern composers not yet arrived on the earth.

'Georges, chess?' Mack had turned his gaze onto his Greek friend, who was now gazing absently across the room, ignoring them both.

'What's the matter with him?' asked Mack.

'I think he's dreaming of revolution.'

Mack gave one of his gulping laughs, more a cough than a sign of amusement. 'Why's that?'

'He's been dealing me a lecture on a novelist called Albert Camus, who supposedly shook the literary world to its core in 1942. He was day-dreaming outside as well, and nearly got himself run over near these very doors.'

'Georges doesn't like nasty shocks. But what's this about Camus?'

'I don't really know. In the rush, he never completed his explanation. Something to do with the death of God, I think.'

'Ah,' said Mack, 'then let me finish it for him. *Camus* is one of his favourite topics. I know it by heart.'

'How?' William was genuinely surprised.

'When you've been around Georges as long as I have, you'll understand all rail tracks lead to the same junction.'

'Which junction is...?'

'Freedom, of course.' Mack waved his hands about in the air, as if trying to evoke this ephemeral nirvana. He continued, 'And in this particular case of Albert Camus, freedom takes the form of man's entitlement to commit acts of unpremeditated violence.'

From Mack's cynical tone of voice, William had already perceived Mack was unlikely to agree with Georges' ideas on Camus, and, on a wider front, that there was little love lost between them anyway; they both probably despised the dogmatic part of themselves they could see in each other.

'So tell me about unpremeditated violence then,' said William. 'No one seems prepared to get to the heart of the matter.'

As William was speaking, he'd noticed Mack had been casting furtive glances across at Georges, no doubt ashamed of encroaching on his friend's territory.

Mack murmured, 'the oracle remains silent. Okay, let me continue for him, and leave the prophet to his meditations. Where were we exactly?'

'The freedom to act violently and without any motive.'

Mack took a deep breath. 'Ah yes. Mersault, our hero. He's like no other character in literature that's gone before. Right?'

'According to Georges, yes; although I'm not quite sure he's got his fact right on that.' remarked William.

Mack was nodding. 'Perhaps you're right, but at all events, he's a villain of unprecedented magnitude.'

'Georges has him as an unprecedented hero.'

'Depends on how you approach it.'

William was tiring of the topic, wondering if this story would ever have a point. From the corner of the room came the closing bars of his beloved Mozart, distracting him altogether from Mack's explanations. For just one moment, he gave thanks to the Almighty for bestowing on him the gift of music, and wondered whether Mack (or Georges for that matter) had any inkling how beautiful this music was. Probably not, he concluded.

Mack meanwhile, realising he was in danger of losing his audience, jolted him from his thoughts. 'Okay, William; forget the music for a moment. Let's get back to Mersault.'

William nodded. 'Yes, sorry. Tell me precisely what this villain (or hero) actually does? What's so bad or so good about him?'

Mack took a deep breath. 'Mersault's a young Algerian, largely minding his own business in life, showing few feelings for anything or anybody. We see him in the opening chapter at the funeral of his mother, bored and uninvolved; and so it is with everything he encounters: an abnormal indifference. As bad luck would have it, however, events overtake him. He gets involved in a minor row with some young Arabs and, by chance, happens to meet a group of them on a beach a few days later. There's just the slightest hint of hostility, and it triggers a display of violence; Mersault pulls out a gun and shoots one of the Arabs dead. Just like that. It's blatantly an unmotivated act, but, worse, he reacts to this crime with the same indifference he's shown to everything else in his life.' Mack paused. 'End of story really.'

'That can't be the end,' remarked William.

'No, but it's the end of our *'Existential'* story. Events have overtaken him, you see. Mersault's arrested and brought to trial. Revealing his true existential colours, he makes little attempt at a plausible defence. The judge finds him a menace to society - as I suppose he is really - and he's condemned to death..' Mack sat back in his chair with a smile. 'That's the simple tale, as I understand it. If Georges were *with* us, he'd probably put another slant on it all.'

William sat in silence for a few moments, prompting Mack to add, 'Georges insists we're all, underneath, like Mersault, strangers to one another.'

'That's pretty good, Mack,' remarked William. 'But look, surely you and I aren't exactly 'strangers' to each other, are we?

Mack just shrugged and grinned, and William suggested blithely, 'Perhaps he didn't mean to kill him. Just scare the Arab off.. Manslaughter.'

'No, there were three more shots. Clearly he meant to kill him. It was a deliberate act.'

William nodded. 'And this book went viral?'

'Apparently.'

William shifted in his seat. 'So what's Georges' point? I think I'm starting to lose sight of the trail.'

Mack shrugged. 'To be honest, I don't know.'

A voice beside them said, 'The world knew Camus was right. That's my point.'

Mack said. 'Georges, you've awakened from your trance.'

'I've not been in a trance, Mack; I've been listening to you two skirting laboriously around the truth.'

'So now you're awake, what *is* the truth?'

'As I've often said, the world recognised in that book what it knew was true. Our world has now become Mersault's. Mersault was the forerunner of modern man, a man for our times.'

William noticed the Mozart had come to an end as well. They'd put on a *Brandenberg*, mercifully restoring a bit of ordered sanity to the chaos of the conversation. 'So then, if Georges here is right,' he said, 'it's not impossible, we'll have to expect, people we don't even know, walking up to us on the beach or on the pavement, and shooting us for no reason other than they just feel like it.'

Georges said, 'That's not impossible, no. Hasn't arrived yet though. But could.'

Mack, who'd meanwhile returned to fiddling with the pieces on the chessboard, suddenly looked up again, the faintest of smiles on his face. 'In fact, although Georges here never mentions it (probably because he doesn't know), Camus wasn't even the first to depict a character of this sort. It happened a hundred years or so ago. Dostoyevsky: '*Crime and Punishment*'.'

'Mack,' said Georges, 'do you always get it wrong deliberately? Or is it just verbal provocation? If you start on that, I'm walking out of here. You just reveal the depth of your misunderstanding.'

'Really?'

'Yes. Mersault's crime is Existential. *Raskolnikov*, in '*Crime and Punishment*'. had a *motive*. The two characters are chalk and cheese. Nowhere near alike.'

'What motive?' said Mack, undeterred by Georges' outburst. 'He just went out one morning and murdered an old lady, didn't he? For the sake of it?'

'No.' Georges was adamant. 'He wanted her money. He reasoned it out. It was fairer, in his opinion, he should have the money, not her, who didn't need it. Money was the motive. Killing someone for their money is commonplace, and always carries a motive with it.'

'Same result though.'

'Yes, but you're being thick-skinned. Look, *Crime and Punishment,* the name of the book itself, implies a motive. Good motive or bad motive. In this case a bad one; one which requires punishment.' He stopped, and then added, 'And guilt, along with it too.

'Okay. And doesn't Mersault's?'

'No, that's the whole point. In Mersault's Existential world, no action carries either condemnation or guilt. Mersault feels no guilt and we are powerless to condemn him. It just **is**. The action itself justifies the effect. We might just as well applaud Mersault's action as condemn it. Judgement's irrelevant.'

'So you can simply do what you like. Is that what you're saying?'

'Yes, *alles ist erlaubt*. The Existentialist, needs no justification. Every act, any act, is justifiable.'

'That's absurd.'

'The Existential world *is* absurd. We're on our own. God dies. All that remains for us then is to act. Every act, no matter what, becomes a creative expression of ones self. Believe me, that's where it's come to. Some of us express ourselves in works of art, others in works of murder.'

'It's a ridiculous concept, Georges.'

'Perhaps. But it's there all the same. We walk alone and without judgement.'

'And Kurt? Kurt Weiler?'

'Nobody judged him. He judged himself. That's what I'm trying to say. Guilt may be always there, a state of mind, but we accept it, in the same way we accept the emptiness of our world.'

'Are you an Existentialist, Georges?'

'I suffer, along with everyone else.' Georges was hauling himself out of his chair. 'I must go. I have work to do.'

As he strutted towards the door and disappeared, Mack looked at William. 'He's a hard man. Doesn't enjoy himself much though, does he?'

William, more seriously, replied, 'He could though possibly be right. I reserve judgement. It's rather depressing.'

'Then cheer yourself up with a game of chess.'

William finally succumbed, while Mack grinned widely, sniffing the chance of a win that evening. They ordered two more coffees which arrived shortly in delicate china cups, along with coloured crystals of sugar and a little jug of cream. After a few minutes, William had over-exposed a pawn, which was removed by Mack, who immediately shifted his bishop into a threatening line. Although William could see the threat, he couldn't see the way to avoid it. His experience was very slim, his game, like most enthusiastic amateurs, limited to scanning the board prior to a move, hoping miraculously to read his opponent's game-plan, before embarking on yet another rather fruitless attack. He was not entirely devoid of strategy, but in limited amounts only, and rarely able to grasp the overall picture.

Mack's grasp on things was wider. 'I'm glad I'm not an *Unteroffizier* in your army,' he said smugly, as he removed another of William's knights. 'Chess is like military strategy. You have to cover your bases, and make sure of the consequences before you move.'

'I don't think I've got the same experience as you, Mack.'

'It's not just experience; it's patience. And planning. You've got to take care.'

William was stung. 'I *do* take care. I don't like losing either.'

'You've got to care more then. You've got to consider the alternatives before moving. It's like life. I'll tell you what, Chess logic is *military* logic.' He pushed another of his pawns forward and sat back, eyeing William condescendingly. 'Remember Stalingrad?'

William smiled. 'No, Mack I don't remember Stalingrad. I wasn't there.'

'Neither was Hitler, but he still went over the heads of the generals. He wasn't there, on the ground, but he still tried to run the show.' William didn't reply, as he spied a pawn of Mack's and removed it eagerly. Mack showed no concern and said, 'Hitler must have been the worst chess player in the history of bad chess players. Dogmatic, inflexible....

William interrupted. 'Did he ever go?'

'Go where?'

'Stalingrad.'

'Course he didn't. Big mistake. If he'd moved his arse and gone there himself, he'd have realised Stalingrad wasn't worth the taking anyway. Just like that pawn of mine you've just removed.'

William ignored the pawn. He felt himself losing interest in the chess as the airless atmosphere in the Teestube started to overwhelm him. 'I assume Germany lost at Stalingrad. My knowledge of World War 2 battles is limited.'

'Good god,' exclaimed Mack. 'They not only lost the battle; they lost the war.'

A strange thing William had noticed about Mack was his ability to combine cool, rational thought and sudden emotional outburst. He wondered if Mack was aware of it himself.

William said, 'A bit of an overstatement?'

'No. True.' Mack was obdurate. 'The historians seem at any rate to think it's true, and it's probable Hitler realised it as well. Wouldn't admit it though.'

'Couldn't afford to, I suppose.' remarked William. He'd taken his mind right off the chess-board while Mack deftly tossed his Knight forward, bypassing William's guarding Bishop, and announced, 'Check.' It was all over. 'Sorry, William. I win once more.'

William smiled, unconcerned now. 'I think you'd have made a pretty good general, Mack.'

'Naa. Too emotional.' He swept the pieces back in the box with an air of finality. 'Don't worry; you'll beat me next time. Just don't be so precipitous.'

William laughed out loud. 'Ha, that's a good one. Hark who's calling the kettle black.'

But Mack seemed almost not to hear. It was as if he'd already put the whole chess incident behind him. He was looking hard, almost staring, at William, curiosity written on his face 'You know, you remind me of someone, William. Strongly. Someone I used to know. Was it in another life?'

William sat there, uncertain quite how to reply. 'Someone nice, I hope.'

Mack continued mechanically to put the chess set away, shaking his head from time to time, for a full minute, until finally a broad grin spread across his face. 'Thought I was going mad for a second. You know who it is you remind me of?' He gave William no time to answer. 'An old teacher of mine. Way back.'

'Not *too* old, I hope. Where were you at school anyway, Mack? How come you've got this American connection?'

I *am* American,' he replied.

'I thought you were. So what's the German link-up? Have you been in Germany long?

'Quite a while. I'm German by origin actually. *Mackintosh Neumann* I was christened. But the christening service took place in America. Wyoming of all places.'

'Sounds romantic as hell. Horses. Cowboys.'

'Yeah, and all that. It *is* quite nice though, Wyoming. Remote. The American dream.'

'How'd you finish up here?'

'I don't know really. It just happened. Came back to see the land of my ancestors. And stayed on. I'm more German than American really. At heart.' He paused for a second, clearing the pieces away. 'Spent most of my youth though in America. Not just Wyoming. We moved around. I was in prep school in the States.'

'Ah. So that's it. That the place where you met my lookalike?'

'Yeah. He was a really nice guy. Spent a lot of time with him.'

Mack was nodding gently, a trait common with him, seeming to retreat for a moment into his own private world. For the first time in months of shared dinners in the crowded Mensa, they found themselves opening up to each other. Their private life. It's hard to say what had triggered it. Perhaps the sudden absence of Georges' lowering presence.

'What do you do here?' asked William.

'Oh, bits of this and that. I'm a trained lawyer. Graduated in the States and then came over to Europe to do a Masters. Never went back. I work part-time here in Hamburg for a law practice and teach a few graduate classes at the University.' He paused for a moment before going on, 'You know, I think really I'm on the run.'.

William was attracted to the phrase. 'On the run from who? On the run from where? On the run from what?'

Mack said, 'All of them probably. There was a girl....' He stopped and then said, 'Isn't there always?'

'I don't know; *you're* talking,' replied William. I'm ashamed to admit I'm a novice in the world of romance. I get my romance from movies. And books.' Mack sat looking hard at him. William added, 'Not from real life, I'm afraid.'

'Yes, I've noticed you casting covert looks at some of the girls in the Mensa. The mark of someone starved of affection. So,' he went on after a pause, 'you're a writer and a Romantic.'

'Not Romantic. Certainly starved. Not sure about the writing.'

Mack guffawed in his usual way, his face splitting into a wide, spontaneous grin. 'I've noticed our mutual friend, Ingrid, comes in for a few furtive glances from you too.'

'Listen, Mack.' William leaned forward, as if what he was about to say could not be shared by anyone in the crowded coffee house. 'Are *you* interested in Ingrid yourself?'

Mack wiped the grin from his face, assumed a serious demeanour. 'Ingrid? No, not really. If even at all, just for a bit of transitory pleasure. Nothing serious.' Now he leaned forward in a similar way, and glanced around conspiratorially. 'Ingrid's a dangerous number. Best to be kept at arm's length. She's one of those girls.'

William for a moment felt a flash of indignation. 'What girls?'

'Don't get me wrong. She's a nice person. I'm just saying I wouldn't personally want to get tangled up with her.'

'Why not?' William was adamant, buzzing, like a bee desperate for pollen.

Mack leaned back again. 'Women can be voracious, you know. Attempt to eat you up.'

'That's what Georges said,' William blurted out.

Mack laughed. 'Did he now?'

'You're not another of those women haters like Georges, are you?' William found himself at last venting his frustration and incomprehension. 'Ploughing a lonely furrow, painting paintings no one can understand or certainly like?'

Mack laughed loudly. 'No I'm not. I can't paint. Poor Georges; I think he had an experience he can't get over. That's what I'm trying to say to you; Ingrid's so nice she'll try to eat you up. Girls like that will change your life, change your plans. They're never in it except for the long haul.' He looked hard at William. 'William, I don't think you're ready for Ingrid. Even if she may be ready for you. Why not go up to the *Reeperbahn*? Have a bit of fun? It makes sense you know, 'business' sex.' He was still laughing as he completed the sentence. William's instant reaction of surprise, almost dismay, at Mack's flippant suggestion, was followed by a rush of anxiety about his own recent trip to the *Reeperbahn*. Had he been found out? However, their laughter had driven away any more thoughts of Ingrid, who'd been discreetly put away in a locked drawer. William said, 'You sound as if you're speaking from experience.'

'About the Reeperbahn?'

'No, not really. About the 'long-haul'.'

'Oh that,' said Mack.' He paused for a minute. 'Yes, I suppose I am. Years and years ago, you know, I knew a girl. A high-school heart-throb. In the States. Trouble was, it wasn't reciprocated. And I made the mistake of letting it change my game-plan. Women can be like that; that's what I mean. They get into you, get under the skin.' Mack fell silent for a minute or so, and they both listened to the piped music and sipped cold coffee, acting as if they'd been to the brink and looked over. Then Mack said, 'Anyway, enough of that. Talking of game-plans, what are you planning to do after Christmas? Staying in Hamburg?'

'Don't know; it's in the air. But, by the way, where was that high school you went to in the States?'

'Texas, would you believe? A funny place to wind up.'

'That's amazing. One of the places my mother - and her sister - often go on about when trying to organise my life for me; there's a little school apparently somewhere in Texas too, where I should apparently go and teach.'

Mack sat for a moment, thinking and then said, 'It's a big place, Texas, I suppose. A lot of schools.'

'Yeah, a lot of schools; you're right.'

Their conversation had, in the natural course of events, petered out. Nothing more was mentioned, either of Ingrid or Texas. If it *had* been, who knows how different William's life might have developed? Mack now got up and stretched. 'Wow, I've been in this place for about 5 hours. I'm off. Presumably see you in the Mensa tomorrow. And, whatever you decide, keep in touch. Wouldn't want you to just wander away from Germany. You never know, things change.'

The conversation they'd had was one neither of them would forget. It went beyond the superficial arguments at the Mensa and had, in some way, entered an area that intruded on their deepest thoughts.

(At Possum Kingdom.) ENTRY FROM ADAM'S DIARY

REFLECTIONS and **CONFESSIONS,** from the pen of 'Sol' the Solitary.
London – the 'Garret' (profile of an artist)

I've been here near on two years, in this dingy flat, this tedious job. Beware. That's a long time and it's not difficult to see how one can become ingrained in a flat, and wedded to a job. A slave to both familiarity and routine.

I've decided to quit the Bureau - even though they seem at the moment to see me as a rising star. How do they come to that opinion anyway? Surely Jack Foreman fits that bill better than I do. However, I'm beginning to believe they're suspicious of Foreman. He's too clever for his own good. They're afraid of his brilliance.. If you think about it, it wouldn't be the first time a guy like Foreman's been deliberately passed over for high office, nudged out by a middle-of-the-road plodder, simply so he doesn't eclipse all those remaining workaday pawns. Yes, seen in this context, I expect Foreman's a meteorite burning out.

I've got to get out of here, rising star or not. I've got to get out and discover for myself what I'm really good at, the doing of which will allow me to grow old and grey and weary with dignity and resignation. Like a gnarled and wrinkled peasant who for years has ploughed the land and one day just chucks in his scythe and ploughs no more. I just know a whole life-time longer at the Bureau won't achieve for me that kind of deep satisfaction.

Anyway, Mrs. Hod, who I went to see the other day with a pile of print-out (Exams season coming round again), came up with a surprising remark, a remarkable remark, a ground-breaking remark, a remark that's worth putting on record, for the Bureau, for mankind in general, and for posterity. I couldn't believe the subversive utterance she let loose in my presence as we sat (she allows me to sit nowadays) mulling over how many candidates should be given a free-ride on the Bureau's current soft and sloppy exam criteria.

'What's the pass mark, Adam.'
'44%.'

'Good gracious. Far too high!'

'It's the same as last year, Mrs. Hod.'

'Then that was too high as well. We can't fail so many candidates.'

'I don't think the examiner would want to lower it.'

'I'm sure he wouldn't, but he doesn't run the Bureau either. We have a responsibility to these candidates. I'd rather see twelve candidates walking round Piccadilly Circus with certificates they didn't deserve, than one candidate... (she hesitates, and I can't resist finishing the sentence for her) ...one candidate *without* a certificate he *did* deserve. Isn't that what you were going to say, Mrs. Hod. But please excuse me for interrupting.'

'How observant of you, Adam. (she calls me Adam after two years of service). I'm so glad we both agree on broad principles. You know, it can get quite lonely at the top, if you haven't got allies' She beamed at me, and then pretended to study the print-out again. 'How many candidates did you say you had in Electrical Technicians?'

'About 23,000.'

Mrs. Hod leaned forward, clutching the print-out for grim death. Our two faces were now aligned no further than one foot away from each other. 'Quite frankly between you, me and the gate-post, I'd like to see all of them with some sort of a certificate.' *That iconic remark should resound down the centuries, but there's better to follow.*

I play Devil's Advocate. 'Good for business, Mrs. Hod?' I raised my eyebrows just enough for her to see the ambivalence of my remark.

'It's nothing to do with business. Have you any idea of the kind of social background some of our candidates come from?' I shook my head demurely, feigning ignorance. She continued, 'Some, not all, but some, are putting their parents' life savings into a course with the Bureau... *Wait for it...* And who are we to set an arbitrary pass mark and fail them?'

'Quite, Mrs. Hod. Perhaps the candidates weren't as good this year as last. It's not their fault.' I lent my whole-hearted support to her somewhat dubious argument and, in the same instant, realised precisely why it is *I'm* a Rising Star now in this Organisation. Unlike Foreman, I go along with whatever's the current thinking. I don't commit.

'And perhaps the exam was a lot more difficult too,' she retorted, handing me back the print-out. 'No. Lower the pass-mark, Adam. There are too many variables in this game.'

'What would you like it lowered too?'

'That's up to you, but...' She stretched out her hand for the print-out again, and perused it. 'I think somewhere around the 37% mark should do it. Lower it to 37 and bring it back in; I'll sign it.'

I nodded. We were conspirators engaged on some fiendish plot. I gathered up the print-out and, on the point of leaving, I heard her say something I still don't believe, will never believe. 'Do you know, Adam, I'm moving more and more towards the American idea of examining, The Americans, bless their hearts, make such a mess of so many things, but I'm starting to think in this respect we may have something to learn from them.' *Would you ever expect someone like Mrs. Hod to say something like I've just heard?*

'Do you mean everybody passing and nobody failing, Mrs. Hod?'

'It's not *quite* so simple as that of course. A scale of one to five. In-course assessment, internal examining, that sort of thing. The teacher, after all, is the person responsible for teaching the candidates. Why should he, or she, have so little say in the examining of them?' *Why should he or she have so little say in the examining of them? Did I really hear that?* She stared hard at me now, apparently waiting for this portentous message to broach my consciousness, gave it five seconds, before answering her own rhetorical question. 'No, Adam, he or she *shouldn't.*' There ensued a brief silence, during which she obviously hoped I'd concur (which of course I did), and, with a gentle smile, she then proceeded to play Devil's Advocate with me. 'I wonder, Adam, if you're thinking we'll do the Bureau out of a job!'

'No, Mrs. Hod, absolutely not. It never occurred to me.' (*One of the lies of the century, I confess. It had of course occurred to me, on Day One at the Bureau, to be precise. I remember expounding that very same heresy across the table to Foreman: Teachers should examine their own students.*) However, I admit I wasn't ready right now to share these heresies with Mrs. Hod, even at this juncture. Too risky. I left her meanwhile to expound her vision for the Bureau of the future. 'Can you imagine, Mr. Riley? This Institution already possesses an enormous objective testing department. We spend thousands each year on it. That's where the future lies. And Charlie Grey (Bureau's stickler for rectitude and the maintenance of standards) had better watch his Ps and Qs. And all the other examiners too. Now be a good chap and put that pass mark down to 37, as we agreed.'

It was a mere formality. I left her excitedly planning a whole new future for the Bureau, and returned to my office, completed another form, and put 37 under *'Suggested Pass-mark'*.

'I guarantee Hod told you about candidates in Piccadilly,' said Foreman, world-wearily.

'She did.'

'She's predictable if nothing else.'

'She also thought everyone should pass.'

'I've heard that one before too. What's the pass mark down to on this latest?' I told him, and he replied, 'She mistakes morbid sentimentality for altruism? She knows nothing about the process of examination. Charlie Grey, for all his sins, knows a lot more. I don't know why she doesn't rely on her examiners; that's what we pay them for.' Because I said nothing, he continued, 'I actually *do* know why she doesn't rely on her examiners. She's scared of them. She knows they know a lot more about the job than she does. It's a pity she didn't stay on at Debenhams.'

'Debenhams?'

'That's where Hod used to be. People in management swop jobs like you and I swop a car. Every now and then they reshuffle, and the Cadillacs replace the BMW's in the executive car-park It's hardly surprising the country's in such a mess.'

The phone on my desk rang. It was Charlie Grey. 'Hello, old boy. Any idea yet what the pass mark on that Technicians' Exam is likely to be?'

I told him. And he said, 'Over my dead body! They were an appalling bunch this year!'

'Mrs. Hod thinks it might have been a more difficult exam this year.'

'Hogwash. They passed it at Moderating Committee, didn't they? Does Mrs. Hod really know what she's doing? I'll tell you what she's doing; she's filling the country with a lot of untrained technicians. I'll be dropping in at the Bureau in a day or two. See what you can do about that pass mark.'

And at that point, I began seriously wondering whether my long-held reservations about the Bureau might, in fact, be valid. I started actively to harbour thoughts of resignation. I suppose it was really Mrs. Hod's apparent susceptibility that had tipped the scales for me.

I went back down the corridor with my 37%. Pekoe was there.

'Ah! Mr. Riley,' exclaimed Mrs. Hod. 'John, Mr. Riley and I were just talking about Objective Testing.'

'Have you seen some of the latest Multiple Choice items sent in?' interrupted Pekoe. 'They're a disaster.'

Mrs. Hod's face turned even paler. 'Throw them away, and refuse to pay the writers.'

'That's what they're going to have to do.'

'They don't deserve to be paid if they can't follow the simplest guidelines. Mr. Riley and I were just talking about some of our older examiners, John.'

Pekoe shrugged. 'We're between the devil and the deep-blue sea. I know exactly what you mean and who you mean.' He shuffled impatiently in his chair.

'I'm sure our new young AO here is going to do splendidly in his job,' said Mrs. Hod, relieving me of the form and initialling it.

'Yes,' replied Pekoe, 'and he's just said he's going to stay on with us.'

'Has he? Splendid! Splendid!'

Had I? I remembered saying that, but it was approximately two years ago. A lot had changed. In my life. In my inner life too, *and,* it seemed, in the life of the Bureau, changing before our very eyes into the flip-side of everything they'd ever stood for. Everything was in flux; nothing could be relied on. It *might* be an exciting time, but I wasn't going to be there to witness it. Truth is, I couldn't really care less about 'testing', in whichever form it came.

Since I might be asked to provide reasons for my decision when it comes, I've been idly turning plausible reasons over in my spare moments.

1. At the highest level, the Administration is divided on itself.

2. Rumour's got around they're going to move me from E Branch (Jack Foreman) to C Branch (Miss Willis). I prefer to spend my hours of the day in the company of an egomaniac rather than a witch.
3. Pekoe's definitely getting dementia, which bodes ill for us all.

On the following Monday, giving myself a little time to list, on a scrap of paper, the possible jobs, occupations, work, open to me, I typed out a letter of one month's notice to Personnel Department, and placed it in the 'Out' tray. My decision would reach its destination via the internal mailing system. Fancifully I wondered if I would feel, in my little flat, the shocks reverberating through the austere corridors of the Bureau. But there were no explosions, no tremors. I marvelled at how simple it all was, and how employees, colleagues, - almost friends really - behaved so naturally towards me in the following days, as if my departing would not stir even so much as a speck of dust from any of the tables crammed into the rabbit warren that was 167. My imminent disappearance would pass unnoticed. At some point, Foreman mentioned he knew about my resignation and considered it to be probably the best thing I would ever do, although he supplied no precise reasons for this valedictory. I think he himself was a young man locked into something he couldn't get out of by the very fact he was so good at it. At least I didn't have that counterbalance to worry about.

It wasn't easy though. Swimming against the tide can never be easy, and those days I'd passed at the Bureau had, in some distorted, inexplicable way, worked to deflect my thoughts from deeper, more fundamental considerations; yes, from the torment of Mary for one thing. Was it maybe the jokes, the stupidity, the company of people locked into a common endeavour, the forced comradeship of people cast adrift in an open boat, or was it even the sheer shallowness of everyday life at the Bureau, which had managed stealthily to take my mind off my own despair? At any rate, in recent days, memories of Her no longer wash over me, out of a clear blue sky, in giant waves of pain, but, oddly, ripple in gently now, as at the tranquil turning of the tide, bringing harmless flotsam and jetsam in their wake, calm resignation replacing harsh anger.

That's where I'm at now with Mary. Rationality has replaced Emotion. Is that the work of the Bureau? Perhaps.

CHAPTER 14

"In which William goes a-courting"

Ingrid, tall, stately, haughty, beautiful, destined surely for the cat-walk, until her zealous parents must have seen fit to place her instead into the more rigid world of academia, because she was clever too. She'd jumped so far all the hurdles in that arena and, although apprehensive at first to mingle with the rowdy men round the table in the Mensa, she'd been relieved to find herself so easily accepted at the table. Like a watchful gecko on some southern wall, she quickly came to bask each lunch-hour in the sunshine of these vigorous men, sucking in their men-talk, while her enquiring eyes wandered undetected around these posturing chaps on their various self-assertive platforms.

However, as time passed, she found her attention, had begun to alight upon the quiet young Englishman who, when he chose to speak, betrayed such rare, yet modest, shafts of insight? As the weeks went by, she'd discovered with consternation that, far from controlling her covert glances and secret flirtations, they'd begun to control her, as each lunchtime she nervously anticipated William's arrival or presence or absence round the table, fiercely hoping his eyes might today, just for once, alight on her.

This new sensation left her puzzled. Could it really be that the gentle young English boy who'd come to stay with the family years ago, when she was a snippet of a girl holidaying with her parents in southern Germany, and who'd quite unsettled her, was the self-same person sitting opposite her at the rowdy table? Absurd idea Quite irrational. She dismissed the thought hurriedly. Yet nevertheless, here again was a young Englishman, so dreamy at times, so ardent at others, making silent in-roads into her affections, threatening to destabilise her ordered life. Unable at present to analyse her disturbing feelings, she'd placed them on one side, concluding that, by some bizarre trait of make-up, some quirk in her design, some errant gene, she was just attracted to this *'type'*, this English boy. Yes, that was it. And so she decided to bide her time and stay out of his way.

...

William, that early evening, couldn't quite believe his luck. Spying Ingrid down the front of the university lecture hall, he hurried down the steps and fought his way towards her among the melee of students heading for the exit. Although it was the opportunity he'd dreamed about for so long, now the moment had come, he didn't know quite what he was going to say. He caught up with her and gave a light tap on her shoulder, hoping he could conceal his excitement when she turned round.

'Ingrid, are you always in this lecture at this time?' The question was non-committal, an attempt to make it seem as if by pure chance he'd bumped into her. She met his gaze with a similarly practised, neutral expression, the kind William had seen so often down the Mensa whenever someone unexpectedly put her on the spot. Had he but known that, in actual fact, as their eyes met, she was struggling to stop her heart jumping out of her mouth with excitement and surprise. 'Yes, of course,' she said. 'Are you too?'

'No. I sneak in sometimes. Just to improve my German. Not to hear the lecture though.'

She couldn't help laughing. His reply was just so typical, the kind of non-committal reply she'd grown used to from this good-looking Englishman, half-answering a question, and often wrapping it in some unusual linguistic image. 'What means *'sneak'*?'

'Oh, sorry.' He raced to find a simile. 'Uhh...how about *'like a thief in the night'*?'

She laughed again. Why couldn't he ever answer a question in straight-forward language? 'So you're a thief, William, are you?'

'Not really. A nice kind of thief, shall we say. One that doesn't steal anything.'

He was slightly alarmed she might take him literally, but thankfully she was quick off the mark. 'Yes, I understand.. You're a... how you say...*ein... ungeladener.*'

It was his turn to be on the spot, but he was quick too at the German. 'Ah yes, you're right; that's. correct. *'Ungeladen'* I'm ... 'uninvited'. I'm not meant to be here at all.' He met her gaze. 'I'm a gate-crasher.'

She laughed again. 'Another of your nice idioms. When you open your mouth, William, an idiom comes out. English is such a difficult language. Gate-crasher. I like that. You're a gate-crasher in the night.... '

'No, not really at night,' He looked around. 'Shall we say in the evening.'

She nodded. 'Yes, and how did we come to meet here just now anyway? Have you been following me, or was it...how d'you say... coincidence?'

It was his turn to smile. 'Sheer coincidence, Ingrid. I promise I'm not a stalker. Please believe me. I come here once in a blue moon.'

She laughed again. 'All these new words. I cannot take them in. Gate-crasher, stalker, blue moon. Perhaps you could give me lessons.'

'That's an invitation I can't refuse. I'd love to.' He glanced around. 'But I think we should leave. Everybody's gone.'

It was right; they were almost alone now in the large hall. William put on his best smile. 'Ingrid, before we go, can I just give you another famous idiom?' She nodded, and he pronounced solemnly, 'Our meeting this evening is a meeting made in heaven.'

She understood and nodded. *'Ach, du bist ein Spinner, Wilhelm.'*

Although he couldn't quite understand this new expression: *'Spinner'*, and was hearing it for the first time, he could make a fair guess at its meaning and vowed to look it up at another time.

They left the Hall and headed for a café. She was saying, 'I think I know somewhere just up this street,' while William was doing his best to explain to her in plain language his presence in the lecture hall that evening. 'What I was trying to tell you in there was that I was in the lecture illegally in fact. I'm really not interested in the niceties of Chaucer's England. I'm only seeing if I can follow what the lecturer's saying. Anything wrong with that?'

She was laughing now. 'Look, it doesn't matter. We're *here*. We're both thieves in the night.'

They finished up looking at each other over two glasses of '*Glühwein*' at a *Weinstube* up the road from the lecture hall, and for a minute or two, as they sat there, they found themselves engulfed in an awkward silence, both instinctively wondering whether they had anything at all in common besides their looks, their obvious feelings and their languages. And, of course, the Mensa. William ordered two more glasses and toyed silently with a whole range of potential topics: the weather, Hamburg, his reasons for being in Hamburg, *her* reasons too, until mysteriously, and beyond logical analysis, all at once a key had turned in a stubborn lock, the clouds had parted, to reveal blue sky above, and they'd both slipped effortlessly into their own honest roles, explaining who they really were.

'I was never really from Hamburg in the first place.' she was saying, 'We moved here from Stuttgart - quite why, I never really understood, something to do with my father's work - and I was placed in a Gymnasium in the suburbs here, and so, finished up at the Uni, and here I am.' It all came out in a rush, and she leaned back with a joyful smile.

'What school, Ingrid? What was the name of the Gymnasium?'

'*Kirchenpauerschule.*'

William was on home territory. 'That's another coincidence. That's where I teach. Now.' Surprisingly, she showed little reaction, and William grasped at thin air. 'It's a very good school.'

That faint smile slid across her face, one he'd often seen at the Mensa when someone made an empty remark, as if the sun had gone behind a cloud. She said, 'Ja, nicht schlect.' (Yes, not bad).'

He assumed her experience there hadn't been the best. 'Did you have a bad time there?'

She shook her head. 'No, it was all right. How you say…it was neither good nor bad.'

William already knew well Ingrid found it hard to put up with empty statements, and unsure now whether she was just plain not interested in the topic, or that something bad must have happened, he chose to change the subject. 'My contract's in fact coming to an end there. I'll probably return to England at Christmas.'

'Why?'

He hesitated. 'I don't really know why, now I come to think of it. Just like *you* finishing up here in Hamburg.'

'Yes, but surely you have a choice. I didn't.'

'Ingrid, I drift.'

She smiled as she instinctively grasped the meaning. 'I drift too, of course.' She hesitated. 'But sometimes I think we just *know* what we have to do without really understanding why. We just do it.'

'I wish sometimes *I* knew what I have to do. I wander aimlessly from one thing to the next.'

'But we have responsibilities. It can't be as easy as that, William Other people.'

'I can't say I have responsibilities. My mother will go on doing the same things she's always done, whether I'm there or not.'

She overlooked this blunt confession. 'You have just a mother?'

'Yes, I never knew my father.'

'Surely that must mean you have even more responsibility to your mother.'

William found her remark hard to understand. 'My mother of course has her friends and routines and interests. But I find it difficult to let my movements depend on my mother. Or anyone else for that matter.'

Ingrid just nodded. 'I wish my life was that simple.'

William felt their conversation was heading up a *cul de sac*. 'Can I get you another drink?'

She looked at her watch. 'I must go home. My parents start to worry when I'm late.'

'Where do you live, Ingrid?'

'In the outer suburbs. Beyond Billstedt. Do you know Billstedt?'

'I pass Billstedt every day.'

She smiled again. 'I catch the bus there.'

'Then let me drive you home. It's on my way.' For a second, an expression of concern crossed her face, and William hurriedly added, 'If you're happy to go on the back of my moped. You can sit there and tell me the way.'

Her glance was non-committal, almost astonished. 'You have a motor-bike?'

'Yes, I go everywhere on it.' He paused. 'That's if it starts.'

'My father would never forgive me.'

'Are you an only child too, ein '*Einzelkind* ', Ingrid?'

She flashed him a smile. 'Yes, why? How did you know?'

'You're like one of those children from Grimm's fairy tales, *Hansel und Gretel*, house-bound, helping their parents, unable to go out.'

When she finally stopped giggling, she said, 'Cinderella.'

'Yes, but the German version.'

That cloud flitted momentarily again across her face 'It's not really like that. I wish it were somehow.' She paused, thinking how to put it. 'You see, my father's older than most fathers of my age. He worries about me.'

'I expect so,' replied William. He didn't want to intrude on what was clearly an intimate revelation 'Most father's do.'

'My father was at Stalingrad. You know the battle of Stalingrad.?'

'Yes, I do,' said William, secretly thankful for his brief conversation a few weeks ago in the *Teestube* with Mack.

'Sometimes I think he never really recovered. He stays at home a lot now.'

'Is he ill?'

That concerned look appeared again on her face. 'Not really ill. How do you say? Ill in his mind maybe.'

'I'd like to meet him.' William had few inhibitions about that sort of thing; he was willing to meet anybody.

'I don't think that would be good.'

'Oh.'

'You're English. It's hard for older people in Germany who remember the War. The bombing.'

He nodded. 'His precious daughter being taken for a drink by an Englishman might not go down too well.'

She looked at him seriously. 'I don't think I'm 'precious', but you're right, it might not.'

'He needn't know.'

'That would be difficult. And the motor-bike?'

William grinned. 'He needn't know that either.'

She glanced again at her watch. 'William, I really have to go.'

'I'll get you home in no time.'

'Where is your bike?'

'Near the Uni. I keep it chained up. I've got to go that way anyway. I live beyond Billstedt too. I'll drop you off at your house, you walk in. I'll push the bike away a bit, and hey presto, no one's any the wiser.'

'You make it all sound so easy.'

'It is easy, Ingrid. No problem.' He paused. 'The one thing that is a problem is that you'll be cold.'

'I have a coat. A good one. Hamburg weather I can take.'

She was getting up. William followed her. She looked around as she glided out. 'So, where's the bike?'

'It awaits you.' He paused and added, 'Up till now, it's most illustrious passenger.'

The smile again, the sunlight. 'Illustrious. That's a good word. Hope it has a nice meaning.'

'More than nice.'

She laughed. 'I'll find it in the Dictionary. I can learn a lot of English staying with you.

'You certainly can.'

They drove that night in the bitter cold, Ingrid clinging tight to him, never saying a word except to point the way. She never complained.

'We're here. Up this street. A little further on.' She indicated a drab little alley as William slowed the motor. 'Can we push it? So your father won't know you've been on a bike.'

'Yes.' She seemed tense.

'Does your bus stop nearby?'

'Yes, round the corner.'

'Don't you feel anxious, walking this bit every evening? It's very isolated.'

'I don't mind. I can take care.' She shrugged the shrug of a pragmatic German girl, used to difficulties. He'd often seen that shrug from her before. 'German people don't creep up on you in dark streets,' she paused, and the smile again, 'like they do in Dickens and London.'

'Okay,' he said. 'Yes, I'm glad of that.' He smiled, but she didn't notice. She was already walking briskly towards the houses and waving her arm back and forth above her left shoulder.

He understood. 'End of the road,' he called, for no apparent reason. And then called again, more loudly, 'We'll see each other at the Mensa then.' She may have heard; he wasn't sure. And he called again, more quietly, 'Hope your Dad's not waiting up.'

She disappeared.

They met again a few times at the Mensa and, although they made no show of it, it was different. They cast occasional conspiratorial glances at one another, as if proclaiming they had a secret. William, in those closing days of December, and realising their time together wasn't long, took his new-found friend once to the Opera. It was part of Wagner's *'Ring Cycle'*.

'So German,' William said, as they made their way to a bar after the performance. 'I love it.'

He heard her laugh in the dark. '*Too* German.'

'Didn't you enjoy it?'

'Up to a point. We Germans can't help clinging on to our myths and legends.'

'Like Dickens and Victorian London,' he said. 'We English are just the same.'

She nodded, and they walked on in silence before William said, 'I'm sorry; I should have chosen my opera more carefully.'

'No, I love being with you. And I love the music anyway. It's just all those tales and nostalgia for the past I don't like. I think we Germans must do less of that.' She thought a bit and then added, 'We have much to forget. We must look around. Be less German.'

'Yes. Don't worry, Ingrid. That's happening. With people like you around.'

She laughed again. 'You're too kind.'

Just for a moment William wondered how great the burden of their recent history must be. Even for those young enough to have played no part. Was this lovely girl only walking out with him because he was English? Just a brief thought and then it passed. And it was at that moment Ingrid said, 'My parents would like to ask you for supper.'

He was taken by surprise. 'Really? I thought...'

She anticipated his thoughts. 'Yes. It's rare. You must be special.'

'A worthy suitor maybe?'

She laughed. 'Not that. But my parents are very formal.'

'But is it all right with your father?'

'Yes,' she said hurriedly. 'He agreed, as much as he can ever agree to anything.'

William pretended he hadn't heard. 'I'd better hide the bike.'

'Yes. We'll catch the bus and walk to the front door.'

'I think they must see me as an interloper.'

'What is 'interloper?'

'Like a gate-crasher perhaps.'

She laughed. 'Certainly not that. I haven't actually told them very much about you. I've just said I'm seeing an Englishman.'

'Very tactful. Not a thief in the night then?.

She laughed again. 'No, not that either. But don't worry. You'll like my mother. She's jolly. Leave me to deal with my father.' After a moment, she added, 'They're just like most parents. They're too protective.'

William said, 'I'll try not to be too English'

'That will be difficult, William.'. They walked on in the silent night until she asked, 'You will come, won't you?'

As usual, William was uninhibited, like a sleep-walker on a roof, unsure of what his own intentions might actually be, and giving little thought to what he was letting himself in for. The promises, the commitments, and all that goes with a relationship. Now that he'd met this girl, he felt ready to place time on hold for once, after what seemed to have been a very long and lonely journey, and he was unwilling to give her up. Nor indeed was she, it seemed; they were Romeo and Juliet, poised on a cliff-edge. 'Of course I'll come.' And with that, she flicked her hand into his - that first signal of physical contact between them - and they walked on silently, locked in their own thoughts, beside the rippling water of the Alster.'

William asked, 'So when then?'

'We'll fix a date. Must be quite soon if you're going home.' She hesitated, 'Maybe best not to mention that though.'

The supper was a sombre affair. The general formality, combined with the lowering presence of Ingrid's sickly father, cast a pall across the dinner table, as Ingrid had predicted. They ate various cold cuts of ham and salami on rich dark bread, a traditional German supper, while they struggled to make perfunctory conversation. Glancing from time to time at the sick man, William gained the impression the sickness might stem from an all-enveloping depression rather than an active disease or even pain.. He wasn't bed-ridden, but chair-ridden. As for the causes of this condition, he wondered whether it stemmed from resentment, anger, frustration, combined with a whole hellish well of ghastly war-time memories.

Frau Spindler appeared to have no such apprehensions. A jovial woman who must once have been attractive and who smiled whenever she had the chance, she met them at the ground floor of their 3-room apartment on the 1st floor. It's likely she'd been eagerly expecting them and had glimpsed their arrival from the single room that looked onto the front of the block, because, as Ingrid placed her key in the lock, the door opened and there stood her mother, doing her best with her English. '*Liebchen*! I am wondering where you have been.'

'*Mutti*, I have a key.' There was an uncharacteristic hint of annoyance in Ingrid's voice.

'*Ich weiss, Liebchen, ich weiss* (I know darling).'

Probably to avoid further sparring with her daughter, Frau Spindler turned directly to William, standing in Ingrid's shadow. 'Ah, *guten Abend, Wilhelm.*'

'William, *Mutti*,' corrected Ingrid peevishly.

Frau Spindler smiled and offered her hand with formality to William. '*Mein Mann ist auch Wilhelm, sehen Sie. Das is 'Zufall'*? (My husband, you see, is also a William. Quite by chance).' She smiled again while Ingrid came up with a better word. 'Coincidence, Mutti.'

'Ach, my English. You must excuse me. I should say rather, what a coincidence, Ja?'

William smiled politely, and both he and Frau Spindler glanced at Ingrid, who said impatiently, 'Mutti, we cannot stand in the doorway. William's German is very good; you can speak to him in German; he will understand.' With that, she more or less pulled William inside, out of the cold.

Frau Spindler received her daughter's admonishments gracefully and, as they entered their apartment, indicated to William a gloomy vestibule, strewn with coats and shoes, which led clearly into a main room.

'I hope you will excuse my English. It's been a long time....'

'*Lass das, Mutti.* (Leave that, Mother).' Ingrid interrupted, 'I've already explained to William he'll have to manage with German this evening.'

As they continued down the hallway, Frau Spindler still attempted to make halting conversation in English, despite the friction it was causing with her daughter. '*Mein Mann* is not well this evening, he is (she turned to her daughter) how do you say? - *ein Kranker*.'

'A sick man' Ingrid quickly responded with the usual slight impatience, clashing this time though with William, who was coming up with an even more appropriate expression: 'an invalid.'

For a moment, Ingrid glared at her mother. '*Mutti, Um Himmels Willen, Bitte sprich mal auf Deutsch.*' (Mother, for heaven's sake please speak German).

However, her mother refused to be cowed, and jumped eagerly on William's interpretation. 'Yes, ein Invalid.'

The two women were sparring, seeming to vie to impress this young Englishman. Ingrid glanced now at him and remarked, 'I thought an 'invalid' was someone who's been injured, William. Or wounded.'

William attempted to dispense with the topic altogether. 'Yes, you're right; it does mean that usually, but it could mean, in your father's case, someone who's more ill than healthy.'

Frau Spindler's face expressed intense pleasure and relief. '*Ja, das stimmt* (yes, that's right).' There was an air of finality in her tone. 'Then, if it's to be German, as my daughter so wishes, let's just forget our little difficulties and call you *Wilhelm* this evening. My husband's name is also Wilhelm.'

There followed a moment of silence before Ingrid exploded. 'Mutti, was ist mit dir? Das hast du schon gesagt. (What's the matter with you Mother. You've already said that,)'

It was a callous interruption by Ingrid, prompting William finally not to intervene at all in this strange interplay between mother and daughter. He felt genuinely surprised, particularly by Ingrid (usually so calm), but instinctively sought to exonerate her, assuming the disputes must derive naturally from a blend of innate female rivalry and the difficulties of living at such close quarters, day in, day out. Nevertheless The visit had got off to an inauspicious start, and could only get better.

They'd entered the small, dark, wood-panelled living-room of Ingrid's home; a sofa, some chairs, a television, another door leading off. They followed Frau Spindler directly into this room, carpet-less but strewn with smart rugs across a parquet flooring, in the middle of which stood a large table. From previous visits with his German colleagues, William had grown used to this masterful economy of space inside the purpose-built German flat: two reasonable rooms, two bedrooms tucked away somewhere, a small kitchen, a toilet, a far cry in fact from his own rambling home in England.

'You must be hungry. We must eat.'

William watched Ingrid stride across to the corner of the room, by the window, and kiss Herr Wilhelm Spindler on the cheek. '*Guten Abend, Vati.*' Her father's face, as Ingrid greeted him, remained impassive, fixed in an expression that seemed to combine a whole welter of emotions. He didn't get up, just stared at his daughter's guest. Frau Spindler muttered something to him, and her husband nodded briefly in William's direction.

'*Komm,*' she now said, 'You are hungry, I'm sure.' On the table stood several plates filled with cold cuts of ham, salami, dark bread, butter. William was hungry, and so was Ingrid, and they attacked the meal, for the most part, in silence. From time to time Frau Spindler aimed some questions directly at William about his status in Germany, how long he'd been in Hamburg, what he was doing there, how come he spoke such good German, and, at one point, she asked, 'Are you intending to make a life in Germany,' following which, William received a gentle kick from beneath the table, as Ingrid glanced at him significantly. The conversation continued in this fact-finding manner, and William noticed that, although the pained and hostile expression on Herr Spindler's face never changed, it was apparent, from a slight movement of his eyes, that he was alert to William's answers. William had already anticipated that any trace of hostility from Ingrid's father towards him would probably be inevitable more on account of his 'Englishness' than from anything else. *Sharing food with the enemy.*

Can she have forgotten those nightly bombardments, transforming our lovely city into heaps of rubble? Is this now my own daughter, fraternising with those criminals, exchanging intimacies with our mortal foe? William himself had always believed the atrocities committed on both sides between 1939 and 1945 would take not just a decade but a century to be forgotten and forgiven. Here, from the man in the chair across the room, was living proof of this reality.

'Where did you study? Herr Bellman.'

William's gloomy thoughts were interrupted by Frau Spindler's friendly question. 'I studied at Cambridge University. German literature. *Faust*, Goethe's lyric poetry. '*Die Leiden des jungen Werthers*' (The Sufferings of Young Werther).'

'Ah, what a book!' Frau Spindler interrupted him. 'I read that story when I was in my teenage years. It made such an impression on me. That poor man; so much suffering for that girl.'

Although they were discussing an early novel written by Germany's undoubtedly foremost writer, and although the situation might be delicate anyway, William simply couldn't restrain himself. 'Very romantic, I'm sure, Frau Spindler, but I have to confess I found *Werther's* attitudes rather self-indulgent, self-pitying really.' There was a brief silence, and William continued, 'After all, men and women have their difficulties; it's common. But it hardly means they have to commit suicide. The characterisation of Werther I find a bit weak.' He stopped, and since Frau Spindler didn't reply, he added, 'You just have to overcome such difficulties and get on with your life.'

Frau Spindler seemed taken aback, almost dismayed, in the wake of this vehement criticism of a much-loved book. In her own sitting-room no less. She made however an effort to deflect the attack. 'Of course, Wilhelm, one must place a book in the context of the time; things, attitudes were different in Goethe's day, and...' she gave it some thought before adding quietly, with a smile on her face, 'we do hope such a thing won't happen to you two lovely young people, but I suppose the book acts as a warning.'

Ingrid, who'd listened but not joined in, now added insult to injury. '*Ich bitte dich, Mutti...* (Really, Mother...). I don't think William's intending to kill himself on my account.' She gave William a conspiratorial glance, while Frau Spindler clearly thought it best to say nothing more, but set her puzzled face in a gentle smile of reconciliation. It was left to Ingrid to add, even more puzzlingly perhaps for her mother, 'We've had enough talk of suicide in the Mensa recently.'

The supper went on its way. Frau Spindler produced gateaux, fruit pies, cream. 'I hope you like the German sweet desserts, Wilhelm. We have, I think, in this country an obsession for them.'

'I love them of course, Frau Spindler. Do you know, I once, when I was younger, went to stay with a German family, as a teenager, and the mother made the most brilliant damson pie.'

At William's words, a shock passed through the length and breadth of Ingrid's body, as if someone had flicked a switch. *Could this possibly be the very same man?* But she wrestled to contain herself and said nothing.

Her mother was still elaborating on the subject of deserts. 'Ah, damson pie. We call it *Zwetschchenküchen*. I know it's a difficult word. They're the little black plums, you know, Wilhelm. A great favourite here. I always used to make Ingrid damson pie.'

Ingrid heard her name mentioned from across ten years of remembering. She was making a desperate effort herself to recover from the shock she'd received from William's account of his teenage 'holidaying'. She made a desperate effort to forget about it as she looked across the table at her mother rambling on about cherry pies and William listening politely, and she hoped he or she might find a way of deflecting her from the topic. Meanwhile her mother, looking earnestly at William, continued, 'Nowadays, of course, my daughter turns her nose up at such treats. She wishes to look after her figure. Young people are so different *heutzutage* (nowadays). Always in such a rush. No time for the nice things in life.'

Ingrid glanced across once more at William as, mercifully, the subject lapsed for want of fuel, until Ingrid unaccountably found herself saying, 'D'you remember, *Mutti*, that English boy who came to stay with us in Stuttgart?'

'Yes,' Frau Spindler came out of her silence, 'You were a little bit in love with him, darling.'

'Not in love, *Mutti*. I was too young to be in love. But he was lovely all the same.' They all laughed, and Frau Spindler said, 'Yes, darling, you have to admit it though; he quite broke your heart on that occasion.' Ingrid didn't reply, and her mother turned her attention to William again. 'Well, Wilhelm, and where *was* this holiday you had.'

'On Lake Constance. Down near Switzerland.'

Ah,' exclaimed Frau Spindler, 'such a beautiful part of Germany.'

'Yes it was', replied William. 'And guess where the family lived, I mean their real home.'

'I can't think.'

'Stuttgart.' William paused. 'Ingrid tells me that's where *you* used to live too..'

'It was indeed.' She sighed, as if she wished to put this cherished memory behind her. 'That's before we had to come to Hamburg. Life is full of coincidences.' For a second, she sat gently shaking her head and repeating quietly 'Memories, memories,' before regaining her composure. 'I expect you'd like some coffee, Wilhelm. Ingrid, darling, please go and make us some coffee.'

Ingrid left the room and Frau Spindler and William sat together at the table in silence, the kind of silence that leaves no room for embarrassment, until she remarked, 'Wilhelm, I'm so happy you and Ingrid have found each other. There's so much discontent in the world. Young people seem so wrapped up in themselves. Things have changed from our time.'

As William was wondering how to reply to this weighty topic, Ingrid stepped into the room holding a small tray with a coffee percolator on it and said, quite loudly, '*Mutti*, William is quite religious, you know.'

William often wondered, looking back on that remark, whether she'd deliberately selected a provocative topic to deflect her mother from an even more provocative one. Whatever the case, William smothered a gasp, glanced quickly at Ingrid, and said as unconcernedly as he could manage, 'Well, yes, I certainly went to a very religious boarding school.'

He was still wondering what on earth Ingrid had been thinking when her mother, perhaps deliberately, chose anyway to steer the matter away from religion and on to schooling. 'What sort of a school was that? Aren't your boarding schools meant to be very. traditional.'

William breathed a sigh of relief.. He had no wish to enter into some sort of religious discourse with Ingrid's mother.' Yes, they have a good reputation. Mine though was a school particularly strong on religion. I think this is what Ingrid's referring to. It was a religious foundation.'

'A catholic foundation?'.

'No, Church of England. C of E.'

Ingrid burst out laughing. 'C of E. The English abbreviate everything if they can.'

'Ingrid, *Liebchen.*' Her mother looked at her sternly. '*Bitte. Seid nicht so unhöflich!*' (Ingrid, my darling. Don't be so impolite).

'It's true, *Mutti.*' She looked at William. 'Don't you call your Prime Minister PM?'

'Yes, of course.' He turned to Frau Spindler. 'Ingrid's right. We play around sometimes disastrously with our own language.'

'My daughter, I think, is sometimes too clever for her own good though.'

William intervened. 'It's good to say things how they are, don't you think, Frau Spindler? Our generation is at least good at that.'

'Yes', she replied, nodding. '*Das stimmt.*' (That's true). There was a moment's hesitation, before she added quietly, 'But perhaps it's better not always to talk about some things.'

The moment had come. William, the orchestrator, the lead actor in this whole domestic drama, knew it was time to leave. He guessed Frau Spindler was getting tired, and her last statement had seemed to stray into heartfelt matters too deep and personal to be aired at that moment. Throughout the whole evening, Herr Spindler had remained silent, although still apparently awake, and it was clear that although Ingrid did her best to help with her father's condition, Frau Spindler was probably left endlessly to manage, impossible circumstances.

However, it was left to this apparently indomitable woman to wind the evening up herself, on an earlier note. 'I suppose you're not so strong on the Catholic faith in England as we are in Germany, Wilhelm.'

'Mainly in the South, *Mutti,*' intervened Ingrid quickly.

'Yes,' said William, 'we sorted out the two churches a few hundred years ago. King Henry VIII. The Dissolution of the Monasteries.'

Frau Spindler laughed outright. 'Is that the correct term? 'Dissolution'. What a wonderful expression.' She repeated it, getting her tongue round the word. 'Your King Henry certainly didn't spare the monasteries. And all that gold and silver.'

'*Stolen*, Frau Spindler, remarked William. 'Daylight robbery.' Frau Spindler laughed again, and Ingrid too. 'But the worst of it,' continued William, 'is all those precious buildings burnt to the ground. You must go there and see for yourself.'

'I'd love to. I've always wanted to go to England. I hope one day before I die.'

'*Mutti*!' exclaimed Ingrid, but her mother said, 'I'm just saying what is true, Ingrid. We all must die sometime.' She turned to William. 'Perhaps Ingrid might go to England herself some day.'

Ingrid quickly tried to deflect the conversation. 'I suppose Germany's too close to Rome to get rid of the Catholic influence.'

'Ingrid, das ist ein irrelevantes Thema.' (That's an irrelevant remark) And this light-hearted rebuke from mother to daughter brought the evening to a close, with the usual thanks and pleasantries and hand-shakes (William never even tried to say goodbye to the lone presence in the corner). Ingrid accompanied William down in the lift, to say goodbye. They stepped together out into the cold air. 'Last bus in twenty minutes. Good timing. Don't get cold.' She put her hand gently on his arm, and tilted ever so slightly her head.

'I won't,' he said, and kissed her gently on the lips, without giving her the chance to respond. Then, as he was turning to go, he said, 'Ingrid, by the way, what was that all about my being religious. You nearly landed me in it.'

'Oh nothing really. I remember you once saying in the Mensa something about the '*Church of One*'. I just remembered that remark, that's all.'

He laughed. 'Elephants never forget, they say. Anyway, I'll explain to you sometime. That's if you've got two hours to waste.'

He turned and waved, and walked down the road, feeling totally happy. Complete.

CHAPTER 15

"In which William faces up to the joys and sadness of courting"

William and Ingrid met once more in the café near the university on a bitterly cold night before William's departure for England. She already knew he had his passage booked and there was an air of solemn finality hanging over both of them, questions unanswered, never discussed, that vital boundary between liking and loving never traversed, nor even considered. William had informed her, some days earlier, that he'd bought his ticket for home, tactlessly disregarding the fact that this placed an irrevocable time limit on their relationship. Was their recent, so-hopeful coming together to be no more than a fleeting friendship between strangers, expiring with a dull 'goodbye'?

As they sat in silence in the half-empty bar, Ingrid, who, on the face of it, had more to lose but no wish either to plead for a stay of execution, asked William, in a neutral tone of voice, what he was planning to do when he reached England.

'I don't know, Ingrid. I need to get back, see my mother. I've already postponed my return for three months. She'll be lonely; you know of course she lives alone. I have no father.'

'Did he just leave?' Ingrid felt bold enough to ask, felt at last that their intimacy justified the question.

'I've never seen my father, Ingrid. He was never there at my birth, or any other time.'

'Is he dead?'

'No, I don't believe so, but my mother never talks about him, never raises the subject; it's as *if* he's dead, to her at any rate. Something terrible must have happened.'

'Don't you want to find out, William? Everyone has a right to a father.' She hesitated. 'Even one like mine.'

He placed his hand on hers, motionless on the table by her glass. 'It's terrible.'

She smiled. 'But *we* are here.'

They relapsed into silence. William was thinking he might just have to get up, ask her not to come to the station, just say goodbye now, when suddenly she said out of the blue, 'What *is* the Church of One, William?' He didn't reply immediately, grappling with even the beginning of an answer, and she added, 'It's something I've wanted to know for a long time.'

He smiled. 'It's a long story.'

She nodded. 'You said it once in the Mensa, remember?'

'Heavens, you've got a long memory.'

'Well, it was such a strange thing to say.' William was plainly hesitating, feeling reluctant to open so sensitive a topic. Ingrid noticed, and added, 'You probably don't want to tell me.'

'No I don't mind. It's nothing really. It's just a phrase I dreamed up when I was younger.' He added after a moment, 'And more religious than I am now.'

'I think you are still religious; yes. Some of the things you say in the Mensa.'

He smiled. 'The Mensa. That free-for-all.'

She ignored the comment. 'What made you dream up the phrase? Who is the 'One' in the Church of *One*?'

He laughed. 'It's me. Or *was* me, when I cared about such things. I suppose it was my childish way of explaining why churches seem so inadequate. So I invented my own.'

He stopped and looked at her, hoping she'd drop the matter. She didn't. She just sat there, waiting, perplexed, and finally asked, 'Why are churches so inadequate?'

He said, 'They're redundant, Ingrid. Churches have become redundant.'

Frantically she said, 'What does that word mean? I don't know the word.'

He thought for a moment. 'It means something is no longer useful. It's been replaced.'

'I understand.' She nodded and sat waiting.

'Look, I was young. We had a lot of religion at my school and religion became important for me at that time.'

'How young?'

'I suppose 15 or16. I'm not sure. But God did become important for me then.' He stopped for a moment, thinking. 'How can I put it? Yes, I found it easy at that time to communicate with this God of my making.' He paused again. 'I suppose I just realised then that churches are unnecessary.'

She laughed a silvery laugh. 'Churches have always been there.'

He threw up his hands in a gesture of resignation. 'Yes, we've just grown accustomed to them. Doesn't mean they're necessary. Why do you need an intermediary to do what you can do yourself?'

'Do what?'

'Communicate with your Maker.'

She laughed again. 'You don't, I suppose. But surely churches help.'

'No, exactly the opposite. They don't help at all.' He'd raised his voice slightly as if in emphasis. 'That's the problem. *How* do they help? They hinder rather than help.

'They spread the Word.'

'Yes, you're right there. Originally they did. But, you see, they sort of claimed God for themselves after a time. It gave them power. The problem, as I see it now, is that Churches believe it their job to communicate with God *for* us.' He paused. But we don't *need* intermediaries. It's that simple.'

'It's not simple, William,' she said quietly.

'Okay, let's say you'd made a good friend; you wouldn't want *me* to talk to him. You'd talk to him yourself, wouldn't you? That's all I'm saying. Churches make it all too simple and yet too complicated.' She waited. 'And as for the matter of dissemination....' (he noticed that look of incomprehension cross her face, and rephrased) 'As for the matter of spreading the Word, well, aren't I doing that right now with you?' She nodded her head gently. He asked, 'Want to join? Make the Church of Two?'

She was laughing now. Perhaps this discussion had helped to expel thoughts of their imminent separation. He would leave perhaps a little bit of himself behind. She said, 'No wonder they call you Luther.'

He laughed. 'Do they? *Who* do?'

'You remember. In the Mensa.'

He shrugged. 'Well, good. If this is what Luther thought, then so much the better. Good for him. And good for me.' He put on a pompous manner and asked, 'Have you got any further questions of a spiritual nature you'd like to share with *Luther*?' He was hoping the jesting manner would bring to an end this rather heavy conversation. He glanced at his watch, while Ingrid replied, 'Yes, actually, I have a question. Well, I think it's spiritual.' His heart sank, as she continued, 'D'you remember that time in the Mensa, when Georges was holding forth about poor Kurt, and kept going on about 'guilt', 'feeling guilty'?'

She went silent, and William prompted, 'Yes, I remember. What about it?'

She didn't immediately reply, and then asked, 'Does the Church of One believe in guilt?'

William was amazed. All this time, two, perhaps three, months, and she still remembered an obscure argument that must long have been forgotten by everyone else who was there. William found himself blurting out, 'I believe guilt is at the heart of all religions, yes.'

She wouldn't leave it at that. 'What makes us guilty then?'

'I'm not, like 'Luth', an expert, Ingrid, but I think there's the guilt Georges was talking about, about Kurt, and feeling you've done something wrong. But then there's another sort,' He paused, and continued, 'It's mysterious, a feeling that's always with us, with every living person, that one has to somehow atone for something, to make it up.'

'Make it up to who?'

'To whoever was there at the time. Your guess is as good as mine.'

She laughed and he laughed too.

She persisted, 'But seriously, who? A god?'

'Yes, maybe. We're never our own, Ingrid. We're always in debt. Like we borrowed money and have to give it back. But who did we borrow it from in the first place?'

A silence followed, and William stood up. 'We've got to go.' He looked at her. 'I've got an instinct right now which tells me neither of us wants to say goodbye, and also tells me I like you very much.'

At that moment he kissed her on the lips, and she responded.

'But you haven't left me your address,' she said, almost panicking. 'Nothing. Your phone number. How do we see each other again if I don't know where you are?'

William was not one in general to leave contact details. In the same way he didn't like taking photographs, he felt the moment belonged only to the moment. Ingrid had laid a piece of paper out on the Formica-top table and was searching for a pencil in her bag. William took a pen from his pocket, stepped forward and wrote down his contact details. He said, 'Forgive me. I forgot. Let's say goodbye and go our separate ways. "*Goodbye is too good a word, Babe*"... So '*lebe wohl*' (farewell).

Ingrid, shsaking her head, took his hand and said deliberately, '*Auf Wiedersehen* (see you again), my instinctive Englishman.'

William turned and, without looking back, headed for the station. Meanwhile, Ingrid watched him till he was out of sight and carefully slipped the piece of paper into one of her pockets.

(At Possum Kingdom.) ENTRY FROM ADAM'S DIARY
REFLECTIONS and **CONFESSIONS,** from the pen of 'Sol' the Solitary.

London – the 'Garret' (Prose-Poet, obsessed with words and rhythms)

Alone. In my little room. My resignation from the Bureau lurking somewhere in the postal system. What have I done? Committed metaphorical suicide. No job, no continuing source of income. I'm heading down a vortex of my own making. And for what? I should have good enough reason, but I confess, I'm following just a dream.

Don't worry, keep your head; think clearly, rationally. Don't panic. The streets of London are lined with 'Employment Agencies' these days. They're all the rage, and new, efficient methods of diagnostic have been devised to point the job-seeker speedily in the direction his/her personality traits indicate. No fuss, nor preliminary small-talk. You're shown into a quiet room and asked to complete, within half an hour, your immediate responses to a set of apparently random, short-answer questions. For example: *'Have you got a sweet tooth?* Y/N *' 'How do you like to spend Christmas? a) with family b) abroad c) in a restaurant.' 'What's your favourite colour? Etc etc.* They feed your responses into an algorithm, and your diagnosis spews out at the other end. Ingenious. Magic. No problem. Supposedly, the theory behind the procedure is spontaneity; that is, if you give yourself time to think about something, you end up with a series of untruths; it's the immediate, unconsidered, instinctive, reactive responses that count and unravel who you really are, and what you really like or dislike.

Simple. I'll give it a try. I owe it to myself, considering my impending impecunious circumstances. Admittedly, I did, in a weak moment, ask myself just how accurate this procedure might be. But I went anyway. To this Agency down the road. Paid a bit of money. They duly posted my responses into the think-tank and guess what spewed out. Something I already knew: "*You'll make a good teacher. Perfect temperament for the emotional cut-and-thrust that kind of work entails.*"

'Okay, I've tried that. But d'you think I could be a Programmer maybe? A computer programmer?' My knee-jerk response issued involuntarily from my mouth.

The guru consulted his print-out, decided, no, the scores rated high enough on logic, but the emotional responses scored even higher. 'Too emotional to be a Programmer. I'm sorry.' He dismissed me with a friendly smile. The great axe had fallen.

What now then? Well, one nagging concern still remained steadfast in my mind, a reservation that had been worrying me before I ever went to that phoney Agency: *I know better what I am and what I really want than any amount of machines.* This blatant truth stared me in the face now. as I made my disconsolate way up the staircase to my garret. And, on opening the door, justification for my concerns stood imaginatively emblazoned on the walls of my friendly room: WHY NOT SELF-DIAGNOSE? YES, HERE AND NOW, IN THIS ROOM, ANSWER YOUR OWN QUESTIONS!

It certainly won't be the first time, and, for sure, this time they'll be accurate. I grab a blank sheet of fools-cap and jot down, as methodically as my recent set-back allows, *all* the jobs I might conceivably undertake in the future, given a slice of luck.

Acting: disadvantaged by ones particular sexual proclivities. (Nothing essentially wrong with that, except that not being in the majority preference might work against you. I added an angry postscript: *"If you don't believe me, then check it out!"*

Computers: Good money. A rising 'industry'. Long-term career prospects excellent *"if that's what you really want"*. The Operator in that Agency had been unconvinced though, so I'd be starting with a nagging doubt.

Publishing: They say some of the best women are in publishing. *"Check it out"*. A plus in itself though. Job slightly effete. Lots of entertaining and obesity-inducing dinners. Quite honestly, not really the faintest idea what is involved. But those girls, a serious consideration.

Advertising: Creative. Lots of women again. Could work from home if good enough. A waste of a serious writing talent if one ever has one. Triviality run riot. But the women!

Salesman: Low status, unless in foreign markets. Fancied the idea of jetting it across the world.

Journalism: Most attractive job of all. But how on earth did one get into it. Too old already. A closed shop. Didn't want graduates anyway.

Broadcasting: Again highly attractive possibility. Again, an impregnable fortress. Too old; should have thought of it before. Previous teaching experience a disadvantage. Full of snobs and arse-lickers (sycophants).

Business Executive: What did that mean? Too late anyway. Should have thought of it before.

Law: Good money. Pernickety. Deep down, despite the good money, *despicable. Shysters.*

Accountancy: No thank you. *Dry as dust, imagination goes to rust.* If you had any.

Social Work: Yuuuuch! Full of misguided philanthropists.

Professional Footballer: Why not? Have the talent. Exciting while it lasts. Keeps you fit. *Was all that 'Education' just for kicking a football around though?*

Teaching: The dumping ground for all those without the *nouse*, the guts, the determination, to do any of the above. A type of 'Prostitution'. *Those who can...**do**; those who can't... **teach**. Was there ever a more damning indictment?*

I reached the end of my enquiries, and quicker than any machine, the surprising result spews out (I write it down on paper): *'I'm born to be a writer (want to be too). Hardest job on earth!'* My mind is racing. I already possess the mechanism for such a trade (words and rhythm), but, more importantly, and despite society's innate reservations about such a trade, I know, deep down, that I *am* one, and that it's a *real* job. Assuredly, lots of phonies who have nothing to say, but the truth is, I'm fascinated by my own existence, and isn't mega mania a vital ingredient for this unusual occupation?

A literary line springs to mind: *For I have that within which passeth show.* Hamlet. Act 1, Scene 2. And I, exactly like Hamlet, have interesting secrets too, and a lot of them, Sometimes I wonder if, among other things, Hamlet was a writer too. He behaves like one. He's dismissive, enjoys leading his possessive girl-friend a merry dance, harboured murderous thoughts: *'Henceforth my thoughts be bloody or be nothing worth...'* And don't I, likewise? With good reason? Am I then Hamlet, and he me? I know I directed *'Hamlet'* the Play, somewhere or other, but was I also one of the characters? The 'Hamlet' character himself.... Our two journeys seem entwined. However, I must bear these intimations silently...for I know I have work yet to do.)*.

Time has moved on; I'm established in my garret now. I make no apologies about my choice of occupation. People sometimes ask me what I'm doing here in London. I reply, 'I'm a writer; I'm an astronomer of the soul,' and I watch their expression go from surprise to curiosity to admiration to disbelief to downright scorn, and I feel I have to protest that, no, it's not a job for idle wasters; it's hard graft; not just 9 to 5, but 24/7, an all- embracing job in fact, which leaves you penniless and wondering how you're going to make out at all. Occasionally I don't tell them I'm a writer at all; better just to reply, 'I live in a garret.' Then there's no misunderstanding; they realise you're scraping along, haven't got enough money, probably on the dole. They still though go away shaking their heads. It's difficult for people, hard-working types, to understand what you mean by 'writer'.

Example: I have a friend. Anthony. 'Tony'. He works somewhere in the City, making fast money. He comes in from the outer suburbs on the main line, and occasionally passes my door in the mornings. I think he feels sorry for me; wants to help, so every now and then he rings the doorbell down below persistently, and wakes me up. We stand on the door-step, me in my dressing-gown, he in his suit, and he shakes his head and says, 'Adam, this really isn't good enough, old boy.' (That's all he can come up with). I tell him I've been working, all night, (which I have; remember 24/7?), and, shaking his head, he strides off towards the tube-station with his brolly and bowler, and pound symbols floating before his eyes, because that's what he's doing: making money, providing for himself and others. It's expected of a man of his status, it's what those former colleagues of mine at the Bureau are all doing. It's laudable, but it's not as valuable a job as my current one, nor as hard work My new job is full-time, never stops, is never halted. My work must by nature occupy my thoughts day and night. Now, can an accountant really say his job absorbs him day and night? Probably not, and quite possibly never absorbs him at all. And what, I ask myself quite frequently, motivated friend, Tony to undertake his line of work at all? Was he fascinated, like me, by Hamlet's erratic behaviour, made comparisons with his own secure life-style? I don't believe so. The pecuniary world doesn't lend itself to such speculation.

(Author's note): It's clear that this monologue was a landmark moment for Adam. His behaviour and diary become more purposeful, less random, as if a distinct gap had been breeched and a goal planted in his disordered mind).

In an idle, doubting moment, I read through that job list again the other day, just in case I'd missed something, and switched on a favourite track from my favourite singer, to restore my sanity, chase the blues away.

The phone rang. *Was it perhaps Mary, ringing to weaken my resolve, persuade me otherwise? (She wouldn't take too kindly to a layabout on the dole).* Angst, in the shape of my ex girl-friend, has started recently slipping in under the door like smoke from a rogue fire. I tear myself away, refrain from picking up the receiver, while that little folk-singer of mine keeps growling on reassuringly, wrapping his eternal truths in musical phrases; yes, that little prophet with the gravelly voice, dredging up songs and words that lie dormant in us all… *(Where, by the way, have I used that phrase '**gravelly voice**' before)?* Something now grabs at my throat. Was it a mere five, maybe six, years ago, in happier times, that I sat in my good friend Bill's house in Krum, listening to that self-same poet spinning his lyrical dreams? I called *him* '**gravelly**' then too. Remarkable how I still remember that distinctive, unique little phrase. A funny thing, memory. It jumps at you unexpectedly. And now, drip by precious drip, it seems to be restoring itself. Is my self-imposed therapy really working? Am I at last awakening from a hundred years' sleep? My heart leaps for joy (tinged, I confess, by an indistinct sense of unease). What is this faint disquiet I feel lately, whenever I take up the pen? Writing was my way out, my salvation, but now I'm not so sure. Are there perhaps situations I *don't* want to remember? I thought my writing would unlock the spirit, release me, but - dreadful thought - are there perhaps other things I really don't want to find out, about my past? What perhaps awaits me around the next corner?

Put it on one side. No good, these vacillating doubts. There's no going back now, and that little singer goes on boldly and beautifully dredging for words and tunes, in amongst the sludge. You know who I mean; I won't reveal the identity of this truth-seeker, this truth-teller, this paragon. Discover him for yourself. He's a household name. His simple honesty is proclaimed now from East to West. Why then, I wonder, was it that my father's generation was so ready to deride this little poet? Heap scorn upon his 'gravelly voice'? It often puzzles me. What was it blunted their otherwise so fine, perceptive judgements? They say: *what's good for some is not always good for others*. Perceptions change, and those parents, that generation, were entangled anyway in other more brutal threads, too busy to heed the lone voices of the poets, too busy dispatching their sons off to fight a calamitous war, not just once but twice in a century. Yes, it was left to us progeny to pick for truth amongst the embers.

Dieu merci, it's different now; we've moved on. We existentialists seek now for gold amongst the sludge, dredge for words, dismiss preconceptions, plumb the bottom, and ignore what lies upon the surface. For, in truth, it's not what you are *thinking*; it's what you're *not* thinking that matters. And then, these days, it's not what you say, it's how you say it.

The phone's ringing again. I pick up this time. It's someone who doesn't know me, but who's met someone at a party who knew Lily Cross - Mary's sister - and they, Lily and Luke, would love to see me again....

It's dangerous, but probably too good to resist. I'll go, of course.

CHAPTER 16

"In which William is fraught with indecision"

A month had passed. Neither he nor Ingrid had communicated. It was a dead time. William was kicking his heels at home in W..., not knowing what to do with his life but aware really that whatever it was to be, it would have to be by the start of autumn - everything started then. He had eight months to kill.

He often thought of Ingrid, but, whenever memories of Hamburg edged into his mind, he made an effort to banish them, compelling himself to close the chapter. He needed to move on. And, besides, logic suggested Ingrid would have contacted him had she wanted to; maybe the impression he'd made on her in those final weeks in Hamburg had been less compelling than he believed.

As he wandered dissatisfied around the big house, he would often encounter his Grandfather in the corridor leading along to his room. The old man scarcely ever came down nowadays except to eat his meals greedily and pass a few inappropriate comments on his daughter-in-law's house-keeping, or rather lack of it. What communication William might once have had with his grandfather had become little more than a tedious duty, as the old man gradually lost his memory and groped to find even the most obvious details of his past.

William met him one early February afternoon, wandering, clearly lost, to and fro in the dark corridor,. He steered him carefully back down to his room and a small light of recognition came into his eyes as he remembered where he was.

'Must have got involved in my painting,' he said. 'Suddenly couldn't remember the way. Come in...he struggled for a moment over his grandson's name... ah, Robert; there's a kettle on. I expect you could do with a cup of tea.'

William had pushed the door open and now followed the shrunken figure into the large, dreary room With Grandfather's fingers clawing at his arm, they crossed to look at a half-finished painting on the easel, and then William watched as the old man hesitantly attempted a brush-stroke or two.

'Never have been able to get clouds right.' It was his inevitable self-criticism as he bent proprietarily over his current work.

William had heard the complaint before. 'The clouds look all right to me, Grandpa.' It was what he always replied. It had become a routine. But this time there was more to come. For some unknown reason, and without any apparent prompting, Grandfather's memory had momentarily been released from its bonds. 'Yes, I seem to remember, you wished to know the names of those landscapes we kept at the house.' He paused for a few moments and dabbed on the canvas with his brush, leaving William to suppose he was already losing the thread. 'The oil paintings, Grandfather?' William prompted.

'Ah yes. As I was saying, we had a discussion about them. You know, it suddenly came to me. Such a funny thing memory, isn't it? Grandma and I had your father's name and his brother's name, one on each picture. Now, what was his brother's name?'

William knew this couldn't be true. He had no uncle, so far as he knew. The old man must be confused, but, in deference, William lied. 'Ah, I remember, one of them was called "*The Haywain*", the other... (He pretended to forget, flicking his thumb and forefinger together). 'what was it now... Ah, yes, "*Norfolk scene by a River*". That was it, wasn't it?'

Little use correcting him. Slightly puzzled, William quietly left the old man dabbing away and went downstairs to join his mother and a bit of sanity.

'Mother, he used to be good once, I'm sure.'

Tessa had her hands in the sink, her back towards him, and seemed to be scrubbing at a particularly stubborn stain on one of his tee-shirts. 'Who did, Darling? You speak in riddles. You seem to have forgotten your nouns and pronouns. I wonder the Germans ever understood a word you said.'

William let indignation wash over him for a moment. 'They did, Mother; I can assure you. I'm talking about Grandfather. I've just been up there. His painting, you know?' He paused for a second wondering how he might put it to his mother. 'He's really not bad. You should have just bought him a canvass and a brush. That's all he needs. Not that dreadful 'numbers' kit.' He paused. 'He might deliver you a masterpiece.'

Tessa took her arms out of the sink and wiped them on the kitchen towel. 'I don't think so. It's all too late for that now anyway. And really, I don't believe he was ever that good.'

William shrugged his shoulders. 'You may not be completely right about that.' He changed tack. 'However, don't you remember those canvasses in their old house at S…. Oil-paintings. They were good.'

'I can't remember any specific ones. And if there were any, they were probably sold off in a job lot when Grandma died and he came to live here.'

William mumbled, 'What a waste.'

Tessa paused for a moment, wishing her son wouldn't be so serious at times. Since his return from Germany, much of his joking, laughing self seemed to have been replaced by something else, something she couldn't quite put her finger on. She said, 'William, honestly, Grandpa's work, it was all just amateur stuff. Done when he was younger.'

'Maybe, but younger is exactly when it counts.' Tessa didn't reply, unsure what her son was getting at. 'Listen, Mother. There was someone in Germany I knew, a real artist, someone who was painting for Germany, believe me.'

'What do you mean painting for Germany? Do they have competitions?'

'No, it's a turn of phrase.'

'Oh, a turn of phrase, is it? Sounds more like speaking in riddles again.'

Once again, William let his mother's sarcasm wash over him. 'Mother, I mean by 'real artist' someone who's made a choice. Chosen painting as a way of life. A career. Taken a gamble.'

'What about him then? Are you sure he was that good?'

'Well only time will tell probably.'

'More riddles, William.' Tessa returned to the sink. 'I don't know what you mean.'

'What I mean is, this guy, Georges, this painter, took a gamble. Perhaps he'll sell them, perhaps he won't. But the point is, he felt fulfilled.'

'Good for him. I hope he was a nice person, William. But I can't for the life of me see what this has to do with you. Or Grandpa for that matter.' She was rummaging around in the fridge. Her voice came out muffled. 'Are you suggesting Grandpa might have become a professional artist?'

'Perhaps, yes. I don't know. Or perhaps he just wasted his talent.'

Tessa came back into the parlor removing her working apron. 'Darling, I think you're letting your imagination take over. Grandpa was never that good. In fact, what I do know is by the time he was twenty and in love with Grandma, he was also a fairly efficient money-making machine. Driving a pony and trap each day, visiting his retail outlets.' She looked almost pleadingly at her son. 'That doesn't sound at all like this Georges person you met in Germany, driven by his art. Believe me, if there ever was any artistic talent in Grandpa, he gave it all up for her. He's worked very hard all his life.'

William said, half to himself, 'That's what I've been trying to say.'

Tessa returned to the utility room to finish the washing, leaving William with his thoughts. What he'd really been getting at was the growing conviction his family, the Riley family, was split between Art and money-making, a fatal, possibly paralyzing defect. After a short while he called to her, an edge of defiance and frustration in his tone this time. 'Mother, I've come to a decision. I really can't just sit around here doing nothing. I shall probably go off and write somewhere. So don't be surprised. I might as well give it a try before I fall in love and buy a pony and trap.'

She laughed. 'Darling, where are you planning to carry out this experiment?'

'I don't see why you find it so funny.'

'Darling, I'm not laughing at your plans. It's just the way you talked about the pony and trap. Where are you planning to go?'

'I'd like to borrow your second car, Grandpa's old car, and drive to Spain maybe. To Seville.'

'Why Seville?'

'Seems like a nice warm place to go. With lots of oranges.'

She laughed again. 'It's a good idea. If it weren't for your Grandfather, I'd come with you.'

William was shocked. 'No, Mother. There's only room for one in what I want to do.'

'I know, Darling; don't worry. I was only joking. One's company, two's a crowd.' She paused. Her son's whole desperate insistence on getting away and working things out had triggered a memory in her, a memory of a time before he, William, arrived, and the constraints began. She said softly, 'You know, I went on the same journey once myself.'

'What journey, Mother?' said William, surprised.

'Nothing really; the journey of footloose and fancy-free. I don't think it'll solve your conflicts, but go. Enjoy it while you can. Course you can take the car. It's just sitting there doing nothing.'

'You're a gem, Mother. Thanks. I knew you'd understand. And please don't feel excluded; I won't be away for long.' He paused, and Tessa thought the subject had finally been brought to a close, until he said, with great deliberation, 'I suppose most reasoning people with any imagination have to face this…this threshold, sometime in their lives.'

Tessa said, anxious to get on with lunch, 'Probably. We're all different.'

'Yeah, we are. Funny, that reminds me of someone, someone else I met in Germany, a guy called Mackintosh. Nothing like Georges. Mack seemed quite happy just to drift. Perhaps he didn't have much imagination. Came from America on a trip and never went back.'

As her son completed his sentence, he had little idea his mother was wrestling with another deep memory that had leapt into her consciousness and just as quickly disappeared. She said softly, 'Funny. I knew a 'Mackintosh' once.'

And then Grandfather came into the little kitchen. Shuffling in, looking at his watch. He was always punctual to the second. 'Is lunch ready?'

(At Possum Kingdom.)   ENTRY FROM ADAM'S DIARY
REFLECTIONS and **CONFESSIONS,** from the pen of 'Sol' the Solitary.

London – the 'Garret' (profile of an artist)

Whether the anxiety, the unease, which descends on me nowadays whenever I sit down to write, whether this is a prophetic warning, a precursor to some dreadful event, I can't be sure, but I've had a disturbing dream recently- a protracted, agonising scene played out in slow motion in front of me - about my dear Mother, she who brought me into the world and lavished unfailing love on me throughout my growing-up. I dreamt I was present at her deathbed. This vision was so vivid, so harrowing I could have been living it for real. It was shocking.

    'She's very groggy,' said my father, as we approached the nursing home. 'They dose her up. I don't think she really knows where she is, but I just couldn't look after her anymore. I couldn't cope.'

    She was in her own private ward, surrounded by flowers. There were a few relatives sitting by the bed, people I hadn't seen for years.

    'It's Adam come to see you,' one of the relatives said to my Mother, but she showed no sign of hearing. She made no movement. I imagine movement of any kind hurt her. Even talking probably hurt her.

    Most of the relatives left. I simply couldn't stand the silence of it all, that awful, unspoken resignation people experience in the face of life's inevitabilities, so I went away from the bed and stood by the mantelpiece, leaving my father by the bedside. Some might say it was cold and unfeeling, but we have to remain strong in the face of sentimentality. Thoughts were in fact racing through my mind and a welter of feelings, but my over-riding emotion wasn't sorrow, wasn't indifference either, no, it was anger, defiant Anger, and somehow I knew my Mother would have understood.

'Is that Adam?' she asked in a whisper from her bed.

'Yes,' said my father.

'I didn't expect to see you here.' She tried to straighten herself up on the pillows. 'I'm sorry to be such a nuisance. How are you anyway? I don't think I'm quite at my best at the moment. But I'll be okay once they can find this thing in me. Dad says I'll get much better care here.'

At this point, I admit I turned my face away and bit hard on my lip. My obstinate anger remained though. She murmured a few times, 'I'm sorry, I'm sorry,' and then lapsed into an unbroken silence. I think she'd dozed off.

The following day there was little change. I went in alone, without my father. Once again there were the inevitable watchers at the bedside. 'It's Adam, Evie.'

Again there was little recognition. I stood by the window, and slowly the visitors drifted out.

'Is that Adam?'

'Yes, Mum.' I went over to the bed.

'I don't know how long it's going to be before I'm better.' She tried a smile and reached for my hand. 'I'm glad you're happy. I'm glad you came back too.' She was lucid. 'You know, we didn't think you were going to make it when you were a small boy. You were the one we used to worry about. You used to have fits in the night.'

'I'll make it all right,' I said.

'I feel so drowsy all the time.'

'They're giving you drugs, Mum,' I said.

'Yes, I suppose that's what it is.'

She dozed off again. On the following day the sun was shining, and I didn't go to the nursing-home. I went out to play golf.

'I'll go along anyway,' said my Father. 'I don't think there'll be much change.'

When I got back from the course, he came out to meet me. 'Mum passed away in her sleep this afternoon at 3.35,' he pronounced quietly. There was no sense of recrimination for my absence.

''Were you there, Dad?'

'Yes, I was at her bedside.'

I was aware suddenly of an immense and inexplicable feeling of relief. 'It's really perhaps for the best.'

'Yes,' replied my Father, and we went inside.

CHAPTER 17

"In which William has an important visit and good fortune"

William never made it to Spain nor a garret in Seville. Events intervened. In early May, as he was trying to complete arrangements to set off - or rather, was trying to buoy himself up to go at all - his mother leaned round the door to his room and said, 'There's someone on the phone downstairs for you.' William showed little sign of moving, and she added, 'Got a foreign accent. German, I would guess.' William headed for the staircase, and she called, 'She sounds nice.'

His mother's voice had an expectant ring to it, and William, descending the stairs, felt the usual surge of irritation at her supposed intrusion - they'd already argued more than once over what William termed 'non-deliberate meddling in his life' - but, on this occasion, he experienced an electric jolt too at the word '*she*'. Women never rang him.

'Hello.' He gave it the usual, non-committal grunt.

'Grüss Gott, Wilhelm.' In contrast to his own rough greeting, this lone voice down the line sang out with the high-pitched clarity of one of those blackbirds that sang each evening by his window, or maybe a solitary flute piping in the hushed heart of an orchestra. It lifted his spirits. He even thought at first it was Frau Spindler, and not her daughter. She'd always been the only one who'd ever insisted on calling him 'Wilhelm'.

'Hello?' William had softened the tone of his voice.

'Es ist Ingrid, William.'

In-grid, In-grid. The blackbird's song had, this time, the precision of a metronome. Ingrid was never less than precise in her speech.

'Ingrid! Wo bist du?' All he could think of was to ask where she was.

'I'm in…there was a pause followed by a short nervous giggle… Muswell Hill.' (About five short miles from where William was standing).

'Muswell Hill?'

'Yes. It is a suburb of London.'

'I know where it is, Ingrid. It's just a short drive from W.... What are you doing here?'

'I decided to come to England in my last months to improve my English. More useful, don't you think, than attending literature lectures in a stuffy hall, and eating stodgy lunches in the Mensa?' She hesitated a moment. 'There's somebody I know in England , you see, who can help me with my English.' One of the attributes William had always admired about Ingrid's linguistic skills was her ability to impart into her speech that English obsession with irony (probably part copied from Mack, he thought, with a slight surge of jealousy) But before he could reply "*D'you mean me?*", she added, with a certain note of concern in her voice, 'You *are* glad to hear from me, aren't you?'

He was more than glad. The long, dreary days until September had, in a single moment, concertinaed, and what small, insignificant plans that were already in place might easily be put on hold. 'Of course I am, Ingrid. But where are you staying? Are you travelling? Are you on your own?'

'I'm an *Au Pair*. In a pretty place called Elstree. What a funny name.' She laughed down the phone.

Within William's brief, rather sad experience of love affairs, there had never been any awareness of the desperate actions a lover can be driven to when separated too long from the object of their desire; that Ingrid, in this instance, might be ready to jump on a ship or a plane, to be in close, physical proximity to the one she pined for, was really quite beyond his scope of understanding. He could quite easily live within himself and allow lonely, nagging desires to slip by, unrequited. He was even naïve enough to believe only *he* could pine, not her. He still had much to learn.

She said, 'Shall we meet? Maybe….'

And at that point, prompted by instinct alone, he interrupted her. 'I'll come and see *you*, Ingrid. Give me your address.'

He left in a rush, calling to his mother that he was just going out for a bit, and he didn't return that night. Tessa wasn't unduly worried, given her son's current bouts of complete scattiness, but assumed his departure had something to do with the earlier phone-call.

He didn't take the car; he found his way to Elstree by bus and on foot. Although it was a place of his youth, as familiar as eating, he couldn't now recall exactly how to get there. He remembered he'd gone cycling once one summer through that leafy North London sprawl of grandiose houses, burgeoning oaks and elms, and greenery, but it was only a distant memory. He got off the bus too early and, feeling as strong and uplifted as he'd ever felt before in his life, walked the one or two miles to the address she'd given him, a large house, set tastefully in a row of others, a unique rural idyll unchanged since war-time.

No one was there except Ingrid. She had, apparently, the large house to herself most days and most of the day. She was looking after two young children, collected them from school, fed them, did the washing-up, kept the house clean, all just a minor intrusion really on someone with as meticulous and efficient a temperament as hers. Her hosts were medics, he a doctor, she a nurse, and for long periods Ingrid occupied this roomy house by herself. What more ideal way could she have devised to see both England and him? A stone's throw from William's own home at W…(an address he'd already given her before he left Hamburg). William could see she'd fallen on her feet (or rather, he wondered, simply looked at a map of London and seen how close Elstree lay to W….). How clever of her.

Her bedroom was large, like the house itself, and tidy, like Ingrid, the main piece of furniture a particularly sturdy, unmade double bed. But even that looked tidy, in its unmade state, and was probably still warm, he fantasized, as if its occupant had stepped from it just a few moments previously,, leaving traces of herself behind.

Is this a fairy tale, he wondered? She closed the door quietly and, like two ardent lovers from another lifetime, they kissed hard, feeling desire creep into every corner of their veins.

Ingrid finally pulled away, breathless, 'We must *do* something today, William. Please. We need to go somewhere.'

'Good idea,' he said, not thinking it was a good idea at all. He had other ideas, and glanced around the bedroom. 'You've fallen on your feet, Ingrid.' He watched her look deliberately down at her feet. 'No, it's an expression, Ingrid. Another of those annoying English sayings.'

'I don't think I'll ever understand this language.'

'You've only just got here. Give it time.' He kissed her again, unable to resist the already familiar scent of her

This time, she pushed him away with Teutonic determination. 'Please stop kissing me. We can do that later. We have the house to ourselves. We mustn't waste the day.'

'Is it really wasting it?'

'William, *Liebchen*, I'm desperate to see you and I'm also desperate to see England. We can pass the day together, *nicht* (can't we?)?' she added quietly, 'And the night.'

Only half believing their good luck, William said, 'Where are your hosts?'

'They're away. On holiday. Spring school holidays. I'm looking after the house.'

For one moment longer, William hesitated, torn between two separate delights, and then came to a decision. 'Okay. I'm going to show you London. Do you know London? Is this the first time?'

Her eyes had lit up. 'Of course it is. How would I know London? I never had an English boy-friend to show me around, did I?' She paused for a moment, searching for an expression. Then said, 'An English boy-friend on tap.' Looking delightedly at William, she added 'That is right, isn't it? *On tap*?'

'It's more than right, Ingrid. It's brilliant. You must have learnt the expression from me. So, I'm 'on tap', am I?'

'Yes, you turn the tap on and out you flow.'

'How convenient. Luckily I must say my feelings are certainly flowing today; like running water. I feel fluid.'

'Then we merge. How do you say?' ... She looked at him enquiringly... 'two streams flowing into each other....'

Caught off balance, William this time sought hurriedly for the word, and happily found it. 'A confluence, you mean...Like the *Rhein* and *Mosel*. A confluence.'

'Ja.' she was nodding eagerly. '*Das deutsche Eck bei Koblenz. Ein Zusammenfluss.*' (The German Corner at Koblenz).She looked up at him again. 'We are a 'confluence', William.'

'I think you're more like a mountain spring than a great river though, Ingrid.'

She gave a silvery laugh and said, 'Why a mountain spring? I think I prefer a river.'

'Your laugh is like a mountain spring. I've always thought so.'

She laughed.. 'How funny; I've never been called a *Quelle* before.'

'*Eine kleine Felsenquelle.*(A little mountain spring),' he said.

'You're too romantic, William. I think this mountain spring wants to get going. We're wasting precious time.'

She was bending down now, putting on her shoes and looking up at him anxiously, as if her haste might be taken for indifference. 'Let's go out today, and then we can come back to this hotel in the evening. I've booked a very expensive room.'

William, ever able to delve into metaphors, said, 'Yes. Five star, I hope.' He had no doubt as to her intentions.

They left the house hand in hand.

(At Possum Kingdom.)   ENTRY FROM ADAM'S DIARY
REFLECTIONS and **CONFESSIONS,** from the pen of 'Sol' the Solitary.

London – the 'Garret' (Lovers, beware!)

I think I must be over-sexed. There's a nasty streak of frustrated aggression in my DNA somewhere, a design fault; and it will be my downfall. I sometimes wonder, for instance, if that afternoon back in Canada, when Mary and I went to the deserted old spa in the woods and 'messed about', whether that marked the moment the rift between us opened irrevocably. We hadn't, you see, been honest with each other. Right from the very start of that short visit of hers with her parents to the Grand Canyon, we'd improvised our relationship, just like beginners do, setting down no markers, exploring our physical relationship as we went along. My fault, I admit, as much as hers. But women don't know what kind of mist comes over a man when he's really going for it. Even markers are overstepped to reach the cherished goal. And, don't forget, I'm no normal man, I'm over-sexed, remember?

Yes, that whole communication failure, on both parts, turned out to be a calamity. Lovers walk upon a knife edge. We should have laid our cards on the table, from the start, in Arizona. *No sex, Adam, until you ask me to marry you.* That's what she wanted, and that's what she didn't say. So, from the beginning, I stopped trusting her. And she stopped trusting me. I *still* don't trust her. I've never trusted her since that moment.

And I *still* didn't trust her when I set off from London for East Anglia that weekend, to visit Lily and Luke, in response to their unexpected invitation. Was Mary still playing a devious game?

I got there late Friday night, very late and tired after a long drive. Lily was proud to show me her house. It was a country estate, large swathes of domesticated agricultural land adjoining. I think Luke, scion of landed gentry, had inherited this plot of land from William the Conqueror. The rooms were vast, with low ceilings and dark corridors leading to the bed-rooms. People were smaller in 1066. They'd modernised it all of course; put in new, smart units, and a log-fire glowed in the fireplace when I arrived. We drank red wine and listened to a few of the latest stage musical hits, all the rage back then.

'Harper Sage wrote the lyrics,' said Lily.

I was surprised because I half knew Harper Sage from way back in Mary's BOAC days, but my time, I suppose, on the Island had left me out of touch. I'm sure Sage had fancied Mary; I'd met him at parties in her flat. Now he'd become a superstar.

Lily handed me the album cover so I could follow the lyrics. 'He comes down here occasionally,' she said with a casual sense of propriety, as if she owned him. 'Usually brings a 'bird' in tow. Different one each time. You can't believe how randy Harper is. He's amazingly randy!' Luke agreed, nodding his head up and down.

'These artists!' I exclaimed, wondering idly if Sage was over-sexed too, like me. The topic bored me anyway. Why did I care about some friend of theirs I'd never really met?

We listened for a while to the music. 'I think the music's fantastic,' I said after a while. 'The lyrics are nothing special though. It's lucky he teemed up with a good musician.'

Lily and Luke cast disconcerted glances at each other as I carefully disparaged Sage's talents, and the conversation lapsed. Luke turned the record-player off.

I said, just off the cuff, 'Lily, by the way, do you remember Uncle Eric?'

'Of course I do,' exclaimed Lily.

'Is he still alive?'

'I don't know. I expect so. Why should you bring Eric up?'

'D'you know, I think he fancied your mother, Lily. I think he'd had an affair with her for years, behind your father's back. It's just a hunch.' I was really going out on a limb with these comments, getting carried away, trying to put both of them down a bit. Luke just sat there with an embarrassed smile on his lips.

'What on earth do you mean, Adam?' said Lily. 'How could you possibly know that?' She didn't seem too upset though. The wine and the log-fire had mellowed us all, and I suspect she'd never been too fond of her parents or Eric anyway.

'I just know,' I said. 'I can't stand *old* people who reminisce about the days of their youth. There's something essentially repulsive about it.'

Lily shrugged. 'Well you may be right. It's unlikely I shall see Uncle Eric for a long time. And it's late. Let's go to bed. I hope you've got everything you need.'

Luke got up. 'I'm pooped. I'm off to bed. We'll see you tomorrow, Adam.'

He left me and Lily in the kitchen, where she was preparing things before going up. I think Lily - feminine instinct - had already understood my actual state of mind, my bold front, my long-term despair. And she was ready to make allowances for it. It says a lot for her. I expect she was comparing my off-hand behaviour and my dismissive remarks to those happier days years ago, when we hurled our way through Kentucky without a care in the world. Where had it all gone?

Getting ready to head up the rickety spiral staircase to the bedrooms, she smiled at me. 'I hope, Old Stick, you've got *almost* everything you need.' She looked me straight in the eyes, and I knew what she really meant. 'And I wish I could give you *that* too. But you can't love two people at the same time.' She came up close and kissed me on the cheek and gently pressed my arm. 'It's wonderful to see you after all this time.'

Next morning was windy, and Luke was already out chopping logs with an enormous axe. In the afternoon we all went for a walk in the Fens. We made small-talk as we picked our way through the tall reeds. Then later, when we were in the garden at the back of the house, having tea, and Lily was inspecting some of the flower beds, she casually raised the subject of her sister. I wondered whether the entire weekend had been engineered for this moment.

'Mary's very happy,' she said. 'They've got a lot in common. They do an awful lot together. Mary's an active person, you know, and so is Alan.' I stood by the flower bed, just listening. She continued, 'Mary went through a very bad patch, you know, soon after you two split up. The Ps were very worried. We all were.'

'Good,' I said, and then again, 'Good!'

From that moment, the die was cast. I simply didn't care anymore. I was angry at the very thought of Mary. Lily and Luke exchanged dismayed glances, and then Lily said nonchalantly, as if it were the last thing on her mind, 'Would you like to see Mary? She'd love to see you.'

'No,' I said.

The speed of my response amazed me. Almost took my breath away. Were they going to roll Mary in, at that moment, from the wings? I wasn't sure how far this whole thing had been engineered.

Lily flushed slightly. 'She's not far from here. It wouldn't be any trouble.'

I was reminded of one of those Shakespeare comedies where the person in question is hiding behind some large Pickett hedge, listening to all the slander about her.

Late on Sunday night, I left. 'Where's your little daughter?' I asked Lily.

'She's staying the weekend with a friend.'

'I'd love to have seen her.'

She looked hard at me. 'It's a dreadful responsibility having children, you know. A terrible responsibility. It changes you.'

'Is it?' I said.

'A far cry from those carefree Texan days.'

'Thanks for having me, Lily. It's been a great weekend.'

'No, it's been *you* that made the weekend. Come again.'

'I will,' I said. But I knew I wouldn't.

It was very late when I arrived back. London was almost quiet. The cars in Baker Street were just a muffled hum at that time of night. A strange thing happened though, something that had never happened to me before, something I would never have thought possible. Maybe it was the whole weekend at Lily's, and my callous behaviour. Perhaps, even, it was that dream I'd had, about my mother, because I realised the dream could have been for real. Maybe it was just the overall emotional content, and because things were starting to open up for me; I was starting to see a crack of light through the darkness. So, as I chucked my coat on the bed, the floodgates opened. I started to cry. I cried on and on, in great gushing sobs, uncontrollably, like surf breaking on top of you, loud enough to waken the entire neighbourhood, until I thought there'd be no stopping it. Mourning is a strange thing, and loss, and loneliness, and you bear them for just so long, penned up inside you, until the dam breaks. When it was all over and I'd cried my fill, I never thought about any of it again. It was a purging.

CHAPTER 18

"In which William sets his dreams on hold and plays the tourist guide."

'It's London Transport today, Madam,' he said to her as they locked up and wandered down towards Elstree station.

'Why do you call me Madam?'

'Well I'm to be your paid guide today, isn't that right?'

She nodded eagerly. ' I don't know; how much will it cost?'

'Whatever you want to pay. *Trinkgeld nicht inbegriffen.* (Tip not included). Okay, follow me. We have to take public transport today.' She looked at him enquiringly and he said, 'Too many cars. Nowhere to park. And exhausting.'

'I don't want to exhaust you, William. It was my idea.'

Strangely, William had grown unused to anyone showing concern for him and his comforts, even in the tiniest of details. Although he knew his mother loved him, at W... he felt himself sometimes just a part of the furniture. Ingrid's unexpected concern flattered him in some way. He wondered whether he reciprocated. Did he make it his business to consider *her* and her well- being. He concluded probably not, and slipped his hand into hers as they set off.

That day, they hardly drew breath They visited Westminster Abbey and St. Paul's as first priorities, going deeper into the heart of the City.

'I feel compelled to show you these sights,' remarked William, 'even though I'm not sure you're interested in seeing them.'

They were standing in front of that giant religious monolith, St Paul's Cathedral.

'I think I am; I've seen only pictures of this building in posters and class-books since grade 1. Is there anything my guide needs to tell me about this lovely building?'

William shook his head. 'Designed by Sir Christopher Wren, and burnt down in the great fire of London. Don't ask me dates.'

Ingrid gave him a skeptical look. 'That information earns you only half of your *Trinkgeld*.'

Inside the building, Ingrid pursued him obediently around like a friendly shadow, murmuring from time to time under her breath.

'What were you murmuring to yourself about in there, Ingrid?' he asked her, as they emerged into the sunlight.

'Nothing really.' She smiled with embarrassment. 'It's always churches in London. So many churches. Big ones and small ones. England must have been very religious.'

'Once, perhaps, maybe.' replied William, unable to resist deflating her enthusiasm 'Come on, I'll show you what's *not* a church. The opposite, in fact.'.

'Sounds exciting.'

They took a launch to Traitor's Gate, and as they strolled up towards the solemn building ahead, William embarked upon a whole historical catalogue of treachery, treason, cruelty, brutality and injustice, encompassing all he could remember about the tales of the '*Tower*': the Two Princes, the Wars of the Roses, Henry the Eighth, and Anne Boleyn.. She fell silent as they wandered among the ancient slabs until he suggested they visit the 'Crown Jewels' section, by way of contrast, to cheer her up perhaps with something glittery.

Ingrid wasn't really interested. 'Whose jewels *are* these?' she asked, as they stood looking at an impossible array of priceless precious-stones, which clearly seemed to her little more than a meaningless display of dubious worth.

'I don't know,' William replied lamely. 'Currently they're the Crown's. That's to say, the Queen's.'

After several silent seconds, she looked at him briskly. 'I'm not interested in jewels, William. Tell me some more stories about your English history. I love them.'

She fell silent again, as he led her up to Tower Hill, place of Execution. He said, 'Anne Boleyn was beheaded here, right where you're standing. She went to the scaffold bravely, they say. Apparently she had a wig on.'

'Why?'

'Well, the executioner holds up the decapitated head for the crowd to enjoy.'

'How horrible!'

'However, on this occasion, so the story goes, the head slipped from his grasp because of the wig, and he was left holding a bunch of hair, much to the horror of the crowd.'

Ingrid just gasped, and William continued, 'Yes, rumor has it, it was Anne's way of having the final word, you see.' Ingrid didn't reply immediately, and he added, 'Defiant to the last. She was a brave woman.'

Ingrid whispered, 'I can't believe they were so brutal. And she was his wife too.'

'Yes. Look, put it in perspective: Anne was a flirt, promiscuous, bit of a bitch. But that was her nature. Only fools would condemn her for that.' As Ingrid waited, looking at him intensely, he remembered something he'd once heard or read about Anne and her final hours. 'Somebody else apparently thinks the same as you and me.' He paused. 'Can you believe, every year a tulip, a single tulip, arrives at the Tower from an unknown donor, addressed to Anne Boleyn?'

Ingrid shook her head in disbelief. 'Who sends it?'

'I don't know. But the benefactor must be a free spirit, someone who appreciated Anne and her bravery and defiance.'

She smiled. 'That's a nicer story than the wig, William. I feel for her, you know.'

'Yes, and you should. Perhaps she's relevant to today somehow.'

'What do you mean?

William took a moment or two to reply. 'Well, look, some modern history writers claim Anne was the first emancipated woman, the original Suffragette.' William watched Ingrid's eyes narrow in incomprehension (a gesture she often made when she didn't understand). He explained. 'Suffragettes chained themselves to lampposts a hundred years ago, demanding women's right to vote.' Ingrid nodded, but didn't reply immediately. He added, 'Anne, with her wig, was claiming the right to be equal, Ingrid. Like you and me, but especially *you*.' He paused and said, 'To sleep with who she liked, for example. Perhaps she started the trend. That whole movement. All the freedoms we take for granted nowadays.'

Ingrid laughed. 'Is that *your* belief or is it general?'

'That last bit's my own humble opinion, I'm afraid.'

She laughed again. 'I'm really glad to hear it. Yes, Anne must have made a start to all that.' She slipped her hand in his. 'And, do you know, in my humble opinion, you're one of the "*Drei Weise*".'

'*The Drei Weise*, who are they?'

'Is there really something you don't know then?'

He sensed the sarcasm. 'Yes, I don't know who the "*Drei Weise*" are. I know there are three of them though.

She laughed. 'In the bible, *Die Drei Könige*. The three Kings.'

He thought hard for a moment, 'Ah, you mean 'The Three Wise Men'.'

'Yes, is that what you call them? How funny.'

'I don't see what's funny. And yes, I'm certainly one of them.'

Ingrid ignored his initial remark. 'But why isn't it the "Three Wise *Women*?" Anne Boleyn would have liked that.'

'You're right, and I agree. But they came a bit before her time unfortunately.'

'Poor Anne!'

She was still laughing when William asked, 'Are you hungry?'

'Another of your good ideas, William, my wise man.'

'You're not going to let me forget that, are you? Well, there're no cafes inside the castle. Let's leave these gloomy stones and find somewhere to have lunch.'

She slipped her hand into his and they walked down the hill towards the waiting boat. As they climbed in, they both turned, to take a final wide sweep of the gloomy tower. Ingrid said, 'The English history, it is all so bloody and violent. I suppose there's a story to tell about the river here too.'

'A million stories. That's for *after* lunch. But isn't German history equally violent?'

'Yes, but the English, they seem to enjoy the violence. There's an anecdote for every event.'

'Perhaps English medieval history is better documented.'

'The horror bits certainly.' She feigned a shudder. 'Please take me now to somewhere the opposite.' For a second she paused and then added with determination, 'Somewhere beautiful.'

'A football match?'

'If you like, William. But maybe some other day for that, I think. You know London so well. I leave myself in your hands. Cheer me up. Make me feel the sun's shining again. Like this morning.'

The sun momentarily had slipped behind the clouds. He said, 'I'm sorry, Ingrid. I didn't think. But you're very demanding.'

She replied quickly. 'Yes, it's just me. I'm being stupid. You'll have to forgive me. Of course I like to see the monuments, but they have such a sad effect on me.' She paused for a second and came to a decision. 'The morning then was for monuments, now make me feel alive and happy.'

He was taken aback by this sudden mood-swing which seemed to have overcome her, and from mere stories and buildings. He'd not encountered it in her before. He thought hurriedly. 'Ah, I've got it. Follow me.' As he said it, her eyes lit up. It was like when one turns on a light in a dark room. He pronounced firmly, 'Let's cast off the shadows. Our destination is Beauty, pure, unadulterated Beauty. Follow me.'

They took the Underground and headed west, across London and away from the traces of its murky, medieval past. At Richmond they alighted, and as they emerged into the sun-shine, Ingrid exclaimed, 'Where *is* this?'

'We're not there yet.'

She looked around at the tall trees, the well-to-do houses, the wide pavements, the green spaces, everywhere the subtle hints of the countryside. 'But this is just like Muswell Hill.'

'Good. Just like home then, Ingrid.'

She smiled. 'But *your* home or mine?'

'Both. I remember parts of Hamburg like this. The *Elbchaussee*? *Dammtor*?'

She glanced about for a moment. 'You're very observant, William. You even remember the names. Yes, It *is* a bit like Germany. Orderly, I think you say.'

'That's the Saxon in us. We share the same preferences. Nice , isn't it? That's why you like Richmond. It's in our blood, you know.'

'Locate Richmond for me, William. I've no idea where we are in relation to....'

He interrupted.. 'Richmond upon Thames. West London. Cozy suburb.'

She let out an almost childish cry. 'The same river as at the Tower?'

'The very same. London's only got one river.'

'Where *is* it then,? I can't see it. I'd like to go there.'

'We'll go for a boat ride. That's the master plan.'

She laughed and slipped her arm in his. 'You're a *master* guide!'

He thought for a second. '*Wilhelm Meister*', yes.'

She laughed. *Das ist wirklich zu viel.* (That's really too much).'

'You know. The *Goethe* novels.'

She thought a moment. 'Of course I know. Every Schüler (school kid) knows that. So, you're the hero in a Goethe novel now.'

'Ingrid', he exclaimed. 'I wasn't trying to.... '

She didn't let him finish. '*Lass das!*' I was only joking.'

All earlier traces of that melancholy had completely disappeared. He couldn't help wondering if there was some truth in the popular idea the Germans are always serious. It seemed to him she was so easily up and down. Like a little child. It was so easy how she came and went, William thought. One moment down and one moment up. Like a child almost. The fanciful tale of a beautiful queen beheaded five hundred years ago? Such historical whimsy was the stuff of fairy stories. and yet Ingrid took it so personally, Could it be that these sudden swift flights, mood-changes, were embedded in the German psyche? Those brooding forests peopled by witches and dark spirits, a land of ponderous hills and mountains, locked forever from the liberating expanses of the ocean? There was a melancholy streak in her, which wouldn't change. He remembered how, in the Mensa, she could sometimes sit for hours saying nothing, a somber expression on her face. However, to be fair, perhaps young women in general were prone to the sensitivity he was noticing in Ingrid.

She drew him from his indulgent reverie; he had a mission to fulfill that day. 'Where are we going now, William?'

'Somewhere to cheer you up. I hope you like it. You asked for Beauty, remember? Well, this is pure, beauty. Unadulterated.'

'Don't use words you know I won't understand. But William, are you certain that exists? We mortals can only take limited amounts of such things..'

'It's gentle, don't worry.. The designer's purpose was simplicity. You'll enjoy it.'

'I can't wait.'

He looked at his watch. 'Then let's go now.. Plenty of time for a boat ride later. Don't worry. You'll survive.'

'I'm not worrying; you're my guide; I trust you. I'm cheering up, remember?'

'And we'll include a cream tea afterwards. For your further pleasure.'

'Cream tea?' She looked at him for a moment, puzzled.

William said, '*Kaffee und Kuchen*'.

'Ah.! coffee and cakes.'

'That's right. But English style.'

'Cream tea. Is that *really* what you call it?'

'Well, it's not quite the same admittedly. Scones instead of cake, and tea instead of coffee. And please don't ask me to describe 'scones'.'

'They're buns, I think.' As she walked, she repeated three or four times in succession, 'Cream tea, cream tea, cream tea…' and William said, 'What are you doing, Ingrid?'

She looked up hurriedly, almost embarrassed. 'If I repeat the word, you see, often enough I don't forget it. I've never heard 'cream tea' before. It's a new expression.'

When William, in Hamburg, had encountered this beautiful, stately female in the Mensa for the first few times, he'd wondered, almost with awe, just how aloof, how unobtainable, a woman could make herself. Now, as she described so naively her simple way of remembering words, methods that had probably served her as a teenager, the womanly veneer just fell away, and he found himself looking almost at a child, all inhibitions laid quite bare. He could only hope and suppose the transformation derived from her present happiness, and their growing intimacy. Was *he* though, he wondered, so ready to lay himself bare? Perhaps, but he doubted it. He still clung firmly to his cozy preconceptions.

They were waiting now beside the wide, busy road. She said, 'Don't you have to cross by the little green man?'

'I can't see one. There isn't one. Let's cross.'

They hurried over and she stood holding William's arm and glancing apprehensively over her shoulder. 'In Germany they would give you a penalty.'

'A *fine*, you mean, Ingrid.'

She was bewildered again, before exclaiming, 'Ah, a fine! *Strafgeld*. I should know the expression. I'm so forgetful.' Standing precariously on the curb, she intoned, 'a fine...a fine...a fine... a fine....'

And William, alarmed for her safety, shouted, 'Mind out; the cars. Be careful.'

'I'm concentrating.'

He steered her gently back onto the curb, towards him and away from the rushing traffic. '*I* know,' he said, 'but the cars don't. You've gotta take care in this traffic, or it *won't* be 'fine'.'

'William, I'm not after all a child!'

'You sometimes behave like one, Ingrid.'

'Do I?'

He wondered if he'd gone too far, offended her. He took refuge in a pun. 'I'll take care of you. You'll be fine if you don't get a *fine*.'

She laughed. 'Thank you, William. You know you make a joke of everything.'

'Life's full of jokes. The English language lends itself to jokes.'

'Yes, it's so typically English.' A shadow flitted across her face. 'We Germans are more serious. We don't laugh anymore.'

'Don't worry. You're just more formal; that's all. It's your Germanic manner.'

She smiled and slipped her hand in his. 'We're getting too serious right now. When are we going to see this 'Beauty' you told me about? I'm starting to think it's not there.'

'It's everywhere, Ingrid.'

They walked silently alongside the smart black side-railings that seemed to grow higher and more impenetrable with every step they took.

'We're nearly there,' William said, struggling to remember when he'd last come to this place (ten years? twenty years?), and whether it had actually changed, and there'd be nothing to show her. 'They certainly try to keep you out with these railings. Don't worry though; Beauty lies within, I promise you.'

'Is it a fashion parade we're going to?'

'I hope not. Why that?'

'It all looks so formal. Fashion shows are formal, aren't they?' As well as beautiful?

'I don't know if a fashion show is beautiful. I've never been to one, The *girls* are though.'

'*Where* are the 'girls'? She turned round to look. She'd clearly not understood. He knew that look well by now.

'The *models*, Ingrid.' He was laughing and looking deliberately hard at her. 'Yes. I can just see you on the catwalk.'

Now she was genuinely confused. 'Catwalk? 'What means catwalk?'

William didn't know the German. 'Where the girls show off their dresses, Ingrid. You know.'

'I *don't* know. Ah, this *English*!' She struggled for a moment to conceal her frustration. 'What is the German, William. You're my guide; *you* should know!'

'Forgive me; I don't.'

'Then I must sack you.' She walked on in front of him, hurrying her pace, and a moment passed. Suddenly turning to look at him, she exclaimed triumphantly, 'I have it now! '*Laufsteg*'.'

William caught up with her, repeating *Laufsteg…Laufsteg….*', and imitating her perfect accent as best he could, while she looked on, astonished. 'It's a new word, Ingrid. You must commit it to memory.'

'*Nein*, Wilhelm!' She laughed. But he was already now striding ahead of her, proclaiming '*Laufsteg…Laufsteg…Laufsteg….*

'You're making fun of me. Wait for me. What are you doing, William?'

'I'm doing it the way you showed me, remember? It's very good.'
He glanced up. 'But come on! I think we've arrived'
The regal gates of Kew Gardens loomed into view....

(At Possum Kingdom.)   ENTRY FROM ADAM'S DIARY
REFLECTIONS and **CONFESSIONS,** from the pen of 'Sol' the Solitary.

London – the 'Garret' (Lovers, beware!)

'Women.' My ambivalent, often biased, subject for today: Women in general, pretty women, not so pretty, and including even the tawdry types, with whom I have recently been impelled to cavort with here in London, shamefully to *'use',* in order to gratify my most basic sexual needs and keep me sane. I wonder sometimes if it's society that drives me (and those like me) through the kind of humiliating experiences I've had to endure over these last few months in the company of sluts and witches, who are only too ready to feed off my solitude, inveigle me to share their own crude existence.

There's a limit to how long one can wallow in the bottom of a barrel. Happily though, I sense the mist is clearing. I catch now and then a glimpse of a light at the end of the tunnel. I'm clambering laboriously upwards in the tortuous world of courtship, towards a new level of womankind. Tier 2. (or, as Dante describes it) Second Circle. In that place reside women from 'nice' homes, with nice educations, nice manners, nice expectations, and who won't put up with anything less than nice treatment from their men-folk

Yes, I've had to take a long, hard look at myself now, and attempt to expel all memories and traces of the forlorn floosies I've been dragging with me through the Pit these past few years. I'm in need of nothing less than a sexual exorcism.

Thus, I've had recourse to a shrink, a DIY therapist, a practitioner in the science of Psychiatry, to release me from the world of vice that I've been slave to, and to restore the spiritual harmony I once enjoyed..

My first and only session turned out to be turbulent, disturbing, not worth the money, (as I suppose these matters often are), and ultimately abortive, for all the good it did me ....

'Doctor' (I begin with 'Doctor' - without a name next to it - to sound more respectful), 'I have to confess from the start, there resides deep inside me a violent streak. a dormant tendency towards violence.'

Following my opening statement, I watch the man shift nervously in his chair, eye the distance between himself and the Exit, and the geometric angle between me, him, and the door. I take little real notice though. 'Yes, Doctor, each time I think of the Desired One, a half of me gets sad, the other half angry. I think I must be a Psycho.'

This doctor of mine, has an office nearby, in Marylebone, and was recommended to me by a friend undergoing a similar crisis; my condition's not uncommon, you see. We sit now in silence for a moment, and I sneak a covert glance at this expert in Psychotic Neuroses. He's lanky, wiry, rather bony in fact, and sports just a modicum of hair round the fringes of his head. I gain, on first appearance, the impression the sole experience of a pretty woman he could ever have had in the course of his pitiful life would be the back of her, hurrying away. We all know the type. Not altogether *my* type, I must admit.

At last he breaks the silence. 'Who is this 'desired one'?'

'Top Beauty Queen, Doctor, winner of more than one of those unfortunate sexist competitions that still haunt society and seek to undermine women's legitimate place in it.' (I lie, of course, partly to impress him with my social maturity, but also to prepare him for the force of my own dramatic predicament; after all, one pretty woman's the same as the next, so why must he have precise details of my current nemesis?). 'She gave me the push, Doctor, with little warning nor explanation. Simply removed herself physically from my life. Walked out and left me high and dry.'

The cards are now on the table. No need for further explanation. This middle-aged starveling in front of me, whose knowledge and experience of women and their foibles can surely be no larger than what you can put into a nutshell, now feigns an expression of concern and offers a lame smile. 'You've come to the right place. You can't, of course, keep things like this bottled up, young man. It's not healthy.'

I have to admit, I'm momentarily impressed by his reply. It's professional, succinct He called me 'young man' too, as if to widen that important gap between doctor and patient. It doesn't do to get too informal.

There follows now one of those periods of sustained silence one hears about in similar psychiatric sessions, moments perhaps of quiet reflection, as in a church at the call for prayer. After a minute or two I grow anxious though; should I say more? should I elaborate upon my condition, give examples? We're two boxers at the weigh-in, I assume, locked in a silent challenge, eyeball to eyeball, to see who'll be the first to lower his eyes, break the stony stare.

'It's me. I can't resist blurting out, 'There's one thing, Doctor, you and I have to understand: This girl I mention has removed herself from my life. Have you any idea what that means: to be pushed over by one of the world's top Beauties? Awful, and it's all very well talking about 'bottled up'. It's worse, I can tell you. She's neutered me, handed me a life sentence, a more than significant dose of hyper-introspection. Bottom line, Doctor: I'm starting to *'fail'*, yes, fail with girls, (this last confession, I utter together with a sort of animal cry of pain).

'How do you mean, 'fail'?'

'Fail. You know, not succeed.'

He nods calmly. 'Impotence, I suppose. It's no crime, young man.'

'It is to *them*.'

He eyeballs me again. 'Now there's one thing I want to make clear: I get a lot of patients in here like you. Think they're going impotent. It's a phase and usually accompanied by a bad acne rash. Do you have an acne rash, by the way?'

'As a matter of fact I do.'

'As I thought. You've got to step back a moment, relax a bit; think more about relationships, less about sexual gratification.'

I was really getting anxious now. Was this bloke any good at all? Was I wasting my money? I tried again. 'I don't seem to want to have a relationship, Doctor. Relationships I go out of my way to avoid. Anything serious, that's the past with me. It's sexual gratification I'm seeking; pure and simple.'

This confession has clearly caught him on the back foot; he's not been expecting such blunt honesty. I drive home my initiative. 'You just can't imagine the kind of trash I've been going out with, simply to avoid a relationship.'

He jots something calmly down on a note-pad and says, 'Uh huh. I see. Self-destructive syndrome.'.

I realise it's time to throw the '*Dwarf*' at him. Jog him from his complacency. 'I tried ringing the 'Dwarf 'again this weekend, Doctor.'

'Dwarf?'

'You remember; the midget Israeli with the tapering hips and massive bosom.'

He nods. Pretends to remember. (He can't remember because I've never mentioned her before). 'I felt the urge to call her.'

'And you feel guilty?'

'Darn right I feel guilty.'

He scribbles again on the pad. 'You definitely need to strike up a more healthy relationship.'

'Doctor, there's a blockage in me somewhere. Against healthy relationships. I can promise you, she can't have been more than 3ft 10 in her stocking feet. It was really bizarre.'

He cluck-clucked, and was shaking his head, as if in condolence. I shouted, 'No, Doc, you're mistaking me. You've got the wrong end of the stick. I was actually *enjoying* it!' (I tut-tutted at him in retaliation, and shook my head from side to side).

A moment's silence, and he said, '*And*, young man?'

'*And* she dropped me, Doctor.'

'*She* dropped *you*?'

'Correct. Believe me, this goes a lot deeper than you evidently suppose. Would I be in this room otherwise?'

He scribbles something on his pad and says, 'A circus dwarf, young man. Has it really come to this? This has gone up a whole new level. You're degrading yourself.'

I played one of my trump cards. 'Listen, Doctor, do you mind if I see your qualifications? It's precisely degradation I seek. That's my problem. That's why I'm here at all.' I allow time for that to sink in, and top it with, 'Don't you know some of the world's greatest artists have been able to find sexual and emotional gratification only in the arms of tramps, sluts, whores and deviates of every nature? Haven't you read your Freud?'

'And *you're* an artist, are you?' he whips back. There's a sardonic grin starting to form on his wafer-thin lips. It's a trap really, one I can't help falling into though. 'Loosely speaking, yes. let's just say I have an artist's temperament; it's subliminal.'

There follows now a more than usual lengthy pause. He's up to his tricks again; possibly figuring out how a 'temperament' can be 'subliminal'. I'm not going to be sucked in though. I know I'm about to give him the Full Monty. 'Right, Doctor, if you really want me to do the talking, then here goes, here's my catalogue of degradation: First, to set the record right, I really *am* a writer. Whether you like it or not. Secondly, don't be surprised about the 'Dwarf'. Even if you don't know it, writing's a powerful aphrodisiac; it stimulates the hormones; it makes you want to have sex. So that's why I phone up the Dwarf. It's a fantasy trip I'm after, you see, with the Dwarf. I don't feel the need to say anything, write anything, just score, silently, and hate myself. If she's not available, I watch TV. Hours of TV. Another form of escapism. My favourite's 'Alias Smith and Jones. Do you know 'Alias Smith and Jo…'?'

He interrupts. 'Your firm? Can't say I've heard of them.' (This charlatan's still awake then).

'No, the cowboy show on TV. One of the highlights of my day. Of my week. They're so direct, so… so unchallenging, so…' I struggle for the appropriate word, '…so unreal.'

'Can't say I watch cowboy films much.'

This is a complete diversion. He's not offering anything. I'm getting that uneasy feeling I'm wasting my time and money. Only one thing left. Shock treatment again. 'Doctor, let me exemplify: If the Dwarf's out, then there's always the New Zealander.'

'New Zealander?'

'Mealy-mouthed she is, and so ugly! These days she's taken to leaving me sort of continually on the simmer. That's exciting too. But the real thing about her is she doesn't believe in undressing. We make it standing up, by the mantelpiece, in the dark, or on the couch, in a hurry, before someone interrupts us. Yes, always fully clothed (except of course for the bare necessities). I think this undressing business has to do with her Puritan upbringing. They're quite puritanical, these Anzacs. Every time I see her, I swear it'll be the last time, and then on the spur of the moment, I suddenly want to ring her; she always refuses to meet me; I persuade her and so on and so on, until she's dragging her feet all the way back to the mantelpiece. We're just playing on each other's weaknesses, enjoying the thrill of degrading each other.'

'But you're a good-looking young man. You could at least seek out someone more physically suited.'

It's quite a fair observation really, but I'm not going to be stopped. I'm in full flow. '*Physically*, Doctor? I don't want to be screwing the female version of Tarzan! It's the weakness factor, Doctor. You're not getting it. We enjoy being *imperfect*!' (I just know I'm going to have to run off the whole string before this quack finally gets it). 'Doc, when was the last time you went to bed with a widow of seven days mourning? Yes, the stuff of Richard III. (I doubt he gets the reference). This particular widow of mine was a fruit waiting to be bitten into. Sad, lonely. I played upon her wretchedness.' (I don't give my so-called therapist the time to comment). 'And before her, came my best friend's sister-in-law. That was another marital history, I can tell you. She was teetering on the edge of madness, a mental wreck, trying to recover from some emotional volcano or other. So I took advantage. We two clambered stealthily between the sheets at my friend's house, (following a good dinner cooked for us by my friend's wife), and in his children's play-room, in their house! Hardly my finest hour, Doctor.' (I think I've stunned him. I go for the jugular). 'An elephant-sized African lard-arse I got lumbered with when I took a business client one evening to Mecca Dancing in Leicester Square?' (I raise my voice slightly to give him the impression things are coming to a head and I am getting angry). 'Would you believe that one, Doctor? This 'lady' wanted to know if I was 'serious' about her. For heaven's sake!).' It's starting to be too much even for this lazy Quack. As I continue, he attempts to intervene, opening and closing his mouth like a bad BBC Interviewer whose not getting the chance to interrupt. 'Then there's the middle-aged Australian barmaid in the windowless bedsit in South Ken. Then…'

'Now wait!' He explodes at last. He's closed his note-pad decisively. 'You're running ahead of yourself.'

I play my ultimate trump card. 'I thought it was me who's supposed to do the talking, Doctor.'

'Stop right there! Let's rationalise all this, young man. We need to analyse the problem.' He's rubbing the top-side of his tongue against his upper teeth. It's a nervous tick. I lie back, waiting for the final analysis - the diagnosis followed by the remedy. His tongue is now right out, pointing directly at me. 'All these females you speak of, is it your opinion they were unhappy in themselves?'

'I don't care if they were unhappy. But yes, definitely unhappy, and funnily enough...' I pause as a thought occurs '... all very international. Very foreign. That must be a fetish too?' I don't give him a chance to reply. 'D'you think that's a fetish, Doc?' Again I've got him on the back foot. 'Did I mention the Canadian nympho with the crimson cheeks and cauliflower lips....'

'Stop!' (It's peremptory. And he's got good lungs. I would never have thought it). 'Young man, the remedy is simple. What we have to examine here is *Cause*.'

I leap from the couch. 'Call yourself a consultant? Who is the Doctor here? You're the one who needs analysing!' I'm on my feet, looming over him, uncontrollably angry. 'Why don't you fucking grow up, you fake. It's peoples' lives you're dealing with here. The Cause is simple. I know the cause all too well.' I pause for a moment, lost in the visions of Mary that are strangely washing over me like a tidal wave. 'It's not unheard of, you know, for an individual to wish to punish himself for an important loss.'

I make for the door, and turn. 'And by the way, when was the last time you had a good meal, you starveling?'

I could have gone on and on with that doctor. My whole string of feminine driftwood washed up on the beach. I'm happily on the edge of dating another sort of girl now though. I feel I'm getting better. I'm on the mend. Can't say why, but it's true. I bade goodbye to the psychiatrist of my imagination. I don't need him anymore. I've become my own therapist, and hope, with my words and advice, I can help the countless others who must find themselves in this same desolate spot, a tunnel that seems to have no exit, *'huis clos'* - as that archetype existentialist, Jean-Paul Sartre, describes it - a space that has no doors, ones own private hell.

CHAPTER 19

"In which William finds a lover."

'It exhibits specimens from almost every corner of the globe,' William heard himself pompously proclaim, as if he were a tour guide, or one of the keepers.

'*Planten und Blumen* (Plants and Flowers),' Ingrid mumbled to herself in response, as if this great garden was familiar to her. They'd walked through the impressive entrance and down the wide drive, large cedars on either side, and were standing now, admiring a giant, bulbous edifice that lay off to the right. 'Do they also have animals then? Maybe that's where they keep them.'

'No, Ingrid; it's not a zoo.'

'*Planten und Blumen* in Hamburg, and in Berlin, has animals too. Did you ever go to *Planten und Blumen*?'

'No,' replied William.

'Why not?'

'I don't know. I had other things on my mind.'

'You're very funny.'

'Funny' as in making jokes, or 'funny' as in strange?'

'Both, I think.'

They wandered in amongst the shrubs, the ranks of over-powering trees, the rose-gardens, occasionally bumping or nudging other visitors as they bent to read the plaques.

'Are these for sale?' Ingrid asked.

William had already noticed her almost meticulous reaction to the enormous array of shrubs and flowers aligned on either side of the path; she literally scrutinized the *flora* and *fauna*, as an expert might examine the display of objects in a museum, allowing no detail to slip past her: the provenance, the English name, the Latin name, the origin of the species. He, on the other hand, just stood breathing in the scents, in much the same way as a casual visitor to an art gallery, might marvel at the lustrous colours and authenticity on display, without necessarily needing to enquire who painted them nor when or where they were painted. Ingrid, he concluded, sought information above all, while he was content to surrender indulgently to the powerful disturbance of his senses.

'No, they're not for sale, Ingrid. They're on display; a collection of the world's most exotic plants. Stand back and let them melt into you.'

She shook her head. 'I want to know where they come from, and I want to *have* one or two of them. How do you say, *own*? I want to *own* them. I want them for my garden.'

'You're a collector then,' he said.

'Yes.'

'Then I brought you here under false pretences.' She looked puzzled. He continued, 'I enticed you here under the label of Beauty. Remember?' He indicated with a gesture of his arm. 'Isn't all this Beauty?'

She smiled. 'William, some of these plants *are* beautiful, of course, and I'm glad you brought me here, but not even the entire collection of flowers and bushes in this whole display can earn the title Beauty.'

'Can't they? Why not?' He was intrigued.

'I don't know; it's difficult.' She sought almost desperately for an answer. 'Let's say, there's too many things, too many different things here.' She bent down and held between her fingers the stem of a nearby orchid. 'This simple flower, to me, is more beautiful than all the bushes and flowers in this exhibition put together.' She looked up at him. 'It's simple. That's why. The Exhibition is not simple enough,.'

'So Beauty is simplicity?'

She nodded eagerly. 'I suppose so.'

'Oh dear, I've failed in my mission then.'

She noticed his disappointment. 'Don't worry, William, I'm just happy to come to such a place. With you. It's important for me.'

So *what is Beauty to you then?* is what he really wanted to ask, but they'd moved on down the path and ducked into one of the giant, domed conservatories, where the oppressive heat and overpowering scents quickly drove all thoughts of anything from their minds.

'It's like being in a jungle and you expect a creature, a snake, to creep up on you from behind.' She grabbed him by the arm. 'Come on, William. Let's get out of here. I can hardly breathe.'

It wasn't long after that before they gave up the whole expedition, heading instead for the lure of the river, the boats, eager to put as much space as possible between themselves and this colossal display of plants and colour, too various and diverse to merit the title 'beautiful'.

'I think you're right,' conceded William, 'it's certainly doesn't fulfill the concept of Beauty. It's something else.'

'It's state-funded Beauty,' she said, in a flash of insight and linguistic brilliance. 'How do you say it? Institution....' She stopped and waited for him to finish the word, before repeating it. '*Institutionalized*'. Yes. Institutionalized Beauty.' She repeated the word, and William added, 'It's one man's, or a few men's, idea of Beauty, you mean.'

She nodded eagerly. 'Yes, Someone else's, not mine. Beauty, for me, is a personal thing. Different for each person.'

'Okay then. You said you like boats. Let's see if each of us can discover it on the river Thames.'

She quickened her step, but he knew, even then, she was still wrestling with the elusive concept. He already knew Ingrid didn't give up easily,.

They drifted on their boat down to Chelsea. They had their cakes and tea, they wandered, together, round the deck, William trying inexpertly to point out famous places; and then they went their own private way for a time, each in their own separate corner of the large boat, wrapped in thoughts beyond the present moment

He finally caught up with her again near the great, sweeping bend by Putney, and found himself intoning, '*Putney to Mortlake.*'

'What's that?' she asked.

'Oh nothing. It's just a phrase. *Putney to Mortlake*. I just know that phrase because it's rooted inside me. From childhood, I suppose.'

'Yes, but what does it mean?' she insisted.

'It's the 'boat-race'. Putney to Mortlake. That's the course.' She still didn't understand, but waited expectantly for William to put this phrase, which carried such significance for him, into context.. 'The university boat-race,' he explained. It's part of the tradition.'

She was already mouthing it under her breath: 'Putney to Mortlake...Putney to Mortlake....'

He said, 'It's nothing really. Insignificant. Certainly nothing compared with all the other majestic things you can see from the boat here.' He was starting to wish he hadn't mentioned the phrase in the first place.

She said, 'So, who races against who?'

'Oxford against Cambridge. Every year.'

He didn't glance at her, fearing some remark that might convey her disappointment, but what he heard instead was 'You see?' Her face was lit up by a radiant smile. She leant her arm on his as they both gazed out across the water 'William,' she said solemnly, 'I'm going to tell you my idea of Beauty. I've just found it again.'

He waited, astonished, thinking how strange and unpredictable women can be, how illogical. 'Well?'

At last she declared, 'It's spending a lovely day in a foreign country with someone I really like.'

Was it at that moment - he often wondered later - that she'd made a decision, one, more momentous and far-reaching for them both than anything to do with the Oxford and Cambridge boat-race. Was this what women did? With their terrible, irrelevant spontaneity? And in the wake of this realization, William understood too that he himself would be embarking shortly on the most strange and mysterious journey a man can ever take in life.

He said, 'I'm sorry, Ingrid, but that's not Beauty, it's Happiness.'

She started laughing. 'Beauty or Happiness, I don't care which. But you're such a pedant - I think that's the right word - and also such a wonderful guide round London.'

'It *is* the right word, and I'm really not a good guide at all. Think of all the history piled up on those river banks over there, and all I can come up with is a boat-race.'

'But it's *your* boat-race, not a history book's. It's part of you.'

They were silent for a minute or two, looking out across the sweep of the river. After a while she said, 'Funny, you know. The German word for 'happy' is the same as the word for 'lucky': *glücklich*. I'm happy today but I'm also lucky, aren't I.'

'What's the word for 'happiness' then?'

She thought for a moment. 'There are many, but one of them is '*Glückseligkeit*.'

He intoned, striding up and down, '*Glückselig ... Glückselig...*' and changed it after a moment to, '*Glückseligkeit ist Schönheit* (happiness is beauty).'

They ate at a cosy bistro in the King's Road, hemmed in, by an array of little wooden tables, between other couples, intent not on the food but on each other, while carafes of red wine seemed to float in mid-air or dangle from waiters' fingers, and the young diners' thoughts spun imperceptibly off towards less immediate, but more vital pleasures that awaited them. William was nervous. But in the end, Ingrid made it all so easy for him

They took an expensive taxi back to Barnet and stood uncertainly on the pavement outside the house until she said, 'Come in, William.'

She closed the bedroom door firmly behind them, and he said, 'Ingrid, are they coming back tonight?'

'No, they're away. I told you, remember. The house is free tonight.'

She started unbuttoning her blouse, quite naturally, as if it were the most normal thing in the world, and turned her back on him. 'Would you like to unhook my brassiere?'

He obeyed, with a little difficulty, fumbling for a second with the clasp, and finally she dropped the garment on the bed and turned to him. 'I'm sorry; I'm ashamed of my breasts.'

William was quite speechless and could only at last utter, 'Why? You're beautiful.'

'Do you like me then?'

'Yes, Ingrid, I do. Very much.'

'Then do you want to take off my other clothing?' She stood still, facing him, as he did as she'd asked, helping him occasionally, a simple procedure, uncomplicated, until William became aware of the frantic beating of his own heart, an immense excitement, his own secret arousal, and he pulled off his clothes, intent only, with desperate haste, on joining her in the bed where she'd somehow gone. Desperate. He seized her and she responded, and for a second they hugged each other in an eternal embrace until William could think only of one sole place his body desired to be. She helped him in, whispering hurriedly, 'I'm taking the pill, William.'

Now he performed effortlessly actions he'd only dreamed about for years, like a seasoned athlete, slowly, gently, stopping, waiting, until at last, abandoning himself, he came, with a giant explosion, inside her, and lay gasping, breathless, motionless, slumped for what seemed an eternity with his head resting against her sweating body.

'William!' She hugged him.

'It's all right; I'm still here.'

And she laughed for a second and he looked up into her face, alight, on fire, with joy.

They dozed. Was it for hours or minutes? They weren't sure. He woke up again and she seemed to be awake too. He said, '*Bist du glücklich?*'

'*Ja.*'

'Happy or lucky?'

She laughed. 'Both.'

'Was that Beauty, Ingrid?'

She hesitated. 'Beauty...beauty is something else. I thought we'd discussed that. Happy, yes. Do you want to do it again?'

They did. And later, William said, 'I'm exhausted.'

'Then sleep, my love.' She caressed his head.

He mumbled something, feeling sleep coming on. 'What strange things we humans are asked to perform.'

'What was that?'

'Nothing. Go back to sleep. I was just musing.'

After a moment she whispered, 'Please don't muse without me.'

And they both fell into a deeper sleep.

In the small hours of the morning, William awoke and climbed quietly out of bed, and fumbled for his clothes. He didn't want to wake her, sleeping peacefully. *She was his love.* He dressed silently and was heading for the door when she called, 'Where are you going.'

'I have to go.'
'Where?'
'Home.'

There was a few seconds silence before she said, just a hint of anxiety in her voice, 'You will come back, won't you?'

He went across to the bed and kissed her on the lips. She put an arm round his neck and he disentangled himself gently. 'My mother. I have to get back. I'll phone you.'

'How will you get back?'

'I'll get back, don't worry.' He closed the door quietly behind him.

(At Possum Kingdom.)   ENTRY FROM ADAM'S DIARY
REFLECTIONS and **CONFESSIONS,** from the pen of 'Sol' the Solitary.

London – the 'Garret' (Gateway to Heaven)

When I was about 7, the whole family went one evening to Wembley Town Hall to hear my Mum's orchestra perform their annual concert. The entire evening, I remember, was one of colossal excitement; you could see my mother up on the platform, squeezed into the row of second fiddles, concentrating so hard, looking so serious. The outing became an annual event after that, and as I grew up, the educational factor inevitably loomed large in my parents thinking, but, in retrospect, those subsequent outings never quite measured up to the thrill of that first visit, a landmark in my life.

It was Tchaikovsky's 1st Piano Concerto (the famous one), and, after a moment or two, I simply stopped glancing across at Mum and became enveloped in the music itself, those unique, breath-taking harmonies, thunderous chords, rippling notes hurrying along like a woodland stream; and all this and everything, each aural adventure, conjured, as if by magic, by the busy band of workers in front of me. How could it be possible?

But yet more wondrous still, I became aware, halfway through the work, of how this massive totality of sound was not just random and mindless, but was metamorphosing into something else, had patterns, like speech, as if the music were trying to talk, to become coherent, make sense, as, every second, phrases you thought were lost were repeated, popped up again, sometimes more slowly, sometimes quicker, coming and going again and again, like old friends you recognize. Until at last, each of these separate elements, in one dramatic moment, join the dance itself, are caught up in the melody and dragged along as each and every element clambers frantically upwards towards a final statement, and then topples down into the conclusion. By the end, it was not just a symphony I was listening to, but a story. Full of thoughts and ideas, and complete, a perfect package of emotional outpouring. As we made our way home in the car that night, I knew something had changed, something wonderful, and taken me with it.

Thinking back now, years later, I find it difficult to say with all honesty whether it had been the 'theatricality', the 'frills', of that first performance which had so captivated the little boy in me, or just the simple purity of the music. Yet now I'm sure that, year on year, it was the grandeur of the music itself I sought, not the paraphernalia which inevitably surrounded it. Music was already flowing through me, and I was cast under its spell. Tucked away in the living-room in front of the radio, legs crossed on the carpeted floor, I absorbed symphonies, concertos, quartets, each different from each other, but, in essence, the same, and all spell-binding in their own right.

As the years rolled by, I graduated to the names, the separate styles, the terminology of that whole classical medium, and could mostly place the identity of a piece within two bars of the start. Of course, in my teenage years, I was lured away by the glitz and glamour of *'folk'* and *'pop'*, but I always returned to that joyful medium which speaks without words, and contains inside itself the entire gamut of human emotion

I'm certain now classical music lies in my genes; I'd even go so far as to say it's what I do best in life, my natural, most effortless skill, my genius. Can I be sure though?

I recently posed the question to that self-created psychoanalyst chap of mine. Pedant he may have been, but didn't he, in some miraculous way, cure me of my previous neurosis? I put to him the eternal question, the one that puzzles us all.

'Doctor, *Who am I?*'

'Hmm. An interesting question, but what exactly do you mean, young man?'

'I mean precisely what I say, Doctor. Who am I? I've recently been having concerns about my identity.'

'Why just now then?'

'Well, I'm starting to wonder if I'm quite the man I thought I was - it's an 'age' thing, I think - and if I'm not that person, then who *am* I exactly? By comparison, for instance, how do you think I measure up?'

'Comparison with what, my friend? Comparison with whom?'

'I mean, all those other guys who walk the planet with me. Career. Success. Respect. Wealth. Was I meant to achieve any of that? If so, then I'm on what you might call the *bottom* tier.'

'Forget comparisons, my friend; that never works. Everyone's different. Everyone has their own stamp and identity.'

'Okay. But I just need to know: have *I* done justice to *my* stamp and identity?'

'I don't know. *Have* you?'

'How do I know if I don't know who I'm meant to be. Life pushes you hither and thither, bends you out of shape and back again, this way and that, until you don't know what shape you should be. *Who am I? What is my real DNA? Can you answer that?*'

'Only *you* can answer that. Ask yourself what you're best at. What you're good at. And stick to it.'

'Hmmm. So life is just doing what you're good at, right?'

'What you're *best* at, my friend. You're probably good at a number of things. But the best of them?

I pause for a moment. The Doctor's doing his job well for once, hauling me out of myself for a moment. In the customary long silence that follows, I ask myself desperately several rhetorical questions: '*Okay. So, what is the thing I love most? My dying wish, what would it be? What couldn't I do without, as I approach the end?* I hesitate, dither with it as usual, try to run the reel of my own life before my eyes, and in a blinding flash, remember that first concert at Wembley. The Doctor, meanwhile waits patiently. 'Yes, I've got it; Doc: it's the sound of the strings and the woods and the brass. That grandeur which claims nothing, commits no slander, but remains the noblest thing on earth. What shall I remember on my deathbed? No, not friends, nor sport, nor partying, nor travel, nor books , nor theatre, the list goes on and on, but the simple answer is: Music. Classical Music. That's who I am. I'm a lover of classical music, that unheralded channel to Heaven.'

'You sure? That was a long speech, my friend.'

'Yes, but one final question before you go.'

'Better make it quick. I've got a dinner engagement.'

'Okay then. If it's all that simple, then *why* am I here at all?'

The Doctor smiles enigmatically, checks his watch and goes off for lunch, leaving me as perplexed as when I went in. To hell with the Quack. I'll figure it out myself.

Recently I've been reading a lot about World War 1 and the more than usual contribution to the well-being of mankind made by those Forgotten Heroes of 1914-18. I wonder sometimes idly if I must first understand them - that 'cream of a generation' - in order to understand myself. Do I for instance measure up at all?

When these brave men returned home in 1918, they were received not as heroes but with veiled hostility; those great soldiers were tainted with the scent of war, they had the smell of war on their fingers, and the country was tired of war, and needed to forget. It was neither grateful nor generous. It had little to offer this 'lost generation', no money, nor employment, nor even hope. Nor was that the end of their problems for, as the country had changed, they too had changed, within themselves. The stain of war lingered and had stuck to them too. It had left its pervasive mark. Although they didn't know it yet,. they'd experienced such horror, fear, degradation that, even had they wanted to, they lacked the words to describe it all; speechless they were, in front of an unsympathetic audience. Still worse, Guilt gnawed at them relentlessly, guilt for the killing they'd done, and also for *not* being killed They were outcasts. They had no *raison d'être*, and finding one would appear to have been impossible. What was to be done?

It seems that a sort of miracle occurred. Mankind is forever regenerating and renewing itself, and these 'nameless' young men from the trenches, abandoning, it seems, those old, tired values - Patriotism, Nationalism, Imperialism, Religion - which had been the cause of their predicament in the first place, were able remarkably to re-invent themselves and, together, find a new *credo* more suited to their temperament and experience. Silent, solitary men, they came to realize that just to exist is all that matters, to trust in oneself and each other, and avoid adherence to groups or brash authority. Too many lies had already been told. *'We walk alone upon this earth'*. This band of men, without knowing it, had discovered the fundamental concepts of *'Existentialism'* before the word was ever invented.

In practical terms, they set themselves a new challenge, this time against an adversary that wasn't flesh and blood, but a lone mountain in far Tibet, called Everest. Each year, as the world watched enthralled, a team of climbers ventured out in the Spring to wrestle with this formidable, undefeated foe, raising not just their own spirits, but the self-esteem of the nation too.

So let me put this in context. I have to believe their dilemma really was the same as mine: they were struggling to regain their identity; they needed to ask themselves the question I ask quite often these days: *'Who am I?'* . Penned in here day after day, one can become dangerously disorientated.

So, the question is easy to ask and hard to answer. Sometimes what you're best at lies hiding. But each individual knows in his/her heart what it is. And, as I told the Doctor, I believe I've started rediscovering it myself: *'I am what I'm best at.'* When those mysterious forces that patched me together and sent me out into the world, I think maybe they said, *'there you are, now you're whole, now you're who you are; you're not there to perform feats on the field of play, on the mountain summit, or in the classroom; these are just distractions, diversions, tedious necessities; music is your genius; only there will you feel at home, comfortable, not lonely. No, not among the teachers will you find camaraderie, they can go their way, not among the golfers, they can go their way, not among the mountaineers and climbers, nor among the scientists; all these are extraneous: it's only alone, in the silence of your room, filled with the sweet sounds of the Composers that you'll find peace. That's your gift; that's who you are. And that, to be sure, is enough. To understand music in its essence.'*

So, although, in my life-span, I may become a teacher, a speaker, a writer, a lover, a sportsman, and onwards…, none of these things will serve me much when I lie waiting to depart. No, I'll put on the headphones, and let me hear the music: symphonies, concertos, sonatas, string quartets, piano trios, requiems, operas, arias, passions, cantatas, sacred masses, an infinite stream of harmonies as I slip into Heaven, my body, liquid music.

CHAPTER 20

*"In which William encounters disillusion and
the harsh difficulties of indecision"*

He walked the five miles back in the early hours, aware of nothing except the thrill inside him. The occasional early morning commuters drove hurriedly past this wiry, wayward-looking figure, striding the pavements as if a colossus of antiquity, ready to shoulder effortlessly a universe on his slim frame. He must have cut a strange sight in the few summer clothes he'd worn the previous day: shorts, a light shirt, sandals. But he was unaware. Could there ever pass again in his life a feeling of such elation? Of such freedom? Of such strength? Of such completeness? The long, arduous, often dispiriting and seemingly endless rites of passage of his youth lay behind him. He'd finally attained manhood. He'd loved a woman and was loved in turn. He was free to achieve, or not achieve, whatever challenges lay in his path. His was the choice now. He was '*Mersault*', that hero in Camus' novel '*L'etranger*'. Memories, for a moment, flitted into his mind of Georges' desperate apologia that evening for his incongruous paintings: "*God is dead, alles ist erlaubt*" *(everything is permitted)*. And then later, his tortuous attempt to describe to his friend and to himself, this indifferent hero.

But had god died?, William wondered. That question would not, would maybe never leave him; he'd already journeyed too far down another road to commit himself to Georges' bleak *credo*.

In the small hours, he crept into the house at W..., found his way to his room and lay stretched out on his bed, too awake to sleep.

'Where did you sleep last night, William?' his mother asked in the morning, 'I heard you come in.' She was trying hard not to sound too prying.

William was surprised. 'I hope I didn't wake you. Mother. I did my best. You must sleep very lightly.'

She just smiled weakly at him. 'I suppose so.'

He'd deflected the question and the need for a reply. 'Don't worry about me, Mother. I'm all right.'

'Yes, but I *do* worry.'

'Then don't.'

The matter was dropped, but Tessa already knew where this secretive son of hers must have spent the night. It had to do with that phone call and the young female voice down the line. In her heart, she rejoiced.

But could William's elation last? He and Ingrid saw a lot of each other during the ensuing weeks. Such regular sexual activity as theirs was new to William and, contrary to what he might have expected, his lust waxed rather than waned, and each fresh encounter seemed to stimulate renewed desire. '*Lust doth feed upon itself.*' Those words rang in his ears and he began to wonder if there would be no surfeit to his desires. Their outings into London that June, July and August became less a pleasurable past-time, more a prelude to that moment when they would cast off their clothes in the quiet room at Elstree and go to it physically, like addicts unable to get enough of their fix. Their attendance at Wimbledon, Henley, Lords, those events that mark the highlight of the sporting calendar of an English summer, came and went, each event appearing to William little more than a tedious duty, as his impatient imagination spun off to the night that lay ahead, while Ingrid, moonstruck herself, followed along, realising, embodying, Rosalind's immortal words in '*As you like it*': "*I cannot be out of the sight of Orlando.*"

But it couldn't last; there was no way it could endure. Lust of this magnitude must eventually cloy. They each changed, William into an impatient boor, and Ingrid into an uncertain and anxious mistress, feeling manipulated and wondering where the excitement had gone.

It must have been Ingrid who first realised her glorious lover had metamorphosed into an addict, one who seeks and finds not just mere pleasure but indispensible relief. And, like the addict, William himself never noticed what was happening. They no longer talked now, but silently, almost furtively, went about their mutual desires with fierce, single-minded determination, feeding off each other until even the most normal pursuits were neglected..

It's quite simple: William had transformed, in a matter of weeks, into someone she scarcely knew, a lovelorn, wearisome, complacent individual, bent on gratification, while she, who in the earlier days of their relationship had looked on her lover with adoration, responded with a desperate sense of abandonment, and, what's worse, started to notice faults in him that weren't really there. *'William, why must you lie in bed until eleven o'clock?'* *'William, what are you – what are we - going to do when the summer comes to an end? You haven't even got a job to go to'.* She redoubled her efforts nevertheless to please him, until pleasing became prying and edging into areas too personal even for their intense relationship. She smothered him with attentions, suffocated him with her presence, and became herself a different person too, because secretly she had already been planning a life together, settling down, those things women do more readily than men, while William had no such plans. Loving someone is a hard learning-curve, a verdant ground strewn with pitfalls, and youth may often rush impetuously in, without regard for consequences. Just another one of nature's little, ironic practical jokes.

It was into this no-man's land of early August that something happened to William's grandfather, plunging the little household into turmoil, and William into more indecision. Up to that moment, Grandfather had always been there, an all-too real presence in the house. When, on those occasions William brought his girl-friend home to visit, they would inevitably bump into him on the landing, the staircase, the kitchen, and he would talk and utter comments and compliments, and often, once Ingrid had left for home, he would remark *'She's very pretty, William. Are you going to marry her?'*

To which William would reply with a quizzical glance, *'Maybe, Granddad.'*

'Well, take my advice; don't leave it too long.'

This was not a response that might have surprised William; it was well-known in the family that his Grandfather's own amorous affairs had not always been straight-forward, and in addition, William sensed that matters of the heart must have been simpler anyway in the old man's day, when courting invariably led to marriage. How could he expect his grandfather to comprehend the modern, promiscuous environment he and Ingrid lived in? *'Don't worry, Granddad,'* he would reply, tongue in cheek, *'I won't. It just depends on when she proposes.'*

Grandfather just shrugged and shuffled on his way.

It was on August 6th that Tessa hauled William aside. 'William, I don't think Grandfather's quite all right. You know how habit-bound he is; well it's changing. I don't know if you've noticed, but he lies in bed often till 11 o'clock, and then comes down for his breakfast.'

'Still fond of eating then, Mother,' William joked.

'It's serious, William. And actually I think he's even going off his food a bit.'

'Nothing we can really do, is there, Mother?'

'No, you're right. But keep your eye open; that's all. I tend to trust my instincts and I have a feeling Granddad is not long for this world.'

And he wasn't. In the middle of August, Grandfather choked on his lamb-chop. The rest, in this context, is history.

The 'council of war' took place not long after grandfather's death, which, for all his joking, seems to have been a watershed in William's life. In addition to the emotional jolt of grandfather's departure, Ingrid's quite frequent remarks throughout the late summer about the impermanence of her lover's life, and the apparent absence of any aim to their own relationship, had left William with a sense of isolation. He knew in his heart Ingrid was right really, but it wasn't in his nature to establish fixed plans. September loomed, and he needed prodding..

The prodding came from Tessa, who looked dubiously at the possibility of another year of her son's indecision, and didn't like what she saw. Was he to go off, as he'd previously hinted, on a jaunt to some far-flung corner, in which to write a novel? Or worse, was she to observe her only son dithering at home in what had seemed to have become a wayward and uncertain relationship with this German girl, perhaps even following the fast-developing fashion of playing poker on-line, or betting, in a desperate attempt to pass the time and to make fast money? So far as Tessa was concerned, to pit your wits against the world's professional layabouts, was to throw your life and money, away, and quite unacceptable. She needed to make it clear to her son.

As luck or blind providence would have it, on this occasion, as in an earlier moment of crisis, Elizabeth, Tessa's sister, was happily present, on a visit from New Hampshire. They met round the table in the small kitchen, all of them still quite sober in view of Grandfather's recent departure. As Elizabeth started by reminding them. 'I'm so sorry, William, for your grandfather's death. I know you were close and you must miss him dearly.'

William nodded his head, but was unwilling to embark on reflections that seemed to have a brick wall at the end of them. In fact he didn't miss Grandfather at all. He was far more preoccupied with his own circumstances, nor was it in his nature to dwell unnecessarily on events that couldn't be altered. Elizabeth meanwhile was not to be put off (although English by descent, she possessed that American gift of speaking plainly, even brashly, when circumstances demanded it). 'I suppose, Tessa darling, you must have mixed feelings really. I know Grandfather was a bit of a trial for you.'

'Yes, it's been difficult, I admit.' Tessa hesitated for a second, then said, 'but he is family. It's the least I could do.'

'Sometimes I think you're too kind, Tessa. You must get it from father. Mother's much more hard-nosed.'

Tessa looked impatient. 'Maybe, but don't let's go into all that. It's William we're talking about.'

William jumped in. 'I feel like a rare insect under the microscope.' He hesitated before adding, 'Look, I've never met any of the other side of my family besides you and Elizabeth here. I'd love to.'

'I know; you will one day, William, but now's not the best time to worry about that.'

'I'm not worrying, Mother, just commenting. You make mountains out of mole hills.'

'Perhaps you'll come out and visit with us, William,' interrupted Elizabeth. 'We sure would push the boat out.'

Sensing the discussion was already drifting from the point, Tessa tried once more to steer it back again, to the Rileys not the Bellmans. 'Well Granddad was the last of the Rileys, besides you, William. Do you realise that?'

'Yes, mother, it's an enormous weight on my shoulders, but…'

'…You'd better get going, William,' interrupted Elizabeth with a hint of a smile on her lips. 'I understand you have a young lady in tow.'

'I have, Elizabeth; but I really don't want to go into that now.'

'Sorry. I wasn't trying to pry.'

'Look, you two,' said Tessa. 'Stop bickering. And anyway, William, you really are impossible at times. Don't be so rude; anyone can see Aunt Elizabeth wasn't prying.' There was a short pause before she continued, 'And anyway, we have to have a conversation about Ingrid. I've been meaning to. She's integral to your life now. I hope you realise that. And, quite frankly, your life is what we're here to talk about right now. Wearisome though it can be at times.'

William retired a little further into his shell. 'Yes, Mother, but don't get so het up.' He turned to Elizabeth. 'Elizabeth, I apologise. I over-reacted.'

'That's all right. Believe me, we've all been in the same place as you sometime or other. It's difficult.'

Trying to remain calm, Tessa looked her son squarely in the face. 'Let's talk rationally about Ingrid. What are your plans? Have the two of you got plans?'

'William replied quickly, 'I thought we were looking at *my* life, not Ingrid's.'

Tessa said, 'She's part of your life now, William. You must understand that.'

William stalled, hoping the topic would pass. 'Look, I'm just not sure.'

Tessa's frustration boiled over. 'You're not sure of anything, William. Life demands decisions. You can't just drop Ingrid. You're involved with her. You have a responsibility.'

'I don't believe Ingrid would see it that way.'

'Of course she would!' Tessa raised her voice a semi-tone. Why can't you *see* that?'

There was a long pause, while both the ladies shifted uncomfortably. Finally William said, 'We're two grown up people, Mother. We knew this when we started out.' He paused for a second and then continued, 'It's hard, if not impossible, to bear responsibility for oneself, let alone for someone else as well.'

The two women sat as if stunned, both wondering if they'd interpreted his meaning right. Finally Elizabeth said, 'You're just finding that out, are you William? Surely you knew that when you started out. I'm so surprised by your answer.'

Tessa said simply, 'Do you love her, William?'

'Love; it's difficult. Who's to say?'

'You are,' said Elizabeth hurriedly.

And Tessa said quietly, 'Then you probably don't.'

He shrugged. 'I just don't know.'

'Well all I can say is, you behave as if you do. Or let's say, you've *been* behaving as if you did.'

William looked at her with as earnest a face as he could muster. 'Passion, Mother. There's a difference.'

Tessa slipped a secret glance at her sister. 'I know there's a difference, William. All too well.'

There was another lapse in the conversation before Elizabeth said, 'You're going to hurt her terribly, William. You know that?'

'It won't be a barrel of laughs for me either, Elizabeth. But I can't sacrifice my young life and my dreams to someone who probably doesn't share those dreams. You have to be hard.'

Tessa cast another look at her sister before turning back to William. 'What dreams are those, William?'

William didn't reply immediately, just sat there, a look almost of resignation on his face. Finally he said, quietly, 'Mother, and Elizabeth too, you know me. I'm no good at decisions, but I also know I have an instinct for things. And I'm good at *doing* things. I know that....'

'...You're lucky, William; yes, you're a very talented person, ...' Elizabeth attempted to intervene, but he gave a gesture with his hand. 'Thanks, Elizabeth; I know, but please let me finish, or I'll never finish; it's difficult....' He struggled for a few seconds to find his train of thought.... 'Okay, I'm potentially a writer, yes? I'm a musician, I'm an athlete...' again he paused for a moment, as if he were going to say something he didn't really want to say ... 'I'm a priest in my own church, even a lover of beautiful women ....' He smiled at his own words and waited, patiently, while Aunt Elizabeth smothered a giggle. 'I suppose I'm even a communicator of sorts. Words come easily to me.... But none of this makes things easier, don't you see? If anything it makes choosing more difficult, because how can I juggle all those things? How can I possibly choose jut one, and throw away what's left? I can't. My only option is to have more time, take more time, go away and find myself.'

William looked up, to see the two women nodding their heads. He knew at that moment that what he'd really wanted to say, he hadn't said: that behind all his apparent talents lay the fear of failure, that all his life he'd toyed with the idea of failure, seemed sometimes to be half in love with it. These women, he knew, wouldn't understand this; women were so positive they held failure at bay by their own boisterous love of life, but within him, for some unknown reason, there flowed what appeared to be a negative stream.

Tessa said predictably, 'I know you're good at all those things, William. You're exceptional.'

Elizabeth added, 'Exceptionally lucky too.'

Tessa said, a hint of a smile on her lips, 'I'm not totally convinced, Darling, about the 'priest' bit, but the rest. yes.' She stopped, as she noticed the doubt on William's face. 'However, that's simply the way things are. Those who are gifted have to make a choice. Life is a barrel of choices; believe me, you have to choose in life.'

'William said desperately, 'But now? Right now?'

A silence came between them again, before Tessa said, 'I was all those things too once, you know. Ask Aunt Elizabeth.'

He glanced at Elizabeth, who was nodding vigorously. Tessa continued, 'With the exception of the 'words'. You have a great gift for them.'

She seemed about to go on, when she stopped suddenly as if she'd encountered a great barrier in her way. William said quietly, 'Go on, Mother.'

Reluctantly she said, 'Yes, okay. If I must. ...I found myself a man once, who seemed at the time more important than anything, anything else in my life, and, well, he chose to dismiss me from his life. Completely...as if I'd never existed.' She hesitated, and the little room resounded with the silence. 'He just dropped me like you apparently intend to do with sweet Ingrid.' Silence again, which none of them seemed inclined to break. At last she went on, 'You see, this man who I thought was mine was just too self-absorbed.' Another long, long pause, as if she were reliving the moment. 'You've got to find someone, my darling boy. Didn't you say you were good at loving? Then my advice is, be a lover.'

'And Elizabeth added, 'Go find yourself a woman. That's enough.'

William replied quietly and deliberately, 'I *have* done, Elizabeth, and it's *not* enough. And I'm going to get a coffee.'

He went into the little kitchen, leaving the two women staring at each other, each struggling to find a way out. Finally Elizabeth said quietly, 'Hillcrest, Tess? What do you think?'

'Yes, I'd thought about that too you know. But what if *he's* still there?'

'He'll be long gone, believe me. And even if he is, what's the problem?'

'I don't think it would be fair on William, Liz.'

Elizabeth nodded. 'But it's one in a million chance, Tessa.'

William came in with a pot of coffee. 'Still deciding my future, I see. And anyway, Mother, what if she dropped me like he dropped you?'

'Are you talking about Ingrid?'

'No, not necessarily Ingrid. Any woman, this fictitious woman I'm supposed to be chucking my life away for.'

Elizabeth said, 'They might do. You've got to be strong. Look, William, forget about all that. It's your life and neither of us wants to meddle. You make your own choices and we're just trying to help.'

William smiled from ear to ear. 'Then let's have a coffee and enjoy ourselves.'

'Thanks, William,' said Elizabeth, and added, 'by the way, Tessa and I have had our thinking caps on while you were in the scullery.'

William looked up at her from the coffee pot he was carefully pouring from. 'And?'

Elizabeth smiled and continued undeterred by her nephew's apparent scepticism. 'We just thought of a place your mother and I had forgotten. It's somewhere that offers you the chance to fulfil all your dreams and find an outlet for all those remarkable talents you have. Plus, you'd earn a good living. This place is honestly made for you.'

There was just a moment's hesitation before William burst out laughing and exclaimed, 'Where is this Nirvana, Elizabeth. Show me, please!'

(At Possum Kingdom.)   ENTRY FROM ADAM'S DIARY
REFLECTIONS and **CONFESSIONS,** from the pen of 'Sol' the Solitary.

London – the 'Garret' (metamorphosis)

So, you think I've got a fixation about women, do you? Well, they do take a rather large chunk out of our lives, don't they?

The last time I looked, I can see I was in the surgery there, with that doctor quack, bemoaning my fortunes with women, all sorts of women, dwarves, Australians, black ladies etc. A whole string of feminine driftwood washed up on the beach. I could have gone on and on with that doctor. I had so much to teach him. However, bear with me; I genuinely sense I'm on the edge of dating another sort of girl now anyway. I seem to have made a break-through. How, I don't know. But I'm in remission .

Do I owe my good fortune to something in my facial features, I wonder? Do I look different? Or have my skill levels just improved? Whatever, but I'm becoming more accomplished, more confident, in this dating arena. I've just returned, as I write this, from an evening with a different sort of girl altogether from the ones I assailed the quack's ears with a while ago. It seems I've moved up a place or two in the league table. I realise it's shameful to categorise kinds of girls into league tables; it demeans them, and, make no mistake, this pursuit of mine's a serious matter for me now. Something's happened. It's no longer just 'satisfaction' I'm seeking, I'm searching for Love. But don't know what it is. I'm confused. I used to know, but don't any longer. It's such a tiny word too - LOVE - so loaded with great import. That little monosyllable, throughout human history, has launched religions, ignited wars, inspired blockbuster movies, inflamed the participators of *crimes passionels,* and, in antiquity, *"launched a thousand ships"*.

Would I recognize that four-letter word if it came my way again? I hope so. I knew I loved Mary the moment I saw her gliding across the airport terminal towards me. And I kind of knew I was only messing with Rita when I chatted her in the typing pool.

So where has that tiny monosyllable vanished to in my life? It's complicated. I should never have let Mary go in the first place. But I'm learning. I'm pretty sure now you don't just love component parts, but the whole. And also how that 'whole' can take one second, a couple of years, or an eternity. There are no short-cuts, but you have to do your best to get the timing right. Between men and women there's a timing imbalance. The thunderclap rarely happens instantaneously to both parties. That time, with Mary, it was me who made a commitment there and then, on the spot. No prevarication. She though didn't. She took a bit of time, chewed it over. Why can't we just meet in the middle sometimes? So, girls, please try not to prevaricate, and please, can't you just refrain from expecting us to perform circus tricks? Decide on the hoof. Take a leap in the dark. We both have a lot to lose. And win too.

*****

In September 1994, William flew out to America and, stopping off en route in New Hampshire to meet the Bellman family, he headed down to Dallas, Texas. Ingrid bravely and steadfastly returned to Hamburg with a broken heart, which would partly heal in time, and went about the business of looking after her ailing father. In October, still assailed by thoughts of William, she signed up for a post-graduate course in Law.

Besides thinking about her son, and his apparent callousness, Tessa often took it upon herself to think about Ingrid too, and about the remarkable similarities between Ingrid's and her own predicament. She came to the conclusion that endings of this sort were not especially uncommon in affairs of the heart, some though were more hurtful than others. But of one thing she remained certain: although her son had loved Ingrid, he had not been *'in love'* with her, whereas *she* had once invested, perhaps impetuously, all her love and future in Adam, naively supposing his feelings had been the same as hers. Perhaps only time would tell.

(At Possum Kingdom.) ENTRY FROM ADAM'S DIARY
REFLECTIONS and **CONFESSIONS,** from the pen of 'Sol' the Solitary**.**

London – the 'Garret' (moving on)

In the Fall of **1976**, Adam, tiring of London and without a proper job, returned to Texas, and, as we've already seen earlier in this tale, acquired a job at Hillcrest .This is the final entry in his journal from **Possum Kingdom**.

In a crisis, nothing relieves the pressure quite so much as a scapegoat, and most of our joys are attained at the expense of others. It's a shameful admission, but it's true. Look at the History books.

Let me put this in context. Each July into August, I venture forth to spend four glorious weeks on the South Coast among colleagues/ friends, teaching my native language to charming, ingenuous foreigners, and reveling in the sun, the sea, and the expansive freedom of it all. My students in the main are men and women of middle-age, combined with a generous sprinkling of wide-eyed foreign beauties, nubile enough to thaw the heart-strings of winter. I've never made mention of this uplifting event or included it in my diary because that document has been so steeped in misery there's been no place for optimism. But now, it's time to set it on record: a thaw has set in in my relationship with Life; I can feel it as each day passes, and the annual Brighton Summer Language Course must have played a major part in restoring me to health. It's taught me to see how important true comradeship is, to be among like-minded colleagues bent on a joint venture. Do all young men, on their journey to true manhood, need to experience the madness that for so long has riven me in two, here in the Garret? I ask myself, because I find it so hard to believe. Comradeship, colleagues, a joint venture. I enjoyed those blessings once in far-off Texas, I remember, but for some reason threw them all away, and chose instead (or did I choose?) to grovel in a mire of self-abasement. Why? I can't remember. Did I chose it or was it thrust upon me? I honestly don't know, but it occurred, and the Summer Course offered a way back, an escape. I have a chance now to regain momentum and perhaps flee this place.

At this moment in time, I'm not *in* the garret, but rather, *on* the garret, up on the roof of the building itself, surrounded by giant Victorian brick chimneys, listening to the distant murmur of traffic passing beneath me. In my mind's eye I see vistas now, stretching across the reaches of West London, sunlit panoramas of new-mown, sweet-scented grass, and rock-hard wickets. And on down again, sliding over the rim of the distant horizon, through those sturdy townships - Brixton, Streatham, Croydon - towards the majestic South Downs of southern England and always heading southwards to the Sea. You see, I've climbed up here, on this gorgeous morning, through a little skylight I discovered in the ceiling of the Garret, out onto the gabled roof of the building, and I sit now alone among the chimney pots, gazing south west, while below, the London traffic throbs, as of the murmur of waves pounding and subsiding upon a distant shore.

Yes, life is good; I must reclaim it. Why, I ask again, did I ever turn my back on Texas? Was it that it was just too good, too simple, for my tortured thoughts, and that I was too young to accept you should just grab happiness when the opportunity beckons? I wanted somehow to create happiness in my own image. I was wrong.

Writing this note here at Possum, I remember it was the start of summer '76, the Summer School of '76, that triggered my recovery. I began then to see the horizon opening, literally and, for me, personally. It marked the end of a long and torturous journey, and prompted me to leave the Garret. That glorious, impossible Summer of sunny days heaped one upon another, cloudless wide blue skies in the vaults of heaven. Pitch-and-putt, ale, trips to the ancient medieval castles, cricket on bone-dry wickets, dominoes, darts, David Bowie and Procol Harum on all the juke-boxes, until we'd lurch from the tavern into the endless daylight of an early July evening. This was a unique summer sent from Heaven. And it cured me. It stopped me on the verge of wintry madness. (There's a short story of mine about that summer course in '76, called '*A Rose in Winter*'*....Should you ever come across it, read it. It's good) .

It's a heart-warming tale of comradeship, chaos and, like most human endeavors, a half-hearted grasp for perfection. It is not my story; I'm not the hero. Selby, our leader, is the man in charge. I'm not unlike him though, I suppose. I could even have been him, but mercifully, am just a minor character, a humble participant, learning the trade, doing my apprenticeship, and, like us all, covertly poking fun at our gallant boss, who inevitably had to be our scapegoat....

* One of the short stories from **"Tales from the Garret"** by Sol Smith

******

PART 3
(FATHER AND SON)

CHAPTER 21

Fall, 1992, Hillcrest School, Texas

William walked down the well-trodden path leading to the Boys' Dorm. The evening was starting to darken, and the usual fierce display of sunset lay silently along the horizon above the top of the school Amphitheatre. He'd not yet quite got over the brilliance of these quiet sunsets, regular as clockwork, as the day mercifully started to release its heat; it reminded him of the finale of a John Wayne movie: assignment completed, Wild West tamed, the lone hero trots off into the fiery distance. William glanced at his watch and nodded: dead-on 8 o'clock, and down the hill all quiet in the Dorms. He smiled: wasn't it *he* now who was the lone rider?

  He stopped at the edge of the squat main building, which, to his right, overlooked the main campus; he hesitated a second, and then entered the little precinct, in which the designers of this pretty, adobe-style campus had squeezed a small bachelor apartment, originally to house a temporary Dorm tutor, but now the permanent residence of Sol Smith, senior member of faculty. These long-termers, such as Sol, who virtually ran the school through their hard work and the respect they received from the students, couldn't just be put out to pasture at the end of their stint of house-mastering; they required somewhere comfortable to live in and call 'Home' if they were to continue to provide the school with the benefit of their years of experience. William already knew Sol was one of these bastions of the school.

  He knocked gently on the door.

  'Come in.'

  It was a muffled sound at best, and William waited. Better not just barge in; he wasn't that well acquainted with Mr. Smith, just knew he liked him and felt the feeling was mutual, even if he'd often wondered why a healthy, good-looking, sporty man like Sol should find himself without wife, children, or a home of his own, as he entered middle-age. Surely romantic opportunities must have come his way. Then why this puzzling solitary status? Circumstance perhaps? Or just plain preference? Both maybe. William was sure there must be a tale to be told there, one, surely, of tragedies and triumphs, a girl maybe, who'd come and gone and left an empty space buried deep. You had only to look at Sol Smith to see the hard marks life had left on him. William possessed a peculiar talent for reading signs in people's expressions; and, in these first few weeks at Hillcrest, it hadn't taken him long to be aware that this solitary, middle-aged man might hopefully be more than ready to share a casual friendship with him. Two solitary men together.

From inside, there came a second call now which sounded like *'enter'*, and he poked his head round the door. It was surprisingly dark inside, so dark he couldn't for a moment get his bearings. A light from what must be a table-lamp did its best to supply a small glow, and some low background music hummed from a speaker somewhere.

A voice from across the room called chirpily, 'Hi, King William; what a surprise. Come in, if you can find your way. Sorry for the gloom.' Another dim lamp came on across the room, revealing Sol in an armchair, a pile of exercise books beside him on a low table. 'I was marking scripts. Don't you find, after a long day, it's sometimes the best way to while away the hours. Might even get lucky enough to nod off.'

'How can you see to mark papers, Sol?'

'Not difficult. You don't *need* to be able to see them to mark them.' It was a good joke. William laughed and Sol continued, 'Grade 8 History.' He chucked a script back onto the pile. 'Meanwhile let's consign them to the ignorant darkness whence they came. Well, King William, to what do I owe this honour? What's on your mind?'

'Nothing particular really. But I hope I'm not disturbing you.'

'Course you're not. I don't get many visits. Pull up a chair and find yourself a space in this jungle. You know, I almost feel ashamed to entertain guests in it. Not that I get many anyway; the odd student or two, and they don't really notice the mess. They don't actually notice anything.'

William grinned. He'd already concluded Sol had an alert sense of humour. 'What's all this *'King'* business, Sol? Which 'William' might you be referring to?'

'I can't remember. How many were there?' He laughed. 'That's rich isn't it, coming from a History teacher.'

'Two, maybe three.'

Sol sat back. 'I'm referring to whichever was the most successful then.'

William smiled. 'Thanks. That's William 1, the 'Conqueror'.'

'Then that fits the bill perfectly. No pun intended of course.' Sol leaned back and spread his legs out. 'So, what's new about town?'

'It's *all* new. That's partly why I popped round. This particular 'King' could do with a little guidance from his Lord Chamberlain.'

Sol gave a little grunt that might have passed for a laugh. 'I'm sorry to hear that. We'd better quickly put that to rights.'

William added, 'I feel more like King John in fact than one of the Williams'.'

'Why John? Didn't he lose the Crown Jewels in the *Wash*?'

William nodded. 'Yes, and I think was a bit of a hothead too.'

'Well *you* certainly don't appear to be a hothead. I hope not; you need to keep a very cool head in a place like Hillcrest. Particularly with all these girl students trying to get a piece of you.'

'Really?' said William. 'I hadn't noticed.'

'You won't; but *they* notice, believe me.' Sol had meanwhile leaned down to reach into a small box-fridge over in the corner, and handed William a beer. 'God, I sound just like your father, giving you a lecture like this.'

William smiled. 'It's invaluable information. I need all the help I can get.'

'Let me see now, wasn't it 'Polonius' in 'Hamlet' who dishes out boring advice to his son…what was his name…?'

As Sol sought for the name, William jumped in, '…*Laertes*, I think.'

'That's it, *Laertes*. I sure hope I don't sound like 'Polonius' then.'

'Actually, although people spend a lot of time criticising 'Polonius', in that particular speech I don't think he was too much of a fuddy-duddy; he was actually giving his son pretty sound advice.'

Sol had sat up a bit in his chair. 'My *Hamlet's* ' a bit rusty, I have to say.'

William thought for a moment. 'Let me see; it's on the tip of my tongue... *'This above all, to thine own self be true, thou canst not then be false to any man.'* William flipped open his can of beer and sat back. 'I think that's how it goes.'

Sol took a long swig of beer. 'Bravo. Go to the top of the class. Fantastic! A *Shakespeare* man.' His face radiated genuine respect. 'If you can just pull up a line like that to quote...'

William interrupted him eagerly. 'Yes, I love Shakespeare. Right from school I've loved it, but I can't say I've got a quote for every occasion. That one luckily seemed to fit.'

'That's the mark of the man, William. Shakespeare's a mine of quotes.'

'Among other things. His metaphors are pretty good too.'

Sol smiled. 'Where did you find your love of Shakespeare then?'

'I don't know. Shakespeare just unexpectedly found *me*, I think. Fitted me like a new overcoat.'

Sol glanced eagerly at the young man. 'Yes. The language just *'comes over you'* doesn't it? Like a blanket.'

'We had a lot of Shakespeare at school. It was promoted. A different production every year. Those plays were so beautifully done too.' Sol nodded, totally absorbed now in his young colleague's commentary. 'It left me for a bit at University; I suppose. Must have been all the other work tumbling down on one's head.' He paused, and Sol gave another quiet grunt of agreement. 'Then all of a sudden, one term, I remember particularly, it seemed as if someone had switched the light on again. There was a Production at the Arts Theatre of ... let's see... what play was it?...yes, of course, I remember, *'A Winter's Tale'*. I can still remember that Production as if I were watching it right now. I just *knew* what they were saying; no longer needed to interpret the language, translate it...' William paused for a moment. 'I was immersed in the words and the acting; as if I were a part of it on stage.' He paused again, while Sol looked fixedly at him from his armchair. 'And that play anyway; what a masterpiece!' William stopped again for a few seconds and then added, 'Shall I tell you what I believe about this whole business of appreciating Shakespeare.'

Sol was listening intently. 'Yes, go on.'

'It may sound trite, but it's when you understand the 'Shakespeare' language that you comprehend the pure magic of all the rest of it. It sort of all fits into place.' There followed a tense silence in the room before William added, 'I think it's good to go and see it alone, don't you? Concentrate. No distractions. Then it's somehow *intelligible*. You dive into that world, in spite of yourself. You're sucked in.'

Sol was lightly clapping, without any sense of mockery. Uncannily it was as if he himself had uttered this precise critique. At last he found himself saying, 'I agree exactly, William. You hit it on the spot. D'you want to give a lecture to the Senior classes. I've tried for years to promote Shakespeare here. I can see you're another enthusiast. You don't just quote Shakespeare; you explain it. Yes, I know all too well myself that uncanny feeling of watching a good performance You're inside it. The language falls away and you're right in it.' Sol's eyes had a distant look in them, as if no longer aware of his friend. 'It's like you're under a spell. I know the feeling.'

'That's what *A Winter's Tale* did to me that time. I came out of the theatre in a different world. And the glory was, I knew I'd actually achieved something myself.' Sol and William laughed together, and William added, 'About the only thing I *did* achieve that first year. Achieving was what it was all about, I remember.'

Sol laughed again. 'Yes, it's pretty scary, University.' They both sat there quietly for a minute probably imagining just how scary. Sol finally asked, 'Will, have you done any acting yourself?'

'No. Never had the opportunity. Or rather, never felt I wanted the opportunity.'

'That's true too. Strange. You can be the world's foremost interpreter of Shakespeare without ever wanting to be a character in it. I know that feeling well enough.'

William had been so wrapped up in explaining his point, explaining part of himself in fact, he'd neglected really to notice the effect he was having on Sol. For a moment he ventured out of himself. 'Is there any acting at the school here? At Hillcrest?'

Sol smiled and nodded slowly. 'You bet.'

'Any Shakespeare, dare one ask?'

'Why 'dare'?'

'I don't know. I suppose I didn't really mean that. It's just that Shakespeare in a high-school in the middle of Texas doesn't sound like the most likely proposition.'

Sol smiled again. 'I love the tactful way you put it. You sound like a professional theatre critic trying to educate a Japanese tourist.'

They laughed together, and William said, straining to get the accent, 'Maybe, Mr. Wong, you should try reading the synopsis first.'

'Exactly!' Sol patted his hands lightly together to and fro. 'A brilliant performance.' After a few seconds he added, 'You know, I think I've got a rival.'

The remark dropped like a stone into a placid pool. 'What d'you mean, 'rival', Sol?'

Sol looked down contemplatively into his lap before remarking quietly, but clearly, 'We have a tradition at Hillcrest: we've put on a Shakespeare production every year since, let me see, 1965, twenty-five odd years ago. With of course a few necessary breaks here and there.'

'Wow!'

Sol raised his hand in the air again. '*I* direct it.'

William said 'wow' again, this time with a deliberate air of respect 'I shouldn't have opened my big mouth. There's me, talking to an expert about his own expertise.' He paused for a second. 'I don't need to be a rival, Sol. Besides; why would I be?. I could always help with the hard graft anyway.'

'Yes, that's true, you could.' There was the faintest note of hesitation in Sol's voice.

William asked, 'When do the plays go on? What time of year?'

'End of spring term. Glorious May. In the Amphitheatre. We have the whole year to get it ready; there are of course one or two other things put on during the year.'

'Sounds great. Any ideas for next May?'

'It's early days, but I'm toying with something. We did a Comedy last year, so I thought we might follow it with a tragedy. Give these Texan Mums and Dads a shock for a change.' He lowered his voice a little, as if he didn't want any other ears to hear. 'Thought I might put on '*Lear*'.'

After a few moments silence, William said, as tactfully as he could, 'That's a very long and challenging play; as well as a very big cast.. Have you got enough students among Grades eleven and twelve?'

'Pretty much. They all come out to audition like lambs to the slaughter. It's a prestige thing, you see; to be in the 'play'. But just occasionally we get two or three gems among the dross.'

William was looking steadfastly at Sol. 'You know, *'Lear'*, in itself, is extremely depressing. I remember reading it when I was in Germany, shacked up in a lonely room somewhere, feeling depressed already, before I even started on the Play..'

Sol smiled. 'What were you doing in Germany?'

'Nothing special. Officially, teaching English in a *Gymnasium*.' He paused. 'Unofficially, wandering the streets of Hamburg '

'Not a particularly salubrious place to wander, from what I hear.'

William looked hard at Sol and said, smiling, '*Finding* myself, yes, that's what I was doing. Hope it doesn't sound too trite.'

'Not at all. Sounds rather exciting, especially those 'Hamburg Streets'. Wish I could have joined you.' He gazed into the distance again, as if already treading the pavements of the *Reeperbahn*. 'Never been to Germany. But tell me, William, why were you depressed? Apart of course from reading *'King Lear'*.'

William's reply wasn't immediate. 'Well, *'finding* yourself' can be a lonely occupation.'

'Darn right. 'There's so much to *'find*! You know, I can just see you somehow, in a cold bed-sit, drinking beer, and reading the *'Complete Works'*.'

'Yes, dead on the button. You've a good imagination, Sol.'

'You need to in this business. Keep on top of the enemy. You don't seem to be lacking in that department either.' Neither spoke for a moment, before Sol asked, 'Tell me, is it 'History' they've got you all the way from England to teach?' He was shaking his head. 'Typical Hillcrest. Nothing's changed.'

'What do you mean?'

'Well you should be teaching English Literature. It's obvious, with your background. It's just typical Hillcrest.'

'I'd certainly feel more at home with that. Or German even.'

Sol shook his head. 'Americans aren't too fond of Germans and Germany. I don't really know why. And *Texan* Americans are even less fond.' Again, a silence, before Sol repeated, 'Nothing's changed though. It's a matter of finance, I suppose. When I came out to Hillcrest - a different administration then of course - I found myself teaching, among other things, Math, to Grade 5.' He paused to let William shake his head in supposed disbelief. 'A general dogs-body, until they got wise, and slotted me into *1st World War*. One of my real specialities.' He looked hard at William. 'In those days, decisions were made on the hoof, if you see what I mean. It's slightly different now, thank god.

William wasn't especially interested in what Hillcrest teachers used to teach, but listening to this Senior colleague of his, this middle-aged loner, talk about himself, stirred something in him he couldn't wholly understand. 'How long ago was that, Sol? When you came here.'

Sol thought for a moment. 'Back in the heady days of the Sixties. I first came here in '63, shortly before the Assassination of JFK.'

'Wow!'

'Yes, but I haven't been here non-stop.' He paused, hesitating. 'I won't go into it now, but it's complicated. Yes, very complicated. For me and for Hillcrest. I'll tell you about it one day.'

William began to wonder if it might be best to leave. Perhaps he'd out-stayed his welcome. He glanced at his watch. 'Sol, I've already kept you from your scripts and your nap. I should be going.'

For a moment, Sol couldn't prevent a look of genuine distress sweep across his face. 'If you must, you must, but it's been interesting. You haven't kept me from anything. You must come more often. We can maybe put the world to rights again sometime. And in years to come, I'll be able to write a learned tract on *'Conversations with Beckley.'* He smiled. 'Just like *Goethe.*'

William wasn't sure of the reference, but grinned, and took up the theme.. 'Yes, *'Conversations with a 'Conquerer'* maybe. But seriously, if you can spare a moment more, can I ask you an important question?'

'We've got all the time in the world. Perhaps you'd like another beer.'

'No, thanks. I'll make it short.' He paused. 'What I really wanted to ask you is: how do you actually teach History?'

For a moment, Sol didn't say anything, just looked at William as if he hadn't heard right. William continued. 'Look, I know it's a strange question, but I mean, what are the mechanics of it, of a lesson? How do you fill forty minutes of teaching History to high-school kids?'

Once again, Sol hesitated before replying, as if bewildered. 'I could fill forty years explaining that, and still wouldn't be at the end. Look, it depends really on *who* you're teaching it to. Haven't you got a 7th Grade History twice a week at the moment?'

William nodded. 'Yes, I know it's not the same as teaching 11th and 12th Grade American History - which I think *you* do.' Sol nodded, as William continued. 'But probably the mechanics of it are the same; the 'method' is what I mean.'

Sol clearly didn't want to appear condescending. He'd never before been asked *how* to teach; he'd often been asked what to teach, when and where to teach, but who was this young man asking *him* to help him with his job? A humble request indeed. William was continuing. 'Do you write notes? Do they copy from the board? Is that how a lesson passes?'

'Yes, largely, I suppose. They copy. Anyway, these kids aren't necessarily the brightest in the barrel.' He grinned. 'Don't worry. You'll be all right. They'll love you; believe me. Especially the girls. And with your accent, they'll be spell-bound.'

That was it. No further advice was forth-coming; William realised he'd need to find his own way into the mysteries of History teaching. He got up from his chair. 'It's been great, Sol. Thanks for the beer. And the company. And the advice. I think I get the picture.'

Sol got up too, and they said their goodbyes at the door, William saying, 'Sounds all quiet on the Western Front out here. I mean the Boys' dorm down there.' He indicated with his hand 'Thank goodness I'm removed from all that.'

Sol said, 'Yes, you're up in that little room, aren't you, in the main block? Far from the madding crowd indeed.' William nodded and Sol said, 'God, if you knew what memories that brings back. I lived there, you know, in that self-same room, when I first came here back in the Sixties.' He shook his head. 'Dangerous things, memories.'

William just nodded and said. 'You know, that play you're going to put on; *Lear*. If you want an alternative, just by chance, why don't you do *A Winter's Tale*. It's a great play; I've got good memories of that. As you now know.' He stepped outside, away from the door, and called, 'Visit me. In that 'little room' in the main block. I owe you a beer. We can chew the fat about Shakespeare.'

Sol was still standing holding the door, an enigmatic smile on his face and his right arm lifted ceremoniously in a kind of salute:

> *'Goodbye young friend, with youthful wings unfurled,*
> *account thee well in this mendacious world.'*

William said, 'That sounds like *Lear*.'

'No.' Sol silently shook his head as William disappeared into the night

******

What Sol had said, was right. After a few weeks, William had established a good working relationship with his 7th Grade History, and each of his other classes too. He'd not mentioned to Sol that first evening about his gap-year experiences at H… in London four or five years previously, and the empathy in the classroom he'd established with those little kids, by means a combination of challenge, humour, sporting prowess, and a sprinkling of creative thinking. Now, here at Hillcrest, with young American kids, he'd found it no different: the 'Authorities' labelled it '*Ancient History*', but William had quickly discovered the truth, that everybody in fact, young and old alike, loves a good story, and so, he'd managed to turn tedious historical facts into legend, engineering a tale out of each lesson, before sending his enthusiastic listeners off to discover for themselves, in the Library, what became of Socrates, Aristotle, Plato etc, not to mention the critical battles between the Athenians, Spartans and Persians, already irresistible stories, long before William Bellman came along.

His relationship with Sol deepened as the weeks went by. They frequently met, and the subject of the Shakespeare play was often the topic of conversation, particularly so, since Sol was already embarked on *Lear* by the time they reached November and Thanksgiving. It was hard for William to put into words the misgivings he felt about this stark, unforgiving play, which Sol was so intent on. It wasn't that he felt Sol couldn't pull it off, but there was something about his new friend which worried him: a certain glance cast perhaps in an unguarded moment, and reflecting anxiety, uncertainty, even sadness; this concerned William, because he'd come to like Sol very much. The point was that, without ever having directed a play himself, William instinctively knew that to spend weeks and months intensely immersed in a drama project, whatever the subject, would clearly rub off on the participants and leave its mark. One couldn't help it. 'Look, Sol, do you think a battering ram of blatant villainy, physical violence, betrayal, hatred, sickness, helpless old age won't affect you over a period of eight months, even if just a little bit?'

Sol, slightly miffed by William's attempt to interfere, was nevertheless taken aback as usual by this young man's unexpected maturity. From where did he derive such knowledge of the Dramatic world and the ins and outs of great literature, if not by pure instinct? William, he'd concluded, seemed to know things even before he'd had the chance to sample them. He tried now, tactfully anyway, to play down William's remarks about the stark truths of 'King Lear'. 'William, it's possible, I agree, but there are many other dark enough Shakespeare dramas? Are we to wipe everything dark and tragic off the slate altogether, just because you're worried about your own psyche? *Anthony and Cleopatra*? *Hamlet*? *Othello*? Why, you'd never, ever put on another tragedy, if you thought that way.'

William, meanwhile, was weighing up the pros and cons of expressing his thoughts openly and possibly losing a friend, or, on the other hand, remaining *stumm* In the end, he opted for the former. He was not to be deflected. 'Okay. Hamlet, yes, with his teasing sense of humour, Macbeth, that almost larger than life swashbuckler, Othello, conniving little, schemer, they all offer at least some light relief, some signs of *catharsis*, as the ancients used to say; but *Lear*, no; it's unadorned, stark, unforgiving, from beginning to end. No light at the end of the tunnel. And also uniquely tragic by the fact that circumstances are outside the hero's control. Makes you wonder what

Shakespeare was going through at the time. Rage, anger. It's a very dark universe indeed.

'Okay,' replied Sol, 'let's suppose you're right, or for whatever other likely reason the play might have to be ditched, what would you replace it with? *Wizard of Oz*?'

Sol clearly didn't take kindly to people meddling in his apparently well-ordered universe. His caustic sarcasm wasn't lost on William. 'Look, Sol, please don't think I want to interfere. It's not of course my business, it's yours. But, if you really *do* want to know what play I'd attempt as an alternative, it's the play I mentioned to you a few weeks ago. D'you remember? *A Winter's Tale*?' He paused. 'It combines light and dark. I'm sure you know it. For me, it's actually far from wintery, whatever the title may be. It's a tale of summer. Two at least of the five acts take place in a warm, rural idyll, among the shepherds. It's mostly joy and jokes and love and dancing. If ever there was a misnomer, it's that play.'

'I have to confess, William, I'm not particularly familiar with the play. I'm sure though it has its attributes and, of course, if it once made an impression on you, it must be something pretty impressive.' He paused. 'But as you've probably guessed, I'm trying to introduce my actors to what you might call 'sterner stuff'. We seem, in recent years, to have done a procession of rather lightweight comedies. Not that there's anything wrong with that.'

'I *do* understand' replied William.. 'The beauty of *A Winter's Tale* though is it combines darkness *and* joy. Light *and* dark. The opening act is one of the darkest sequences in all Shakespeare.' He waited for a response, but Sol remained stubbornly silent. William went on, 'But although I haven't of course read Shakespeare's entire works, the ending to *A Winter's Tale* must be almost unique in Shakespeare: full of happiness, forgiveness and reconciliation. It makes you want to cry.' He rounded the statement off with a smile. 'Everyone feels good at the end.'

Sol's final, non-committal comment on the matter was, 'Interesting. I must certainly pay that play another visit.'

They were walking together up from the football pitch where William had been watching one of Sol's renowned soccer practices. Sol - 'Coach Smith' - had quite a reputation with the sporty students (and indeed with non-sporty ones too) for his inventive and creative soccer sessions on the bottom field most afternoons, and, not wanting to interfere, William had deliberately kept his distance, in spite of his love for the game, and his wish to be a part of the school team's success. The team, at this early point in the year, had already reached an impressive stage in the State Play-offs, and William hadn't been slow to notice Sol's usual loud, post-session enthusiasm most evenings in the crowded dining-hall, surrounded by his equally loud and jostling players, as if the practice were still underway. Sol was enormously popular, and the girl students were already bursting to form a team of their own. *'Sir, Mr. Smith, could you coach us too?' 'I'm already coaching the boys' team.' 'We could all play together, Sir.' 'I'll speak to Johnny.' 'We want **you**, Sir, not Johnny'.*

Above and beyond all this, it hadn't taken William long to discover Sol went off most Saturdays to play for a Dallas side himself, which lent an additional gloss to his popularity rating among the sporting ranks. William, of course, could only watch enviously as Sol headed off down the school drive with his kit-bag. He'd never been someone to thrust himself, uninvited into any set-up, but it had sometimes occurred to him to wonder why Sol had made so little effort to involve *him* in his 'soccer world'. Was it just pure absent-mindedness, or could there be another motive?

That afternoon, a glorious early October temperature, William had been unable to resist the lure of the games-field, and taken himself down to watch one of Sol's coaching sessions, which seemed to have produced such startling results this term. 3.30, as the sun started to lose its intensity, he stood on the touch-line, and watched the boys randomly kicking balls about, taking loose shots on goal, waiting apparently for the session to begin for real. Coach Smith himself was even larking about with the boys, taking a few shots on goal and generally join in; it was as if strangely they were all in limbo, waiting for something to happen, for someone to push a button and get the session underway.

At last, the moment came. Immediately stealing the limelight, 'Johnny', assistant coach, jogged onto the scene, neatly dressed in the latest gear, a large net of balls slung over his shoulder and a firm expression on his face. The boys stopped kicking around, and, as

Johnny reached the edge of the pitch, he sent several balls spinning in their direction.

'*Hi 'Coach'*. Johnny briefly acknowledged Sol as he continued to stride in amongst the players. '*Okay, take a ball, you know the drill.*' Johnny continued to advance towards the centre, while the kids silently collected a ball each, and went to stand in a circle round the Coach. Johnny wasn't tall, nor in any way remarkable in his appearance, but he seemed to exercise an almost hypnotic effect on the boys, addressing them now in an endless stream of words, and firmly in control. '*Don't waste time waiting for my arrival; just get on with it!*'; he sent them off dribbling, each with their own ball, trying to keep it under control on the parched grass. Johnny called them in. *Okay, you' all know the drill*. His right arm shot into the air, fingers raised. *How many fingers? Three*, roared out the boys in unison. Johnny moved abruptly the digits on the end of his hand. *One*! Shouted the boys. Johnny brought his arm down, slight smile on his face. *Okay, you know what to do. We're for real now. A lap for the kid who shouts out last.* William watched as the boys, unbidden, took their ball and started dribbling again within the perimeter. Unbidden, Johnny's right arm shot out into the air, four fingers raised. *Four*! came the chorus. And so it went. It was very simple really, as Johnny manipulated his fingers, the boys shouted out the number.

Johnny finally called the squad in and they sat round in a circle. '*Okay, you were all too slow. Let's go. One lap round the field.*' When the boys returned, Johnny got them sitting round him again. '*Okay, gather round*'. They came in an instant and sat panting at his feet.

'Okay, what are we doing that drill for? Remind me.'

Silence, until someone shouted, 'You gotta watch *two* things all at the same time, Coach.'

'What two things?'

'The ball and *you*, Sir.'

'Why?'

'It's the only way to dribble.'

'Why?'

'Cos you gotta be aware of your team-mates on the field of play, at all times!' They were all shouting it out together by the end, because they knew the drill.

The Coach relaxed. 'Right. To be a soccer player, you gotta have eyes in the back of your head. You gotta be able to see *wide*.' Silence, while the admonition sank in, and the Coach rounded it off, 'You gotta be *aware*.'

More glorious silence, until the most daring among them asked, 'Have *you* got eyes in the back of *your* head, Coach?'

'I do when I'm walking with my missus, and I see a pretty girl.'

Howls of laughter, and Johnny takes the opportunity to send them all on two laps of the field.

It was so simple really. Sheer genius. That afternoon, William watched awe-struck from the touch-line, while Sol, largely uninvolved, jotted down a couple of things here and there, and otherwise took no part. Meanwhile, Johnny, in the course of twenty minutes, led his troop, with military precision through other such skills and practices, all hitting at the very core and essence of the game: *Use the wings, switch the ball, keep your formation, find space*. He finally checked his watch and started kicking random balls out of the field of play. '*Okay, let's play!*'

It wasn't Sol who did the coaching. It was Johnny, the 'pro'. Then why was it, William wondered, that Sol should take all the credit for the team' success? He had little time to wonder; the practice game got underway. Sol put his note-book away and joined in. It was clear to William he was very good, dodging, feinting, finding space, doing it seemingly with all the time in the world. Johnny refereed, and at one precise point, one of the Seniors called over to William on the touch-line, '*Hey, sir, why don't you join in?*', and William needed no second asking and at last, after six weeks, got a chance himself to perform, winging past the static kids, emerging with the ball at every corner of the field, shooting goals, a natural ball-player in his prime.

Johnny finally blew the whistle and, without another word, they all marched up the hill for supper, as the sun began to dip, and along with saying goodbye to the 'Coach', a few of the Seniors wasted no time in approaching William, to complement him on his obvious playing prowess.

Sol checked there were no stray balls or sweatshirts floating around or lying behind the goal, and walked up the slope towards the dining-hall with William, now totally buoyant and on fire. 'Marvellous practice, Sol. Where does that guy Johnny come from?'

'Lives in Dallas.'

'He's an amazing coach.'

'He is, isn't he?' Sol gave a grunt of a laugh, 'Funnily enough, he talks a great game, coaches an even better one, but isn't actually a very good player himself. It's a strange game, isn't it?'

'Yes.' William, from the touch-line and then later from the actual game they'd played, had formed the impression Sol was innately good at soccer, had once been *very* good, but was now reaching the time when aching limbs and a slowness on the ball occasionally intervened., He himself was still good *and* lightning quick, faster by far than Sol or any of the boys, He knew this fact himself. He also had the wit to realise Sol's value to the side lay not in the coaching, but in the overall strategy, the day-to-day management, based on years of experience: Johnny coached, Sol managed. This combination worked fine, he thought, until the time came when Sol's strength, skills, and interest would fade with age, and the admiration, almost awe, he was held in by the students might dwindle. This would be a very hard pill indeed for his friend to swallow, and a situation hard to relinquish.

'You're a pretty good player yourself.' Sol was cutting in on his thoughts.

'Yeah, I played a lot at school and then at college.'

'Where were you at college?'

'Cambridge.'

Sol gave silent acknowledgement of his respect by nodding wisely. 'Did you play for the university?'

'Once or twice. Mainly for the college though.'

Sol nodded again and the matter was dropped. As they reached the top of the slope, Sol stopped abruptly, as if he'd come to some conclusion. 'Listen, would you like to come one Saturday with me to a game?'

'Your team?

'Yes. Of course.'

'That would be great. I'd love that.' William didn't need asking twice.

Sol said, 'I'll have to square it with the management down there, but they're always looking for good players. You'd have no trouble.' They walked together into the busy dining-hall as Sol continued, 'Look, I'll take you down, maybe this Saturday. How's that? You doing anything else?'

'Just a mere matter of weekend duty,' replied William solemnly. 'Church run.'

'That's Sunday. I'm talking about Saturday.'

'Movie run then. Same annoyance.'

Sol thought for a moment.. 'Swop the weekend then. We'll sort something out.'

William had no intention of missing this chance. 'Okay. That'd be great.'

'You can meet the guys. You might as well take your kit, you never know. Might get a game.'

It sounded magic to William, who for a few weeks had done little with his weekends except walk the well-trodden paths of the campus. His life was taking a sudden turn for the better. 'I'll bring my kit'

He glanced at Sol, who, after having initiated this weekend invitation, had suddenly gone strangely quiet and seemed preoccupied. William wondered if he'd put a foot wrong or whether there was something actually the matter with his friend. He was certainly not his usual buoyant dining-hall self, but seemed immersed in private thoughts and quite unaware of his immediate surroundings. He was wrestling with an errant memory which had come momentarily to plague him. The memory of a young, red-headed girl who once, years ago, he'd invited to accompany him to watch one of his football games in Dallas. Sol now made a determined bid to thrust away the thought. He knew he couldn't afford to allow these *déjà vues*, to linger, but recently they seemed to recur more frequently. '*I must shun that; that way madness lies.*' A line from *Lear* spun into his head, as he wondered sardonically if he too was going mad? Memory playing tricks perhaps?

CHAPTER 22

The relationship between William and Sol had up until now remained relatively superficial. Apart from that first evening, weeks ago, when they'd both discussed their various enthusiasms for Shakespeare, and this recent dialogue on the soccer field, they'd never really talked on a personal level and still knew very little about each other. However, as winter came on, the two of them met on a regular basis most Saturdays on the field of play in Dallas, finishing up in the bar that sponsored their side: The Rheinischer Hof FC.

That first Saturday, back in October, when William had accompanied Sol to the match, had been an eye-opener for both of them, particularly Sol. While William had never doubted he wouldn't make the grade with this little local team, Sol had been genuinely surprised at how well his friend had integrated, and how very well he played. His fellow players were more than excited by the contribution William was making on the field, and the Management of course quickly saw in this young man not just a very accomplished footballer, but also a precious signing for a club that needed constantly to rejuvenate and attract new players. They weren't in a major league or anything like that, but of course no team of footballers, however insignificant, enjoys losing and languishing at the bottom of the table. The Rheinischer Hof FC took their game very seriously.

They'd even got into the habit now of automatically replacing Sol at half-time with William, until in some games William even started, while Sol indignantly watched the whole match from the touchline. What's more, the mid-week selection phone-call to Sol often left him in no doubt that it was William they wanted, not him, which understandably had sometimes left William making the trip to Dallas, and Sol excusing himself on the pretext he had other important matters to attend to. William was young, fast, a goal-scorer, and in truth did everything on the field of play as well, if not better, than his older colleague. It was even remarked, on one such occasion, that William must be Sol's *alter ego,* so alike did they sometimes play and look on the field.

Sol though, although he had to confess he resented William's replacing him (to the point where he wished he'd never even taken him down to Dallas in the first place), took solace in the thought that he could devote more time to his other weekend relaxation, namely his frequent visits to *'Possum Kingdom'*: this great recreational lake, in the heart of West Texas, and the little place he'd discovered beside the lake, where he could go alone, feel free to be himself, write his diary and rid himself of obsessive thoughts. Should there ever be a time when he had to choose between his beloved soccer and this *Shangri La,* the latter would take pride of place.

And so William played throughout the winter almost every Saturday afternoon, occasionally accompanied by Sol, but more often on his own. He'd become integral to the team, controlling like a predator that narrow rectangle of space (the 12 yard box) where all attacking moves eventually funnelled down to, and carefully aimed through-balls were speedily despatched now into the back of the net by this eager front-man. It wasn't long before it became widely known at Hillcrest that William played in the local league in Dallas, which did wonders for his prestige among the students.

Out of habit mainly, William would retire to the RH Bar in downtown after the match, drink two or three lagers in a corner somewhere, and discreetly eye the habitual clientele, many of whom were adherents and members of the club anyway, spectators and management, and followers of the club's fortunes, who respected William's privacy for the most part, and were happy to leave him alone with his drink after a good match. However, the weeks went by and William started to feel more confident among these rather sedentary middle-aged 'regulars'. Later on, he began to notice that the drinkers who remained tended to split into two distinct groups, the older management who enjoyed their beer, and a smaller group of silent, surly characters, who in general seemed to rotate like satellites around a heavy, thickset man with reddish hair, who sat silently scanning the scene in front of him, making no attempt either to drink or even to communicate with his supposed acolytes. The man's facial hair was so wide-spread and bushy that a spectator might suppose it was intended to disguise his identity. William had already nick-named the man 'Red beard', or 'the Baddie', with reference to the kind of character in a 'Western', who's just ridden into town and is now scrutinizing the lawman across at the bar (William, in this case). William had already taken a dislike to this 'Santa-Clause', who, for all his cosy image, carried a malevolent glint in his eye and said nothing.

On one-such post-match evening, William happened to get up to order a beer from the crowded bar, and found himself looking directly into the steely eyes of 'Red beard'. For a moment, neither of them wanted to break eye-contact, until the big man said quietly through his jungle of hair, 'You sure had a good game this afternoon. Mighty impressive.'

William was thrown off guard, particularly since the remark had been delivered with empty eyes and to the accompaniment of smothered giggles from his side-kicks. He could think of little to say in reply. 'You were there, Sir. I'm glad you liked it.' Red beard's nodding continued, but his eyes remained empty, revealing no trace of friendship. William headed away with his beer.

For a couple of weeks, there ensued no further attempt at contact until, in the wake of a particularly tiring match, William found himself watching, from across the room, Red beard's hand moving involuntarily backwards and forwards, as if detached from his body, and realised he was being summoned over by this arrogant 'cowboy'. In spite of himself, he crossed the room on the pretext of buying another beer.

'You sure are a mighty fine player, Boy.' The man nodded his head slowly up and down in his usual manner and in response apparently to nothing. 'Where d'you hail from?'

William found himself reluctantly blurting out, 'from England.'

Red beard nodded on, showing little sign of having heard, and the two of them eyed each other silently until Red beard said, 'Where's your friend today?'

He was still nodding, and, as if hypnotised, William was compelled to reply, 'He doesn't play every week.'

'I sure have noticed that.' Another silence, until Red beard remarked 'You're a better player than him. You know that?'

William forced himself to smile now gently at this compliment, imagining in a flash this man, this 'talent scout' from one of those prestigious Californian soccer clubs, would hand him the thousand dollar 'sweetener'.

'He's from the school up yonder, ain't he?' Red beard was continuing his interrogation, and William, coming back down to earth, debated whether he should exchange personal information like this with someone he already violently distrusted. Red beard meanwhile added, 'You from there too, boy? You sure are look-alikes, ain't he boys?'

The 'boys' nodded uniformly, and one of them added, in a surprisingly high-pitched voice, as if he were a fully-grown adult who'd never quite thrown off adolescence, 'Yeah, boss, they sure do look like kith and kin.'

William forced himself to play safe. 'No. No relation. We're just friends, colleagues.'

'You teach there too boy?' There seemed almost a genuine note of surprise in Red beard's question. William nodded, and Red beard continued, 'You sure are young for a teacher, Boy. Better stick to football, to my mind.' A soft murmur of laughter from the acolytes followed this remark, and Red beard persisted, 'Where does he go then?'

William hadn't understood. 'How do you mean?'

'Go. You know, at weekends?'

'I don't know; I've never asked.'

'You'd do well to know, Boy. Might be off with *your* lady-friend.'

This remark received a round of full-blown laughter from the acolytes, and William, intimidated, couldn't let on he didn't in fact *have* a 'lady-friend at the moment. 'I don't think so.'

More laughter, while Red beard watched him walk away, calling, 'You better get back to your beer 'fore you start spilling it. You sure seem clumsier holding a glass than kicking a football.'

William retreated, and, at the same moment, determined he positively didn't like this red-bearded fellow and would never again allow himself to be the butt of his humourless wit.

Sol, that weekend, that moment perhaps, was taking a long, deep breath and looking out through the large pane of glass onto the placid stretch of water. Possum. His beloved place, his privacy, his isolation, his writing, his getaway, his personal solitude... his loneliness? No, not at all.... That last thought needed thrusting back, down to where it had wormed its sneaky way to the surface. Yes, solitude, but not loneliness. They were different, two separate meanings. How though? He'd often wondered about the distinction between those two words, and struggled with the ramifications. *'Solitude'* was simple: the absence of another human being in your immediate vicinity; that was a fair enough definition. *'Loneliness'*, though, was different. You could still feel lonely even in the presence of thousands of others: a railway station, a football game. He often had. But loneliness implies also the need for someone, the missing of someone, the wanting someone, and is always accompanied by an absence of peace of mind, contentment, and all those other blessings he himself currently enjoyed on these weekends.

However, on the last two recent weekends at Possum, he'd actually been aware of an unusual restlessness, a trace of impatience with himself, which he sensed could quickly tip over into loneliness. Why?

He decided to leave these reflections for another time. He performed now his usual checks on the place: making sure windows were as he'd left them, not tampered with, shelves (needed dusting), his writings tucked neatly away between two cupboards down in the corner, vital material, if ever one day he might look for a publisher, and certainly vital material to be hidden from the prying eyes of anyone else, particularly since they were as yet unfinished and were very personal too, a testimony to his wanderings in the wilderness, and (not to forget) the truth about his real identity, his name, his unorthodox return to Hillcrest, the whole subterfuge in fact of his present comfortable life, which, if ever challenged one day, would lead him into legal proceedings. Wasn't he, after all, a person who didn't really exist?

He checked again the bundle of papers wedged tightly between the two wooden cupboards and interlaced with old local newspapers, so as to render them insignificant jottings and cuttings to anyone coming upon them unawares. Anyway, nobody except himself ever entered the shack without his knowledge. Hadn't he himself ascertained over so many years, that the place had been abandoned?

He took another deep breath and looked out onto the water as he always loved to do. He felt a sense of welcoming from the way the water beckoningly moved on the placid surface: nothing harsh, just a gentle lapping. He went down onto the deck and wandered along the wooden jetty to where the motor boat lay in its habitual place. All safe. Checked gas. Half a tank at least. He might have to motor down to the nearby gas point; just to be safe....And, as he stood there on the deck, looking at the vast, inviting stretches of water, little headlands, creeks, leafy places to explore, to sit outside of in the glare of the early spring sunshine, moving over later as it got too hot, and then either falling asleep in the shade or heading up the lake looking for new channels. And then...? For the first time ever, he involuntarily checked his customary, easy reflections, and wondered '*then what....?*' He realised uncomfortably that the day's plan just didn't sound as inviting as it should. Something missing. He tried to tell himself he was tired after a hard week's work; perhaps he should spend the day doing odd jobs, go in the boat tomorrow, and yet, all the while he was trying to dismiss a niggling, persistent thought, which insidiously hovered on the edges of his mind....*William*. Yes, it was his friend, William, he was thinking of. Would he perhaps enjoy a weekend at Possum too? Would perhaps his whole day now with the boat be rendered more exciting if he had someone to share it with? Yes, Share it. Something Sol wasn't used to; sharing, hadn't, for reasons known only to himself, ever been an activity that came naturally to him. Too much to lose; too many secrets. And now, for several seconds, he lost himself in difficult matters involving decisions: this young man, young colleague, for example, wasn't he already making in-roads into his, Sol's, solitary life? Should this be allowed to happen? Wasn't that why he'd called himself 'Sol', those days far back when he'd needed to re-invent himself? Sol, the Solitary One, but for sure not the *Lonely* One.

However, standing there by the boat, he couldn't quite dismiss the whole fact, the reality, of this young man, with whom he already felt an inexplicable bond; William, so enthusiastic, so energetic, so instinctive, so...just like he himself must once have been. He actually experienced an uncanny sense, not just of friendship for William, but of kinship. They played soccer together, they coached the team together, they delved deeply together into important interpretations regarding Play production, they whiled away the long evenings together with cans of beer. It had already progressed this far; was he now to deny William the opportunity of sharing these weekends together? The matter boiled down right this moment to a decision that was black or white: Should he invite William one weekend? To share his precious sanctuary?

As the nagging thought refused to leave him, he made his decision there and then, broke his own cast-iron rule never to invite anyone to share Possum, and decided to invite William the moment he got back on Monday morning.

Consequently, that afternoon, he didn't while away the hours sunbathing or drifting around the lake, but moored the boat up, and went for a stroll to the local store, bought some items, met a few 'locals' (while hoping not to), and then wandered on further, as far as what he called the 'metal church', the tiny, unattractive, temple-like building that stood at one of the few crossroads in the area, and which, according to the large wooden sign outside was called the 'Seventh Day Adventist Temple of Zion.' *'Seventh Day'*? Presumably this reference in the Bible, in Genesis, to *'God's creation of the world in 7 days'* wasn't, to the founders of this building just metaphorical, but *literal*. From Sunday (first day of the week) to Saturday (Sabbath). Furthermore, why was this a 'Temple'? What on earth was that anyway? What was wrong with the plain, honest word 'Church'? How were they distinct? And, as for 'Zion', wasn't it actually spelt with an '*S*'? Where exactly *was 'Zion'*? He stood idly for a few minutes wondering what Zion meant, and why it was related at all to a church set in the very heart of rural Texas. More biblical gobbledy-gook no doubt. He stopped in his tracks, realising pedantry was overtaking him; he was being pedantic - like any typical teacher. Nevertheless, were William to come, better keep him away from such strange types of church. He'd already had to suffer a few moans from his young friend about the numerous and various churches around Denber, and the tedious business of having to ferry the kids to them in the school bus on Sunday mornings, dropping them off at their *preferred* church. According to

William - they'd often talked about it - it was quite unnecessary for there to be so many different 'churches' anyway, because all of them were irrelevant to 'true religion'. William was always very forthright about this for so young a person; indeed, William seemed very set in his ways about Religion. *'Churches are unnecessary. Detrimental, in fact. Your God is inside you. Why do you need to go to a special 'house of God' to worship? I doubt the kids could care much what church service they go to, just so long as it's short and they get back in time for some of Mrs. Doublejoy's pancakes.'* These were William's final cynical words on the subject the last time they'd discussed it. He feared that if William were inadvertently to encounter a temple-goer' here at the Zion Temple, there'd be a god-holy argument. Quite amusing really. Religion surprisingly hadn't actually hit Sol yet, even though he was already moving on in years. He guessed he was probably too concerned with his own introspection. However, he did to a certain point agree with William; he figured it wasn't ever any good being 'persuaded' into a belief; whether in church or out, Religion would come to you whether you were looking for it or not. It certainly hadn't reached him yet.

Sol returned to the lake and the shack along the dusty back-roads. Everything in order there; nobody prowling around. He lived in fear of finding one day smoke issuing from the chimney and the rightful owner warming himself by the fire, but this had never happened in all the years he'd used it, and he didn't really suppose it ever would. Just a small, forgotten property, simply overlooked perhaps by a lawyer sorting out a will. He'd got lucky.

Sol returned to his writing, with trepidation it must be said. It wasn't that he had no more to say. Too much in fact. However he had to confess, all those endless days in Canada, in London, trying to restore a broken memory and to re-create one particularly elusive moment in his past, all this exhausting endeavour simply hadn't really worked: that moment still lay dormant in his mind, the memory still lay broken and elusive. *How had he come to be there at all?* Until finally, he had started to believe the answer might prove too terrible for him to cope with. The dredging up of memories, things done in ones life, and things left undone too, perhaps they should be left to lie. He was assailed over and over by this same puzzling question as he picked up the pen these days. *Don't re-awaken the dead. We are frail creatures; we cannot bear too much grief.* "*The first time we sniff the air we waul and cry....* That prophetic line from *Lear* slid into his mind. For what does that child cry? That clarion call of every human ever born is not one of joy, but of *pain*....How does that line go on? Sol was remembering those difficult moments he was having out there in rehearsals these days out in the Amphitheatre...Yes: ..."*that we are come unto this great stage of fools".* It's a cry of pain the child makes as it gazes for the first time upon the Earth. Is it perhaps remembering what it's left behind? Better then perhaps to rake over the ashes, leave memory undisturbed.

He thought long and hard that afternoon and suddenly, like a spring flower opening, it occurred to him that he had a real friendship established now, someone who seemed to like him and was ready to share his life with him: Perhaps William was the answer. In truth, there already seemed, from the start, an unusual bond established with this young man. An instinctive connection

William put his papers to one side, and took the boat out on the water on what remained of the beautiful evening. He felt at ease; strange how important thoughts can set your mind at peace and yet be triggered by such trivial things as a rusty old church. Perhaps, he wondered, I might attend a session there one Saturday. In that melting pot of the 'hot gospel'.

'Who won Saturday, Will? I trust a satisfactory result.'

They'd met up in the noisy staff room for coffee at break. 'William' had become 'Will' for no accountable reason. Perhaps, thought William, it was because Sol had had a relaxing two days at Possum. He occasionally wondered what it was his friend enjoyed so much about this mythical paradise of a lake. He also wondered if *he'd* ever get an invitation. In which case, he'd have to give up one of his beloved soccer Saturdays. Difficult decision.

'Three nil. We're still top of the league. Don't worry. They were asking about you, the lads. Want to know where and with whom you're spending your weekends, these days.' Sol laughed and William added, 'As a matter of fact, there was another guy I bumped into in the RH Bar; he also wanted to know where you were.'

'Who was that then?'

'I don't know what his name was. A weird sort of chap covered in facial hair. A red beard; I almost mistook him for a woolly mammoth.'

'Sounds like one of those 'King Williams' we talked about. William Rufus, perhaps? They called *him* 'the Red'. He was a nasty piece of work, I believe.'

'This guy certainly was. Looked at you straight out of steely blue eyes.'

The more Sol heard, the less he liked what he was hearing, even though William made a joke about it. He didn't like people enquiring about his whereabouts. 'Can't say I've seen anyone like that at the RH Bar. Must be one of the locals.'

'I think so too; I don't believe he was one of the club; never even mentioned the game. And he was surrounded by a bevy of side-kicks. Just like someone out of a Western. Anyway, he wanted to know where you were. So he definitely knew you.'

Sol had been thinking hard. 'Hope you didn't tell him,'

'No. Top secret.' He thought for a moment. 'I might have mentioned Possum Kingdom in passing, but I can't remember. It's not important, is it? Even if I did. I doubt anyone would've heard of it. Not that group anyway.'

'Don't believe it.' Sol replied adamantly. 'They would.'

'So why does it matter if they know the place.'

'People are inquisitive, that's all. Not possible in this world to have secrets.'

'I don't think you need worry. Best thing is not to *have* any secrets, isn't it?'

He went to refill his cup from the large urn in the corner. When he came back, Sol said, 'I don't really care either. But it's surprising people won't leave you alone sometimes.'

William nodded. 'That's quite nice sometimes, to be left alone, isn't it?'

Sol didn't seem to have heard, but said, 'D'you know, when I came back here, years ago, to teach, I received a phone-call within about two weeks of being back. Guess who from.'

'From the tax man?'

Sol laughed. 'From Rheinischer Hof, more like.'

William thought about it for a second. 'I didn't even know you went away; let alone you came back.' He paused, 'Just shows how inquisitive *I* am.'

Sol meanwhile was suddenly thinking he might have just given something away. His paranoia often got the better of him. He made now an attempt to deflect William from asking any more telling questions. 'Yes, It was Rheinischer Hof. Don't know how they got my number. They wanted to know if I was up for any more soccer.'

'And were you?'

'I said I'd think about it.'

'Sounds like you were indispensible back then.'

Sol laughed. 'Sort of, I suppose.'

'How long'd you been away then?'

'Well,' Sol replied reluctantly, 'it's a long story. With which I won't bore you right now. Maybe another time.' He made a show of looking at his watch. 'Time for class.'

As they were going out onto the Breezeway (the passage which led to the classroom block), William said, 'Sounds like that phone-call must have been worth it. They got their man back.'

Sol nodded, relieved the topic didn't seem to be going any further. He knew though that one day, if he were to extend this friendship, William would come to know about his past, and *vice versa*, he'd know about William's.

A Senior boy came hurrying past, calling out to William, and deflecting Sol from his thoughts. 'Hi Mr. Beckley, sir. You going to play for us in the match this Saturday?'

'What match is that, Bill?'

'The state play-offs, of course.'

'I'd like to. But I'm faculty. We'd get found out.'

'No disrespect, sir, but you sure do look young enough to play for us.'

The boy went on his way to class, while Sol looked across at William. 'There you are then. That's indispensability for you. You make me feel like a dinosaur.

They were heading due west on interstate 20 in Sol's large estate car. It was three weeks later, Saturday morning, and neither of them had anything else in mind but to put as many miles behind them as quickly as possible, away from the hurly-burly, the duty-bound environment of a weekend at Hillcrest. Free. Liberated at last.

William essentially always liked the idea of getting out, seeing new places; nevertheless, this was a rare outing indeed. Over the last few weeks, he'd become so immersed in the day-to-day school routine and in his soccer commitments in Dallas that he'd never found time to plan anything beyond the immediate vicinity of Denber. Now, as he gazed through the car window, he was amazed how fertile even Denber seemed, in contrast to these needly, scrubby bushes poking up from the arid earth outside, all bent and twisted, as if old before their time. It was almost desert country. Maybe in the actual process of becoming desert right this very minute, as he watched.

Sol noticed him looking. 'Pretty arid, isn't it? Not like the Cotswolds or Devon. Trouble is, you need rain for places like that. And here, you hardly get any rain.' He turned to glance at William. 'Take your pick. You can't have it both ways

William nodded. 'Where are we exactly?'

'About 30 miles west of Fort Worth. Probably almost exactly in the dead centre of good ol' Texas. Another two hundred miles, and you'll be in oil country. Midland. Odessa. The power-houses of the Texan economy. It gets even drier there. Apart,' he added, 'from the occasional biblical deluge.'

William laughed. 'Why 'biblical'? That's a strange turn of phrase.'

'I don't know; just sounded good. Those biblical fellows didn't do anything by halves.' He paused for a moment. 'Which reminds me; I want to show you the Zion Tabernacle in Possum when we get there Don't let me forget.'

'I didn't know there was a Zion Tabernacle in Possum. You never told me. In fact, I don't know what a Zion Tabernacle looks like anyway. Sounds very grand though.'

Sol laughed. 'That's the irony of it. It's just the opposite of 'grand' really. The zealots who frequent 'tabernacles', I've noticed, seem to like exaggerating everything; and it all just becomes grotesque.'

'Really?' William had little idea what Sol was talking about. He waited for him to continue.

'Yes, their basic, fundamental belief is that the world was created in precisely seven days. They take the Bible literally.'

'I've heard something like that.'

Sol nodded. 'Yes, it's too fantastic to believe. They're the Seventh Day Adventists. The world was created by God, not via the lengthy process of Evolution, but literally, *in seven days*.'

William didn't reply immediately, and then said quietly, 'Just one more church to confuse the issue.'

'That's a nice way of putting it, I suppose.' Sol paused. 'Their Sabbath is Saturday, not Sunday. Today, in fact.'

'Why's that?'

'All part of the same basic idea. You've got seven days in all, and for some unknown reason, God created the world Sunday through Friday, and rested on Saturday, their Sabbath.'

William didn't reply immediately, and then said, 'well, whether it's six days or seven, I suppose, if you think about it, it's quite a fanciful notion, playing around with this '*seven days*' obsession. Lends itself to the imagination and makes everything seem so simple. Artists like 'simple'.' He paused for a moment. 'Haydn took advantage of the idea, you know,. The great Joseph Haydn. Wrote a majestic musical work based on that same image.' He smiled. 'And he was probably a staunch Catholic. I suppose when you think about it, imagery cuts right across religious divides.' Sol didn't reply for a moment, concentrating on the road, and wrestling with what William had just said. William went on, 'Imagery kind of lends itself to artists. The simplicity of imagery makes the story all the more believable.'

'Go on.' Sol was not ready to commit himself on this one.

William laughed eagerly. 'Well, *The Creation,* Haydn's *magnum opus*, in a musical way, allots to each separate day one of God's tasks, over the seven days. It's a great idea. As well as great music.'

'You're a musician too, are you, along with all your other talents, Will?'

William laughed. 'Not really. I just happened to play in the *Creation* one or two years ago. In a school orchestra.'

Sol took his hands momentarily off the steering wheel and gave a couple of light claps. 'Then you really *are* a musician. Is there any end to your talents?'

William laughed. 'Don't go overboard. I didn't have a solo or anything.'

'I'm still impressed.'

They'd been progressing steadily along the Interstate, and Sol finally took the run-off from the highway.

William, glancing round, said, 'You don't need the map? All looks just the same to me.'

'I certainly don't. I'm just a humble traveller, you see. That's *my* claim to fame. Not music. I can't compete of course with the '*Creation*'. But I drive this particular route at least twice a month. Probably more. And, in the greater picture, I won't count the many times I've headed directionally westwards from Denber to other venues. Journeys long and journeys short.'

'That's a good word, '*Directionally*'. Deserves a clap too.' William raised his hands and brought them silently together again twice.

Sol smiled. 'Yes, I suppose *in the direction of...* might do better.'

The two of them fell silent, Sol concentrating on the road, until William asked 'Have you been to the States before? Before *this* time, I mean?'

Sol said, 'How do you mean, 'this time'?'

'Well you told me once, don't you remember, how you got a call from Rheinischer Hof?'

Slightly anxious, Sol thought about it for a moment. He knew the big, wide questions, like this one, were inevitably coming. He'd already decided that to ask William to join him at the weekend at Possum Kingdom meant things would begin to loosen up between them. He was bound to have to share experiences like never before with anyone else. He'd come finally to a conclusion that he could trust this young man. Straight-forward, no tricks nor deviations. He did things he said he'd do, fulfilled promises, and kept no cards up his sleeve. In fact, Sol thought wryly, he'd make a terrible poker player, but he makes a good teacher. That's why the kids like him.

He finally responded to William's question 'Yes, is the simple answer. At least twice before. I can't really remember whether it's twice or three times. America is my adopted country, you see. I think we probably all, in our lives, *own* a country other than our real one. I mean a special place you kind of inherit as your birthright and never let go of.'

William said, 'That's a new notion to me.'

'Yes, it probably is. It's just my fanciful idea. Like your 'imagery' idea. *Your* special country though is probably a different one from mine. It's just a question of one's experience.' He glanced sideways at William. 'Possibly Australia, I guess. Australia is more in the public eye than America nowadays. Perhaps America's fading a bit. Too much bad press. And anyway, it seems a birthright shouldn't last more than a century. America's century was the twentieth.'

After a moment's silence William said, 'You seem to have thought it all through.'

'Not really. It's just a whim. Anyway don't forget, I've had longer than you to work my theories out.'

'No, I think it must be the History teacher in you talking. The rise and fall of empires, that sort of thing..

Sol laughed. 'I'm actually a linguist.'

'Ah well, can't win.'

They both laughed, and Sol said, 'Theory or no theory, the truth is I love America. I feel it's my home; it fits my personality. That's what I was trying to say.'

William wasn't surprised at this confession. He'd learned you never quite knew what Sol was going to say next.

Meanwhile the country beyond the car windows had caught his attention again. It seemed if anything to be increasingly 'spikey'. Sol veered suddenly off onto a back-road.

William said, 'Where exactly are we going?'

Sol, tongue in cheek, replied, 'We're going to Possum Kingdom. I've already told you.'

'You know this place pretty well then. How did you find it.?

'William, Don't ask too many questions about this place. I just *did*. Okay?' There was a faint edge to his voice, and William knew better than to overdo the questions. Sol continued, 'This Lake is a sort of vast reservoir from the Brazos River. Typically Texan.'

'What's typically Texan? The Lake or the River.'

'Both actually.. The Texans have a lot of these kinds of recreational lakes.'

William nodded and said, 'Maybe because they're so far from any other kind of water. I wanted to ask if there's a town in the area. Seems like you could drive right by, if you were on the Interstate, and never notice'

'A town? Who needs towns in this picturesque countryside?'

'Hardly picturesque surely, Sol. But certainly different.'

'Wait until you see the Lake, the water. You'll forget all about 'needly' and 'spikey'.

'Great!'.

They journeyed on down interminable back-roads, narrowing and twisting, to reveal at each turn a new enormous panorama of water. William finally asked once more, 'How did you ever get to know of this place? It's certainly in the middle of nowhere.'

Sol knew there was no way he was going to be able to conceal the history this place held for him. There was bound, sooner or later, to be a *big* question from his friend, striking unwittingly at more than one of his vulnerable points. He thought hard for a moment and said, 'Okay, listen hard, I've lived three separate existences in this house on the Lake. In an earlier existence, I used to come and visit this place; just like we're doing now. It belonged to a friend, a Texan family, who I got to know. She brought me here on one trip and then seemed to lose interest in me and the place. And, in return, I suppose I lost interest in her too. We split up, that's all.'

He paused for a moment and William said, 'And the second existence?'

'My second 'existence' here was *more* than a mystery.' Sol's voice had changed and William glanced up to see if this was one of Sol's little jokes. It wasn't. His friend was eying him intently 'So mysterious in fact you won't understand.' He hesitated and then said, 'Because *I* don't understand it either. Still, after so long.'

'Why not?'

Sol shook his head and uttered a deep sigh.. 'Look, I suffer memory loss occasionally. Real forgetful moments. And, in this case, I can honestly say I have no idea how I got here to Possum in my second existence. But I *did*.'

'That's weird, Sol. Was that a long time ago?'

'Very. Yes, very.' He hesitated. 'Mid-sixties. Seems like ages. I had a girl-friend at the school then. A senior student.'

'Really!' exclaimed William.

'Don't sound so surprised. Even dinosaurs had girl-friends, you know.'

William laughed heartily. The spell was broken. 'I'm sorry; I didn't mean it like that.'

'I know how you meant it. Don't worry.' He stopped for a lengthy moment, as if in search of some wayward memory. 'Yes, an American girl. Lovely girl.' He stopped again, searching, and then said, 'Tell me, is there a line of poetry which sums the whole thing up?'

'What whole thing?'

'My sentimental trip down memory lane.'

'Yes, there is. Very much so. Listen.' Without hesitation, William proclaimed, '*If you're travelling in the North Country Fair, Remember me to one who lives there.*'

'Perfect!' Sol repeated the phrase, *Remember me to one who lives there*. God, who says Dylan isn't a poet? He encapsulates more emotions in one song than a whole clutch of academics on a fortnight's poetry seminar.'

'Yes,' said William, 'Or how about a gaggle of nightingales in an enchanted Grove. Or, better still, *In some melodious plot of beechen green.*'

Sol laughed. 'That's beautiful. Where's that line from?'

'Keats, of course. '*Ode to a Nightingale*'.

Sol laughed. 'Your 'imagery' genius once again,' while William, after a moment, said, 'We're getting off the track. I'm really none the wiser, Sol, about your second existence, except there was a girl involved in it. That's fine; it's a good story.'

Sol, shaking his head, looked at him hard. 'It really *is* shrouded in mystery; you've got to believe me.'

Okay, Maybe one day. And what was your third existence? You haven't told me anything about that.'

Yes, my third existence was much more straight-forward, more obvious. When I came back to teach at Hillcrest again I came here alone to Possum just to take another look at the place. The house was still here, and, would you believe, not even locked. I don't know why. Maybe the lady died and forgot to include the property in the inventory. That's far-fetched, but it may be true. I've almost claimed it for myself now. It's that simple.'

It hadn't of course been simple at all, but meanwhile they'd arrived at their destination and driven the car into the slot overlooking the little house. They sat contentedly for a moment surveying the sight of the rockery garden and the vast stretch of water beyond.

Sol said, 'Nice eh? He hesitated. 'I vote, we leave the 'existences' for another time. We've got a whole weekend. Come on; let me show you the place.'

They went inside. Sol showed him the little living-room, the galley kitchen, the little bedroom at the back. All immaculately tidy. As though professionally maintained.

William was surprised. 'Who cleans this place, Sol?'

'I do of course,' said Sol. 'Who else?'

'This is fantastic!'

'If you think that's fantastic, come outside. On the jetty.'

They went outside, down the three little steps onto the jetty, the little motor-boat bobbing on the water at the end, as if begging to be released. William said, 'It's all so well kept, so neat, Sol..'

'Did you expect it to be a recycling tip?'

'No, of course. But the fact you just found yourself here. It's pretty surprising.

Sol nodded agreement and they wandered down to the little boat. William said, 'Does this really go?'

'Course it does.' Sol grinned. 'Except of course when it doesn't. And sometimes when it runs out of gas in the middle of the lake.'

William grinned. 'That's human error.' He turned round to look back at the little house. 'This though is divine perfection. Error free.'

'Maybe,' said Sol. If anything in life ever is'

They both stood in silence, looking at the beautiful contours of the lake as they wove mysterious shapes as far as the eye could see. William finally couldn't resist asking, '*How* did you say you came by this place? You *can't* have forgotten. It's too precious.'

Sol looked at him earnestly. 'I have. Not forgotten the *being* here, but the getting here. I've tried. I've travelled, I've written reams, to try to awaken my memory, disturb the blockage. It's fixed and fast though.'

William stubbornly persisted. 'Can you remember *when* this happened then? And what led up to it?'

'Certain details, vividly. There was a party. Faces I know. Things leading up to the party perhaps.....There was this girl...I *know* the girl. She's stamped indelibly. And then the memory goes blank. Memory is a strange thing, you know; it remembers what it wants to, not what *you* want it to. Sometimes I wonder if something terrible occurred.... too dreadful to remember. If so, perhaps I shouldn't think so hard. It might re-appear.' Sol looked fixedly at William a moment. 'Look, come inside. I want to show you something.

They went inside and fetched their things from the car. Sol dumped his small case onto the *chaise longue* that took up one whole side of the main room and overlooked the water. How conveniently placed this couch was, thought William, as he watched his friend. Just suppose someone fell asleep on this couch, they'd wake up to this wonderful panorama of water.

At the very same moment, as if by some telepathic process, Sol said, 'See this sofa? You know, all that time ago, I can still remember this self-same couch. It's the couch and the view, I remember.' He paused just for a moment, as if uncertain whether to continue. 'I remember I woke up, alive, and found myself here, in the house. Alone. Completely unscathed...' he paused again briefly... 'but with absolutely no recollection of how I came to be here. I promise I wasn't drunk or even hung over. No, I was fully sane, fully aware, and in good shape.'

For the first time since they'd left Hillcrest, Sol thought he noticed just a hint of scepticism cross William's face, and felt, in return, a trace of irritation, even anger, that he was unable to convince his friend of this bizarre event. Why could it not be believed? Was he to keep this improbable tale locked up for the remainder of his days? Was it, after all, really so hard to believe? If this young friend of his could only pretend to believe it, then how hard might it be for him one day to convince a court of law, if it ever came to that?

Sol reached a decision. 'Sit down on the couch, right there, for a moment, Will; I can see you're never going to believe me. Close your eyes and open them when I tell you.' William, surprised, did as he was asked, while Sol hurried across to a gap formed by the side of a desk and the end of the sofa, and rummaged in some papers for a few moments. William had meanwhile opened his eyes.

'Ah!' Sol turned triumphantly to William and handed him a piece of foolscap. 'Look at this. This sheet goes back a very long way. It might even have a date on it.' He took the sheet back from William. 'Yes. I thought so. 1967. twenty-five whole years ago.' Then he handed it back to William, who took the paper silently and sat back down on the couch, while Sol continued, 'I wrote that actual letter in 1970, although the events it describes go back even further. Three years back.'

William looked up, uncomprehending still, and Sol said, 'Don't worry; it's not important. But I think what's written there first saw the light of day...let me see...yes, May 1970 it was.' He grunted. 'I sent it to that faceless pretty girl I told you about. Remember? The Bob Dylan?'

William returned his attention to the paper, and read: "***At Possum Kingdom, West Texas, Summer 1967***

"*Dearest Tessa, I woke to the sound of wind and lapping water - that sound you and I remember so well - waves against the hull of a boat. Slap...slap. I was on soft bedding, in a lake-house on the shore of Possum Kingdom....*

Those vital words he'd sent ...

Sol had waited for William to slowly read what was on the paper. When he finished and looked up, nodding, Sol said, 'It tails off; it's the end of the page. I'm sorry. But it's strange isn't it, how I can remember there was a girl, and this paper even tells me what her name was, but I've no conception of *who* she was.' William continued nodding, while Sol added with a faint smile, 'Desperate, isn't it? Perhaps she was important to me. I wonder if it'll ever come back to me. If only it would.' He took the paper and carefully replaced it in the pile over in the corner. 'Let's go for a cruise. I want to show you round this pond.'

Although he didn't say it, William had experienced a convulsion. That name. The name of the girl. Could it be? William was far from putting two and two together. It was all too improbable and wrapped in mystery. A coincidence, no doubt. But he determined there and then he wouldn't let it slip away, out of reach. He would find a way to hound down the truth. But it must remain unknown to Sol. Might it, he wondered, be possible to find a way of spending a little time here in Possum on his own?

They glided quietly around the creeks and inlets of the big lake, from time to time opening up the throttle of the powerful motor, or silently mooring up in a creek, to laze in the warm sunshine.

William was amazed at the seemingly endless perimeter of this man-made reservoir. 'You know, if you idled all day in these creeks and corners, it wouldn't be long enough to see them all.'

Stretched out on the grass, Sol said, 'Yes, idling sounds like the most appropriate word for us two. I used to be pretty energetic when I came out here. Even had friends to pull me on the back of the boat on the skis.'

'Have you got skis?' asked William, sitting up quickly.

'Long gone. Along with my energy. I think I sold them off, not knowing some young blade would be coming along one day.'

William smiled. 'Didn't know I was a young 'blade'. Feel more like a crusty old teacher these days.'

'That's me, not you.' Sol paused for a moment. 'Particularly with this mighty play bearing down on me. Sometimes wonder if I'll ever get it done. Mid-March! Two more months and it's show time! It's scary.'

'I've neglected to ask you how things are going.'

Sol remained silent for a moment and then said, 'William, if ever one day Doublejoy comes into the faculty room and takes you on one side, believe me, it'll be to ask you to put on a play. Just say no.' He'd sat up and was looking William straight in the eye. 'Of course I know you'd make a good stab at it, but it's all those hidden things like lines not learned, or punctuality, or just plain mucking around. They're the things that get you down. I think I've already aged by about five years.' William glanced back at Sol. What his friend had just said was true: Sol looked indefinably weary. He didn't reply, and Sol continued, 'You have to interpret every line; not explain - they understand well enough usually- but *interpret*, on the actual stage, walk them through it. They can't do that for themselves. The 'blocking', if you k now what I mean.' William nodded and Sol added, 'And this play, this particular play, has the added hurdle of 'age'. They're young and the play's about old age.' He paused for a moment, and said, 'Do I look like King Lear yet?'

William was polite enough, sensitive enough, not to reply; nor did he like to say the words '*I told you so*', even though he knew them to be true. Instead he said, 'If you'd like me to come to a rehearsal or two, help out, do that 'blocking' for you, I'd be more than willing. Just say the word.'

Sol didn't reply for a moment; just nodded his head slowly. Then he muttered half under his breath, 'The first time in twenty years I've had to ask for help in a Production.'

William said, '*You* didn't ask. *I* did.'

Sol grunted. 'But *I* didn't decline.' He smiled. 'Sure, you're welcome. Come anytime. I'll let you know when there's a particularly obscure or heavy passage in rehearsal.' Then he said, out of the blue, 'You know, I think I'm going to bow out of the soccer; I don't feel the same burning desire any longer. It's become a bit of a drudge. I think it's all too much.'

William waited silently for Sol to explain, but Sol just looked at him, almost interrogatingly, as if to ask if this was the right thing to do. William said, 'D'you mean school soccer or Rheinischer Hof soccer?'

'Both maybe. But we'd need to get the Boss's permission anyway.'

'How about Johnny?'

'I don't think Doublejoy would agree to that.' Sol shook his head from side to side. 'Johnny's all right. But I don't think he could manage the whole thing. How about you?'

In the space of fifteen minutes Sol had theoretically unloaded one half of his extra-curricular commitments onto William's shoulders. William wondered whether, in the broad light of day, Sol really intended that. Meanwhile, he didn't reply to Sol's proposal, but said, 'How about a swim?'

'Sure. I'll drive, you swim. And I'll hold the life-belt too; in case you get caught in the reeds or attacked by a large fish.'

He laughed, and William took no notice. They started up the engine and glided out into the middle. William stripped to his underwear and dived lithely into the murky water. For a while he duck-dived, slipped beneath the boat, came up the other side and set off with an energetic crawl. All the time, Sol stood in the boat, watching, a bit like a hired life-guard. William swam on, heading for the very middle, occasionally diving under, to see if he could see anything in this water; he couldn't, and then he began to wonder if he could make it to the other side, sort of like a dare to himself. Right to the nearest shore. It might be further than he thought, almost out of sight in some corners. He knew Sol was watching though, and decided he *could* do it, but then hesitated and decided he didn't want to keep Sol waiting. Not now then; another time. He reined his enthusiasm in and glanced back for Sol and the boat.

It wasn't there. The surge of adrenalin that rushed through him was accompanied by mild alarm. His instinct prompted him to look harder. Nothing immediately in front, but quite a long way off a power boat seeming to head fast away, in the opposite direction. William had never experienced moments like this before; he'd read about them and heard about them, but he'd never himself felt the real blind panic, which in the space of a second, confronts cool reason, looks it straight in the face. He knew though that, if he were to survive, reason must prevail. Yes, he *could* make it to the shore, and besides, wasn't that a distant boat veering left in a wide circle? The adrenalin dissipated as quickly as it had come. Yes, it was. *Their* boat, and coming to collect him. William trod water calmly, as the boat roared straight towards him, decelerated, and drew up alongside his head, bobbing on the surface.

Sol was grinning. How can one describe that grin? Not totally friendly but a grin tainted slightly with exhilaration and excitement. Dare-devil. 'Just kidding' came out of Sol's mouth, and William watched him hook the steps onto the stern of the boat. Even in this predicament, this humiliating moment, as he trod water, his innate personal discipline was such that he resisted the temptation to scream abuse at this older man, his colleague, his friend, and compelled himself to continue to trust him. What else could he do? 'I could have made it to the other side anyway,' he said, forcing a smile.

'Yes, I knew you could; just putting it to the test.' Sol was busying with the steps. 'Next time, you know what to do.'

'What? There was a hint of irritation in William's voice now.

'Swim for it, of course. What else?' He paused and then said chirpily, as if the incident had never occurred, 'C'mon. Let's go.' He yanked William out of the water. 'Let's get back and have a beer. I wanted to show you that Temple, remember?' He checked his watch and handed William his clothes. 'They'll be singing now, no doubt; full of the joys of life. We'll go for a stroll there.'

The moment was over, trust restored and that sour taste of panic and terrible sense of loneliness in the water, forgotten. The truth is, such was William's confidence in his own physical strength, he could afford to brush aside any open resentment towards his friend, even though a slim residue of caution and distrust remained towards this man who could want to play such a trick. One doesn't easily forget things like that.

They showered back at the house, drank their beer and set out for the Tabernacle, a short stroll away, in what appeared to William, as they approached, to mark the centre of this tiny community. Sol, for reasons unknown, was already heaping scorn on what he called The *'Adventists'*, while William, alongside, was struggling to understand quite why his friend felt such earnest hostility towards people who surely couldn't impinge directly on his own life. 'They're a type, you know, William.. Almost a different species. Strait-laced, literal, humourless. You wonder really what planet they come from.' He spat the words out, each image in some way ringing true to William, and bearing a certain validity. In his young life he too had met such colourless people as Sol was describing. 'Hypocrites too,' Sol was continuing. 'You know, I remember we used to call them, back in the early days, the 'Dinosaurs'.' He laughed. 'It may sound funny now, but it wasn't funny at all back then. They played such an integral part in our lives. They ran the school, ran Hillcrest, these sorts of people. Would you believe?'

'What? Bible-bashers?'

'Of that type, yes. Bible-bashers is just a general term for a whole variety of born-again Christians in this part of the world.. 'Pentecostal' is perhaps a more universal name. They split from the main church, and then split again. But each sect is characterised by narrowness and intolerance.'

'So how come they ran Hillcrest?'

Sol for a moment marvelled at William's apparent naivety, and yet persistence too, but attempted generously to remember how naïve he'd once been all those years ago. 'They were local Texans, William. They held positions of power in the local community. It stands to reason they were Members of the Board of Hillcrest. To these people, Hillcrest was just another school in its infancy. And the local people, accordingly, needed to keep control, make sure it was on the straight and narrow, and ensure that this new educational establishment wasn't harbouring blasphemous intentions. What better way than to be at the heart of the place?' He shook his head slowly. 'Can you imagine that? Veto on anything that smacked of the unconventional. Quite how our students ever advanced educationally at all, I sometimes wonder. These men were an extinct species, both educationally, socially and morally.' William had never heard his friend so passionate. He sensed that somewhere inside him it was personal. Sol was continuing, 'They were a bar to any sort of progress. Fortunately there were enough great faculty members to counter-balance the influence of these barbarians.' He paused. 'We put on a *'Hamlet'*, did you know? We read lewd American poems. We studied Lady Chatterley. All kinds of unacceptable material.'

William said, '*You* were on the faculty too, weren't you?'

Sol laughed. 'Of course I was. That's why I feel so strongly.'

'Sorry, you seemed to be excluding yourself from this 'great faculty.'.

'No. I didn't mean to.' He was still smiling. 'I played my part; let's say we *all* held it together somehow, even though some more than others. A few dedicated outlaws.'

'Sol, I can't see you as ever being an outlaw.'

'I was once. Yes.' That glazed look that William already knew so well, drifted momentarily over his friend's face. 'When I think about it, they were good days. And education must have rubbed off on at least some students.' They walked on a bit in silence, until Sol returned to this theme he clearly found difficult to leave. 'Don't ever get the wrong idea, William, about these kinds of people we're homing in on right this moment. They were supposed to be responsible for the moral welfare of the kids. Don't believe it. They're hypocrites. Some of them were personally into some really bad stuff. Which in fact never came to light.' His eyes glazed over again. 'In particular, one, I remember. But I don't want to go into all that.'

William had noticed that Sol, at these particular moments of outpouring and condemnation, always followed them with what appeared to be an intense personal effort to drown out the memory. Perhaps they were too painful, or for fear of what he might find if he went too far.

They were standing now outside the 'Tabernacle'. He didn't recollect how he'd got there, so engrossed had he been in Sol's diatribe.

Sol remarked, 'They'll all emerge in a minute. Washed clean.'

William, by way of support, added, 'Off, each Sunday - or is it Saturday? - to pay their dues to the Lord, and then lie and cheat for the rest of the week. Doesn't sound much different from the Catholic Church.'

Sol laughed. 'Yes, forgiveness on demand.' He paused. 'But worse. We're not just talking about religious practice. Don't forget, these guys, these dinosaurs, hold office. In the community. Have power. Tell us where to park our car, tell us how much tax to pay.' After a moment, he asked abruptly, 'What was that famous play? You know, the Scopes Trial?' William didn't know and shook his head. Sol said, 'They made a film of it. I forget the name. Anyway, a teacher, just like you and me, a Science teacher in fact, called Scopes, is put on trial somewhere in the Deep South for teaching the theory of Evolution. You know, Darwin's theory: We're all descended from monkeys.' He laughed. 'That idea, I suppose, was too much, too unpalatable, for the Pentecostal worshippers back then in Scopes's day. In exactly the same way, in fact, as 'Lady Chatterley's Lover' was for the Hillcrest Board.' Sol had started to shake his head slowly, and William knew he was going into one of his reminiscences, as if daring to confront his memories. William asked hurriedly, 'So, who won?'

Sol looked at him. 'What d'you mean?'

'Won the trial.'

'Ah yes. I never finished the story, and therein lies a tale.' He gathered his thoughts a moment. 'Scopes did. What had started out as a show trial, put on by the authorities to declare to the world their ignorant truths, finished up as a fiasco. Scopes had a good, enlightened lawyer. The forces of evil were driven back into their den by the powers of Reason. Scopes was acquitted.'

'Marvellous!' exclaimed William. 'And very nice imagery, too, Sol, if I may say so. I like the *'forces of evil'* bit. A great metaphor.' They stood now looking at the ugly metal erection in front of them, and William added, 'It's a shame they don't *always* lose though.'

'Ha ha,' laughed Sol, 'You know, I reckon that little story, that little triumph in the Deep South, in some way epitomises the whole simple message of Religious faith, if we only realised it.'

'Wow! That's a giant statement. How's that then?'

'Well, Christ, on trial in front of powerful, ignorant men who couldn't or wouldn't recognise the Truth, even if it slapped them in the face. There you have it. In a nutshell.'

William replied, 'I think you're right, except that in the Scopes story, truth triumphs.'

A smile spread across Sol's face. 'Yes, shows maybe the human race must be learning something slowly. But surely, in the biblical tale too, Truth triumphs, doesn't it?'

William thought for a moment. 'Yes, I suppose so. But it's taking a long time for the message to get through.'

The sound of voices proclaiming their own particular brand of truth - a strangely rhythmic, lilting incantation - was by now, on this Sabbath day, emanating loudly from inside the Tabernacle, probably the final stage in this ritual of worship, or whatever else it was.

The two men listened for a moment until finally William said, 'It just doesn't sound right, that singing, does it?

'How do you mean?'

'Well, we sing songs too in our churches, but this singing's not solemn at all. Like ours. Not respectful. It's flighty and basic, the kind of thing you hear on the radio. Pop music.'

'Yes,' said Sol. 'But at least it's chorus, not solo.'

'Worse still,' replied William. They stood for a few more moments listening to the boisterous sound until William said, 'What I suppose I'm really trying to say is ... this music is basic, literal. Like this building itself. No subtlety. Everything is as it seems. No mystery, nothing spiritual about it.'

Sol agreed. 'Well that's like the beliefs they profess of course. Everything is at face value. Seven days; you can take it or leave it. It's just dogma.'

The singing inside the building came to an end. Everything went suddenly silent, and William and Sol were left standing, looking at the ugly building and wondering what kind of species might momentarily emerge. William broke the silence. 'Merciful release. You know, if it weren't potentially harmful, this kind of sham carry-on could be very funny, like a Chaplin film. I can just see it: Women in long dresses, hems sweeping the ground; men crammed into black suits which didn't fit. And all following in the wake of some enormous giant of a guy with the ugliest mug you've ever seen.'

Sol laughed loudly. 'A great image, William. Laurel and Hardy. You've hit the nail on the head. That's probably precisely what will emerge from over there.'

'Yeah, I suppose so. What is it about images, descriptions, which link in with all this paraphernalia?' Sol didn't reply, not quite understanding what his friend meant, and suddenly William gasped, 'Yes, that's it! It's images again. I'm beginning to understand. I'm starting to get it'

'Get what?'

William indicated the group of people milling happily around now outside the church 'Yes, I begin to get it. The image of 'Seven Days'. How can these people be so simple as to believe such a message?'

'That's easy,' said Sol. 'God said so. In black and white.'

'Precisely. A simple, mind-boggling false premise. Therein lies the great error.' Sol sensed, his young friend was about to hit the nail on the head again, and didn't interrupt. 'You see,' continued William, 'God never mentioned Seven Days. The Bible did. But God didn't write the Bible.'

'Don't, whatever you do, tell that to those people down there,' remarked Sol.

'I won't, but I'll tell *you*. These people's whole faith is founded on a false premise; that is, on the belief that God wrote the Bible. He didn't! A *man* wrote the Bible. A humble man, a writer, like you and me.' He turned to face Sol, and added, 'Well, like you, Sol. Not me. And being a writer, he used imagery.'

Sol nodded. 'It's a tool of the trade, I agree. We all know that.'

'Yes. It depicts ideas. And the point is, Seven Days in the biblical context is nothing more than a piece of imagery; it's that simple. However, along comes some willing but unimaginative zealot and invents a new religion on the basis that what he reads in the Bible is God's whole word.' William was shaking his head slowly. 'Was ever so simple a deception used to fabricate so giant a lie?' William laughed and turned to Sol. 'Sol, who *was* this person? Do you know?'

'In fact, I believe it was a couple. They were an ardent middle-aged man and wife living in New England some time in the mid-nineteenth century. You're right though. It's downright frightening how easily people can be persuaded into believing a lie.'

While William had been speaking, the full congregation had been making its way into the open air outside. The two of them watched for a while, until William said quietly. 'Yes. It's a dangerous thing to confuse Imagery with Truth. I can't believe your two humble Victorians imagined the trouble they were going to cause. I can't believe they imagined anything very much at all. But to make such a mistake, just to play safe and not antagonise God.'

There was no immediate reply from Sol to William's latest outburst. Expecting some feedback, William was surprised to see his friend silently focussing, not on him for once, but on one of the congregation who'd emerged, and was standing in a small group a few paces away. Sol wasn't merely looking; he was looking intently.

William glanced in the same direction and exclaimed, 'My god. It's Red beard. What's he doing in a place like this?'

Sol meanwhile had remained as if transfixed and still taking little notice of William, his eyes rooted on the stocky, red-bearded man a few paces away.

It was William who took the initiative. 'Let's go and say hello, even though he's not my favourite person.' He walked a few paces towards Red beard. 'Hello there. Out talent-spotting, Sir?'.

The steely blue eyes William knew so well, looked up, flitted briefly to and fro, and came to land on William's eager young face. 'Do I know you, Boy?'

'I don't know. *Do* you?'

The eyes, unused to getting curt responses, took on a new level of hostility. 'If you know me, Boy, then what's your business? If you don't, then stand aside out of my way, and let me get on with mine.' The Eyes turned in the direction of his three young acolytes. 'Ain't that right, boys?'

The acolytes predictably nodded as if their very lives depended on an up and down motion of the head. William, unwilling to allow the initiative to be wrested from his grasp this time, said, 'Well I remember *you*, without fail. We met down-the-ways a tad. In the great city of Dallas.' Red beard's expression remained blank, and William added, 'You were advising me on how best to kick a football, or some such other useless thing our elders and betters see fit to lumber us with.'

The faintest of lights flickered in Red beard's eyes. 'I remember well. You're that little teacher who looks like he's too young even to teach diddly squat.' The acolytes found that funny and giggled appreciatively..

'Yes, the world's indeed a fickle, topsy-turvy place,' replied William. 'Some of us too young and some too old; so old in fact they get troubled by bad memories and wear red beards to disguise their unappetising faces. But have no fear, Sir; they say God sees even into the heart and soul of the most hardened of sinners, and can surely recognise you, beneath your facial accoutrement. Have you by any chance found the Lord today in there?' William indicated the Tabernacle. 'Or has He, as is more likely, found *you*? For in the words of that observant writer, William Shakespeare: "*We are arrant knaves all, crawling between heaven and earth*". Something like that.'

'It don't do to abuse the Holy Word, Boy.' The response was abrupt, and revealed, William thought, if not panic, then a desire to get off the subject.

He replied, 'Would that be the Holy Word or the Holy Word*s*? One, or many?'

'You know well what I mean. The Word of the Bible.'

'Just one word then. But is not every word in the holy book God's word?

'Every one of them.'

'Then God must indeed be very busy. A prolific writer. I too attempt a modest line from time to time, as does my friend here,' he indicated with his arm to where he believed Sol was watching, 'but I fear even just a page of foolscap takes me one whole day and a welter of effort. Is God a writer perhaps?'

'I don't get your drift, Boy.'

'All I mean to say is, how did God find time to do all that writing and still complete Creation on time? How many days was it it took him?'

'Seven Days and Seven Nights. It states in the Holy Book.'

'See what I mean then?'

It was obvious Red Beard didn't see at all, and was starting to get irritated by this quick-fire questioning. 'Boy, I know your type, you and your friend, parading your easy words round as if they were Manna from heaven. You may fool some, but you don't fool me.' An appreciative ripple of laughter was enough to indicate the acolytes were still there and listening to every word from their master. Red beard took a few steps towards William. 'I've no time to stay and bandy words here with you, my friend. Let me pass. And talking of 'friends',' he looked around, 'I notice *your* friend too seems to have tired of your company.'

He pushed past William, closely followed by his cringing accomplices, while at the same time William noticed that, indeed, Sol was nowhere to be seen. He must have slipped away. Puzzled, William hurried back to the house by the lake. There too, there was no sign of his friend. The place was empty. Without even thinking about it, William found himself over in the corner of the room and stealthily reaching into the pile of papers he knew were wedged between the couch and the table. He pulled the first sheet on the pile out and read: <u>At Possum Kingdom, West Texas, Summer 1967:</u> *Diary of Sol Smith.*

"Dearest Tessa, I woke to the sound of wind and lapping water - that sound you and I remember so well - waves against the hull of a boat. Slap...slap. I was on soft bedding, in a lake-house on the shore of Possum Kingdom." Those vital first few lines...

William looked up now, seeking a continuation of this letter in the little pile of papers. He'd already this morning seen and read this opening part of Sol's apparent diary, a few hours before, in Sol's presence. Perhaps the continuation might give him a clue as to who this mysterious 'Tessa' was. William hurriedly pulled out the next sheet from underneath, and read on, all the while keeping his ears open for Sol's return.: *...I remember sending in a letter to Tessa so long ago (was it 6 years? 7 maybe?) and which remain now, hard-wired in my mind, like an errant phrase of music. But beyond those few brief watery images, no clues as to the desperate events that had preceded them and had left me stranded, unconscious, upon a bunk in the self-same room where I now sit. How had I come to be here? Who had placed me here, and why? Had I been saved? And, if so, from what? It was a void then, and remains to this day a void. Negligently, I'd kept no copy of the letter, but was certain it was the key to it all; yes, and I half remember there'd been something intimated, either in the letter itself or even somehow prior to it, some telling piece of information, which I need to know, but which stubbornly refuses to reveal itself.*

I glance around this so familiar room. Little or nothing seems to have changed; all is as if, for seven years, the little lake-house has slept, remained unoccupied, even unvisited; an ideal place perhaps to come and write, to rid myself on paper of the emotions, the sadness, the despair, the hopes I've carried within me these past few years of restless wandering. They say writing, or talking, can ease the pain and longing, bring release, perhaps even restore memory. Maybe, with time and care, words might complete the jig-saw and lend me some peace. It's been a long time since I've written anything of substance at all or kept a diary. Gone are those heady days at Hillcrest in the 60s: Bill, Hamlet, the thrill of Mary, the Assassination, when I...

The indecisive start of Sol's diary. Here, the page ended. William sat enrapt. 'Who, I wonder, was this 'Bill', this 'Mary', and this enigmatic 'Tessa'? In particular, this 'Tessa'? And, of course, what was that '*telling piece of information*', which Sol had found so elusive? these questions, and others, still preyed on his mind since the morning. How might that '*Dearest Tessa*' be related to Sol? Could it just be co-incidence? Or was it.....

He heard the car approaching the car-port and hurriedly replaced the page and stuffed the bundle back where it came from. Sol entered, scratching his head. 'I had to go back up to the Tabernacle, to catch a better look at that 'Red beard' you call him. All that facial hair. I could swear I've seen him before. He's in my memory. Somewhere. It's unbearably frustrating.'

'Did you find him?'

'No, he'd gone. You'd do best, William, to stay away from him. That's all I know. There's something in his eye that makes me mistrust that ancient hippie.' William could see his friend was upset, striding anxiously backwards and forwards in the little room, as if uncertain what to do next. He seemed suddenly to make up his mind. 'I've just got to go out; see to the boat. Get your things together. We're going.'

'I thought we were staying tonight.'

'No, I need to get back. I've got to do some blocking on the Play. Important rehearsal Monday.'

'You should have brought it with you.'

'I know. But let's go.'

They drove fast and in silence, Sol at the wheel. William got the impression his friend wanted to put as many miles as he could between himself and whatever menace lay at the Lake. He wondered if it was Red beard that had unsettled him.

After several tense miles, William nonchalantly remarked , 'Who's 'Tessa', Sol?'

Sol turned quickly to look at him. 'Why do you ask?'

'Well, you know that sheet of paper you gave me to read?'

Sol didn't reply immediately, just kept his eyes fixed firmly on the road. Finally he mumbled, 'Just some girl I used to know. That's all.'

William didn't believe him, but dropped the matter. It wasn't until they reached the outskirts of Fort Worth that Sol dropped the bombshell. In a cold, hostile tone, like giving a firm rebuke to a recalcitrant student, he said suddenly, 'Don't ever look at my private notes again without my permission. Do you understand?'

William was taken aback; this voice, this hostility, was not the Sol he knew; more like a stranger. To add to his confusion, there lay the nagging question mark as to how he'd been found out. He was certain he'd put the bundle back tidily. He blurted out, 'Yes, okay, I'm sorry. My mother's name is Tessa too, you see. I couldn't resist looking.'

Sol made no immediate reply, kept his eye on the road for a further bout of unbearable silence. What made it worse for William was that his instinct told him something had changed irrevocably between the two of them at that moment and would never again be restored. And all his fault. Nevertheless, as they approached the school that night, his curiosity got the better of him and he couldn't resist asking, 'How did you know?'

To which Sol replied, 'You'd placed sheet 2 on the top of the pile. That's how.'

*****

Sol continued to behave strangely over the succeeding weeks, one moment exuding an unfathomable sense of paranoia and anxiety, the next, flying into unapproachable rage over matters that were quite trivial. Even the students had noticed the change. *'What's the matter with Mr. Smith, Sir?'* More than once William had been accosted by a Senior student with this question, particularly those who had to bear the brunt in play rehearsals.

'I don't know, Sophie; but what *is* the matter?' William might attempt to observe some form of neutrality, as befitted an impartial member of faculty. 'Can't say I've noticed anything. Perhaps it's that time of the month.'

The girl, an attractive blonde who did her best to appear each morning in Assembly looking like Britney Spears, struggled to suppress a giggle. '*Really*, Mr. Beckley! I don't think it's that. But in play rehearsals nowadays you can count on at least one tantrum and one memory blank. And the way he looks at Hayley with his mouth watering. It's embarrassing. Everybody's noticed it; not just me.'

William felt a shock run through him at this last remark, but decided to ignore it. 'You're in the play, aren't you, Sophie.? What part have you got?'

'Oh, just a courtier really. A few lines. But honestly, it's a mad play. It's *meant* to be mad; I know that. But Mr. Smith's making it even madder. Why doesn't he play the part of the mad king himself? It's all Troy can do to manage it anyway.' (Troy was the unfortunate 18 year-old allotted the lead role, grey beard and all, and Sophie evidently, along with the other cast, had already come to realise the insuperable mountain this had left Troy to climb).

'Stick with it, Sophie. I'm sure you're making a good job of your part. Things'll settle down. It's the way of play productions.'

This was William's final word on the subject, delivered, it's true, without ever having had any experience of producing a play himself, and not really believing what he was saying anyway.

However, he had, himself, gained the impression over the past weeks that Sol seemed to be in the grip of a mild form of dementia, a condition not uncommon in the teaching profession, and one William's own grandfather back home had suffered from in later years. Add to this crippling condition the enormous pressure that lay in wait for Sol with the Production, and William knew something might at any moment snap. Sophie meanwhile went on her way with the question, 'Why don't you come to a rehearsal, Mr. Beckley? Mr. Smith sure could do with your help.'

William now remembered that a month previously, Sol had casually tried to enlist his support anyway. Although that plea for help, he realised, had since then probably been withdrawn, during the notably silent relationship they now shared, William had watched Sol indirectly throttle back on some of his other school duties, leaving William to take over; he hadn't gone near a soccer ball, neither at the school nor in Dallas, and had left William to do the job of coaching the boys' team, alongside Johnny. '*I've got too much on my plate. You take over the soccer; I'd appreciate it. And anyway, the boys are bursting to have you out there rather than me.*' The bitterness of these few final words had been evidence enough for William to believe Sol was not himself.

Neither this bitterness though, nor Sol's apparent hostility towards him, had managed to quench William's own thirst for the wide open spaces of Possum Kingdom. It had started to exercise a powerful allure, and in addition he felt the need to get to grips with the pile of writings he'd discovered lurking at the Lake, and to discover more about the history of this increasingly strange man. He'd not been able to forget that word '*Tessa*', which had sprung from the page that evening before they'd left the Lake, nor Sol's apparent unwillingness to talk about it. He'd become instinctively convinced that somehow his own life too might be linked to Sol's in a most unusual way. He couldn't dispel the thought. Nor could he brush aside that astonishing remark down at Sol's place one evening (before their friendship had gone awry). They'd been sitting drinking a beer together when Sol had started to wax eloquent about his family and particularly about his *'Painter'* father: *obsessed with putting brush on canvas, and not to forget his keen love of sport....'* Just those few words had been enough to trigger memories in William of his *own* artistic grandfather: *'the two landscapes fixed on the living-room wall... his name inscribed on the back...part of his inheritance'*. These not insignificant little details, given the context, had shot like a bullet through his head. Surely this reference to *'painting'* and *'sport'* had to be more than mere coincidence. Could it in fact be possible that Sol's *'father'* and his own *grandfather* were one and the same person?'

William could of course have simply written home, asked his mother right out; but something warned him against the turmoil that might unleash. How would he have put it anyway ...? *'Mother, I've made friends, (platonic, of course) with a senior member of the faculty here. I believe we may be related in some way. He's called Sol Smith....* No, his mother, by such a blatant action, would have been left none the wiser. There are many people in the world named 'Smith'. And anyway, how could he himself be related intimately to someone called Smith? Unless, that is, Sol had changed his name somewhere along the line? It got too confusing, and what's in a name anyway? He too, as a matter of fact, wasn't bearing *his* own name either, but had changed it on a whim, in the sheer excitement of arriving at Hillcrest, when he'd signed in with his Grandmother's maiden name *'Beckley'*. Just for a lark.

Lumbered with all these question marks and deliberations, William had eventually decided to lie low and see how the land lay between himself and Sol. The matter was too highly sensitive. Could there ever be a matter more sensitive than the relationship between father and son?

*****

William sat down on one of the wide concreted steps in the centre of the school auditorium. Dead centre. This open-air auditorium had been designed not for acoustics, he guessed, but for scenic value. The view from the top of the wide sloping arch of the auditorium, where he was sitting, was enough to take you breath away on any summer evening, with a sunset blazing in the West above the simple wooden structure that formed the backdrop to the stage. Any audience coming out from town to see a play couldn't help but admire the unique panorama as they made their way down from the dining-hall, or - for the elite among them - up the path from the Head's apartment, where they'd been dined or cocktailed, prior to strolling, in the short-sleeve warmth of the evening, to take their seats precisely where William was sitting now.

True to his word, he'd come to watch a rehearsal of *'Lear'* in progress, even perhaps lend a hand on stage or take critical notes to share with Sol after the players had left. He was drawing on a small cigar, which he thought might lend him the 'Director' image, as well as provide a soothing counter-balance to the earnest role of critic. Right that moment though, he was busy trying unsuccessfully to make out the scene, the lines, actually in rehearsal at that moment. Sol had briefed him only with a copy of the text, not the rehearsal schedule itself. He'd been there already ten minutes without being able to pick out the precise spot in the text, nor had his ears yet discerned any actual spoken 'Shakespeare' at all coming from the players on stage. Were the acoustics that deficient, he wondered? There were five or six players grouped on stage, centred around Sol, who seemed to be engaged in a rather agitated discussion with a Senior boy called Ched. From his limited theatrical experience, William already knew that voice projection was all important for live performances, particularly outdoor ones, and he felt at that moment like calling from his seat at the top of the amphitheatre: *'Speak up. Can't hear you!'*, but realised that would be one intrusion too far; Sol, after all, was already aware of his presence, having shot him a despairing glance the second he'd arrived in the auditorium, the kind of pained expression, William idly thought, *'Gloucester'* might have worn, as his second eye was removed forcibly from its socket by his daughter *'Goneril'*.

The rehearsal clearly wasn't going well. If you want a good rehearsal, you've got to actually *want* a rehearsal in the first place. Sol clearly hadn't; it was for him just one more chore, another hopeless struggle with an unwilling cast, out of its depth in an experience quite unsuited to its inclinations and maturity.

'Sir, how're you going to tackle the castle scenes, the palace, all this indoor stuff like we're doing today? You going to do a film backdrop? It'd look pretty smart.'

Ched, cast as '*Gloucester*', was asking a not completely irrelevant question given the circumstances, and certainly neither rude nor even provocative.

Sol replied, 'First off, Ched, what *d'you* know about stage sets?'

'At my last school we had a Supremo stage manager, Mr. Smith, Sir.' The student thought for a moment. 'Come to that, we had a good Director too.'

That was clear provocation. One of the Senior girls, Hattie, playing *Cordelia*, and genuinely indignant at Ched's comment, cut in. 'Ched, that wasn't called for. Mr. S. is doing his best. He knows a lot more about putting on a nice stage-set than you ever will.' She looked around the small group and raised her voice. 'C'mon you guys. Wake up. You've gotta put your backs into the play or we won't even have a play. It's so embarrassing.'

Sol, a gentle leer on his face, stood listening patiently to Hattie before intervening.. 'Ched, we don't want to start a discussion about sets; let alone a slanging match about them. We don't have time. Your question is theoretically a good one, but.leave me to do the sets and I'll leave you…' he stopped, hesitating, and then, addressing the entire group, he said, 'I'll leave you *all* to learn your lines and try to understand your character and put it in context. Because we're not getting anywhere at the moment. You're terrible. The rehearsal's terrible, the performance will be terrible, if you don't get your act together.'

This time, William had little difficulty hearing the lines, because Sol's voice was raised, if not in anger, then in the promise of it. Sol's words might have been lifted directly from the text, and were received by his students with a subdued dismay. Nor did Sol leave it at that.

'You've been like a row of dummies this evening, no, wait, I'll correct that, a row of *zombies*, mouthing gibberish.'

'But Sir...'

'Let me finish! 'You're actors, not dummies. You're supposed to interpret lines and emotions. But what you've been saying this evening, what you've been mouthing, bears no relation whatever to what's in the text.'

'Sir, it's a difficult play.' Another Senior girl, Hayley, playing '*Reagen*', remarked despairingly. 'You've got to show us *how* to say it. Teach us.'

'Much as I would love to mimic every single one of your lines on the night, Hayley, I don't think we'd get away with it, do you? Haven't I the right to expect a little bit of intuition from each of you?'

Silence. Then the boy, Ched, said, 'That's it, Mr. Smith. You just don't encourage us.'

William, assumed Sol would have the sense to leave it at that, call the kids to order and get on with speaking '*Shakespeare*'. But no. In a calmer voice, Sol now proclaimed unexpectedly, 'Ched, in answer to your original question, do you want me to tell you *how* I'm going to manage those 'castle' scenes you so correctly referred to?'

The boy was taken aback by this sudden change of manner and context, and probably expected a trick. 'Sure, Sir, If you like.' There was a naïve grin on his face.

'Okay.' Sol paused and continued, 'Then I'm going to tell you. I'm going to do precisely *nothing*.'

Nobody got the drift of this remark, and all waited breathlessly for at least an explanation. It was Ched who finally had the courage to ask, 'Is that because you don't know yourself, Sir?'

'By no means. I just happen to think '*Lear*' is not a play that needs refined and intricate stage properties.'

Ched answered, head now held high, 'Now you're talking, Sir. Why not?'

Sol for once seemed to have the whole group's attention. And William's too. 'Okay, here's what I plan to do, I'm going to take three large rocks, find them or have them made out of *paper maché*, and simply place them strategically around the stage.'

'Won't that be a bit bare, Sir?' asked Sophie.

'It will, Sophie. But, believe me, bare is how it should be.' He waited, and then pronounced, 'You see, this play, 'King Lear', is so bleak, so utterly devoid of hope, that it strips the characters down to nakedness, and the set too.' He stopped for a moment, recalling a line from the play. *'poor bare, forked animal, such as I am.* D'you remember that line, Ched?' Ched nodded thoughtfully while Sol continued, 'Well, it says it all, doesn't it?' You could have heard a pin-drop as Sol continued, 'What you need to understand is that in Shakespeare the set has to capture the mood of the play as a whole.' He looked directly at Ched. 'Then, Ched, what more appropriate properties might there be for this play than three elemental boulders strewn at random across the stage? Let the drear language do the rest. And don't forget, in the supposed prehistoric setting of this history, there were hardly any trappings anyway, except what nature provided.'

Following a general silence, someone said, 'Sir, why haven't you told us all this before?'

'I played you the movie, didn't I?'

At this precise moment William felt it appropriate to intervene. All eyes looked up at him, a solitary figure in the auditorium, as he said, 'Yes, Mr. Smith's right, but of course movies can't give you the whole picture, can they? Just look at this whole rocky stage here, where I'm sitting; it's pretty bare too, isn't it? It's a perfect setting for the scene Mr. Smith's got in mind. With a little adaptation it might ....'

Sol however didn't let him finish but broke in abruptly. 'Right, we've talked long enough about sets.' He glanced at his watch. 'Let's get back to the text. See if we can rescue something from this fiasco. *'Reagen'*, Page 24.' He looked across at Hayden. 'You're about to evict your absent-minded father from his own home...deliver him over to the bare elements. Let's get on.'

For William, it was obvious he'd been deliberately cut out of the rehearsal, for whatever motive. And rudely too. He was left wondering what precisely Sol considered his supportive role to be, sitting up there, a solitary figure, listening now to a session that had reverted to a play-reading exercise: no blocking, no movements on stage, no acting. Instinctively, William knew this whole undertaking would never work, nor his collaboration in it either. There just wasn't time any longer.

He felt hurt. His mind wandered off, and it wasn't until the students started to pad past him on the steps and until he received a few respectful *'have a good evening, Sir'* that he realised the rehearsal was over. Sol came striding past, making a deliberate gesture of ignoring him. Then, a minute later, suddenly there stood Hattie, a good kid, respected by both faculty and the student body, sitting down beside him now on the stone steps.

'Hi Hattie.' Despite the disastrous evening, William felt determined to put a positive light on the matter if possible.

'Hope you don't mind, Mr. Beckley sir. Could I speak with you a minute?'

'Of course.' William shifted over to give her the chance to sit down clumsily alongside him.

'Oh, I do just hate these big concrete seats they have here, don't you, sir? It's a wonder they get any audience at all to plays.'

William grinned. 'You're right. I think they put cushions, pad them up a bit on the night. Anyway, what's on your mind, Hattie? Not too good a rehearsal this evening.'

'It never is, Mr. B, sir. It's always just arguments. We never get anything done.'

William nodded. 'No. It's not easy; I can see that.'

There was a short silence, before Hattie said abruptly, 'Is there something perhaps wrong with Mr. Smith?'

William shifted in his seat and looked straight at her. 'It's not easy to say, Hattie. I haven't probably known him as long as you. You're a Senior; did you come all the way through the school?'

'I've been here since Grade 9. Mr. Smith has really changed this past year or so. He used to be so calm. He was wonderful. Dynamic. He's become so...' she looked for the word... 'so moody.'

'In class too, Hattie?' William didn't want to appear to confirm the whole situation. He knew it was sensitive.

'No, it's okay in class.' She laughed. 'It's a different situation there. We *expect* the teacher to bawl us out in class.'

William laughed too. It relieved the tension. 'Hattie, have you come here on your own accord?'

'No, not really, Sir. Some of the other girls asked me to come and talk to you. They all feel the same, And the boys too. We need someone to really direct us. Teach us. Mr. Smith just goes over the top if we make a mistake.' William waited for her to continue. 'We all can see it' a lovely play. A great play. But we really wonder if it's for us, if you see what I mean.'

William pretended to give it a moment's reflection, unwilling completely to concede the girl's point 'You see, Hattie, it's tragedy. It's hatred, betrayal, anger, even madness. All those kinds of emotions.'

'That's just it, Mr. B. I can see how wonderful the words are, but the emotions, I mean the situations, aren't really ones we encounter in our own lives. They're just too drastic.' She looked at him. 'I can't really explain what I mean.'

'No, you're doing a great job, Hattie.' William was actually amazed at Hattie's maturity. 'I understand exactly what you mean about the play. Perhaps nowadays we've found ways around those drastic situations. In *real* life, I mean. We have doctors, we have judges, we have civilisation.' He looked at her, grinning. 'Perhaps we're just plain and simply nicer.'

'That's exactly what I mean. It's not relevant to us nowadays. So why go there then?'

William found it hard to answer the question. At last he said, 'Look, Hattie. It's not altogether irrelevant. Whatever we like to think, anger and betrayal haven't just gone away. Those emotions still exist, it's just that maybe we control them better.' He paused for a moment. 'Dramatists aren't all that practical, you see. Particularly when it comes to tragic situations, like in our play. If you go back a long way, ancient dramatists actually believed showing audiences terrible things had a good effect on their audience. Made them better people.'

Hattie was shaking her head. 'I can see you know a lot about this, Mr. B. But I just can't get my head round it; we're just not like they were.' She hesitated, before launching the key question. 'Why don't you take over from Mr. Smith? We'd all get on much better.' She smiled. 'Might even try a happier play.'

'It's not all that easy, Hattie. That's all I can say at the moment.'

They both sat there silently, watching the final strip of pink slowly fade to nothing in the West. William was quietly wondering whether Hattie's suggestion might even be a relief to Sol if it happened. He'd already almost made up his mind anyway on the course of action Hattie was proposing. 'Do the others think like that too. Hattie?'

'They sure do, Mr. B. In fact they asked me to come talk with you.'

After a moment or two William said, 'Look, I appreciate you coming. Would you leave it with me. I'll talk to Mr. Smith.'

Hattie went off, but William didn't immediately go back to his room. It was peaceful out there. He sat thinking again about that conversation earlier in the rehearsal, when Sol, in a quieter, more lucid moment, had been explaining to Ched about stage settings and how they imitated the essence of the play itself. He was trying to piece it together in his head....

William was found early next morning by the Headmaster, Mr. Doublejoy, and his dog. The dog had gone up and sniffed this figure, wrapped in Hattie's jacket and curled up on the stone steps, fast asleep. It turned out that, before dozing off, William had been thinking about a performance of '*A Winter's Tale*' he'd once watched as a student, that joyous play, he remembered, with a joyous ending, so unlike the harsh conclusions of '*Lear*', with the scent of death always prevalent. How, he'd wondered, could one expect seventeen- and eighteen-year olds, in the prime of their young life, to grasp tragic drama, the epitome of wretchedness and hopelessness that one confronts in Act V? It was beyond their scope.... So, if he were to cut large parts of the dialogue of *A Winter's Tale*, shorten it, invent a Narrator to move the play on, make it all into a story rather than a play, the student cast he'd seen that evening could possibly, at this stage, pull it off .... He'd tried juggling in his mind the trappings too, the set ... make it a bed-time story, an opening and a closing of a book. (The stage director could easily fix a flap, make it seem like the cover of a book)...yes, and the floor of the stage would look good painted black/white, in chequered squares, resembling a kitchen or hallway, and reflecting overall an ordered, well-established setting, certainly not the end-of-life, as in *Lear*... Yet, over and above these various superficial adaptations, in William's mind before he fell asleep, lay like a beacon, the message itself, at the heart of the play: the theme, the author's statement: a play of joyfulness, a statement of forgiveness and reconciliation, of coming together, of Life not Death, an affirmation of love....

******

PART 4
(THE CATALYST)

CHAPTER 23

It wasn't through careful planning but apparently quite by chance that Mack Neumann bumped into Ingrid Spindler in Hamburg in the early spring of 1994. Strange how chance can devise ways of intervening in matters of great significance to those involved, radically transforming their lives. Wasn't it after all by chance that Lenin met Trotsky or that a man like Hitler should stumble unexpectedly on the Wall Street Crash of 1929 to launch his destructive platform.

Spring was already coming to Hamburg in all its amazing scents and sights in March 1994, as Mack made his way from the Mensa, and headed towards the Alster and the heart of the City. Although now a well-established lawyer and partner in a practice with offices in Berlin and New York, he still chose to 'steal' a student lunch whenever he visited Hamburg. Thus, after a wholesome lunch and finding himself near the *Neuer Wall*, he was immediately reminded of those carefree days when he would hurry into the *Teestube* and lose himself in a chess-game with his friend Georges, the Greek, or alternatively embark on a lively religious altercation with his foreign friend, William Bellman, that enigmatic student from England they'd all universally nick-named 'Luther'. Where had those heady days all vanished to, when he could idle away the hours, and not need to account on a spread-sheet for every working minute and expenditure? He was losing touch with his carefree youth, and worse, losing touch with that uninhibited band of colleagues; all in the dubious name of 'success'.

On the spur of the moment, that Spring day, Mack chose to ignore his vigorous accounting ritual, and decided to drop into the *Teestube* for a post-prandial coffee, as in the old days. However, it was at that precise moment that Ingrid, checking her watch, headed for the Exit to the same coffee house (in order to attend her afternoon array of lectures on 'Family Law') and either Chance or Providence had arranged for the two of them to cross, he on the way **In** and she on the way **Out**. In an instant, Mack realised he knew that tall girl squeezing by, while Ingrid, even quicker off the mark, knew precisely *who* the tall man was brushing past her, and, at the same moment, came to the decision *not* to acknowledge him. She was like that; modest and unassertive, and a bit shy . Fortunately for Fate however, Mack himself possessed none of those three attributes, and exclaimed *'Ingrid'*, with all the elation and surprise he could muster.

Her heart beating fast, Ingrid shook the proffered hand, smiled a lot, blushed even, and swopped her telephone number with this old friend, promising him she wouldn't slam the phone down if he called her. Mack did phone, and they agreed to meet up one evening - *'this week,'* - to catch up on the myriad events that had invaded their lives over the past two years. Ingrid, of course, made sure to propose an alternative venue to the one from which she'd said goodbye to William Bellman some fifteen months earlier.

They met. Among the many other things they discussed that evening - their shared interests in the legal profession for instance - Ingrid was naturally keen to tell her newly-discovered friend, after a bit of gentle probing, about her brief relationship with William Bellman a year or two before, and about her subsequent trip to England. Mack, of course, had always had a shine for Ingrid himself back in those days, but, in the interim, he'd finally come to terms with his loss and had to admit defeat at the hands of a younger, more enigmatic man, who at the same time possessed 'foreign' allure. 'That UK trip sounds fantastic, Ingrid. Where did you stay?'

Ingrid felt a slight surge of pain at the memory of that brief romance, but compelled herself to forgive and forget, as she had stoically done already for so many months. 'Oh, it was cheeky. I took the bull by the horns and just turned up in England. He couldn't very well have sent me back then.'

Mack was puzzled. 'He wouldn't really have wanted to, would he? Someone like you arriving unannounced on his doorstep would be like manna from heaven.'

She smiled. 'It wasn't of course quite like that. I had a job to go to. An *au pair* job very near to where he lived.'

'How did you know where he lived then?'

'We swopped notes hurriedly in a café, before he left Hamburg that December.'

Mack paused for a moment. 'Where *does* he live then.'

'It's a town called W.... Near London really. I did my homework with a map before I accepted the *au pair* job.' She smiled.

'As any careful-thinking lawyer might well have done.'

'Yes, London was the main thing, William came second.'

'Are you quite sure, Ingrid?'

Mack laughed and Ingrid replied, 'Ah well. Maybe.'

They paused for a moment, and then Ingrid said, 'We've only had the briefest of contacts since I came back - perhaps a letter or two - but, so far as I know, he's not doing much at the moment. Trying to find his feet.' She looked hard at Mack for a moment. 'But don't feel sorry for William, he's living in the lap of luxury. Typical William. Lovely big house. Mother cooking for him. Grandfather keeping him company.'

'And father too, presumably?' said Mack, a questioning note in his voice.

There passed a few moments of hesitation before Ingrid said quietly, 'He doesn't have a father, Mack. Didn't you know?'

'Everybody has a father, Ingrid; or, at any rate, *had* a father. Did he die then?'

'No, I think he's alive, but from what I could gather, it seems his father disappeared sometime soon after his birth. Tessa briefly mentioned it, but of course I don't know the full story. I *do* know though Tessa brought William up all by herself. She's a lovely, clever lady.'

Ingrid's words dropped like a stone into a pool, and shook Mack more that he'd like to confess. After a moment, he asked, 'Did you say 'Tessa'?'

'Yes, Tessa Bellman. William's mother. I thought you knew.'

'How should I know?' Mack's question was abrupt, almost unintentionally forthright. It was his turn to feel a surge of pain, at the mention of Tessa. He pulled himself together and said, 'I know William's mother then. I know Tessa Bellman. I know her more than just '*know*' her. I was at school back in the States with someone called

Tessa Bellman. Way back when. Is this the same Tessa? How many Tessa Bellmans can there be in this world, for heavens sake?'

Ingrid said, smiling, 'Mack, I really don't know if she's the same Tessa. But that's who I stayed with, and got to know. Have you seen *your* Tessa since then?'

'How could I? I've been in Hamburg since I left the States. We lost touch.'

'When was that?'

Mack thought for a moment. 'Must have been 1970. Almost twenty-five years ago. Yes, I last saw Tessa in....'

He didn't finish his sentence, lost suddenly in his memories of those seemingly so distant years. He'd not forgotten how much in awe he'd always held her during that short time they'd lived together in Canada, she with her tiny child, he just discerning for the first time the responsibility of manhood, of caring for another human being, protecting them. Both he and Ingrid sat now for a full five minutes, sipping their coffee, locked in their own thoughts and scarcely able to believe the chain of events that had just unfolded before them.

At last, Mack murmured, 'Can this be more than just blind co-incidence?'

And Ingrid said, 'Mack, now I've found you again, promise I won't lose you like you seem to have lost Tessa. That's not meant to be.' Mack was nodding his head, and Ingrid added, 'Look, I'm very fond of William, as you must know. You are apparently, from what you say, fond of William's mother, Tessa. Then why don't we both pay them a visit, presuming they're still there. I think I could fix it up.'

'Really? Are you sure?'

'She can only say no, can't she? But she wouldn't. I know. I can phone her, say I'm coming with a friend and could we drop in?'

Mack continued to nod as their story moved on another notch. 'Listen, I'm due a bit of leave. They're sending me to New York. The firm has an office there.'

Ingrid quickly replied, 'Couldn't we then arrange to tie that in with a visit to England? Just a day or two, and you could fly on to the States.'

Two days later, they caught the morning flight from Hamburg to Heathrow. Ingrid, uncertain whether to mention Mack immediately by name in this forthcoming sensitive encounter, and eventually deciding not to, had called Tessa, telling her she was '*coming to London, with a 'friend', and wondered if they 'could drop in for a 'cup of tea and a chat.*' Ingrid hadn't deliberately intended to be deceptive about Mack; she just felt unsure how he and Tessa really stood. She'd continued, '*It'd be so lovely to see you all again, Tessa, but don't go to any trouble. My friend will be flying on to New York in a few days, and wanted to see a bit of London en route.*' That was how she'd left it.

Tessa of course had been overjoyed. The loneliness of saying goodbye to both her foster parent and her precious son, in the space of a month, had hit her quite hard. 'I'd love to see you, Ingrid darling, and catch up on your news. You know the way, and you'll have a car. Give me a ring when you leave the airport.' Tessa, as ever, had been kind and practical. 'We'll never have time to squeeze all our news into one cup of tea. You *will* stay over, won't you?' This last comment was more a plea than a question. 'You'll have your old room back. You could even share with your friend.' She'd left Ingrid with some brief directions on the route from Heathrow, and said, 'About 45 minutes to an hour. Head for W....'

As they drove up the wide avenue, still so fresh in Ingrid's memory, the cherry trees were just coming into blossom as if welcoming her home, and already lending an auspicious air to the visit. In the driveway, Ingrid took in, at a single glance, the big house, the little front lawn, the thick picket hedge sheltering the house from prying eyes. Nothing had changed. Of course, William's presence then, and their intimate relationship two years previously, had surrounded everything for her in a magical aura, and now, just for a moment, she felt a twinge of nostalgia and nervousness, but compelled herself to focus on meeting William again in such different circumstances. She was determined not to dwell on the past, but to take him how she found him. All these thoughts and emotions were racing together as she and Mack stood in the porch and she pressed the door-bell.

Tessa must have been already aware of their arrival. Ingrid remembered a small, convenient little window set into the doorway, which allowed a view, from within, of any visitors outside. A wise precaution, she thought. She hoped desperately now that, on this occasion, they, inside, liked what they saw.

There stood Tessa, framed in the doorway. 'Ingrid, Darling!' A radiant smile was already starting to light up her face and eyes as she caught sight of her good friend, and then she noticed the tall, stern-looking; early-middle-aged man standing behind Ingrid. And, For a tense moment, her broad smile faded for a second, to be replaced by uncertainty and hesitation as.she failed to recognise Mack. And then, as recognition returned, she was whispering beneath her breath 'Mack. Mack. Is it really you, Mack? But you've changed so much. It *is* really you, isn't it? I just can't believe it.'

Ingrid wondered for a second if Tessa might faint, but fortunately Mack, brushing bravely forward and past Ingrid, proclaimed reassuringly, 'Hello, Tess. Yes, it's me. I hope, by the way, I've changed for the better.'

Tessa smiled but still remained speechless. Ingrid blurted out an explanation as hastily as she could. 'Tessa, darling, I didn't know whether to mention Mack by name, when I called. I just hoped it would be a nice surprise.' She indicated Mack. 'Mack and I recently met up in Hamburg after just two or three years only. But I believe it's about twenty-five years since *you* last saw Mack. I do hope this isn't too much of a shock for you.'

Tessa still didn't say anything but remained looking steadfastly at Mack, as if, by doing so, she might stop him from disappearing again. At last, she took a pace forward and grasped him between her two outstretched arms and hugged him as if she'd never let him go. Ingrid, in this moment, knew and understood how much Mack meant to Tessa, and how the past can occasionally combine with the present in one enormous and overwhelming wave of sentiment.

Tessa at last broke away from Mack and reverted briskly to the role of hostess. 'Come on in. I think I've just got to sit down and draw breath.'

Mack, smiling, followed her into the house. 'I never used to have this effect on you, Tessa.'

They all three laughed loudly, and that glorious but overpowering enchantment of unexpected reunion was mercifully broken. Tessa, leading them through the large hallway, said, 'It's as if Hillcrest and

Redemption

Texas just walked through the door.' She turned quickly to Ingrid. 'Well, not Ingrid exactly, but of course, in my mind, I can't help linking *you* Ingrid, with my son, William.' She paused for a second and added, 'And he's in Texas too right now.'

Ingrid, unable to conceal her dismay, blurted out, 'Isn't William here then?'

Tessa didn't fail to notice Ingrid's disappointment. 'No, it's such a shame. I'm on my own. William's gone out to Texas, and Grandpa passed away just about the time William left.'

Ingrid, swallowing her own feelings of sadness, said, 'I'm terribly sorry, Tessa. He was such a lovely man.'

'Yes, he was hard work too though; but strangely I miss him a lot. I was forgetting you met him occasionally too Ingrid, didn't you, when you were here that time.'

'Yes, a number of times. William often took me up to the 'painter's sanctuary'.

Tessa laughed. 'Grandpa's inner sanctum.' She turned to Mack. 'You must think us two mad, Mack. Sorry. We're talking about Grandfather's room at the top end of the house. Where he lived with his precious painting kits.'

Ingrid said, 'He tried to give me one of his paintings once, you know.'

'*Show* you, more like, Ingrid. He could be very possessive. Quite a recluse too. Scarcely left the room towards the end.'

Mack said, 'I'd love to visit this great room. But what about William, Tessa? Tell me about my good chess buddy of Hamburg fame. Where precisely has he gone?'

'Sorry. I was forgetting. He's at Hillcrest. Left here last September. Couldn't make up his mind where to go, so eventually my sister Elizabeth and I made it up for him. Virtually pushed him out.'

Ingrid, feeling this conversation about her former lover was slipping away from her and awakening old wounds, asked rather desperately 'Where's Hillcrest?'

Tessa said, 'Of course. Sorry, Ingrid, we're leaving you out in the cold. Hillcrest's my old school in Texas.' She smiled, 'And Mack's too.'

Ingrid nodded. 'What's he up to out there now, Tessa? Is he teaching?'

'He was, at the last call, but I hear from him so seldom, he could be doing anything by now.'

'Yes, he never was very good at communicating, was he? Let alone making decisions.' She turned to Mack. 'I never knew you were brought up in Texas.'

Mack nodded too. 'I think there's a lot we three don't know about each other. We'll have to catch up. I'm a dark horse, you know, Ingrid.' A teasing smile had spread across his face. 'Tessa already knows that, but you don't, Ingrid. And yes, in a previous life, I went to school in Texas and I grew up in Wyoming' He paused. 'I suppose that makes me an American.' He smiled. 'Along with Tessa.'

Tessa said, 'Don't let's talk about me and America right now.' She looked earnestly at Mack and Ingrid. 'Tell me about yourselves. And I'm terribly sorry, I never offered you that cup of tea. Let me get it now. Is tea all right?'

She disappeared into the little adjoining room as the other two shouted, '*Of course.*' And Mack added, 'A real cup of good old English tea.'

Tessa ignored Mack's hint of sarcasm and called, 'And what are *you* both doing? Not in the past I mean, but in the here and now. And don't worry; I can hear quite well in my little inner sanctum.'

Mack called, 'We're lawyers, Tess. Both of us. Good old boring lawyers. Not adventurers and travellers, like you and your son.'

Tessa said, 'Hah. I may once have been an adventurer, one time in my life anyway, but not any more. Tell me, are you both working in Hamburg?'

'Hamburg and Berlin for me,' replied Mack, and I think Ingrid's mainly stationed in Hamburg at the moment. Don't forget, we've only just met up again ourselves. We're all in a state of reuniting. It's quite intriguing actually.'

'I suppose it is,' said Ingrid softly. 'An interim stage between coming and going, I think you could call it. But Tessa, I'm certainly not quite the high-flyer in the legal world that Mack is. I'm sort of still apprenticing.'

Tessa placed the pot of tea on the table, remarking, 'Say what you like about English tea, Mack, but they really *do* do it best.' She paused. 'Anyway, talking of 'best', I assume you're the best lawyer in town too, Mack.' Still pouring the tea, she turned deliberately to Ingrid. 'You know, I always thought Mack would turn out to be a straight-faced lawyer. No insult intended of course. It's just that he's so logical and practical.' She paused for a moment. 'I already knew it when I was seventeen and he was eighteen, and we were putting on the 'great play'.'

Ingrid, sipping her tea, was nodding. 'You're right about the tea, Tessa. We Germans never quite make the grade with tea. But tell me, what's this *'great play'* you're referring to?'

Needing no prompting, Tessa replied *'Hamlet'* actually,' and added, 'Much too difficult for adults, let alone school kids. But we think we pulled it off pretty well.' She glanced at Mack. 'When was it? 1965? Yes, Mack's senior year and my junior year. Two years after the Assassination.' She smiled, looking at Mack. 'Good times. But I knew in my heart practical Mack would be something like a lawyer when he refused even to come out for a part; just chose dreary old Stage Manager.'

'I remember there was another person who started off her stage career as 'stage manager'. She was called Tessa Bellman.' He turned to Ingrid. 'But you should have seen her when they finally realised she was a brilliant actress, and gave her a main part.' He glanced at Ingrid. 'I, of course, knew from the start that I never had the imagination to act.'

Tessa said, 'But, don't forget, they gave *you* a part too in the end, Mack. A very important one, I remember.' Mack seemed puzzled, while Tessa jogged his memory. 'The *'Mime'*, Mack. Have you forgotten?. The *'Assassin'*?'

'Oh that. That was nothing. Hardly a lead role, like yours.'

'What was your part, Tessa?' asked Ingrid.

Mack jumped in. 'Nothing less than *Ophelia*.'

Ingrid thought for a moment. 'Even *I've* heard of that role. I wish I'd been there, to see you perform, Tessa. Everyone seems to know about *'Hamlet'*, except me.' She looked hard at Tessa. 'So you're a great actress too then, Tessa. Along with all your other talents.' There was a brief silence, until Ingrid added, 'You know, I believe that's where your son, William, gets his imagination. I love imaginative men.'

'Too much imagination, I sometimes think,' remarked Tessa, while Mack said, grinning, 'So that's where I missed out, is it Ingrid? I see it clearly now.' He was shaking his head, the grin still on his lips. 'A dreary lawyer. How could I ever have stood a chance with a handsome, young, imaginative Englishman like William around?'

'The two women found Mack's plaintive comment rather amusing, and Ingrid, a faint smile on her lips, said, 'All that time, Mack, and I never realised your true worth.'

There followed a short pause before Mack added, 'In fact, I'm starting to think that's where I missed out on Tessa too.'

Tessa looked him directly in the eyes. 'What on earth do you mean, Mack? Were we ever an item?'

'Oh, I 'm just kidding. But all this talk about being 'practical' and 'unimaginative', let me remind you, Tess, looking back a few years and thinking of that time we were both together out in Canada, you with your baby, you didn't mind my being *practical* now and again, mending a few doors and windows, mowing the grass, carrying the heavy loads, even protecting you and your baby from intruders in that desolate place.' The smile flitted across his face. 'No, then I was just big, bold Macintosh.'

Tessa was laughing whole-heartedly. 'What's all this '*Mackintosh*' business, Mack? I never called you that. That's not a name, that's what the Brits call a raincoat if you really want to know.' She paused. 'And as for 'protection', I seem to remember one occasion, when I thought a bear was actually lolloping towards me, you were typically nowhere to be seen.'

Mack was genuinely puzzled. 'What occasion are you referring to, Tess? You've really lost me.' He waited, together with Ingrid too, who'd been drawn into this interaction in spite of herself.

A questioning note in her voice, Tessa finally replied, 'Sam?. Have you forgotten Sam?'

'Sam?' Mack remained silent for several moments, genuinely struggling to remember the name that had tripped so lightly off Tessa's tongue. Then he came to life again, as suddenly as he'd left it. 'Sam.

Yes, Sam, of course. The messenger. I really had forgotten him, Tessa. Believe me. I hardly remember him being a *bear* though.

Tessa smiled. 'He might have been, for all you cared, Mack. As you well remember, there were quite a few stray black bears in that neck-of-the-woods in those days; when I saw Sam striding towards the cottage, I honestly took him for a grizzly at first. And me, defenceless, with a tiny baby on my lap.'

Mack just grinned and said, 'Hardly, Tessa,' while Ingrid, who'd been following this intriguing dialogue eagerly, and starting to regret she'd not been able to share this apparently vital episode with her two new-found friends, remarked, 'You two seem to have lead very exciting lives.'

Tessa noticed her discomfort. 'I'm sorry, Ingrid. We're both getting carried away down memory lane. Hopes and failures.'

Mack, however, with the true lawyer's instinct, was turning over in his mind seemingly trivial links in the past, vital leads that might actually have remained relevant even up to this present moment; this sudden, rekindled memory of Sam had taken firm root once more in his lawyer's brain. And Tessa too meanwhile couldn't resist replaying in her own thoughts that desperate little scene in the cottage at Elk, where the young black man had poured out his heart and soul to her, as William played contentedly on the carpet.

Mack broke the silence. 'Yes, Tessa. I shouldn't forget Sam, you're right.'

Tessa said, 'Tea anybody? Have another cup of tea. Have another two cups of tea. Stay and have dinner. Stay the night. Stay as long as you want to. It's definitely too late now to be booking somewhere, and we've got room enough in this big house. We can even all sleep in separate beds, if that's the general wish.

Mack felt a surge of desire at the ambiguity of Tessa's words, but said, 'That'd be lovely, if that's okay with Ingrid; I've got a flight to catch to New York the day after tomorrow. That's all.'

'Wonderful. Then stay two nights; and I've got a surprise for you for the rest of this afternoon. It's near at hand, I promise. We can all go for a walk through Cassiobury Park, and down to the canal. A short stroll. And I *have* to show you where my son used to do his football training.'

'Please don't tell us any more right now, Tessa,' said Ingrid. 'For me, it's too much to take in, in many senses. I seem to have missed out on most of your two lives, but I'm determined not to miss out on any more.'

Tessa seemed to be awakening from a long sleep; as if, like a chrysalis, she was emerging into the sunlight of her two old friends' reappearance in her life. As they walked down the small road together, she was already pointing out landmarks that could only possibly be relevant to her and her long struggle with solitude.

'*There*!' She was pointing to a non-descript house on the opposite side of the road. 'That's where William's Granddad lived. Almost right on top of the entrance to the Park.' She smiled. 'Not to mention the precious town football pitch. A vital venue of course.' They walked on through the narrow passageway leading into the park. No-one could fail to be impressed by this giant, wide-open space, almost in the centre of town.

'Where William came each day to jog and do his calisthenics.' Tessa laughed. 'I'm sure he probably frightened off a few old couples with his weird physical jerks.'

'It's a public park, Tess. I could do with a bit of calisthenics myself.' He patted his stomach. 'Just sitting in an office all day.'

'Then, keep walking, Mack. Let's head for the Canal.. Walk it off..' She indicated in the direction. 'Way down the bottom end of the Park. The Grand Union.'

'Sounds very grand, Tessa,. It certainly is a lovely park,' said Ingrid. 'And don't worry about Mack. He'll be off running; just like your son.'

'Mack said, 'No, I won't. I'm listening. I'll stay with Tessa.'

Tessa seemed scarcely bothered either way, wrapt in memories of her son.. 'Every Saturday, at 2.30 pm, regular as clockwork, William and Grandpa strode out together, on this precise pathway, to their beloved football.'

'A nice tale, Tessa,' said Mack. 'Was that why William was doing his 'calisthenics'?'

'Mack, I sometimes despair of you. Of course it wasn't. The town soccer pitch, I'm talking about.. William was only young then.'

'I'm getting confused, Tess. Don't forget, I'm a lawyer now. I need precise details. Time and date.'

'A pedant, more like, Mack.'

They all laughed, and headed off in the direction of the Canal. It was during this short walk to the Canal that Ingrid strayed off on her own, attracted by the band-stand and a small plaque that stood at the entrance to the grandiose building. Mack meanwhile found himself alone with Tessa.

As tactfully as possible, he seized his chance to ask her something that had for a long time puzzled him. 'Tess, I don't want to pry, but since we've met up this time, you've always referred to 'Grandfather' when the topic of William has come up. You never mention William's *father*. Do you mind my asking...' he hesitated for an instant, ...'who is William's father, and where is he? Your former husband supposedly? I'd love to know, not as a lawyer, but as a friend.'

Tessa smiled and said quietly, 'You remember that time we lived together in Canada. I often wondered then why you never asked this same question. You were so tactful, Mack; you always are. And I'm grateful.' She paused again. 'I never had a husband, Mack. That's why you never had an invitation to the wedding.' She paused again. 'But surely you must have had some inkling.'

'I did, of course, as we all did. But I never actually knew.'

After a moment, Tessa replied, 'It was Adam of course; it couldn't have been anyone else.'

'That's why I never wanted to raise the matter. Because, of course, I *knew* he was dead.'

At that moment, they caught up with Ingrid. 'It really is a beautiful park, Tessa. You're so lucky to have this on your doorstep.' She indicated the bandstand. 'That's a fascinating custom, a band-stand. Truly English. I've never seen one before. Do they still have concerts?'

Tessa replied calmly, 'Yes, but not so often. Perhaps on ceremonial days.'

'Did you know, that plaque apparently commemorates the death of the late Duke of Buckingham.'

Tessa was nodding. 'I think I did. Yes, I am so lucky. In so many ways.' She glanced up then at Mack, who was by her side, and said calmly, 'Adam isn't dead, Mack. He didn't die.'

Mack said, 'I watched him die, Tessa, in Slater's apartment all those years ago. He must be dead. I attended his funeral.'

Tessa didn't reply immediately. 'Yes, I know. But, although I don't know where he is now, nor where he went, I *do* know he didn't die at Hillcrest on that dreadful afternoon.' Mack simply couldn't believe what he was hearing. He was aghast at Tessa's words, delivered in an almost toneless way, with no sense of emotion. Just pure fact. Tessa continued, 'I received a letter from him affirming that fact in, I suppose, 1968. *After* William's birth, and before I left for England.' She stopped, and looked at both of them, listening, riveted, to this unbelievable story. And then said, 'He acknowledged nothing and explained very little in that letter. And asked even less.'

They reached the Canal, hidden by the leaves of giant elms and oaks just coming into bloom. The water seemed to flow unaided, and all three stood silently for a moment, hidden from the comings and goings of the world outside as if in some dark grotto. And slowly, a giant sadness began to grow in Mack, a man not prone to deep emotions; a sadness for this girl, Tessa, his friend, almost his lover once, who'd been condemned to spend her days alone, uncertain of the whereabouts of the man she'd once loved, but forever buoyed up by the sole consolation of her precious son, around whom her universe rotated.

'This is where William, in the school holidays and bored stiff, used to come and play golf.'

Ingrid said, 'What? In amongst all these big trees?'

'Look, on the other side of the canal, there's a lovely golf course, where William played, usually alone, and where, I believe, his grandfather used to play too, in his younger years.' She looked at both of them. 'They're great sportsmen, you know. Like father like son.'

Again, sadness overtook Mack for a moment, but the sadness was already turning to anger in this usually placid man, an increasing desire to go wherever it took, and to right the wrongs done to this woman. Was it sadness, was it anger, or was it perhaps love that had so suddenly gripped him?

'Tessa said, 'We'd better go. They shut the gates to the Park. So you're both staying tonight, and tomorrow night too, yes? How lovely; I might even persuade darling Ingrid to stay longer.'

The three of them turned away from the canal and headed home, mostly in silence and locked in the intimate warmth of their friendship, their fellowship, and envisaging happier days.

*****

Hillcrest. Early April

Matters had gone from bad to worse with the school play at Hillcrest. Rumours had begun circulating about Mr. Smith's unpredictable behaviour during rehearsals. William, worried for a friendship which had already fallen on rocky times, had surreptitiously gone out and watched a second such evening rehearsal, skirting unseen the amphitheatre several times. He saw Sol predictably lose his grip after a very few minutes, challenged by one of the students about his particular interpretation of a line and, by another student, about some clumsy, even impossible blocking Sol was trying to impose on them. Sol refused to consider, or even *pretend* to consider, the actors' viewpoint, but dismissed their objections out of hand, until the students had fallen into sullen resentment and started to transform tragic scenes into some trivial comedy of their own invention. It was like wilful children at play.

'This is not a comedy,' bawled Sol, suddenly 'It's a tragedy. A travesty, more like. I wish I'd never embarked on this production.'

A pregnant pause, until one of the Senior students was bold enough to reply, 'Mr. Smith, sir, some of us wish we'd never embarked on it either. It's too difficult.'

A further silence followed, while the actors waited to see how Sol might react to this latest humiliation, and at last he said, in a quieter tone, 'Rehearsal dismissed. Go back to your rooms. Study Hall is still in progress.'

This cannot have been the first occasion this sequence of events had occurred because a few of the students were already on their way out. Those however who were still on stage heard Sol solemnly pronounce, 'I'm going to have to reconsider my whole position on this play. I feel let down and unwilling to put up any longer with your childish behaviour. I have better things to do with my time.'

Most of the players had already vacated the amphitheatre, but one or two, from the top of the amphitheatre stairs, watched Hattie approach Sol and say, 'Mr. Smith, we've got less than two months to put this production on, and almost all of us believe we should drop '*Lear*' and try something easier.' She seemed about to leave but turned back. 'Sir, I don't think it's us who are childish; a number of us believe it's you who's showing immaturity. And, on another matter, all of us, but especially the girls, are not happy about your behaviour with one of the girls, Hayley, who herself feels uncomfortable in your presence. It's embarrassing to say the least.'

Sol waited, and in the same cold tone as before, said, 'Hattie, you realise you're out of line here. This could be a disciplinary matter. As I said, the rehearsal is dismissed and you need to get to Study Hall.'

William hurried away from the amphitheatre, remaining hopefully unseen. He felt he needed to act, quickly, but was uncertain how. He knew though already that Hattie wasn't 'out of line'. Nor had it escaped the notice of other members of the faculty that Sol seemed fixated on this pretty girl.

As it transpired, the matter was taken out of his hands anyway. The rumours had reached the ears of the Headmaster, a man respected throughout the school, and normally reticent about intervening in matters pertaining to his trusted faculty. He felt though in this case obliged to act, fearing, amongst other things, that the rumours might drift beyond the school perimeters. He called the girl, Hayley, in, hoping to establish the truth direct from the horse's mouth, without having to disturb the general smooth-running of the school: things had been going well; admissions were up and there was a happy atmosphere about the place, not to mention the encouraging state of the school's bank account.

Hayley initially burst into tears. This was, in the eyes of the broad-minded and worldly-wise Doublejoy, not necessarily an admission of guilt, but a delicate situation nonetheless.

'Hayley, let me see if I have a tissue. Yes, here we are. You know, nobody's accusing you of anything. We just called you in to try and establish the facts. Now pull yourself together and let's try to get to the bottom of this.' Hayley continued to sob and, after a while, Doublejoy quietly left the room to call in his wife, a sympathetic and experienced woman, and when Doublejoy re-entered, it was accompanied by Mrs. Doublejoy

Hayley had stopped crying and assumed a firm and steadfast frown, as if ready to take on nothing less than the Spanish Inquisition. By the time the two of them had sat down, Hayley had, herself, assumed the initiative, blurting out, 'Mr. Doublejoy, Mrs. Doublejoy, I'm innocent.'

'We know you're innocent, Hayley,' replied Doublejoy; what we're trying to establish is whether Mr. Smith's innocent too.'

There was a brief silence, until Mrs. Doublejoy intervened, her face wreathed in a broad smile. 'Everyone's innocent my dear, until proven guilty,' to which Doublejoy added, 'It takes two to tango, Hayley.'

'Mrs. Doublejoy, Ma'am, I would hate to get Mr. Smith into trouble. He's a very good teacher, even if he's having a bit of a hard time with the play production.'

Doublejoy's expression changed in an instant to one of real concern. 'Ah yes, the Production! Tell me, Hayley, is the production at the moment a matter you think will resolve itself?'

Hayley was slightly taken aback by the question but did her best to explain diplomatically. 'I think it will resolve itself, sir; especially if Mr. Beckley comes out and helps.'

Doublejoy nodded sagely, while Mrs. Doublejoy said, kindly but firmly, 'That's a great relief, Hayley. Now, I think we must focus on the question in hand, don't you? Let me ask you a straight-forward question: Has Mr. Smith ever tried to touch you or behave towards you in what you might call an inappropriate manner?'

Hayley couldn't help blushing slightly, but replied, 'Oh no, not at all. He's been giving me some extra-curriculum coaching recently, and we seniors sometimes get to go into Mr. Smith's apartment for some refreshment. That was of course before he turned 'funny'. But really, I'm sure nothing inappropriate has happened, or at least I don't think so.' Hayley finished her reply with a somewhat bemused expression on her pretty face.

'How do you mean by 'funny', Hayley? asked Mrs. Doublejoy.

'He's not been himself lately, Ma'am. He's a bit irritable and impatient. I think perhaps he feels under pressure.'

Mrs. Doublejoy was nodding. 'An interesting observation, Hayley. We must look into that; meanwhile can you tell me when the last of these 'extra-curricular' sessions took place?'

'Mr. Smith, last night, helped me, not with my school work, but with my part.'

'Which part is that, Hayley?' Mrs. Doublejoy was quickly on the scent, like a barrister in a murder trial.

'You know, Ma'am, my part in the play.'

'Ah. Were there any other students getting help?'

'There sometimes are, but often I'm on my own.'

Following a brief silence, Mrs. Doublejoy said. 'You've been most helpful, Hayley dear. I think that's all the questions we need ask you at the present time.' She turned to her husband, who was already nodding, and added, 'Perhaps it might be wise, given the circumstances, to take fewer extra-curricular sessions with Mr. Smith. That is, of course, until this matter can be resolved, which, I'm sure, won't be too long. Meanwhile, Mr. Doublejoy and I wish you all the very best in your play production.'

After Hayley had left the room, Mrs. Doublejoy turned to her husband. 'Edward, that was rather inconclusive, and I must confess I don't feel completely happy with poor Hayley's replies.' Edward Doublejoy nodded, and his wife concluded, 'I think there's nothing for it but to have Sol himself in; although of course one doesn't want to rock the boat until absolutely necessary. We must be careful to get the timing right.'

'What must be, must be, dear,' sighed Doublejoy, and his wife concluded, in a sympathetic tone of voice, 'She's a sweet kid, Hayley, but I'm not sure she'd know she was being abused even if caught *in flagrante delicto*.'

The potential abuse scandal settled down somewhat, but the school play production didn't, and went from bad to worse. Doublejoy himself had noticed an unaccustomed irritability, a nervousness, a tension, about Sol Smith's general manner; it wasn't hard to pick up on for someone as experienced as himself, and suggested that all was not right with his Senior member of faculty. Although Doublejoy knew full well he couldn't have an abuse scandal - even the slightest whiff of one - on his doorstep at any time, the possibility however of this occurring at this critical moment when his beloved annual school drama production might be at risk was simply more than he could bear, and he realised full well the need to act quickly.

However, rather than summon Smith to a formal hearing and risk all sorts of anger and confrontation, he felt it more positive to invite him informally to dinner with himself and his wife. They'd talked it over and concluded there was probably no way they would obtain any straight-forward admission from Sol over the matter of sexual misconduct, and in Doublejoy's heart lay the hope that the rumours could be attributed to nothing more serious than a harmless flirtation. After all, teachers often flirted with their students by design, superficially at any rate, in order to wheedle more effort and better results from them. However, both he and his wife, had no doubt as to the precarious state of the Production and the need to find out precisely why Smith was behaving so oddly. Margaret Doublejoy described how, walking past the amphitheatre in the early evenings after school supper, she'd often played the innocent role of 'spy', and how, almost inevitably, there'd been *no 'Shakespeare'* - as she put it - but more often just talk and explanation *in plain English*, sometimes even with voices raised. 'After all, Edward, if you want to learn a language, you can't just *talk* about it, you have to *speak* it. Surely it must be the same with plays and Shakespeare.'

Edward Doublejoy had nodded wisely, knowing full well himself the pitfalls of producing a school play. 'You're right. But if Smith's not up to it, for whatever reason, have we any alternative, short of a disastrous cancellation? Who else do we know could step in at such short notice? I feel almost certain we'll find Smith under too much stress, but we must have a card up our sleeves.'

'William Beckley, dear.' said Margaret Doublejoy immediately. 'I think he's our man. Why, quite often when I'm spying at my end of the amphitheatre, I notice William spying at the other. And don't forget, they're thick as thieves anyway: Soccer, English, I've even heard they sometimes play football together in Dallas at weekends. At least they *used* to. Perhaps, on the grape-vine, there's been a slight falling off between them recently; but that could just be yet another rumour.'

Doublejoy smiled. 'You know, Margaret, your network of spies never ceases to amaze me. You'd have been perfectly at home at the court of Louis XIV. However, on a more serious note, whatever's the matter with Sol, we need to get it out of him. They say the way to a man's heart is through his stomach. And who could resist your cooking?'

Sol made no attempt to deny his difficulties. From the very start of the evening he was experiencing an unusual sense of apathy and absence of his usual energy. 'It's a difficult play though; Edward; don't let's forget that.'

He clearly expected his boss to agree with this absurdly brief diagnosis, but he didn't. 'Rubbish, Sol. It's the greatest play in the English language; probably the best in world literature. Come on now. You'll have to do better than that.'

'Will I?' replied Sol hurriedly. Am I then on the carpet?' His question came out like a bullet from a gun.

'No, Sol, no, not at all. But this 'apathy' you hint at; it worries me. I think we three need to examine together what might be the cause. If King Lear is able to turn off my top English teacher, then there must be something badly wrong. Have you had a health check recently?'

'It's not physical, Edward. I still eat three good meals a day and run around after recalcitrant students all day long. No, it's not that.' Sol thought for a moment. 'I think perhaps, like Hamlet, the problem lies within: "*I have that within which passeth show...,* ". You recall the quote?'

'Oh come on, Sol,' interrupted Margaret Doublejoy. 'I know you've always been a 'Hamlet' man, but it can't be as bad as that.'

Sol glanced at her and nodded. 'It is, Margaret. It is.' He looked at her earnestly, half pleading for her understanding. 'I think I'm ill. Degeneratively ill.'

Mrs. Doublejoy couldn't help exclaiming. 'How awful, Sol, I've always thought you in the best of health. All your soccer, and extra-curricular activities. I'm so sorry to hear this.'

For a brief moment there was silence between them. Then the Headmaster intervened, 'Sol, what do you think precisely is the matter?'

'I may be right and I may be wrong. I'm not really sure. I've always been under the impression you and Margaret knew about that terrible incident when some of the faculty were poisoned, and the school had to go into closure; it was some years ago, shortly before you took over,' There ensued a pregnant pause before he added. 'Well, I was one of them.' Doublejoy was by now theatrically closing his eyes and shaking his head, as if in sympathy and an unwillingness to revisit those dreadful events. Sol though hadn't yet finished. 'I was held for dead. Yes, and miraculously I recovered. But I often wonder if my recovery was complete.'

Margaret Doublejoy was shaking her head, along with her husband, as if to annul such thoughts. 'Sol, I'm so sorry. And what a brave recovery you made.'

'But did I? At the moment when it was assumed I was restored, I'd forgotten almost everything; a complete loss of memory, and what it boils down to now is that my memory still comes and goes; and, in addition, sometimes I'm on top of things, while at others, I'm down in the depths. I fluctuate.' He paused for a moment, seeking a final, telling symptom to clinch the matter. 'And that's not all; nowadays ironically, when my memory seems at its best, I feel as though things might overwhelm me, like an enormous wave.'

The two Doublejoys appeared genuinely shocked by this admission. Nobody said anything for a while. At last Doublejoy said, 'And we never knew, Sol. You conceal your problems remarkably stoically. Have you thought it might be Depression? Many people suffer from that. *You* perhaps, by the sound of it, And worse than most.'

Sol, aware he might have confessed too much, tried to make light of it. 'Don't worry; I can hold the job down all right, as I hope I've proved over the years. Hopefully this is just a phase.'

Again there was no immediate response. Both the Doublejoys were thinking a single thought: *Where, then, did that leave the play production?*

Edward voiced these concerns. 'Sol, we are both very sympathetic and will help in every way. We know some good doctors. And with the summer vacation coming on...' He hesitated a send... 'how do things stand with the Play? Are you going to pull it off?'

It was Sol's turn to look shocked. 'Of course. What else?'

Doublejoy felt impelled to repeat the question. 'What else indeed? You see, there are voices raised about getting behind schedule, finding someone else to take over or even about changing the play. We can't just ignore these voices.'

'Voices from whom?' Sol seemed genuinely puzzled.

'Well, Margaret's been approached by one or two of the cast.'

The tone of Sol's voice was rising slightly in intensity as he said, 'The cast, despite their beliefs to the contrary, don't know the first thing about production. Surely you can't rely on a bunch of kids to drive this matter forward.'

'It's difficult to ignore them either, Sol,' said Margaret. They give up so much of their time.'

'Time,' mimicked Sol. 'They'd almost certainly be wasting time if they *weren't* in the play.'

A brief pause followed while both parties retired to their corners and took stock of the situation. Finally Doublejoy said 'Leave the students out of it. It's just the plain facts of the matter that can't be overlooked.'

'What facts?' Sol's voice had a ring of desperation about it.

'Well, for one, there's your friend, William Beckley. He's made no secret of his....'

'Sol exploded. 'Beckley! Beckley's no friend of mine. The little rat! He's already taken over my football, and now he's scheming to take over the Drama activity too. Never!'

'We thought he was a good friend of yours,' exclaimed Margaret, greatly shocked. 'Being a compatriot.'

Sol hesitated, taking stock of things, before replying almost in a whisper,

'Compatriot' he may be, but whenever I'm in William Beckley's company nowadays, I inevitably feel a sense of anger.' He looked down at his feet, almost as if in shame.

Mrs. Doublejoy exclaimed to nobody in particular, 'We just can't have that!' And her husband added, 'The play, Sol; let's get back to the point. What criticism there has been, is not just Beckley's; in fact hardly his at all, to be fair. There've been other general voices on the faculty. It's wrong to suggest Beckley's to blame for everything. Your choice of friends is of course entirely up to you and none of our business. However, we need a decision. And quickly, or we won't have any play at all.'

They sat in silence again, over an excellent dessert. Edward Doublejoy, being a conscientious man, felt he had no option but to deliver the crowning blow. 'Sol. I regret to say, changing the subject slightly, that we have also received rumours that you've been behaving with Hayley De Vriess in a manner not altogether suitable for a member of faculty.' For a moment a hush fell on the room, before Doublejoy continued, 'There's no smoke without fire, Sol.'

Sol erupted, his expression passing, in quick succession, from horror, to fear, to menace, until all those emotions became wrapped in one desperate package. He stood up abruptly from the table, overturning a wine glass. 'I suppose it's that little rat again!'

He stormed out of the room.

Mrs. Doublejoy exclaimed tearfully, 'It's unheard of', Edward,' while Doublejoy, trying to maintain a balanced judgement, said, 'At least, Margaret, we now know what we have to do, regarding the play. As for Hayley, we'll have to remain very vigilant.'

Margaret replied, 'Believe me, Edward. There's nothing in that at all, On this occasion, there *is* smoke without a fire. But as for the rest....' She shook her head.

The following day, during morning break, Doublejoy spotted Sol Smith and pulled him over to one side. 'Perhaps we could adjourn to my study, Mr. Smith, and reach a positive conclusion about the play. On-going.'

They left the faculty room and went into the quiet, dark interior of Doublejoy's sitting-room, a place no doubt specifically designed against the intrusive heat of summer. With a hurried gesture, he indicated to Sol one of the comfortable armchairs, and sat down opposite.

Before Sol had time to apologise for his behaviour the previous evening, Doublejoy said, 'Sol, this matter of the play schedule, not to mention, as rumour has it, the apparent disruptions that have been going on at rehearsals, has led me and Mrs. Doublejoy to reach the decision to replace you for this year. Last night, you remember, we batted the breeze, and we are obviously very worried by your own situation regarding health, and really do believe you are in need of help. Mrs. Doublejoy was extremely upset yesterday evening....' At this moment, Sol attempted to interrupt, but Doublejoy raised his hand earnestly. 'Let me finish. We have come, in the light of this, to the conclusion you should take a sabbatical, starting immediately, and find yourself some professional help, as well as restoring yourself with adventures new, so to speak. The sabbatical can be for an unspecified time, although we imagine it might be until the end of the current school year. You need rest, Sol. This sabbatical will be at the school's expense and we will obtain a replacement member of faculty to take on your courses.'

Sol remained silent now, and the Head continued, 'Please accept this enforced break not as a dismissal, but, shall we say, 'time-out'. Let's hope and pray it will be beneficial to us all.' They sat for several tense moments in silence, looking at each other across the gloomy room, until Doublejoy added, 'For right or wrong, this decision is not open for discussion, but please bear in mind it's your well-being the school places first and foremost.' Once again a silence ensued, until at last Doublejoy eased himself out of his armchair and said, 'Thank you, Mr. Smith, for all your effort this trimester. We wish you all the best. I think you should make plans to be off campus by, shall we say, the middle of the week?'

Sol climbed out of his steep armchair and headed, pale-faced, to the door. Doublejoy called, 'If you need to find accommodation during the next few weeks, I'm sure the school can offer some suggestions.'

Sol stopped and turned to his boss with what might be called an enigmatic smile. 'Don't worry, sir, I know where I'll go.'

*****

William already knew what play he would do, and how precisely he would do it, before Doublejoy even approached him on the Breezeway on Monday morning and asked him to: 'take over the Production this year. I'm busy right now, William, but I'd like to fill you in on the details later today. Knock on my door in the late afternoon some time.

I just know you're our man.' He'd looked William straight in the eye: '*Once more unto the breach, dear friends....* I know I can rely on you to close the wall up, eh?' He strode off towards his office.

William had already fixed in his mind an outline of how the Production might pan out. There was no time (six weeks) for a complete play. Abandon *'Lear'* then. Put together a skeleton version of his favourite play, namely *'A Winter's Tale'*, in two short acts, presented by a 'Narrator', who would recount, in summarised form, the *'tale'*, laced with lines and mini-scenes borrowed from the original text. No great strain on the actors then: short rehearsals, short passages honed to perfection. It was all there, stamped on his imagination, and, with the bold naivety of youth, already a project assured of success. William had little doubt he could pull it off, and who knows what wondrous magic might he encounter on his path to transform this bare promise of success into a living, dramatic miracle. When he met the Principal later that afternoon and outlined his idea, he entitled the Project, on the spur of the moment, **A Story Play**. 'That title, sir, should fit easily into Shakespeare's title.' The Head had nodded with approval, and William added, 'Don't worry, Mr. Doublejoy; leave it to me.'

Sol meanwhile took two days to prepare for departure, lurking, like the Dragon in Wagner's *'Siegfried'*, and dangerously wounded. Who knows what hurt and anger lay festering in a mind, muddied already by deficient memory and half-remembered triumphs, and now severed at the bone. He lay in wait for the knock on the door he knew would come.

William, buoyed up by the golden opportunity Doublejoy had suddenly heaped on him, and yet, it must be said, still relatively naïve in his understanding of mature relationships, had hit upon the idea of a final attempt to restore the bond of friendship that seemed unaccountably to have been snatched from him for reasons unknown. For someone like William, already feeling invulnerable, a visit to his once-precious mentor seemed the most natural step in the world, and the least he could do to try to put their former relationship on an even keel. And so, on the self-same evening he'd been entrusted with the Play, William descended the hill and knocked gently on the door of Sol's apartment.

It opened quickly, and Sol stood outlined in the doorway. 'Ah. I've been expecting you. Come in. Make yourself at home.' There was no trace of a welcoming smile on Sol's face; William was met with a blank page and two terse directives. He went into the darkness and found a chair. This same toneless voice came at him several seconds later from an uncertain direction. 'I suppose you've come here to gloat.'

'To gloat, Sol? I don't know what you mean.'

'To gloat at my demise.'

'What demise, Sol?'

Sol didn't answer him, but continued, voice raised unnaturally, 'How innocently he speaks. But for the darkness in here, I imagine I'd see a face as guileless as ignorance itself. How cleverly those most guilty conceal their crimes beneath a blanket of innocence.' His words were precise and clear-cut, as if he'd been long rehearsing them. The voice went on, 'I seem to remember a quote to that effect. Something in *Hamlet*. I'm sure with your superior knowledge of Shakespeare you'll be able to help me out.' The sarcasm filled the room, almost suffocating William. He was about to reply but Sol cut in. 'Ah yes, I have it. Hamlet to Ophelia. Act III. *"For wise men know well enough what monsters you make of them."* I think that fits the bill, doesn't it? Such innocence beneath a cover of such deceit?

'Sol, your words make no sense to me. Of what am I guilty and where is my offence?'

'Still deceitful then? No repentance? *'Alas, how sharper than a serpent's tooth it is to have a thankless friend.'*

'I think, Sol, the line finishes with the word *'child'*.

'Yes, you are right.' His voice dropped a semi-tone. 'There is that too.' Not understanding at all Sol's dismissive final remark, William waited, realising it would be pointless to intervene in this muddled stream of empty accusation But the stream became a torrent, as Sol continued, 'You know, I can date my demise, my loss of favour, my loss of pride itself, from the day I first set eyes on your impish little face. Yes, the so-called 'King William' in that childish little sketch we invented together. Remember? That was the day too that I lost my own self-respect. I can see now how it's all part of a plan. To steal away first my prowess as a footballer, my success as a coach, and then, as if that's not enough, to steal away in plain delight, before my very eyes, the respect owed to me by my students. And all accomplished as if it were the most commonplace proceeding in the world.' He was nodding his head at his own words. 'The youngest must first topple the oldest before they can replace them. I see it all now. Is it not then betrayal? I lent you my friendship and you betrayed me. *"how sharper than a serpent's tooth...."*. You find that good, eh?'

This fierce diatribe seemed to have drained Sol himself, because, sitting down, he lapsed into what seemed the silence of sleep. William, after a minute or two, realised he was the only person awake in the room, and yet the vehemence of Sol's accusations had so startled him that he sat on, trying to make sense of it. At last, something, some noise, must have startled Sol, for he jerked out of his coma and fastened his wild eyes on William. 'Get out. What are you doing in my room if it isn't to steal my possessions as well as my heart? I swear - I forget your name - I swear, traitor, I will do you harm.... Hasn't that poison potion already done its work?'

William, in a sudden moment, knew his own life may already be at risk. He raised himself out of his chair. 'Poison? What is this?' Mercifully he could remember no offerings he might have received that evening from this madman, but knew such an eventuality was not impossible. He looked at the figure slumped in the chair and backed away towards the door. Sol was mumbling to himself as if now unaware of William's presence. 'The little traitor. Did I fall asleep? I must be on my guard.' A heavy silence ensued, as William stood with his hand on the door, wondering how he should proceed, until the sick man, seeming to emerge from his reverie, and noticing a shadowy William by the door, lurched forward in his chair. 'Ah. What are you still doing here? Didn't you hear me? I do not want to be anywhere near you. Little rat. Or have you come to rob me? Have you not robbed me enough? I cannot look at you without disgust. Get out, and take your impish little face with you, and never again darken the portals of my house. I swear, if I ever set eyes again on your treacherous visage, I shall not be responsible for my actions.'

William had already concluded there was little help he could give Sol in this state. What if he had a gun or a knife hidden somewhere?

He took one last look at the desperate figure in the chair opposite him, and, slamming the door, fled into the night.

CHAPTER 24

'Good morning. My name's Neumann, Mack Neumann. You won't know me, but I'm an alumnus of Hillcrest. Graduated 1965.' Mack was surprised how formal he sounded. He wasn't used to these kinds of phone-calls anyway, and after so long in Germany, he heard himself adopting the more rigid European manner of speech. There was silence at the other end of the line: a Receptionist also not used probably to such formality. Mack prompted. 'I'm on a business trip to the States, and just thought it would be nice to revisit the old school. It's been nearly thirty years; a lot must have changed.'

He waited, still wondering if there was anybody there on the other end. It wouldn't do to get off on the wrong foot with what he had in mind. He knew well, from his own legal work, the world was starting to go crazy about security, and guessed that in the educational field this was doubly so. The school wouldn't take kindly to some stranger drifting around unannounced. On top of that, he himself felt unaccountably nervous.

The voice, at last, down the line was friendly. 'Real nice to hear from you, Mr. Neumann; Mack, was it? We'd sure welcome you down in these parts. I think you'd find us much the same as ever.'

'I look forward to it then. I believe too a good friend of mine from Hamburg - that's where I live - is on your faculty. Name of Bellman.'

'Hold the line, Mack. I'll check the program for today. Bellman, you said?'

'Yeap.'

She came back on the line after a minute or two. 'Strange; there seems no record of a Mr. Bellman - nor Mrs. Bellman - on our faculty.'

Mack found himself up against the kind of brick wall he'd least desired. 'That's certainly strange. Let's see.' His usually lightning-quick brain wasn't coming to his aid that morning. 'Bellman...

Bellman…Tessa Bellman…that's my friend's mother's name….' And then his brain clicked into gear. 'I know. Try 'William'. Have you got a young man, Englishman, by the name of William on your staff?'

This 'password' did the business.. 'Sure have, Mack That'll be William Beckley right enough. I must have misheard you first time '

Mack thought it best not to argue the toss. 'Sure. It's not a good line. Either that or William's changed his name.'

'My, I don't think he'd do something like that.'

Mack in reality knew better. William wasn't beyond changing his name, if indeed it *was* the same old enigmatic William he knew. However, he thought it best once again to agree. 'That's wonderful then; I should be with you tomorrow at about 11.00.'

'Just fine. I'll let our Principal know. 11.00's our coffee break. Mr. Doublejoy can take you into the faculty room himself. He meets his staff there at that time. William's bound to be there. Shall I also mention to Mr. Beckley you're coming?'

'Probably best not. Let me arrive first. I'll recognise my old friend anyway, no matter what he calls himself.' There was a short laugh at the other end and Mack replaced the receiver, more than relieved his visit hadn't been aborted at birth. He was over the first hurdle.

He'd made, in fact, no mention of another even older friend, Adam Riley. His circumstances - he knew from Tessa - lay in the mist, but he couldn't shake off the feeling that probably his old mentor had somehow re-invented himself and found his way back to Hillcrest. If so, no point in confusing the Receptionist further: Adam would almost certainly long since have been living under a new identity. However, both his friends working under assumed identities, and he a lawyer, left him wondering if he wasn't anyway straying into dangerous areas; he couldn't dismiss the uncomfortable feeling that what had started out as a short trip, might well be turning into something a lot more like a mission, and that he might need to tread very carefully. Standing there now, as he replaced the receiver, he tried to put the trip next day to the back of his mind, but was aware even this chat with the Receptionist had left him unusually over-excited.

Little though did he anticipate either the life-changing revelations that awaited him at this little school, or the full significance of his journey there.

That receptionist lady had been right: 'nothing really *had* changed.' Up the old driveway in his hire-car, maybe things looking a little bit tidier, but all the familiar land-marks still in place: soccer fields, dining-hall, sports hall, swimming pool at the back. The last time he'd driven up this track had been around the time of those dire events in '67. He shuddered at the thought and hoped his welcome would be a little more genuine on this occasion, and a lot less treacherous.

Mack recognised William almost straightaway in the busy faculty room, alone over in the corner, a cup of coffee in his hand. Mack hadn't really been sure how he'd be received, whether it would be the same cheerful, positive William he remembered from the Mensa. But one look at the figure slumped in the chair, and his anxieties were allayed: that same intense young man, watching the world with a puzzled expression on his face, seeming to wrestle with demons others never noticed, but beneath it, a solid, immovable confidence, and a character almost impossible to ignore.

'Good morning, William.' William looked up, immediately on the alert, and yet, for a moment showed absolutely no recognition at all, as if he were in another dimension altogether. 'It's me, Mack, your mate from the Mensa, your buddy from the *Teestube*.' A wide smile had suffused Mack's face, and still William looked on, unknowing. Perhaps at another time and place there would have been instant recognition, but William was still reeling from the events of the past few days, that final terrible, malicious encounter with Sol, and his own sudden, unexpected elevation to the rank of Drama Director. His life had changed in an instant, not drastically nor permanently, but enough to knock him off balance. Slowly, as the chatter in the room, the familiarity of the accustomed surroundings, brought him back from his thoughts, he became aware of the tall man looming above him, a shape and face he recognised. 'Mack. Is it Mack, from Hamburg? What are you doing here? In the Wild West? Or is it me, not you, who's been transported?'

Mack laughed. 'No, you're still here and it's me who's been - what was it? - 'transported'.' Still laughing, Mack put out his hand, shook William's proffered one, and half-hauled his friend out of his armchair. 'Don't do a heart-attack on me, William. Let's look at each other full in the face.' He glanced round the busy, stuffy room. 'And let's get out of here. Find a quieter corner in this little building of nooks and crannies.'

William began to smile for the first time in days. 'You'd better come to my cranny then, along here in the main building. Just room enough for two. I've got a free period now, and then I'm on all day. No respite.'

Mack said, 'Sounds like nothing much has changed then.'

'I don't know how it was then, but that's how it is now. I think we'll have a bit of free space this evening. Where are you staying by the way?'

'I've booked into the *Holiday Inn*.'

They adjourned to William's small room, scarcely place enough for two to sit comfortably. 'Okay, Mack. You belong to Hamburg and the Mensa; please tell me how you belong now to the heart of Texas.'

'In short, I'm on a business trip; in detail, it's a long story, with many twists and turns. Which I'll bore you with, but spare some of the detail.' He stared now hard at William, reminding William of those sceptical, sometimes unbelieving looks he used to receive, whenever he'd launched into an argument or some impossible religious rant in the frantic back and forth of the student dining hall in Hamburg. Mack was continuing, 'Here's how it came about, William, and some of the characters in it you'll recognise. You won't believe it though.' He paused. 'Okay, I bumped into a mutual friend in Hamburg a month ago. Yes, someone you know well.' He made William wait, and then concluded, 'Ingrid Spindler. Remember her?'

William's eyes widened in joyful astonishment. '*Oh, brave new world....*'

'Yes, brave indeed. She was the one I believe I took second place to in our mutual rivalry at that time.'

'Mack, I never even knew you fancied her, let alone that we were rivals.' He laughed. 'Wouldn't have made any difference though.'

'It's in the past. Let bygones and rivalries take second place to this miraculous tale of mine.' He paused, seeming to wonder how best to continue. 'She brought me to England. It's that simple.'

'Is it?'

'She took me to meet your mother.'

'Where? In England?'

'Wait. Let me finish.... Your beautiful mother, lovely woman. Living on her own, and much forsaken by a son who can write only two letters in the space of one year.' There were groans of embarrassment and regret from William, as Mack continued, '*Your* mother, Tessa, as it turned out, was nothing less than my old high-school colleague and crush, and that particular high-school was the very same place we're sitting in right now.' He gave a wide sweep of his arm. 'Here. And the rest, I suppose, is history, which you and I and the girls are in the process of making.'

'What caused you to come here though?'

'I'm on a business trip. To the States. I'm a lawyer. I thought how good it would be to combine business with pleasure and come and visit you. End of story. I hope my explanation wasn't too boring.'

'Mack, can these circumstances really be true? It's a coincidence beyond imagination.'

'It's certainly unusual. A lot more refreshing than the usual stuff that lands on my desk each day. And those two ladies of yours are probably right now sitting together in the parlour of your lovely home in W....'

'How come?'

'Ingrid decided to stay on a bit, and both of them hit it off real well. They're probably right now hatching a plot to come out and visit. She's keeping your mother company anyway.' He paused. 'Let me say though, Ingrid, strangely, wasn't entirely unfamiliar with W... nor the house. Seems like she'd already spent some time there. How come?' There was the trace of a knowing smile on Mack's face.

'William, nodding, said, 'I miss her, you know. But better left unsaid about that bit of the story. Another shameful act on my part.' He mumbled beneath his breath: '*Oh, brave new world that hath such people in it.*'.'

'Yes, I suppose Shakespeare's a fitting conclusion to a story like this.'

William looked hard at him. 'You're right, Mack. Funny you should say that. Hope it won't be a Tragedy.'

Mack frowned. 'Why? That sounds ominous.'

William was wearing now that kind of intense expression Mack knew so well from their Mensa days, a look which pre-supposed one of his difficult and convoluted tales. 'Listen, Mack, I'm going to tell you a secret. Keep it to yourself. I'm putting on the school play in a month. And *you'll* now be in it.'

Mack laughed. 'No I won't. How come?'

'It's a long story, like yours was, and I'll definitely tell you the full tale sooner or later. But briefly, I've been landed with an impossible drama mission by the Head, in one month's time, and I realise, right now, the only way I can pull it off is to include, in the cast, both you, along with some other mutual friends. I've just had a good idea, you see. And I need you, and other various stand-ins, in my play.'

Mack was shaking his head. 'I'm a lawyer, William. Feet firmly on the ground, remember? Not on some rickety stage. And in a month I won't even be here.'

William was nodding. 'Yes, I know. I'm just a desperate man kind of getting carried away. Okay, let's, for the moment, forget I ever raised the matter, and not mention it again. There's little sense for us poor mortals to play hostage to fortune There's no knowing what might happen.'

'Fine words, William. As usual. And true too. More than true. Who would have thought yesterday I'd be sitting here in Adam Riley's old room with Adam Riley's son.'

That final remark of course was lost on William, and he thought little about it anyway, and took Mack and his suitcase over to the nearby *Holiday Inn*, arranging to pick him up at 6.00. 'You can eat in the school with me. The Doublejoys won't mind; they're hospitable people. One dinner serving won't be missed. I'll pick you up and then we can come back later to the motel or go to a bar and get a drink together.'

The dining-hall was, as usual at that hour, a vibrant place, full of hungry jostling students. Not unlike the Mensa, Mack was thinking, as he guided his tray to an inviting table overlooking the beautiful view down to the bottom end of the prairie and the horse stables.. William followed him into a corner table, and, unexpectedly, there was the largish shape of Mr. Doublejoy looming above them, wondering if they minded if he sat with them.

'Of course not sir; it would be a pleasure.'

'I don't want to intrude, Mr. Neumann. You two - he indicated William -.must have a lot of catching up to do. I understand both of you have links with Germany. Perhaps William here should offer a German course in the next semester. Or an outline of modern German history. It would go down very well with the students.'

William remained politely silent, unwilling or unable to enthuse about the Principal's proposal, while Mack clearly understood it was just small-talk on Doublejoy's part. He attempted to draw the conversation back to more realistic maters. 'It's a lovely view from these windows. I think, as a student, I never ever realised how uniquely beautiful this campus was.'

Doublejoy spooned a portion of soup into his mouth. 'Yes, Mack, we think so.'

Mack replied, 'Nothing changes, does it? I could be a young student sitting here several years ago, wondering which assignment to tackle at Study Hall.'

Doublejoy clearly liked the comment. 'Yes, we haven't done much to the campus. Cleaned it up a bit, added a few things here and there. So you're a lawyer, Mack, are you? Which specialism may I ask?'

'Company law. A lot of work and not a lot of play.' He smiled weakly.

The conversation was already in a cul-de-sac. None of them seemed to want to confront the actual reason for Mack's purpose in being there at all at this odd time in the school calendar. Doublejoy however nodded politely at Mack's comment, and after a moment asked, 'When was it you were here at Hillcrest, Mack?'

Mack responded without hesitation, as if that particular period of his life was branded forever on his mind. '1965, Sir. I graduated in '65.'

'Seems a long time ago, but I expect in your busy life it seems like yesterday.'

Mack nodded. 'But fortunately it's not.' He smiled at Doublejoy.

'What makes you say that, Mack?'

'It's not the year itself specially; it's all that followed in its wake: the closure of the school; you know.'

Doublejoy nodded. 'Yes, I *do* know. They were difficult times.'

'The school's made a miraculous recovery since those events.'

'Did they affect you, Mack. Personally, I mean?'

Mack went unusually quiet in the wake of this question. Then he forced a grin. 'I suppose you *could* say yes.' He placed special emphasis on his ensuing reply, as if nobody could ever forget the disastrous disruption in the years following '65. And all the while, William sat quietly listening to the conversation, but understanding little of its content. Doublejoy seemed unwilling to pursue the topic further anyway, and brought it to a close with a masterpiece of understatement. 'Yes, they were trying times, I know, but we pulled the fat from the fire. It would have been criminal not to resurrect such a beautiful location for a school.'

William was left wondering what they were talking about, and the supper came to a close. He said, 'Mack and I had better get off to Denber. I'm dropping him at *Holiday Inn* and then we might have a drink or two. We've got a lot to talk about, and Mack's already threatening to leave prematurely.'

'Not prematurely,' Mack added tactfully. 'Just *soon*, William. I'm not on almost permanent long vacation like you teachers.'

They left the dining-hall.

They sat silently on high stools in one of the few public bars in Denber, savouring the casual indifference to their presence of everyone else in the bar. Mack appeared almost to be revelling in the atmosphere, rediscovering the relaxed manners and behaviour of his beloved Texas. He finally broke the silence. 'Not like I remember from those movies of old, where strangers like us in town would have put the sheriff on high alert in a matter of minutes.' He gestured with a wave of his arm. 'See? Here, we just fit in. This is more like a modern-day bar in Hamburg or Berlin. Nobody takes any notice of you.'

'Thankfully,' replied William, remembering his own recent experience at Rheinischer Hof. 'It's not always like that, you know. You still get the occasional inquisitive cowboy.'

Mack grinned. 'I won't forget to bring my holster next time.' Their conversation lapsed again until he said, a sceptical expression on his face, 'Okay, William, fill me in on what all this business about 'names' is. And get me another beer.'

William went off for the beers and came back with what appeared to be a deliberately ingenuous expression on his face. 'What 'names', Mack?' he asked.

'Yours. There's no 'Beckley' is there? He's fiction. You can't expect me to believe that.'

William smiled. 'I expect there *is*, actually. There isn't probably a '*William* Beckley', but there're certainly Beckleys around.'

Mack wasn't having any of it. 'You're beating about the bush. It can be quite confusing to others, you know, changing your name. What's the matter with 'Bellman'? Isn't that what you called yourself in the *Teestube* in Hamburg?'

William was shaking his head. 'I don't know actually. Did I? I don't remember calling myself anything formally over there. Strange how one can get on without a surname among friends. It was just plain 'William' and 'Mack' from what *I* remember.'

Mack nodded. 'Yes, but hardly the same in a small town like Denber though, and especially for someone paying your wages.'

His eyebrows were raised, and William was clearly uncomfortable. 'Alright,' he said, 'I'll level with you, Mack. It was a spur of the moment decision. It meant nothing. I've always had a bit of a complex about carrying my mother's surname, and as for my non-existent father, I've no idea what he was called. So I borrowed my Grandmother's maiden name. *Beckley*. Make a new start somehow. Nobody asked any questions, nor were they any the wiser. No deceit intended.'

Mack realised suddenly he was treading on thin ice with William on this topic, now that he knew what Tessa had told him about William's fatherless upbringing. He back-tracked. 'Okay. It's none of my business really. Just a lawyer's nosey nature, that's all. I get your point. End of story.'

William took a long swig on his beer, and smiled. 'What's in a name, after all? *A rose by any other name*....' They sat silently, both reflecting on the mysteries of identity.

Mack finally got off his stool and said, 'It's my round,' while William, changing the topic, remarked 'I'd better take it easy on the beers. I've got a game in Dallas tomorrow. They rely on me scoring two goals a game. Why don't you come? You could see downtown if you don't want to watch me scoring.'

'Sounds great. Forget the beer then. That's important, I can see. You've got to get your priorities right.'

After a moment's pause, William said, 'I try. Anyway, I think it's my turn to ask *you* a question now.' And Mack, smiling, said, 'Go ahead. I've got nothing to hide, like *you*.'

'You sure?'

Mack laughed. 'Lawyers never tell lies, William. You should know that. What's the question? I don't come cheap.'

William hesitated a moment. 'Then tell me, what *did* happen in '65? You know, that year you were talking so earnestly about, back in there with Doublejoy.'

The almost permanent smile on Mack's face disappeared for a moment. 'Yes, you should know anyway.' He paused a moment. 'Well, besides the fact that, in that year, *I* graduated, and the world held its breath, and wait, yes, we also put on a great play, directed by a guy called Adam Riley. Does that answer your question?'

'No. I mean the bad stuff Doublejoy was referring to.'

'That was '67. Two years later.' After a moment, he continued 'It really is a long and complicated story, a two-year odyssey. But the gist is, we, the guy called Adam, and your mother, and a few of our better students, went on a youthful jaunt, in order to right what we believed were wrongs.'

'And did you?'

'No. We got quite far, in all honesty, but finally it became deadly serious, believe me. And we all dispersed, wiser, but licking our wounds. That's it, in a nutshell.'

'The jaunt proved pointless then?'

'No, we unearthed some very dirty laundry on the way.' He was nodding again, as if starting to recall the true weight of their endeavours. 'People were killed and the school had to close. It was that bad.'

'My mother never told me this.'

'I'm sure she wanted to spare you the details. It was all very messy, and we got on with our lives as best we could.' He took a swig of his beer. 'A little microcosm of life itself, you might say. The whole enterprise, a gentle fable.' William laughed, perhaps at his own ignorance of this strange story, and Mack said, 'That's my story and now please tell me what this school play is all about.'

'Mack, it's in production, on-going if you like.' William indicated with his forefinger a point on his forehead. 'In *'here'*. I'm having to do it all, you see, but I think it'll come out marvellously in the end. What I envisage is a rehash of a particularly favourite Shakespeare play of mine, one I hope will deliver an enlightened message to the audience. Full of forgiveness and expiation. It may sound pretentious, I know, but I intend to present nothing less than my own interpretation of the *'Enlightenment'*. Just as *'Goethe'* did.'

Mack was shaking his head. 'You're losing me. I never studied any of that stuff.'

'Goethe'. You haven't heard of him? The great German poet, who ushered in the German *Enlightenment*.' Mack didn't comment, so William continued, 'Don't worry; it'll be clear when you see it. However, I *am* going to want to enlist your help, in a very minimal way.'

Mack hesitated, waiting for details, but clearly William had come to the conclusion not to elaborate now, at this precise moment. Instead, he said, 'I think I need another beer. You too?'

He ordered up, and, on his return, Mack said, 'You know, William, I've been thinking; you're a versatile fellow, but all this drama stuff!' He shrugged. 'Don't you think it better to stick to Religion? Do what you're best at?'

William experienced a surge of annoyance at Mack's apparent unwillingness to take his drama project seriously. He couldn't resist however rising to the teasing challenge implicit in Mack's question. 'Mack, you want a 'Religion' rant, do you? Like in the old Mensa days? Well I'll give you one.' After a few moments he waded in. 'This is hot of the press, okay? My latest religious update.' He paused a moment, and then said dramatically, *'Behold, I tell you a mystery....* Whether you like it or not, Mack, there *is* a God, okay? It's obvious. No question about it. A god just not like we imagine though. We look in the wrong place, that's why we all find it so puzzling. Endlessly seeking a god decked out in medieval pageantry and living at some fixed abode somewhere.'

Mack, as once he'd been in the Mensa, was already locked now intently on his friend's simple and persuasive words; it seemed to him as if William lived right on the edge of his beliefs.

'It's no longer like this.' William was continuing. 'We've moved on, or *should* have done. The world has moved on, even if, in some quarters, its beliefs still haven't kept up with the pace.' He hesitated a moment. 'Everybody knows, or *should* know, we carry our own God inside us. We *are* our God; we don't need anyone to intercede for us. That's why it's so simple; there's no clash, or pointing the finger, or interpreting. If the thoughts are bad, they belong to us, and equally, if they're good, it's us who own them.' He stopped mid-stream for a moment and seemed to become almost belligerent There was a glint in his eye. 'And as for trying to locate the Almighty at some fixed point, like a church or wherever, the idea's simply ludicrous. How could God be in just one location? You'd have to queue for hours to get an audience. No, *our* God's in touch at any time of the day or night Most convenient. Like modern life. 24/7....' He looked up at last with a grin on his face. 'Here endeth the lesson for today. That's all I've got to say on the matter, because right now I've got other problems on my mind. I'll leave you with the old adage: *He that hath ears to hear, let him hear.*'

Mack, remaining spellbound as he'd listened, made no attempt to disguise the fact. 'God, you're magic at that, William. You hold your audience. Wow, I can just visualise you in the pulpit at the Vatican, in front of those bishops and prelates, eating out of your hand. You're destined for a great career.'

William smiled. 'Except that I've got this Play to put on first.'

'You can't do everything.'

'Well, the theatre's a whole lot more compelling, I must admit. I really can't see myself putting on a surplice and stole again, and all that ridiculous dressing up.'

'No different from putting on a doublet and hose though, is it? Anyway when did you last put on a surplice?'

'How d'you mean?'

'Well you said 'again' just now. When was the last time?

William grinned. 'At school.'

Mack looked sceptical. 'Ah, brainwashing of little boys.'

'You could call it that.'

'I *do* call it that.' He paused. 'You know, I don't want to cast aspersions on your obviously remarkable talent and instinct, but, as a good lawyer, I have finally a duty to ask: How do you explain religion, without some basic proof. Where's the proof?'

'A broad smile spread across his friend's face. 'Faith. You take it on faith, win or lose. And, if you can't accept that, then take a look at human nature: Who else but a wise god could have created the kind of nature we humans have been landed with? Every little part of it, if we're honest, binds us to realise our helplessness.' He drained his glass. 'And here endeth the lesson again. I'm tired of being a counterpart Luther.'

'You win, Luth,' said Mack, draining his glass too. I should never have brought the subject up; promise I won't do it again. Subject concluded.'

'Fine, but nevertheless don't overlook the fact that the 'real' Luther, that great swash-buckler, had to contend with medievalism and ignorance. For *us* though, it's much more plain-sailing: whether it's Religion or just Drama, we're on the verge of a second *Enlightenment*, a sort of Redemption.'

'Are we?'

'Yes, a new dawn; watch, and just go with the flow.'

Mack got off his stool. 'Show us the way then, William.' The two of them headed determinedly for the door, having arranged to meet for the football the following day.

They met as arranged and headed for Dallas. Mack, slumped in the passenger seat, said nothing for a while, no doubt regretting the unaccustomed amount of beer he'd consumed the previous evening. William, younger and fitter, was less inclined to feel sluggish, more used to the rhythms of his body. About halfway down the highway and heading for St Luke's, he attempted to stir Mack into life, 'Mack, who is this Adam you mentioned last night?. Remember? Adam Riley?'

'I don't remember anything very much,' growled Mack, 'but, yes, it's hard to forget Adam. We two were as close as you and I right now (he indicated the gap between the two car-seats), and in fact, that's not a bad analogy either, we were so often in a car, your mother, or

Adam, or I, anchored in the driving seat, shuttling between here and Santa Fe.'

'Why? What was so important about Santa Fe?'

'It's where a lot of that happened.'

'A lot of what, Mack?'

'Our quest, our journey, out mission, call it what you like. And Adam was an integral part of that, the driving force in fact. He drove us all along with him.'

William nodded. 'He was a young teacher at Hillcrest, right? I think I've got that far. But *who* was he? What was he like? That's important, isn't it?'

'Very. Okay,' Mack paused for a moment, a lawyer about to deliver his crucial summing up, '6ft tall, shock of dark hair, slim, mentally alert, imaginative, moody, passionate, loved soccer, talented, an inspiring class-room teacher by all accounts, loved women, music, theatre, inclined to be a bit scatty on occasions. D'you want any more about the man?' Mack finished with a wide grin on his face. 'Now, who does that remind you of, eh?' William, focussing on the highway, didn't reply but just shook his head, and Mack stated calmly, 'You. It reminds me a bit of you actually.' He lapsed into silence for a few moments. 'However, no matter how much talent we all had, it served in the end for nothing. Our quest ended in disaster, real, desperate disaster, and I lost sight of Adam at the end; I thought he was dead, and subsequently don't fully know what happened to him. We lost touch.' He paused, as if confronting a barrier he didn't want to cross. At last he said, 'I've always believed he died, but very recently I learned from your mother - *his* girl-friend - that, despite everything, he didn't die, he's still alive. She doesn't know where, although she's got some theories.'

William had been listening more than intently to Mack's description. 'She was his girl-friend? This guy, Adam? How come? I never knew, never was told.' William, shocked, went silent for a while, and Mack said, 'Keep calm; don't forget, you're at the wheel, you've got a soccer game to play.'

And at last, William broke his silence. 'You won't of course have a photograph of this Adam Riley?'

'No. Why should I, William? I don't do photographs as a rule.'

'Just thought you might, being a friend of his.' William was undeterred as they approached their venue and ran off the freeway. 'If he taught here, at Hillcrest, for long enough, there's bound to be a team photo anyway, a school photo, a faculty photo. There must be one hanging somewhere on a wall at the school.'

'Isn't my description good enough for you?' Mack was laughing.

'Yes, of course it is; just thought it might seal the matter.'

It was Mack's turn to go silent, leaving William desperately racking his brains as to where there might be a photo of this *'Adam'*. Finally Mack urged, as they neared the ground, 'Priority number 1, the game. Don't let all this talk put you off your game. Nothing can be more important than that.'

'I won't. You're right. One thing I've certainly learned is to block out everything extraneous once on a soccer pitch.'

While William played, Mack took the car to see again something of the remnants of that fatal event, already fading fast in people's memory, which had occurred near Stemmons Freeway in November '63. He, like many people his age and mentality, still regarded the assassination of Kennedy as something special, a pivotal moment in the western world, and not merely just another drama.

When he returned, the game was over and some of the players, including William, were already emerging from the locker room. 'Good timing, Mack. Pity my timing in front of goal didn't match up. Another lesson learned: Don't drink too much alcohol before an important game, nor discuss other important matters. However unimportant the match may be. It destroys both co-ordination and concentration. *And* helps you lose.'

'*You* lost then, I presume.'

William nodded. 'Badly.'

'Well. If it's any consolation, we did cover a lot of interesting ground last night in the course of our disgraceful indulgence. And this morning too. I must admit I owed myself a bit of relaxation. Been working my butt off since I arrived.' William nodded, and Mack asked, 'Where do you go after a match?'

'Our sponsor's pub. The Rheinischer Hof.'

'Let's go then. Show me the way. It's my round.'

The Bar seemed abnormally crowded. William said, as they entered, 'Usually only like this if we win.' He looked around the room. 'Strange. Must be the oppo celebrating. That doesn't happen often.'

They sat for a while, quietly drinking cordial and eyeing the milling crowd. William said, 'Have you ever noticed how people always find themselves the same seats?' He looked across at Mack. 'You're sitting in Sol's place, you know. That's where *he* usually sits.'

'Sol, I take it, being the guy at Hillcrest who introduced you to this Club,' said Mack. Funny name though.'

William nodded. 'And - breaking news - he's also the guy I'm replacing on the school drama production.'

'I didn't know that. Why do you have to replace him then?'

'He's suffered a minor break-down. He's going through a bad patch.' William hesitated. 'Sol's been a close friend of mine for a number of months, my mentor really. For reasons I can't quite understand, he's recently turned against me Really moody and unpredictable; resentful almost.' He paused. 'It's been upsetting his work too. I'm sorry, I should've mentioned this before Anyway, the Head's offered him a sabbatical, thinks he needs a break. And consequently, his annual play production has landed in my lap.'

While the crowd and the noise in the Bar gradually diminished, William explained in more detail about his growing friendship with Sol and the unusual events leading up to his apparent break-down. Finally, Mack asked, 'Where is he now then? Sunning himself in the Bahamas, I suppose.'

'Don't worry, I *know* where he'll be. Even if no-one else does.'

Mack intervened. 'I'm not really worrying, but I'd certainly like to check out this photo you say might be floating around in the staff-room, or somewhere. Just to make sure we're talking about the same Adam.'

'Yes, I'd half forgotten that, but ….' William broke off in mid-sentence, as he realised Mack had suddenly stopped listening, wasn't even looking at him; instead he was staring intently at a spot across in the far corner of the room. William said, with a hint of annoyance in his voice, 'Sorry, Mack, I didn't mean to bore you. I'm a bit tired. Is anything wrong?'

But Mack seemed not to hear even that, directing his gaze fixedly across the room. Then suddenly he muttered beneath his breath, 'Good god! That must be Hateley. It cannot be anyone other than Hateley.'

William followed his friend's stare and found himself looking at the familiar and obnoxious face of the 'cowboy', Red beard, ensconced in his usual spot and accompanied by several of his cronies. Mack, meanwhile, in an apparent state of alarm, had risen from his feet, and was speaking softly and urgently to William. 'Let's get out of here. Quick.' Not waiting for a reply, he strode across the room and out through the door, with William, bewildered, in pursuit.

It took just a short time, as they headed back to Denber, for Mack to explain to William who precisely Hateley was and his role in those events that had destroyed people and places, at Hillcrest and elsewhere, in 1967. 'On that 'mission' I mentioned, Hateley was always our target, and we failed to get him, but, it seems, just maybe, fate has landed him in our lap. Would you believe it? We have another chance.' He fell silent, processing perhaps in his orderly brain the way forward, until they neared Hillcrest, when he finally emerged from his thoughts. 'William, this is even more urgent now than you may quite understand. This man is a criminal, responsible for many a death in this part of the world. A slippery customer.' He thought for a while. 'Look, the first thing is to identify this character, Sol. Take me to that photograph you think might be in the faculty-room, or somewhere around. I've got suspicions. It's vital I identify this guy, Sol. He probably doesn't realise the danger he's in. And all of us.'

Sure enough, on a wall in the back of the faculty room, half hidden by various other framed photos, was a picture entitled "**Faculty of Hillcrest. Spring Term, 1975**". William put his finger on a spot on the photo. 'That's him. That's Sol.'

He glanced now at Mack, who asked firmly, 'Are you certain, William? Absolutely sure? There can be no mistakes.'

'Of course I'm sure. I should know, shouldn't I? I've worked with him for months. At close quarters.'

Mack was shaking his head now, an enigmatic expression on his face. 'Get ready for a shock, William. I can assure you that's not someone called Sol. It's Adam Riley.' He looked intently again at the photo. 'Yes. Funny thing. You know, I've had my suspicions for a while now, particularly since my visit to your mother. Just instinct, not thought.' He looked straight into William's eyes. 'Yes, that's an older version of the man I once knew so well.' He paused, before gently placing his hand on William's shoulder. 'That's your father, William.'

It took William a short while to feel the impact of the news Mack had brought with him. Initially came a feeling of intense surprise, almost relief, that at last he could feel normal and complete, a man, like most other men, with a mother and a father. For so long, that deep-seated awareness that he was odd had been a part of his make-up, of how he saw himself and how he related to other people. Now he had a father, whom he might or might not resemble, might look and behave like, a pillar in his life, on which to lean, and either copy or reject, the choice was his. It was a relief beyond all measure.

Then came the doubt. How could these things be true? He had only this clever friend of his to rely on. Supposing he was wrong. This discovery was too enormous for there to be mistakes. His mother's lover of twenty-five years ago, mysteriously materialising. It was a fairy-tale, and we all know the flimsy substance of fairy-tales.

He met Mack next morning, busy as usual, but as if all were normal and the world still turned on its axis. 'Mack, you know what you told me last night. That about my father. Are you sure?'

Mack smiled in reply. 'You can take my legal word on it: that man you call Sol is the very same man I call Adam Riley. The picture doesn't lie; so, as long as your index finger doesn't, yes, you have a father.'

CHAPTER 25

Mack, that morning though, had already been to the Post Office in Denber on other business, to request them to place a notice in the LA Times.

'You'll need to do that yourself, sir. Find the newspaper's telephone number for advertising and personal notices; they'll insert your message.'

Mack had thanked them, at the same time humbly realising how a simple phone call nowadays had replaced the clumsy process of telegrams. It was that simple. In fact, Mack, even earlier that morning, had simply reached Tessa in W... by phone, to ask if she remembered a certain Sam Toms... *'...or perhaps, Tessa, going under the name of Jackson. You must remember Sam. The black guy who visited you at Elk that time, years ago. I'm sorry, Tess, to bother you; it's a bit of a long shot, but something's come up. Something vital, (too complicated to tell you right now). The long and short of it is: I need to know how, or what, if anything, Sam left when he left you that day. An address maybe?'*

'Mack, Darling, of course I remember him; how could I forget him. It seems just like yesterday. Let me think, for a moment.'

'Tess, he maybe gave you a phone number or a code or something?'

Tessa, down the line, asked him to wait, not to hurry her... *'It's years ago, Mack.'* Then, in a moment, she was coming back on the line. *'I remember precisely: He didn't leave anything. But better, he told me something in that message I found on the table. Here it is, it's locked in my memory: "Place a notice in the LA Times, and mention in it '***Grave News***.*"' Yes, I won't forget that clever play on words either.'*

Mack breathed a short prayer to his Maker, thanking Him for making women so practical-minded. He exchanged a further gentle word or two with Tessa, deliberately omitting to tell her about the revelation of 'Adam'. He knew it was bound to upset her; better to wait for a more convenient moment to deliver that bomb-shell.

The procedure functioned correctly to Mack's relief, with no hitches, and he despatched his 'message' to the newspaper, adding his own personal phone-number for Sam Toms to reach him, still however remaining slightly sceptical that this distant, informal arrangement of Sam's with Tessa so long ago (just a note left on the table), might have any hope of success. Nevertheless, he remained positive, and turned his attention back to William, wondering how the shattering news he'd received might have affected his young friend. In addition, there remained still some vital details he needed to get from William, before he could put his newly-formed planned in motion.

He found him alone in the faculty room, examining again the tell-tale photograph that had changed his life. 'William, I'm going to go see Sol, your father. Did you mention yesterday you knew where he was'

'Yes. I know.'

'Did he tell you before he left then? I need to be sure.'

'No, he *didn't*, but I know. There's only one place he'd go. It's called Possum Kingdom.'

'Where in heaven's name is that?'

'A lake, a hundred miles from here. I've been there with him. He has a house by the lake. He'll for sure have gone to ground there. Lick his wounds.'

'Will I find it? Sounds like the lair of a desperate wolf.'

'You have about as much chance as an umbrella in a tornado. What do you want to find him for anyway?'

.The question came out surprisingly blunt and angry. William had spent half the night trying to come to terms with this new, enormous discovery. His feelings were ambiguous though. After having at last established and accepted exactly *who* this father of his was, there'd followed in its wake a multitude of disturbing questions as to *why* Sol/Adam hadn't behaved like most fathers, but instead had chosen to live a lie, a life *in absentia*. What enormous calamity must have occurred to compel a man, in the prime of life, to absent himself life-long from a wife and son, until his shenanigans finally caught up with him? For sure, something beyond his ability to avoid. Had he been detained in prison perhaps? Then better a father released from prison, than no father at all. There was such a thing as forgiveness. And now, what had this father become, this snarling, envious creature who'd chased his own son out of his room with threats and menaces? In the absence of answers, William had started already to wonder whether this rapacious father was someone he wanted in his life anyway.

'We need to go and find him now, William,' said Mack calmly. 'Without him nothing will make sense at all.'

'Did you say 'we'.'

Mack nodded. 'Yes.'

'He's dangerous, Mack. He was threatening me the last time I saw him. He has it in for me. My life.'

Mack thought for a second. 'I won't find him without you. We'll drive together and take two cars. You can show me the place and return straightaway if necessary.'

The suggestion was met with silence, as William considered the feasibility of this plan. 'The geography of the place doesn't lend itself to secrecy. It won't be easy. If we do it, we'll have to do it in darkness.

'We can't avoid this, William. It's vital I find him. He's my close friend, my former teacher. He won't bear *me* ill-will.'

'I hope not; that's all I can say. I'm certainly not going to go in there myself.'

They talked it out, and it was agreed. William would take the lead car, but, on arrival, Mack would slip down into the bay while William remained back up the lane a little. It would be Mack who knocked first and hopefully entered. 'I'll suss out how the land lies and send you a signal, William, if it's safe. I have a flashlight. If you see it go twice, get back in your car and get back to the school. You need anyway to get this Shakespeare off the ground. Time's against us.'

William nodded uncertainly. His entire demeanour seemed to have shrivelled and lost its youthful gloss in the space of twenty-four hours. 'If I return here, and you are left to somehow negotiate with Sol, please don't forget to tell him the most significant fact of all: that *I am his son*. Surprisingly enough, I still don't believe he's figured that out. The subject never came up.'

'You get your Play going. Leave the rest to me. I'll coax the wolf from his lair, and be back with you in a day or two with the beast in tow.'

But it wasn't to be like that. They headed off the same evening, driving west into the setting sun. As they neared the lake and the shack, they stopped, and swopped positions, Mack leading now, as agreed. William's nerves had already started to fray at the edges, but Mack, never having forgotten those endless fraught days of manoeuvring with Tessa and Adam on the trail of Hateley, managed to remain cool. He slipped the car down as silently as possible into the solitary parking bay by the house, engine already off. In the back room, lakeside, he spotted a dim light, indicating the presence of someone. He knocked lightly on the door and waited. The light inside seemed to go off and then, a moment later, was switched on again. Nothing stirred. Silence. He was already starting to wonder how he might gain access, with or without the aid of an uncooperative occupant, when the rickety wooden door was suddenly flung open and Mack, in the gloom and semi-dark, looked into the two barrels of a shot-gun, and, behind, a shadowy figure holding the gun. Seconds ticked by before he heard a voice. '*Stay exactly where you are. Don't make a movement, or it'll be your last.*'

Mack, slowly, calmly, raised his hands in the air. 'Don't shoot, Sol. I'm unarmed.' Endless moments elapsed, until Mack's voice broke the silence again. 'I'm Mack. Remember? Your former pupil at Hillcrest. Mack Neumann.'

Mack heard the unmistakable sound of two hammers on the barrel deliberately pulled back, and the tense voice behind the barrels came again. 'Tell me the name you knew me by at Hillcrest, quickly, before I expedite you on a journey to eternity.'

Mack stood, at that moment, as if on an unsteady cliff-edge ready to fracture and crumble into a million parts. But this ultimatum of Sol's, delivered in the clipped, precise tones of a careful school master administering his class, worked to minimize, rather than emphasize, the deadly threat, and reminded Mack of schools and classrooms, and TV quizzes. Instinctively, he blurted out the only response he could think of, which probably saved his life. 'Could you repeat the question please? It's kind of important I don't get it wrong.'

The shaft of humour latent in this reply, and delivered with a boldness he didn't feel broke the tension and restored a moment of sanity to this whole ridiculous, but deadly stand-off,. The edifice held firm, and Mack knew, in that split second, he was safe and that, moreover, Adam too could probably be saved.

The voice came again, impatiently. 'Hurry. My name, the one you called me at Hillcrest years ago.'

'Adam. Adam Riley.'

The spell was broken; the barrel was slowly lowered. 'What do you want?'

'I came to see you, Adam. And I came to tell you some remarkable news. If you turned the light on, we could sit down and talk.'

A dim light was switched on somewhere, and the two former friends stood facing each other in the doorway, not three yards apart. Adam, still very wary, said, 'You're lying.'

'Why would I come all this way just to lie to you?' Mack hesitated a moment and then added, 'You have a son, Adam.'

'I have no son.' The reply was instant and adamant, almost too much so 'I never had a son. Why have you come here to taunt me?'

After a moment, Mack replied, 'Because we two once risked our lives together, and what's more, as my teacher, I once liked and respected you. Isn't that reason enough? I tell you again, you *have* a son. This is not a lie.'

Adam looked hard and straight at him, clearly unsure of his next move. At last, as if a great weight had been lifted from his shoulders, he said, 'Let's go inside; we can't talk here.'

'Put the gun away, Adam. We have much to tell each other.' They went into the little sitting-room and Mack said, looking around, 'Nice. If I can make you trust me, is it too much to ask you for a bed for the night?'

There was the faintest hint now of a smile on Adam's face. 'That's not impossible, but I must warn you, this is not five-star hospitality. Just a sofa bed.'

'Any bed will be welcome.' Mack remembered there was something important he still needed to do. He said, 'I'll go outside a moment to the car-port. Get some luggage.'

'No funny tricks, Mack.' That apprehensive expression had appeared again on Adam's face.

As Mack disappeared outside to send William the agreed all-clear, the irony wasn't lost on him that this was indeed a 'funny trick' He flashed twice with his torch, and watched for a moment as William slowly backed away and disappeared into the night. Mack came back inside and the two of them sat down. He'd already concluded that Adam was neither mad nor even on the fringes of lunacy; fraught, that's all.

Adam leaned back in his chair. 'Okay. There are a lot of questions, Mack. First off, how did you know where to find me?'

Mack, aware now he needed to tread slowly and carefully, replied, 'Your son guessed correctly. He showed me the way here. He's gone back to the school.'

There was a long pause, as, very slowly, a glimmer of a smile appeared on Adam's face. 'Yes, my son. Tell me, what 'son' is this? I don't remember having a son. Nor a wife. Is this a virgin birth?'

'William Bellman is your son, Adam.' Mack sat looking hard at Adam and shaking his head gently from side to side. 'There's no Beckley. His name is Bellman, William Bellman. And his mother is Tessa Bellman, whom you and I know all too well.'

'It can't be true. Give me evidence; give me proof, and I might believe you.'

'Simple, Adam. We - you and I - know each other, and I know William; and I know William's mother too. I'm the link. What further proof do I, or you, need? Believe me, William is your son.'

The sceptical expression on Adam's face had been replaced, for the first time, by one of anticipation, almost excitement. 'Tessa is this man's *mother*?' He repeated the name, still incredulous, while Mack slowly nodded. 'Tessa Bellman?'

'Yes, Mack, the very same.'

Adam repeated again the name. 'Tessa. Can it be true, or a fairy-tale?' He raised his hand, as if uncertain what to do with it. 'Don't take offence, Mack; I'm starting to believe you. But you must have been on a long journey to tell me this.'

Mack nodded, and said simply, 'I have.' For many minutes, as Adam sat spell-bound, Mack recounted the whole coincidental chain of recent events which had led to this moment 'Suddenly I was meeting your mother again, and arriving in Texas, and simply making the connections. With William's help.' He paused and went on. 'One thing in all this still puzzles me. Tessa, at W..., a week and a half ago, showed me a letter from you to her, written twenty-five years ago, in which you made no mention at all of her apparent pregnancy. Even though, you must already have known she was pregnant. *I* knew, at that time, and so did many others. You can't just *not* have known, considering your obvious - how shall I say it - 'involvement' in this pregnancy. It must have been in your mind. But nstead, if my memory serves me right, you just dismissed her, and even disregarded your own past, in that letter.' He paused. 'The other parts of the letter I can half understand, but no mention at all of a possible child, that's impossible to understand.'

Adam had got out of his chair, as Mack had been speaking, and was fumbling with a bundle of papers, now in his hand. He held up two of the sheets. 'D'you mean this letter?' He gave it to Mack.

'Yes, the same. Tessa kept it. For obvious reasons.' Mack hesitated for a moment, before pursuing his argument. 'You mention your 'new' life. But how can that have been so important to you, by comparison with your old one?'

For a few seconds Adam didn't reply. Then he just shrugged and said, 'Guilty as charged, your Honour. I guess it's just me. As you can read in the letter, I had things to do. My '*old*' life didn't offer me that chance; a new one did.'

Mack remained silent for a moment. 'I hope it was worth it.'

'How do you mean? I had a decision to make.' There was a new edge to Adam's tone. 'Tell me, when was the last time *you* died and were then reborn? This bizarre event wasn't that simple, and the circumstances surrounding it had a massive impact on my life; not just mentally, but physically too. And not always good, I can tell you. I don't believe, in retrospect, that blame comes into question.'

'It's not exactly blame, Adam; the two words that come into my head are 'curiosity' and 'responsibility'. Do you feel no regrets? I mean, the nothingness you left Tessa with?'

Adam was shaking his head. 'The student now teaching the teacher, I see. Life is hard, Mack. We have to be strong.'

Mack played his trump card. 'What are you going to say to your son? How will you explain your actions.'

Adam's fierce, stubborn expression had returned as fast and wildly as wind on a stormy day. 'I still don't believe I have a son. But if it turns out I have, I'll tell him what I've told you.'

Mack interrupted. 'William Beckley, at Hillcrest School, at this very moment in time, is your son. There can be no doubt. If you have to, take a DNA test; but it will return the same verdict.'

Adam hesitated. 'For the moment, I have to tell you, I feel no joy then . That apparently untrustworthy young person you mistake for my son has left me with a sense of betrayal and distrust. I have no fatherly feelings towards him. Just dislike.'

'How come, betrayal? In what way has William betrayed you? He's simply, in the most natural manner in the world, taking over from you. He's been apprenticed with you, now he's replacing you. It's common; the young always replace the old. Hell, you have to come to terms with your ageing. Your son has no inklings of betrayal; he's on the edge of his greatest challenge, this Play. Can you remember how you felt at Hillcrest, when you produced '*Hamlet*' all those years ago? I have to say that, in my opinion, your feelings and motives are cowardly and misguided and selfish, and your hasty reactions must be totally incomprehensible to him.'

Adam was nodding his head. 'Mack, what do you really know about it?'

'I know what I know, and for the rest, my intelligence leads me to presume.' He paused. 'I see from your expression you don't agree. Let me put it another way: all my experience leads me to think getting older and the effects of ageing can sometimes lead to subtle misconceptions. I categorically believe you've been unjust to William, your son, and that you need to make amends, ask his forgiveness.'

'Never!' It was a harsh reply.

Mack hauled himself out of his chair. 'It's pride, Adam, and I'm tired. It's been a long day. Maybe we should sleep on the matter and not lead ourselves into more biierness at this stage.'

Mack woke next morning plagued by the thought that he'd never really asked himself why he'd come to visit Adam in the first place. What was the actual purpose of this stressful visit? Of course, since that moment at W..., when Tessa had shown him the mysterious letter which confirmed beyond all doubt Adam's strange 'resurrection', Mack's prevailing emotion had been curiosity. To return from the dead, after all, is no common human experience, and almost certainly has to involve a third party, some kind of human intervention. But by whom, and how, exactly, in this particular case? In addition, the puzzling fact that his old friend, once reborn, had apparently shown no evident signs of wanting to rejoin the human race, but chosen instead to stray into the paths of illegality and assume a whole new identity: new name, new passport, new life, this tickled of course Mack's restless, legal mind, despite his genuine friendship, and impelled him to find out more..

On an altogether new level though, what he found difficult to ignore, or forgive, was the blatant fact that, since that time, Adam appears to have stubbornly ignored or denied the arrival of a son in his life and a woman who had given birth to this child. Surely he must have known Tessa had been pregnant on that fateful day in '65, and, what's more, pregnant by *him*. This, for Mack, was less easy to overlook.

All these reflections, however, faded, in the face of the one main reason that had beckoned Mack to this beautiful lake and an encounter with Adam Riley: it was the hope, after all these years, of rekindling his relationship with his old friend, someone he'd shared common thoughts and goals with in those far-off days at Hillcrest, and with whom he'd stalked the hills and plains of Texas, placing their lives at stake on the trail of a dangerous criminal. He and Adam hadn't been just friends, but partners, in a unique endeavour, and Mack, since his recent rediscovery of Hateley, earnestly desired they might be that again. As he lay on the couch by the window, he knew it would take all his wit, humour and tact to rekindle that relationship, but realised he had to. He knew too he needed Adam's help.

He'd slept deeply, and feeling refreshed, looked out through the large bay windows, and noticed Adam, already up and tinkering with a boat at the end of the dock. Unwilling to delay any further, Mack determined to plunge in like a swimmer into cold water, and not prevaricate. He would tactfully allow Adam to be the genial host, while he played the role of an enquiring but forthright guest, eager for new sights, sounds and experiences.

Adam called from the end of the dock, 'C'mon, let's go out in the boat. It's what I usually do in the morning. Takes the place of a stroll in the park. Less strenuous too.'

The tense confrontations of the previous evening seemed already to have been forgotten. They chugged across the empty stretches of the lake, Adam steering unswervingly towards a jutting promontory, until Mack asked, 'Where are we heading?'

'My special place. It's always deserted; no one seems to have noticed it.'

They reached a little island opposite the main shoreline, a couple of small overhanging trees, a bit of grass to sit on. Mack said, 'Wow, a desert island idyll. You can see the enemy coming too.'

Adam laughed. 'I have no enemies.'

'You did last night; me.'

'You can never be too careful, Mack.'

'D'you greet everyone like that then?' As Adam didn't immediately reply, Mack added, 'If so, you wouldn't have many friends left.'

'I suppose all strangers are potential enemies, aren't they? It depends on the level of your paranoia.'

'True. Would you have pulled the trigger?'

'I'm not sure.'

'It's a dangerous game, Adam. Were you expecting someone else perhaps?'

Adam was shaking his head. 'Who? I don't get many visitors here. That's why I like it.'

Adam was clearly beating around the bush and Mack knew he too was getting no nearer the real Adam, an Adam without the veneer. He abruptly changed the topic, hoping to get a reaction from his companion. 'Talking of friends and enemies, do you remember Charles Hateley?'

There was a moment's pregnant pause before Adam exclaimed, 'Could I ever forget that criminal?'

'I saw him last week.'

Although Mack was expecting this 'bomb-shell' to be received by Adam with shock or dismay, it was Mack who received the shock at Adam's reply, 'Yes, me too.'

'You've seen him too? Where, for heavens sake?'

'I've seen him twice. I'm convinced it's him. I've seen him at a football game with William, and remarkably, I actually saw him round here, where we are now, in this isolated spot. I'll show you exactly where later. I was with William again, walking, and I'm almost certain it was the very same man.' He hesitated a moment. 'So, where did *you* see the slippery eel?'

'At a soccer game in Dallas; just like you. We're following in each other's footsteps.'

Adam laughed. 'Yes. That's where he hangs out, I suppose. William's already acquainted with the man. He calls him 'Redbeard'. After a moment, he added, 'I believe William knows, on one level, who this guy, Redbeard, is, but he doesn't know *who* he is, if you get my meaning. I don't think he needs to know either, at this stage. Don't you agree?'

Mack nodded. 'Yes, I do agree. He needn't know. We'll keep this matter to ourselves.'.

'The question really is, what are we going to do about it?'

'Adam, don't worry. You've got other things to think about, and I believe I might already be on the case. You're right. We can't afford to let him off the hook twice.'

They lapsed into silence, re-living perhaps the destructive part Hateley had played in both their lives, until it was Adam who broke the silence, 'C'mon; I'll show you a bit more of this placid lake of mine. We can't let Hateley ruin any more of our day; thoughts about him don't exactly go with the innocent solitude of this lake.'

Mack nodded. 'Couldn't have put it better myself. Yes, it reminds me of Texoma; it reminds me of those days we spent there with Bill and the students. Do you remember?'

'Do I remember Bill? Adam repeated scornfully. 'What a question. Course I remember him. He was integral to all of us: you, Tessa, even the kid; William; we're all about Bill when it comes down to it. We wouldn't be here if not for him.'

Mack cut in. 'Your memory doesn't sound quite so bad as you think, Adam.'

Adam smiled wryly. 'Well, I may forget most things, but those early days at Hillcrest somehow remain locked in my mind somewhere. Trouble is, I can remember the good times; it's the bad ones I forget. They'll catch up with me one day, I expect.'

'Sounds the right way round though. Doesn't do to dwell on them; nostalgia's a dangerous force. Best to move on.'

'Great idea. Let's 'move on' then.' He'd stood up and was pushing the motor-boat down the slope and into the water. 'Come on, Mack, or I'll leave without you.'

They set out again across the lake. Adam seemed almost buoyant, the old Adam Mack once knew. 'So you became a lawyer, Mack. I really don't recall how I knew. But I do.'

'It's written all over my face, I suppose.' Mack paused for a moment. 'What's the matter? Don't approve of lawyers?'

'No, it's nothing.. Nothing at all. Just wondering how you got into that career?'

'Wasn't cut out for anything else, I suppose.'

'That's the way I feel about teaching sometimes.'

Mack nodded. 'Yes. But you're cut out for it, Adam: imagination, an all-rounder.' He paused. 'I could never do teaching. I had a bit of a try once but realised I didn't have what it takes. I'm too straight-laced. Too one-tracked.'

'So you make a good living?'

'Yes, the money's good. Particularly in Germany.'

Adam laughed. 'They're *all* straight-laced over there. So you returned to your roots after all. D'you remember that evening we went to Fort Worth, to the German restaurant? The kids gave you such a bad time; they were all over you about your Germanism?'

'Yes, I do. I also haven't forgotten I gave them as good as they gave me.'

'You did. Always the fighter, Mack.

Mack, from the comfort of the stern of the boat and watching Adam guiding it expertly in and out of the little creeks, realised he needed to steer the conversation away from himself, back onto Adam, who seemed to be increasingly occupying centre stage. 'Adam. I've been meaning to ask you, hope you don't mind, but why d'you think the Play proved quite difficult for you this year?'

Adam reacted, heard the question, and, leaving the boat gently chugging, replied, 'It's hard to say really; a number of reasons. Perhaps I've been at it too long. Found it all getting stale. I also believe the play itself was probably wrong for me at this moment in time, even if not for the kids. The mad 'King Lear' was starting to remind me of myself.'

Mack laughed loudly. 'Come on. I hope you don't treat all your Shakespeare characters like that. Let them get to you.' He paused. 'I have to admit though, you did sometimes think you were *'Hamlet'*, back in '65.'

'Maybe, but I should know better now. Seriously, I've started to find this past year weighing on me. Don't forget, year in, year out, a school gets a very varied selection of good and bad students. Talent-wise, I mean.' He hesitated. 'This year's mediocre bunch played a major part in turning me off altogether.' There was momentarily complete silence in the boat, and in the lake, and in the universe, an absence of sound, as the stone dropped into the pool at this midday hour. Adam's blunt, damning remark had left him stunned and speechless. It was as if a dark cloud had floated across the sun. How could a teacher write off an entire year-group with such a comment? Adam probably felt it too, and, as if wishing to change the subject, said half-heartedly, 'Anyway, let's get on. I'll show you the rest of the Lake. D'you want to steer?'

'No thanks; I'm quite happy playing the tourist.'

And then Adam, unprompted, said, 'I believe William played his part in it all too, you know,.'

'His part in what? How do you mean.?'

'In unsettling me.'

'He's told me he thought he was just helping out.'

'No, he thought he knew better than I did. That's the truth of it.' Adam almost spat the venom out. 'However, it was the kids mainly.

They too thought this nice young teacher, who was all smiles with them, knew better than I did. It became impossible in the end.' Mack thought he'd finished, but Adam added vehemently, 'It was the same with soccer. William just took over. Won over the kids, damn it. They stopped listening to me.'

Mack was astonished by how quickly, like a sudden change in the weather, Adam's mood could swing from this to this. They lapsed into silence, staring mindlessly at each other, or the bottom of the boat, both surprised by the harsh direction their conversation had taken. Finally it was Adam who firmly turned the key on the motor, and they drifted slowly, rocking on the water. 'Look, my old friend; I know where you're coming from with all this. You think I've lost the plot, and can't cope anymore, with my work, my so-called son, whatever. Right?' He gave Mack no chance to reply, but continued, 'Let me explain. You remember, I was poisoned, by that bitch. I should have died, but somehow I didn't, and the truth is, I still have no idea why not. Nobody can ever know. Except perhaps the person responsible. But I believe that person somehow contrived an antidote. We can't of course be sure, but, nonetheless, I personally am certain it *is* so. He or she administered that antidote, and placed me here,' He waved his arms dramatically at the lake. 'Here, in this place. He or she dumped me in this spot, to recover. Like God does sometimes, I suppose.'

He smiled bitterly, and Mack said gently, 'So you recovered. Why the problem then?'

Adam shook his head. 'You still don't understand, Mack. I won't employ you as my lawyer, or my surgeon, if it ever comes to that. Seriously, though, I wasn't completely 'recovered'. The medicine, the antidote, was only to a certain extent effective. It left me with a damaged memory. Irreparable. I couldn't remember anything about those final events. I still can't. I remember many odd things before and since, but that moment remains a blank. And so I've had to live with this handicap. For years.' This last statement was delivered with an anguished cry

.At last, Mack said, 'We all have trouble with our memory, Adam. We don't let it worry us though. It's called ageing; we have to accept it. And perhaps some people feel it earlier in life than others. Dementia.

Dementia can bring powerful bouts; not just of memory loss, but of paranoia as well.'

Adam was shaking his head. 'Are you telling me I'm a paranoid maniac as well as having dementia?' He shook his head determinedly. 'No. I'm not paranoid. I've just got a defective memory.'

Mack let the outburst go, and attempted to make light of the topic. 'Well that's a relief. They say if you worry about having dementia, then you haven't got it.'

'Yes, but I *don't* worry, Mack. I just suffer from it. So where does that leave me?' He too laughed. 'But I can assure you, I've been on journeys all my life, hoping to recover what I'd lost. I've tried writing. They say, writing aids memory. I've tried that.' He paused. 'I'll show you some of my writing, my journal; it's back at the house over there. But I'm afraid it didn't help. Not in the long run.' He showed a little gap between finger and thumb. 'I think I got *so* far...' he indicated with his fingers ...'but it was late, too late.'

They sat on in silence until Mack said, 'You probably never will reach your own personal Nirvana. We all suffer from that. There comes a moment when you've got to just shut your eyes and stumble on in the dark. But it's never too late to do that. That reminds me though. A question, as a lawyer, I've long wanted to ask. Why did you change your name, your identity? Was that necessary?'

Adam gave a weak smile and shrugged. 'A new start, a new kind of life; I hoped that might help restore my memory. Anyway - you should know, as a lawyer - it's not just the criminal who needs to change his identity sometimes; there must occasionally be justifiable motives too.'

Mack was shaking his head. 'I'm afraid not, Adam. Not under the Law.' He glanced up at him and repeated. 'I'm afraid not. Don't be surprised if that doesn't catch up with you some day.'

Time passed slowly at the lake. For several days, the two friends meandered around the perimeters of the water, occasionally in the boat, but often strolling along the gentle verges. And, very gradually, trust seemed to grow between them again, and the tension began to go out of Adam. His smiles no longer resembled the pinched, fearful glances of a sick man, but had come to resemble the true mirror of a man at ease with himself, happy, courageous, exhilarated, the Adam Riley of old, as Mack remembered him. His recovery seemed almost complete.

For Mack though, the recuperation of his former friend wasn't the only vital marker on his agenda, just one of many; he was constantly mindful now that time was closing in on him and that there was still much to accomplish.

One afternoon, they found themselves in the vicinity of that village focal-point, the Tabernacle. The ugly Temple reared up like some monstrous spider in the middle of the Square. Adam, who was of course already familiar with the place, but had actually surprised himself to be inadvertently there again, exclaimed, 'Ah, the Tabernacle. How strange. Here we are again.'

He turned abruptly to Mack, and was about to embark on a description of his previous visit there, with William, when Providence, in the shape of a shrill phone-call, intervened. His mobile was urgently ringing, and, glancing at the dial, he said, 'Just a moment, Adam; I've *got* to take this.' He stepped away, leaving Adam impatiently waiting in the vicinity of the Square and the Tabernacle.

Down the phone came a deep voice Mack didn't recognise. 'This is Sam. Sam Toms. I picked up your message in the LA Times. Is that Mack Neumann?'

'It is.' Mack could hardly control the excitement in his voice. 'Where are you, Sam?'

'California. But I haven't forgotten your friend Tessa. How could I ever forget her in fact? Her comfort, back then, in my hour of need.'

There was a surge of crackle on the line, and Mack, desperate not to lose the connection, said hurriedly, 'You've got my number, Sam. In case we lose contact. What are you doing at the moment?'

There was a gruff laugh at the other end. 'What am I doing? I'm having a coffee in Hollywood, and talking to you on the phone.'

Mack joined in the laughter. 'Sorry; I mean on a more permanent basis.'

'I know; I was just having a laugh. I run a law firm here in LA. But you sound quite fraught. Nobody's *ever* fraught outside of California.'

'They are, and I am, Sam. Look, let me explain, in case the line goes dead. It's a tall order; I'm in the middle of Texas right now, with

Redemption

my friend, Adam Riley. I need you to come and meet us in Santa Fe. We: me, you, Adam, have important business there.'

A silence followed, and then the sonorous voice down the phone, 'Santa Fe's a long way, Mack. But go on.'

Mack added tersely, 'We've located the guy who murdered your mother. Among other little crimes. He's here in Texas. Charles Hateley. Does that ring any bells?'

'It sure does.'

'I think we have a chance at last of bringing him to justice. We need your help though'

Another silence followed, suggesting someone not entirely comfortable with news he's received.

'That crime's not small, Mack. I get your sarcasm. But.my help? How, and where?'

Mack realised in a flash that Sam, in distant California, was quite probably ignorant of the dramatic events that had taken place at Hillcrest all those years ago, and of Hateley's role in them. It took Mack several minutes now to describe how they'd gone on the hunt for Hateley, and how it had all gone sour.

Sam said, 'I read somewhere about a killing spree in Texas. I guessed it might be your school, but had no contact number. Why weren't the perpetrators brought to justice at that time?'

'Hateley escaped, went on the run.'

There was hesitation down the line. 'You say you've located him now though? What's Santa Fe got to do with it?'

Another hesitation; this time from Mack. He realised he needed to be concise; although friendly, Sam, was clearly dragging his heels. He needed coaxing. 'The evidence wasn't there, Sam. We couldn't indict Hateley at that time, link him to your mother, even had he been in our hands. We had no real evidence to pin on him. We have now.'

The two men were business-like now, confronting each other like lawyers, unwilling to commit to anything. After a few moments Sam asked, 'So what's changed?'

'Sam, I take it you've heard of DNA.'

'Sure have.'

'The DNA evidence is up there. In the hills near Santa Fe. I know it.'

'So what do you need me up there for? Go up and find it.' There was a longer than usual pause and Mack almost thought Sam had hung up on him. But no, the deep voice finally came back. 'I imagine you already know, Mack, this DNA is strong stuff now in a court of law,. You find the evidence. Get it back down to Texas. I'll sure come then and indict this bastard. Prosecute him. These are Texas crimes; they need to be tried in a Texas court of law.'

Mack, overjoyed at last by Sam's positive spin on the matter, said, 'You'll prosecute this guy for us?'

'Sure will. You get him in, and the evidence with it, we'll try him in Dallas together.' Pause. 'Mack, I know people in Dallas. State Prosecutor. Some guys in the police too. You give me a call when you're ready, or before, if you like, and we'll talk. I gotta go. I've finished my coffee. Hope to hear from you.'

The line went dead.

Unbeknown to Mack however, Adam had stood casually listening to parts of the phone conversation, and overheard Mack's references to 'DNA' and to 'Sam'. In a rare, crystal-clear moment, he knew at once who this was on the other end of the line and what the two men were discussing. It was but a small step more for him to make the link and realise the relevance of this conversation and the reference to Hateley, his avowed enemy. He knew what he had to do. He wandered off, went through the open door, and entered the Tabernacle, which, inside, resembled any Episcopal church in Denber or, for that matter, any Church of the kind he'd once been compelled to frequent in his own boyhood in England: a porch, where prayer-books and hymnals were always on display for private use by members of the congregation. Surprisingly, the Tabernacle seemed empty at first, but after a few minutes he was accosted by an earnest-looking young man.

'Good day, Sir. are you new in this locality?' Before Adam had a chance to reply, the man added, 'I'm one of the lay-messengers here.' He offered Adam his hand. 'Adoniram Ebenezer Jones. Folks call me E.J. or Eb,. for short. You can call me Eb.'

'Well, Eb, right nice to meet you. I was just idly looking round your nice church. I've recently moved here, although I confess I'm not exactly a Believer in your faith.'

'You're welcome, sir. Sure hope you can join one of our prayer meetings. And what is your name?

'Smith. Just plain Smith. People back home call me Smith the Smithy.'

'Are you a smithy, Sir? A noble trade.'

'Yes, but not of horses, of people. I shape young minds.'

'Nice way of putting it, sir. That leads me to suppose you must be a teacher.'

'Correct. I wonder if I might ask you a question.' Without waiting for an answer, Adam continued, 'I have a good friend at my former abode, an old red-bearded gentleman. Much facial hair. I believe he hangs around these parts too occasionally, with a few younger friends of his, and is an ardent adherent to your Pentecostal faith. I even think he might sometimes frequent....'

Eb interrupted him. 'You're right, sir. Hiram. C. Parham. A faithful believer, adorned with a unique name.' Eb smiled. 'And, if I may say so, a unique beard too. We often see Hiram here.'

'That's what I thought,' replied Adam, slightly amused there were other people, besides himself, adept at hiding their real name and identity. 'Another question, Eb, before you go. Is it the custom at your prayer meetings to lend out from the table here, (he indicated the array of biblical literature beside him) your books of song and prayer?'

'It is indeed. We have regular attendees, like for instance, Hiram, who even have their own dedicated edition, and guard it very jealously. They associate, you see, the true book with their true Maker. It's precious to them.' He looked at the table nearby and picked up a particular book, and handed it to Adam. 'This is Hiram's very own edition. I even see his name inside the cover.'

Adam pretended to examine the book closely. 'This surely is a valuable memento. Let me peruse it for a while, Eb. I'll be sure to replace it where it lay.' He pretended to leaf through a few pages of the text.

Ebenezer offered a slight nod of the head and went on his faltering way. No sooner had he disappeared from sight, Adam, who'd had no intention of returning the book, left the Tabernacle and made his way back to Mack, clutching his prize.

Mack was at the same spot, looking anxiously for him. 'Ah, Adam! Thought I'd lost you.'

'Sounded like an important call. Business, I suppose.'

An elated Mack replied, 'Yes, Adam; business indeed. C'mon; gird up your loins. We've got business too, in New Mexico. We're going bone collecting.'

They left early next morning, taking the route north-west to Lubbock, and from there due North to join Interstate 40 at Amarillo.

Mack said, 'Old hunting grounds, Adam. You'll recognise that desolate road to Santa Fe before long. D'you remember? You, me, and Tessa on our desperate way to the Pueblo, with the 'Weasel' on our tail. We stopped at Clines Corner to throw him off. Remember? Must have been at least twenty-five years ago.'

Adam, who'd sat slumped silently in the passenger seat since they'd left that morning, said, 'Could I ever forget it? It was the low-light of my life.'

'Don't you mean 'highlight'?'

'No, low-light. When I think of that whole journey, it still fills me with dread. It's part of me.'

'Really?' Mack showed genuine surprise. 'You ran our show, Adam. You were always so self-confident. I didn't think you were afraid of anything.'

Adam made a half-hearted attempt at a smile. 'It all changed though, didn't it? For me, at any rate. In that dreadful moment. Let's not fool ourselves.' Mack knew well what 'moment' he was referring to, but let Adam finish. 'You know, I'm certain that moment lies in wait for me,' he paused. 'to strike again. The full replay in glorious Technicolor. And I'm terrified by the thought of it; I sometimes think I don't want my memory back, if that's what it's going to entail.'

Mack nodded in sympathy. 'Yes, but the difference is, it's *we* now who're on the trail; we're the ones in control.' They both, for a second, let the thought sink in, before Mack added earnestly, 'But that knowledge's got to come as a surprise to Hateley. He must suspect nothing until it hits him with the same impact he hit you on that 'Gamesday' at Hillcrest....Huh, 'Gamesday'. He repeated the word with all the sarcasm he could muster. 'What a farce!'

'For some, I suppose,' retorted Adam ruefully, squeezing even further down in his seat, as if expecting the enemy to rush him at any moment. 'You know, over the years, I think I'd reconciled myself to believing Hateley lay forever beyond our reach. I find it difficult to accept that now; it's the reverse. Here we are, on *his* trail. How've you done it, Mack? What's the difference?'

Mack replied quickly, 'DNA's the difference. Plain and simple. That is, if we can find it. And don't forget of course that fortuitous phone-call from Sam, yesterday. In the hands of a good lawyer, his evidence, together with DNA, will act like dynamite in a court of law.' Mack took a quick look at the route map by his side. 'If we can find it up here.'

They drove on silently for several minutes before Adam said, 'Tell me. What is it about this DNA. I think I've been out of touch.'

Mack said, 'It's crucial evidence that clinches cases in court. I discovered it like a bolt from the blue. An article from a newspaper in a dentist's waiting-room; or somewhere like that. You know how you can randomly pick up an article and find yourself absorbed. It was only a brief story about someone who'd thought he'd got clean away on a charge of murder, only to find his DNA matched the prints on the gun. It's common nowadays, especially in criminal cases, because of it's nearly irrefutable evidence. I read up about it later in Britannica. Great things, these encyclopaedias. Apparently 1986 was the first key-date for the effective use of DNA evidence in a murder trial. It got someone off on a charge, and a year later, helped bring the actual perpetrator to justice.' For a long time Adam didn't reply and Mack wondered if he'd fallen asleep. 'You awake, Adam? Has my long story put you to sleep?'

'No' came the immediate response. 'I've been following what you say. I'm just working on the relevance of it to our predicament.'

'There's many things we know about Hateley which we've never been able to prove. DNA opens the door.'

Adam replied after a moment, 'How long does DNA evidence remain before it gets wiped?'

'Thousands of years apparently. Even on rocks. So long as water and stuff doesn't get to it.'

'Okay. So, DNA hadn't appeared on the scene by the time we were getting poisoned by Charlene at the dinner table.'

'Correct. And even if we'd been able to catch the perpetrators in '67, the true turn of events couldn't be proven.'

Adam smiled, 'Sure. Even though Hateley's finger-prints would have been all over Slaker's knives and forks.'

'Precisely.' Mack paused for a moment. 'Adam, let me give you the full picture; right now. Even though I know you'll have figured it out yourself soon.' He paused again, wondering how to begin. 'This guy Sam - the guy I was talking to on the phone at Possum - he's key to everything. Okay? You must understand that. Not only is he an influential lawyer, he's also personally involved in this whole operation. You remember we all went digging one night years ago at Texoma, looking for a grave. Sam's mother's grave. We found the location, but the evidence then would have been inconclusive in a court of law.' He paused. 'Now, we can find the DNA. We'll have to re-visit that grave all over again' He was silent again for a few moments. 'Do you see now? We can't do it all without Sam's help.'

Adam seemed almost nervous. 'Okay, I'm with you. I hope I won't let you down this time though.'

It was a solemn moment, and Mack took his hands off the wheel and they both looked hard at each other for a second. 'You didn't let us down last time either, Adam.' He paused and returned his gaze to the road. 'What I'm counting on a great deal though is that that cowboy murderer of ours won't ever have heard of those three capital letters, let alone their significance. He'll wander into court wearing that ignorant grin. So, let him meanwhile enjoy his football before we hit him with all the evidence we can find.'

'How're you going to get him there, Mack? Into court, I mean?'

'This guy Sam'll do the business. Hell, he's got a big enough motive, hasn't he? He'll have to stand up in court and tell his childhood story all over again.'

'So why in fact, if the evidence lies at Texoma, are we heading, right now, to Santa Fe?'

'Trip down memory lane for one,' said Mack with a wide grin. 'But seriously, I guess there're a number of relevant bones among the murky rocks at the foot of that precipice. We know all the various tales. Hell, you and I, both, know 'Mongrel' went over, for starters. I shoved him there.'

Silence, until Adam said, 'Yes, *'that guy made love to his employment'*.'

'He did indeed. That particular piece of DNA though will have to be kept quiet.' He paused. 'We know however we'll uncover the bones of someone called MacDiarmid. He's linked to the death of Sam's mother too. And we registered our suspicions years ago with the Press about his involvement, remember? This additional evidence will only strengthen our case.'

Adam said, indicating his head, 'My memory's complaining, Mack. So many names. It's like the end of an Agatha Christie story.'

'Okay. I agree. Let's keep it simple. We'll gather what we can here at the Pueblo: human remains, animal remains, whatever. We'll serve a summons on Hateley in the Rheinischer Hof Bar, get him behind bars and then into court.' He hesitated. 'You know, it's shocking that I, a lawyer, don't even know what Americans call that word 'summons'.'

Adam said, 'I think it's 'indictment', but perhaps 'arraignment'. Don't worry; a Californian lawyer's bound to know, and to know the procedure.'

'You're right; leave that to Sam.' They both fell silent, reflecting on the imminent success of their project. Mack said, 'This work at The Pueblo's not going to be all that pleasant though. Be prepared to get your hands dirty.'

And at that moment, Adam was quietly putting on some light gloves and reaching inside the glove-box, and holding up a finely-marked prayer book. 'This might help.'

Mack said, 'What's that?' And Adam replied, 'It's the personalised prayer book of a mutual friend of ours, called Hiram, alias Redbeard, alias Charles Hateley. All the way from a place called Possum Kingdom Tabernacle. Our first piece of real DNA evidence.'

*****

Three phone calls.

For three days the two of them ranged the murky undergrowth that lay at the foot of the giant cliff of the Pueblo. As Mack had guessed, amongst the thick foliage lay strewn many bones, skeletons even, testifying to the carelessness, the dirty work, the savagery, the nature, of both humans and animals, throughout perhaps centuries.

They finished with two sturdy bags, which no doubt, under analysis, would carry age, type, time of death, and even, in human bones, an identity of some poor unknown, which could become vital identity if a matching 'partner' could be found somewhere on the national DNA database.

Securing one of the bags, Mack said, 'Hateley, I'm assuming, isn't on the national database; he should be, but he won't be. And not in this bag either; he got others to do his dirty work for him all along, remember? But - and it's a big but - we have our own database now; hopefully his DNA will be all over that holy book.' Adam laughed at Mack's irreverent turn of phrase as he continued, 'Our great hope now is to hurry down to Esther's grave at Texoma. It's a big gamble, but I feel confident. All those decades ago, Hateley surely can't have been so squeamish about getting his hands dirty.'

'Adam laughed again. 'Why have we bothered to come all this way up to Santa Fe?'

'Mack had no hesitation replying. 'I've already told you; to give you a holiday and visit old haunts. And just perhaps we might also find a few other interesting matches on these bones here. You have to be thorough.'

'Who's going to plough through all these?' He indicated the sacks.

'I don't know. I'm relying on Sam to help us.'

They stood in silence for a minute, looking west at the mighty view, as if two believers sending a solemn prayer of gratitude and hope to their Creator. Mack said finally, 'C'mon. Let's be off.' And Adam, slightly panicking as one can, when leaving a place in a hurry, said 'Have you got the grid reference and the code Mr. Jackson left in his letter? Or we'll never find Sadie's grave again.'

Mack grinned. 'I posted them, along with the rest of the stuff we sent to the newspaper, in a separate envelope. *Just in case*, remember?'

'Where's the envelope?'

'With the newspaper, we hope.'

'Did you keep a copy?'

'Of course. I carry it everywhere on my person; for memory's sake. Strange isn't it?'

Adam replied gruffly, 'It's the lawyer in you.'

That same evening they packed and headed south for Denison and Texoma.

May.15th

Mack stopped somewhere near Wichita Falls, and was standing beside the car, checking his mobile for connection. He dialled a number and after two or three seconds, the clear, strong voice of William answered. 'Hello.'

'William, it's Mack.'

The voice went up a semi-tone. 'A voice from the past.'

'Yeah, but coming back down into the present.'

'Where are you?'

'Wichita Falls. Not too far from Denber.'

'What are you doing there?'

'Looking for bones.' Mack hesitated. Time was not on their side; he didn't want to waste some of it by going into lengthy, improbable explanations. 'I'll tell you about it later. How are you?'

'Fine.' The response conveyed the usual brimming confidence, a tireless sense of certainty, that Mack had grown so unused to after several weeks in the company of the unpredictable Adam Riley.

'And the play? Coming along okay, is it?'

'It's great. It's going to be fine. What a wonderful team of students they are.'

As he listened to this voice down the line, Mack was experiencing a déjà vue from twenty-five years back. It was uncanny how William's voice resembled his father's; along with the irrepressible enthusiasm Adam had always displayed at rehearsals back in those days; it could even have *been* him,

Mack quickly brushed away any trace of sentimentality. 'We haven't got long, William. *'Time, like an ever-rolling stream...'.'*

'No, don't worry, we're on target.. I'm working on it. I'll have it ready. Last weekend in May.' The conversation seemed to have come to an end, but William added, 'Did I tell you? You're in it. I'll need you.'

Mack didn't want to appear negative, but could hardly conceal his consternation. 'I'm no actor, William. Thought you knew that.'

'You don't have to act, just be there.' Then William added, 'That guy you call my father, I'll need him too.' Then he added puzzlingly, 'And any other interlopers from home would be useful.'

Mack wasn't about to argue the toss; he had other worries, and time wasn't on his side. He just replied, 'Okay, let's say your father will be watching the play, I hope. But not acting in it. However, what will be, will be. It all sounds very inventive.'

'It is. By the way, I never asked: How *is* Sol?' He hastily corrected himself. 'I mean 'Adam', I mean my 'father'.' This final word was wrapped in disbelief and irony.

'Recovering, I think. Look, I've got to go. I'll keep in touch.'

Mack was on the phone again, late evening, somewhere in the precincts of Lake Texoma. It had taken him a while to filter in his mind what William had been trying to say at the end of that phone-call. He was not the kind of person to dwell on statements nor rely on instinct, he was always far too straightforward and logical, but in this particular instance he'd gnawed on William's enigmatic bone for the past hour or two; he knew there was a hidden meaning in his word '*interlopers*'. What had he meant? And then it had come to him; he knew what he had to do. He checked the map which lay on the back seat of the car, while Adam sat passively, seemingly lost in thought, or dreaming. 'We're going to change direction, Adam. We'll leave William to get on with things; he sounds all right. We'll head now direct to Texoma. Do the business there.' He looked upwards at the red streaks crisscrossing an otherwise clear sky. 'No rain or bad weather to prevent us from doing what we have to do, stealthily. We'll find a motel later, in Sherman.' He seemed about to get back into the car, but said, 'First, another short phone-call though.'

He stood outside, listening impatiently, until his line finally switched to *ansafone*. 'Hello. Tessa, is that you? Hope this call doesn't get you out of your bed. I'm busy with some important things right now and can't take long. We're all fine.' He hesitated for a moment. 'I wanted to tell you, it's time you came out here: you, and if possible, our lovely mutual friend, Ingrid. It'll be worth the visit, Tess. Things are coming to a head, and you both need to be here. Check the final weekend of May and go back at least a week. Book yourself some tickets and a car, and head for Hillcrest. I've gotta go now: *"The curfew tolls the knell of parting day..."*. A poem Bill Jackson got me to learn in my Sophomore Year. Anyway, I'll ring you again in a day or two. I'll explain all then. Sleep well.'

He concluded his hurried ansafone message, wondering why Tessa hadn't been there to answer in person. He hoped her telephone system would be able to cope. She'd get it in the morning, hopefully in a good mood. In some strange way, Mack seemed suddenly to have been gripped with the urgency that certainty can bring to a project; he'd glimpsed the outline of what now he understood was William's secret objective, and realised that delay, on his own part, could be fatal. William, he knew now, was secretly orchestrating nothing less than a grand finale, the jubilant bringing together of all the participants in what he conceived as his very own drama, a grand statement redolent with reconciliation and forgiveness, and perhaps, just perhaps, a cure for all his father's muddled ills. These were his *interlopers*.

They reached Texoma. No room for delay; they both had work to do. They predictably found the grave again, tucked away amidst the riotous growth of Spring, Sadie's sleeping place lay undisturbed throughout those twenty-five years when they'd last visited her. She'd slept soundly.

As Adam uncovered the remains and hurriedly dismantled the tiny skeleton, Mack went to the car and returned with the two sacks containing the bones from the Pueblo. As he lifted one of the sacks and prepared to empty the contents carelessly inside the now empty hole in the ground, Adam shouted, 'What are you doing for heaven's sake? Is that wise?'

Mack stopped and looked at him uncertainly. 'Maybe you're right. But I don't think we'll be needing these bones any longer.'

'What? After all that work up at the Pueblo?' Adam registered his astonishment.

'I know; I'm sorry. But, thinking about it more carefully, the bones in this sack, from the Pueblo, might be worthless to us anyway;

they'll probably have our own DNA all over them, and they could be the cause of endless delays, which we can't afford. I think we're going to have to rely on Sadie's bones to do our business. She won't let us down, and we'll arraign Hateley on that sole count.' He cast a glance at the gravel and rough brushwood surrounding them. 'Where can we get rid of these bones in the sack then?'

Adam said, 'Well, you can't just tip them into the empty hole. This grave's bound to get opened sooner or later. And anyway, you can't just desecrate Sadie's grave. It means something to us, doesn't it?' He was vehement, fully involved.

Mack stood there, holding the sack full of bones. 'You're right, Adam, but we need something to carry the bones in. And anyway, where am I going to put these?'

All their thought, all their planning, all their work of the past few days, seemed to have been thwarted by an unforeseen detail. They stood there, wracked by indecision

Finally, Adam said, 'Chuck them in the water, Mack. There's enough of it. I've an idea. Not far from here I know an ideal spot.' He looked up at Mack, standing over him with the sack. 'Trust me, my good friend, I know what I'm doing.'

Mack, for the first time in his life, felt helpless, almost paralysed. 'You'll have to make it quick, Adam. Time's of the essence.'

They set off with the bags through the undergrowth along the line of the lake and, miraculously, after a few minutes, reached a promontory where the edge juts out far into the water. Adam said firmly, 'Empty them here. Precisely at the edge here. They won't be lonely, believe me; this place - folklore has it among the inmates of Hillcrest School - bears the nick-name 'Deadman's Rock'.'

'I don't know how you know that, Adam, but it certainly looks a likely spot for our purposes.'

They tipped the bones into the Lake, and found their way back to the grave. Mack checked his watch. 'Barely fifteen minutes. That's okay. Let's cover over this spot and be off.'

They left the grave as they'd found it, and made their way towards Sherman, with Sadie's bones snugly in the remaining sack. Adam, slumped in his seat, said, half to himself, 'Now the 'dead man' will have a bit of real company at last.'

Mack was pacing up and down in the corridor of a motel in Sherman, hoping this unexpected in-coming call would have better connectivity than the recent one in the great outdoors at Texoma. Was it perhaps from the office in Hamburg? Or from Tessa? Or William? Time nowadays was of the essence, and he dreaded any unforeseen interference which might upset his careful planning.

It was the deep, throaty voice of Sam Toms. 'Hi, am I speaking with Mackintosh Neumann?'

'Sam, great to hear you!'

'How's your work been going, Mack? Are we getting any nearer to landing the big fish?'

Mack laughed. 'I assume, Sam, you don't mean the one Hemingway tried so hard to catch.'

'No, no, but every bit as slippery. Hateley'll do me fine. So where do we stand?'

'We've moved a giant step forward, I believe. We've captured his original DNA from one source, and from another, less reliable source, a possible match-up.

'How possible?'

'Let's say probable then.'

'Then let's move on Hateley. No delay. Listen; Police Chief Anderson's your man. Leroy Anderson; works out of Dallas and Houston, but you'll find him mainly in Dallas.'

'Can he handle DNA?'

'You mean analyse? Probably not, but he knows people who can.'

'Our case rests on it, Sam.' Mack's voice betrayed a note of concern. 'In the hands of a good prosecutor we....'

The interruption came back, firm and assured. 'The best, Mack. Don't worry. We'll have the best. Leroy has many strings to his bow. He's a popular man in the channels you and I move in.' There was an abrupt, sudden silence, leaving Mack cursing the inefficiency of the little piece of metal in his hand, and all those involved in the manufacture of it. After several anxious seconds however, Sam's reassuring voice came on the line again. Mack, I've told you, I'm committed to this business. I've got a couple of weeks leave and will shortly appear in your neck of the woods. I ascertain that, with Leroy's assistance, we should aim for trial in the early weeks of next month.'

Mack's heart leapt. *So soon.* 'So what do I do meanwhile?'

'I'm texting you, right this second, the number you can reach Leroy on, along with a password which will lead you direct into his confidence.' Another hesitation, while this time Mack gave all computer nerds, wherever they may be, his blessing for an uninterrupted phone-call, and Sam's voice continued, 'Meanwhile, you see you get your evidence validated, at all costs. Even if it means going to the ends of the earth. Bye for now. I'll be in touch.'

The line went permanently dead this time, and Leroy missed Mack's response: '*I've already been there.*'

A small buzz on the mobile, and there stood a phone number and a short password, which Mack, like the hero in the TV series '*Mission Impossible*' thought he'd better commit to memory before it sizzled and burst into flames.

*****

Mack had to drive to Houston to meet Leroy Anderson in person, leaving Adam to drive all the way back to his hide-out at Possum and close up the place there. In a difficult conversation, Mack had at last persuaded Adam that his occupation of the beautiful place by the lake was illicit, and that sooner or later his presence there would be discovered, which in turn would lead inevitably to embarrassing legal proceedings against him, plus the possible disappearance of his precious diary entries. As Mack pointed out, in no way could Adam, given his current situation, afford the possibility of lawyers crawling all over him asking importunate questions about his identity and legal status in the United States. 'At all costs be sensible, Adam, and lie low, as you've done for so long anyway. And above all, return in two days maximum to Denber to play your part in your son's Production. He's counting on you.' These had been Mack's final words as he watched his friend drive off into the West with an enigmatic smile on his face. Mack seriously wondered whether he would ever see this unstable character again.

However, he had work himself to do, and had begun to feel his days in Texas were coming to an end; whether they might be joyous or disastrous he couldn't honestly say. He was aware that, since his arrival in Texas, he'd been travelling down a long, narrowing tunnel, at the end of which stood a pin-point of light, which could either broaden into glorious day, or glimmer, fade and go out altogether. Two priorities vied endlessly now in his head, each clamouring for his attention: either to focus all his efforts on William's Play, and the consequent coming together of his friends, or to go after Hateley, now he at last had the chance, and bring that Gorgon-headed monster immediately to justice, leaving the promised grand reunion to look after itself. However, as he watched Adam's car disappear into the distance, he realised he'd done as much as any man could; the rest must be left to Providence. He'd given Sam his word, and he'd go to Houston, and keep his appointment there.

Leroy Anderson was a large, amiable black man, large in every way, not unlike Mack's imagined picture of Sam. Leroy had clearly been well-briefed by Sam and was impatient to get on with the business. He had a lot to say - a man used to being listened to - and a lot of important questions about the feasibility of the whole project..

'What have you got for us here, Mack, in this bag?'

'Bones.'

'Yeah, I can see. And whose are they?'

Mack experienced a slight trace of the frustration and impatience that had been building up in him over the past month. 'Didn't Sam explain to you, Leroy?'

'Yeah, but I want to hear it from you.'

'Okay. It's Sam's tale really, not mine. The bones are his mother's, discovered years ago by me and my friends, at a shallow grave at Lake Texoma - there's evidence in the local newspaper near Sherman to prove it - and subsequently dug up and placed in this bag a few nights ago by me and my friend. His mother, it seems, was murdered by a gang of white thugs. Indiscriminately, and for the fun of it.' He indicated the bag. 'These are her remains.'

With Leroy, there was little time for pauses. 'When was this?'

'We guess some sixty years ago. Somewhere around the late thirties.'

'Precisely, Mack. There's no room for guessing. You're a lawyer yourself. The devil's in the detail. You know that.'

'I do, but, as I said, it's Sam's story. He's alongside us in this enquiry, isn't he? He'll be able to tell us precisely. I thought perhaps we could just skate round the edges right now, so we know where we're heading, and leave the details to later. It's a very long story, and a lot of details. We need to get on fast with the business.'

'Okay. You call it. So this guy, Hateley, then a young fellow, had a hand in Sam's mother's death. Right?'

'Right.' Mack waited.

'What else have we got? The murder, perpetrated perhaps by one, perhaps by more than one...'

Mack interrupted....'Yes, but it's dubious we'll ever know those fellow-criminals or bring them to justice, but we know it was instigated by Hateley, and possibly carried out by him'

'How do we know?'

'Sam personally witnessed the crime.'

'So Sam's testimony will be critical in this. An eye-witness. Always works well in a murder case. But has to be handled carefully. Who will prosecute this business?'

The frustration nagged again at Mack. 'I thought you'd discussed that with Sam already.'

'Okay, probably him then. Could work. Right. What are we doing with these remains here?'

'In my opinion, most of our case will rest on our finding Hateley's DNA somewhere on these bones.'

Leroy pulled out a handkerchief and wiped his brow. 'A long shot. But yes, possible.'

'Have you got a process for all this, Leroy?' said Mack, handing the bag over to him. It's vital. Without this evidence, Hateley's going to be walking free with a smile on his face and a gun in his pocket. I don't want to be around in that event.'

Leroy nodded, grinning. 'Sure we have a process. I'm in touch with a laboratory here in Houston. They're expert, they're quick. If *I* ask, then they'll be quick at any rate.'

'How quick?'

'Couple of weeks or so.'

'Okay, let's suppose we *do* obtain the evidence and establish Hateley's DNA's on the bones, and we find a match....'

Leroy jumped in. 'You aint going to find Hateley's DNA on these bones, or on anything, if you don't already know what it looks like.'

Mack pulled out the prayer book from the Tabernacle. 'We know. Hateley's DNA will be crawling all over this little book here. I can guarantee that. Trust me.' He handed the book over to Leroy.

'Okay, seems like you guys have been doing a thorough job.'

Mack repeated, 'How long, Leroy? If we find the evidence, how long're we looking at for an indictment?'

Leroy hesitated. 'I gather from Sam this DNA isn't the only count we're attacking Hateley on. Isn't that right? Isn't there also an identity fraud question, and some matter of a nasty affair at a school somewhere upstate....'

'You're right, Leroy, but how long then? Needn't be specific. Roughly, I mean.'

'We're looking at several weeks, maybe months, to do a good job on this piece of shit in a court of law. We're going to need at least a couple more meetings between us three. I gather you're on leave from your work back in Europe.'

Mack nodded. 'What's your first step then, Leroy?'

'The bones, the DNA evidence. Let me take them with me, and this little holy book and we'll let you have a result on that in less than a week. Before you need to go back home at any rate. That's step one. Let's close this meeting now; shall we? I'll be in touch with you in a matter of days with the DNA testing.'

They shook hands, and Mack prepared to head for the airport. 'It's good of you to help in this case, Leroy. We're really thankful.'

'Sam's an old friend of mine; when he asks, I jump.'

'I'm sure you're very busy.'

'Darn right I'm busy. The felons in the state of Texas don't leave us in peace. They're quite inconsiderate.' He grinned. 'Talking of criminals, that reminds me: considering what Sam and yourself have told me, Mr. Hateley's already a man on the run. Isn't that right? We don't even need to build a case against him to arrest him. He's already outside the law. He's a wanted man. Let's think about that; we might just get to the point I like most in my line of work - that's arresting criminals - in just a day or two: Even without the DNA. Does anyone know his whereabouts?'

'We do, Sam; just let me know when you're ready to move on him. I'll lend a hand with the location.'

Mack left, driving off in a taxi in the direction of the shopping malls in downtown; he had a ring to buy, an expensive one

———

CHAPTER 26

Culmination

They hadn't experienced anything quite so novel and exciting at the 'New' Hillcrest, since its happy foundation in the wake of the disastrous events of '67. William's drama production was of a new kind altogether, including the vital ingredient of a 'narrator', guiding the audience through the story, while often interspersing his narration with the live enactment of a pertinent short 'Scene'. This innovation allowed the Director to cut the running time of a long play, and, more importantly still, vitally reduce the burden of line-learning on his young and inexperienced actors. With this unusual flexibility, William was able, on that beautiful evening in May 1994, to introduce, as well, some most unusual participants in the school performance.

Mrs. Doublejoy had been the first actively to notice the busy comings and goings, both out on the rehearsal stage and occasionally in the dining-hall, of various mysterious adult strangers, which had left her worried enough about security to mention the matter to her husband.

'Another body in the dining-hall tonight, Edward. Nice enough looking, but I certainly don't remember ever having set eyes on her. Seems like we're feeding the five thousand.'

The Headmaster, still concerned more about the success or failure of his precious end-of-year Production than about the unscheduled appearance of strangers on campus, replied, 'I'm sure, Dear, that, at this busy time of year, we can leave the vetting of personages in and around the school to William, particularly since any unknown face is almost certain to be involved in the Production; as you well know, parents often come from afar to get a preview of their little '*Jimmy*' spouting Shakespeare; and then there are always painters and carpenters from town lending final touches to the stage. Don't worry, Margaret, I'm sure William will have matters in hand. I just hope he's got the budget in hand too.'

'Even so, Edward,' replied his wife, 'we ourselves should still be informed about foreign bodies floating around the place, just as a matter of courtesy, not to mention the matter of Insurance. And besides, we have a duty of care.'

'You'll be eating your words in a couple of days, my Dear, when you're enjoying an exciting production of 'A Winter's Tale',' he paused for a moment, 'or should that be *'The* Winter's Tale'?' No one ever gets the title of that play right.

Despite her husband's flippant response to her concerns, Mrs. Doublejoy had nonetheless been alert and correct in noticing the presence of a number of unaccounted-for adults on campus. Several days prior to the performance, not just Tessa and Ingrid had arrived and been happily and hurriedly secreted in the Holiday Inn in town by William, but, in addition, Elizabeth, Tessa's American sister, and, quite improbably, Georges the Greek, that old Hamburg acquaintance of Mack's, who had joined the party, hoping, as he later explained, *'to do and sell a few existential portraits.'*

Mack, finally returning from Houston (and on William's request), had swiftly made it his business to secrete all these old friends at the Holiday Inn, where they'd no longer be observed on campus either by the Doublejoys, or, more importantly, by Sol/Adam, who'd (temporarily, it seems) taken up residence at Sherman. *'I want their presence to be a surprise'* William had tried to explain, and, what's more, had then persuaded all the new arrivals (even Georges, but with the exception of Adam), to *'take a very small and undemanding role in his Production. Very few lines to learn.'* And that's why Adam, sitting up, solitary, in the back row of the amphitheatre on the final Saturday in May, surrounded by parents and people from town, actually believes, as the performance gets underway, that he recognises, in person, the actress, the graceful woman, playing 'Queen *Hermione'*. *'But it can't be; how could it be?'*

As Doublejoy had predicted, The Play *was* remarkable. William, with his unique, instinctive flair for the 'different', had contrived to conjure nothing less than a subtle depiction of his very own family experience at W..., set however against a, fictional background, dreamed up by a master playwright of four hundred years past. It had originally been William's intention to include his father in the play, by offering him the main part (*King Leontes*), but unsure of Adam's unstable condition, had finally decided against this move, and had picked the best of his male students to take that leading role, that murderous, short-sighted, obsessive, neurotic 'King' villain. Thus, as the plot remorselessly unfolded before his eyes, Adam was left with the painful task of looking into a mirror and seeing himself. Yes, Sol is inadvertently condemned to sit up in the amphitheatre, the one he's for so long dominated, and to watch the folly of his own lonely life played out before him on stage.

The house-lights dim, the sizeable audience is hushed, and the Narrator, spot-lighted in fanciful doublet and hose, proclaims: '*Welcome to this strange tale of light and dark, of winter chill and happy summer.*' He strides, accompanied by the spotlight, across the stylish, chequered flooring. '*Behold, observe the royal palace of Leontes, King of ancient Sicilia, vibrant now with a royal visit from Polixenes, King of distant Bohemia, and in the company of a gentle gathering of lords and ladies ,all now happily basking in the regal presence of the two Kings. Ladies and Gentlemen, let our play take you there.*

Let us watch Leontes and his beautiful wife happily revelling in the adoration of their subjects. Joy compounds joy, until a cloud seems to steal unexpectedly over the gathering, as, all at once, we are witnesses to a scene as improbable and uniquely disturbing as ever in all Shakespeare: we observe this King 'Leontes' transform from white into black in one violent, unaccountable fit of jealousy, as he observes his wife's friendly, harmless banter in the garden with her royal guest. Through suspicious eyes, Leontes converts this dalliance into a flirting ritual. Believe me, ladies and gentlemen, not one of us here can find reasonable excuse or explanation for this fit of rage, on which our play turns. However, for a moment, I leave you, as the spotlight catches our King, in his hidey-hole, together with a courtier:
    (Leontes) "*Ha'not you seen, Camillo, My wife is slippery?*
If thou wilt confess (or else be impudently negative,
To have not eyes, nor ears, nor thought), then say

My wife's a hobby-horse, deserves a name
As rank as any flax-wench that puts to
Before her troth-plight; say't, and justify't".
Observe now how the servant, Camillo, is as shocked as anyone in the audience by this unjust outburst:
(Camillo) "I would not be a stander-by, to hear
My sovereign mistress clouded so, without
My present vengeance taken" ;
And yet, behold how the immovable Leontes sets his seal upon the unfolding tragedy:
(Leontes)"Is whispering nothing?
Is leaning cheek to cheek? Is meeting noses?
Kissing with inside lip? Horsing foot on foot?
Skulking in corners? Wishing clocks more swift?
Hours, minutes? Noon, midnight? Is this nothing?
Why then the world, and all that's in't, is nothing,
The covering sky is nothing, nor nothing have these nothings,
If this be nothing" !

(Up in the gallery now, solitary 'Sol' is witness to this unjust travesty, as he watches this noble, faithful Queen, bearing the King's child and already proud mother of a young boy-heir, betrayed by her husband on little more than a whim, a fancy, and is denied, in a trice, the simple, womanly pleasures of normal life, condemned to years of solitude, by a man who refuses to be father to his own children. Surely Sol, up there, isn't so muddled that he can't make the obvious connections: a tale parallel to his own cavalier behaviour of years ago).

The plot proceeds: Matters go from bad to worse for the Queen. Sentenced, together with her boy-child, to a life in jail for infidelity, and that unborn child already in her womb sentenced on pain of death, to be set, new-born, upon a rocky shore, at the mercy of what fate may bring:
<u>*(Leontes)*</u>*"We enjoin thee*
As thou art liege-man, that thou carry
This female bastard hence, and that thou bear't
To some remote and desert place, quite out
Of our dominions, and that there thou leave it

Redemption

*(Without more mercy) to its own protection
And favour of the climate".*

Meanwhile, dear audience, Queen Hermione, in despair, watches her young son, heir to the throne, fade away and die from grief. However, amongst the court, outraged voices are secretly raised, courtiers determined to bring reason into play and justice to their Queen. Swayed at last by the death of his heir, and the persistence of the court's unrest, the King is persuaded to place his earlier rash judgement into the hands of Great Apollo, fount of all wisdom. Before the whole court the King's guilt and the shining innocence of his once-wife is proclaimed by the Oracle:

(Officer proclaims) "Hermione is chaste, Polixenes blameless, Camillo, a true subject, Leontes a jealous tyrant, his innocent babe truly begotten; and the King shall live without an heir, if that which is lost be not found".

But, still worse, and pressing upon this earlier news, the Queen's fearless hand-maid, Paulina, arrives to announce to the court the death, from sheer grief, of her mistress, the Queen.

*(Paulina) "O Lords,
When I have said, cry 'Woe!'; the Queen, the Queen,
The sweetest, deasr'st creature's dead; and vengeance for 't
Not dropped down yet".*

Yes, dear gentles, too late, Leontes realises the terrible mistakes he's made, and retires to spend the rest of his days with an heirless throne and a life of loneliness, regret, and repentance.

*(Leontes) "Once a day, I'll visit the chapel where they lie,
And tears shed there will be my recreation".*

Our **Interval** *is reached, and not too soon to bring us, dear audience, blessed relief from the terrible ills that have befallen, one upon another, the Kingdom of Sicilia.*

Margaret Doublejoy, helping out in the dining-hall with refreshments for the audience, bumps into William, who's already taking much praise from all quarters for his 'original interpretation'.

'William,' she says, 'what a disturbing play you picked. Unadorned tragedy, isn't it? Edward and I don't happen to know the play that well.' She smiles impishly. 'I have to ask you; will things get better in Sicilia?'

William smiles. 'I'm glad you like it. Yes, it's certainly light and dark, isn't it? Except, of course, the other way around, so don't worry; although things don't improve in Sicilia, they certainly do in Bohemia. You'll see, the second half switch to Bohemia, full of light, laughter, dancing, simple country pleasures. But I mustn't spoil it for you.'

'Sounds so exciting. William, I've been meaning to ask: who is that person playing *Hermione*? She's very good.'

William smiles again. 'I'm ashamed; I've been meaning to mention to you for the past week, I've had some old friends and relations from Europe threatening to visit me here in Texas for so long, and now they've finally arrived; so I told them they'll have to earn their passage by taking a part in the play. That's Elizabeth, the sister of my mother, who's playing '*Hermione*'. She's very good, isn't she? And in the second part, you'll see *me* too, and a good friend of mine, Ingrid; then there's Mack, of course, who you already know, who plays the stern Polixenes; and - I almost forgot – there's my and Mack's old friend from Germany; he's here too; he's the one, poor bloke, who got killed by the Bear incidentally.' Margaret smiled at the thought of the farcical 'Bear' scene she'd just witnessed, and William continued, 'I'm really sorry to have sprung all these people on you; I should have explained earlier, but everything's been so hectic.'

'No matter, William; we love to have guests.' She hesitated. 'Could I be so bold as to ask if your mother's accompanying her sister?'

William had been afraid she might ask that question. 'I'm keeping the answer to that question, Margaret, under my hat.' He smiled and placed his index finger on the edge of his nose. 'Mum's the word. Is that all right?'

'Of course it's all right; as a matter of fact, it's more than all right. Listen, William. Edward and I've been thinking of having a little celebration to mark such a successful play and the end of a successful year. Why don't we all - that's your guests and a few of the students in the play - join us for dinner after the show this evening. It would be really lovely to meet all your friends, once you've got your make-up off, or whatever you actors do after shows, and then all come down the hill to our apartment. We'll commemorate '*A Winter's Tale*' with a slap-up feast.'

It was an invitation not to be declined. But Mrs. Doublejoy had yet one more question to ask. 'William, I'm certain I know that man sitting all on his own up in the Amphitheatre, watching the play. Is it really Sol Smith?'

William for a moment hesitated, thinking how best to put it. 'It is, Margaret. But don't worry; It'll be all right.'

Her voice lowered.' Yes, William, but is *he* all right?'

'Yes, I *mean* him; he's recovered. Back to normal. Have no fears. Amazing what a small break can do. So I invited him back to the school to watch the play.'

'That's wonderful. The poor man though; all on his own up there. Should I ask him to join us afterwards, perhaps?'

William tried to conceal his alarm. 'No, don't do that; he's fine; and 'A Winter's Tale' has yet another surprise to reveal to us all, including Sol. It'd be advisable not to rock the boat at this stage.'

She nodded, but said firmly, 'I understand, William. However, I really don't see why Sol shouldn't be involved. Please make sure he accompanies you to our party.'

'All right; if you say so, I will indeed.' William looked at his watch. 'I think I'd better get this second half on the road.'

She touched him gently on the arm. 'Don't forget, after the show; say 8 o'clock. Good luck, or perhaps I should say, 'Break a Leg'.'

The 'Narrator' steps onto the stage as the lights dim.

Welcome, guests, warmly back to our story and allow me, if you will, to be your guide for our exciting finale.

The little child-princess, left to die upon the rocky shore, doesn't die indeed, but is rescued by a shepherd and brought up as a shepherdess in beautiful Bohemia. As if by magic then, we jump 16 years, and Perdita, now in the happy Kingdom of Bohemia, is in love with the young prince, Florizel, son of King Polixenes and heir to the throne of Bohemia.

(Florizel speaks) *"But come, our dance, I pray;*
Your hand, my Perdita: so turtles pair,
That never meant to part."

To cut now a very long but happy story short, after much to-ing and fro-ing, the young couple find their way back to distant Sicilia, where the joyous reuniting of Perdita with her more than repentant father, Leontes, brings to both audience and actors a lump in the throat, The tale resembles indeed a fairy tale, and, but for the sad absence of the Queen, Hermione, all will indeed live happily ever after. However, nothing can bring the dead Queen back, and, as a commemoration to her memory, kings and courtiers alike, royal guests, both new and old, progress solemnly down to the temple, where Perdita and Florizel will be wed, and Perdita will at last 'find' her mother, if only a commemorative statue of her.

It goes without saying that, as this optimistic second half of the play warms up and joy, young love and rural happiness edge out the steely gloom of Sicilia, Mrs. Doublejoy, sitting with her husband and occasionally casting a glance behind her at the solitary figure in the back row, cannot resist getting up and softly finding a seat next to Sol. He, truth to tell, has been overcome by many of the events he is witnessing, but, above all, by the irremediable loss of *Hermione,* and the shadow that has cast on the scene. He is quietly sobbing, tears brimming over and hurriedly fought back.

'Sol, I do hope I'm not disturbing you; a little bird whispered in my ear that you were better. It's so lovely to see you back at Hillcrest.'

Sol, with difficulty, attempts to suppress his emotions. 'Hello, Margaret.' He pauses. 'It's such a moving experience, isn't it, the conclusion to this play? And all these half-familiar faces who keep appearing; who are they? William's been so clever, integrating them like this into the play. Some I seem to know, some I don't. Mack, and William himself of course, as *'Florizel';* however, his bride, *Perdita,* I've never seen her before. Isn't she pretty? I believe she may be German, from the accent. The genuine happiness of the two lovers, I have to confess, brings a lump into the throat. How on earth did William manage to cobble all this together and be *here* at one and the same time?'

'These 'strangers' you refer to are old friends of Mack and himself, he tells me.' She laughs. 'In *real* life, that is.'

'Are they?' Sol is speechless for a moment. 'Well, at least I know Elizabeth... the woman playing *Hermione*. I met her just once, years ago in Connecticut. 'She's actually the sister of a girl I once knew.' He attempts to sound casual, but his words produce momentarily a smothered sob, and he coughs elaborately. 'I'm sorry, Margaret, I'm quite overcome. I wonder if *she's* here too, that girl, I mean. She was a good actress herself once, believe me. And if Elizabeth's here, why not her sister too?'

Margaret looked hard at Sol. 'Well, in the interval, the Director told me there were still some surprises in store, at the very end of the scene. Perhaps she is indeed here, Sol. It's such an imaginative plot. I do hope these surprises will be nice ones.' She touches Sol gently on the shoulder and gets up. 'And don't forget; we're having a little party at our place afterwards; to which you're naturally invited. I'd better hurry down now and be with Edward for the conclusion. I think it's a clincher.'

Sol was about to ask what she meant, but she'd gone as swiftly as she'd come, and the play moves inexorably towards the grand *finale*, as *Leontes, Polixenes, Perdita, Florizel*, and the assembled court, process solemnly down to the temple (a large white curtain has been cleverly drawn across the grass alongside the amphitheatre) to behold the commemorative statue of the dead *Hermione*. Everyone, players and audience alike, watch spellbound now as *Paulina* draws back the curtain to reveal the perfect, more than life-like *Hermione*. There she sits, graceful and statuesque, but Sol is already on his feet as he strains to see for himself what perhaps he already knows in his heart: Yes, only he can see; the statue down there on the grass a few metres from him is not 'Elizabeth' at all;; it's her sister, Tessa, sitting as still as any statue.

A gentle murmur ripples through the assembled courtiers at the sight of their once adored Queen, and Sol, caught up in the action and thinking he too is witnessing a dead figure, is suddenly overcome by a string of uncontrollable emotions; far removed from just this theatrical moment, but of a whole life spent chasing empty dreams, impossible memories. He utters a great sob at the very moment that, from the players on stage, encircling the statue, comes a collective gasp, as *Hermione*, at *Paulina's* touch, rises from the stool and walks gracefully towards her daughter and son-in-law. A walking statue. A living '*Hermione*', concealed all this time, far from the precincts of the Palace, by Paulina, and played now, in real life, not by Elizabeth but by Tessa. It's of course just a clever dramatic contrivance, but, as the incontrovertible truth bears down on Sol, it's all too personal. Is it joy he feels, or grief? After all these years of silence, it's Tessa out there, and alive.

*****

It was William first out of the Green Room to visit Adam, still in the back edge of the Auditorium, watching the excited audience slowly filing out, as the applause subsides. He was standing alone, immersed in the shattering and all too personal theatrical events that had flashed past him in the last two hours: a child he'd never known, grown now to adulthood and marrying a stately girl; was that real or just fantasy? But most telling of all, the mother of this child of his, the lover he'd abandoned once upon a time, returning now, coming back from oblivion, alive and well. Adam was still unsure of what to make of what he'd seen; he was finding it difficult to separate fact from fiction. Nor did he remember quite where now he was meant to be for the remainder of the evening. Deeply confused.

William approached, slightly nervous and apprehensive, but so buoyed up by the success of the evening he was ready to carry all before him. 'Hi Father, is it all right to call you father, or Dad?' He gave one of his wide, open smiles which were always so hard to resist.

Adam was also ready with a smile, that of one in need of help and kindness. He was more than ready to accept and restore the reality of his former relationship, and secretly relieved that at least something might be salvaged from the desolation he found himself in. He looked William squarely in the face. 'Let's come clean, William, and put an end to the charade we've been playing. It's Adam, as you seem already to know anyway, not Sol, not the solitary Sol, but Adam Riley.' He hesitated for a moment. 'And that makes you William Riley, that is, if your mother will allow it.'

'Then okay, Dad; let's put Sol firmly to bed; let's shake on it and let bygones be bygones and let me introduce myself: your son, William.'

Adam smiled and shot out his hand, and they shook and seemed momentarily to achieve the miracle of reconciliation that had for so long eluded them. Adam said,. 'It was a masterful production of yours. No weak links, and all put together like a master craftsman.' He paused while William basked in the sunlight of praise and success from his father. Adam continued with a wistful smile, 'You know, at one point in the evening I almost thought you'd deliberately chosen this particular play to make a statement of some sort. That's not true, is it?'

William shook his head. 'Not really, just luck. And it *is* a particular favourite of mine, as you know. So probably just plain self-indulgence.'

'There's more to it than that, William.'

William shrugged. 'Not really. Come on; we can't just stand here all night; we'll turn into statues ourselves.' He smiled and then added, 'Locked forever in stone, and keeping watch over the Hillcrest amphitheatre for future generations. I think I prefer to join the others and get down to the party.'

As if in sympathy, the others were already processing down the series of wide steps which led to the Doublejoy's apartment. William watched his friends for a moment, and added, 'C'mon, Adam. Let's join the Immortals in Elysium.'

Twilight was coming, and the last rays of the setting sun were casting glimmers onto the now silent amphitheatre, as they caught up with Mack and Georges, accompanying the ladies through onto the patio, which lay adjacent to the main entrance to the apartment. That patio, still indelibly printed on Mack's memory. For just one moment, as he entered the large dining-room, table laid and full of the happy noise of the young students who'd been invited, Mack experienced an eerie reminder of another time, another occasion, fraught with horror and anxiety. It was the very same place where it had all happened so long ago. No, he hurriedly chased the memory away, consigned it to history, along with so much else. Hadn't they all moved on, he and his generation, from those ambivalent days of the Sixties, when the Assassination cast its long shadow, and emerging America still struggled to cast off the memory of a primeval, brutish war. Those days had been his adolescence and growing up, but, like so many of his generation, he'd grasped new, hopeful opportunities and turned his back on such suffocating memories, proclaiming now boldly to the world an end to indiscriminate violence, prejudice and despotism. It was a new world now, with new people in it, merely a few short years from a new millennium. *"The world lay all before them, theirs to choose and Providence their guide...."*

As Mack pushed forward into the room, he wondered if Adam too had been assailed by such debilitating reminders of those dreadful days. No, there he was, talking calmly to his son, William, choosing a seat to sit on, clearly enjoying the vigorous, vibrant chatter of the students, smiling and casting his eyes across the table where his freshly-discovered friends were taking their places and sipping their cocktails. It would, Mack thought, take something particularly fateful indeed to shatter the confidence he and Adam had built up over the past few weeks.

The Doublejoys had come in from the kitchen to greet them all, those two most, excellent, modest people, who'd taken over the little school in the dark days, and, by dint of hard work, reformed it and transformed it into an enlightened, successful enterprise.

The impatient buzz of his mobile, that symbol of the new world of his dreams, brought him back from his meditations. It was no use; he would have to answer it. Who could be ringing him at this time of night? He gestured across to Margaret, his hostess, and tapped gently on the appropriate button of the apparatus in his hand. She smiled across, and he headed out, back to the patio, to take the call.

It was Police Chief, Leroy Anderson. 'Hello. Is that Mack Neumann I'm talking to?'

'It is.'

'Give us the pass.'

Mack repeated the word they'd arranged as security for such conversations. Dropping his alert tone, Leroy proclaimed four short words. 'We've got him, Mack.'

'Got him?'

'We've got that felon, remember? Not forgotten him already, have you? Hateley, Charles Hateley, going under the name of hell knows what, Kilman, I believe. He came like a lamb.'

After a short pause, Mack replied, 'No, I haven't forgotten him. Believe me; I could never forget that guy. That's great news, Leroy. How did you do it? Where?'

Mack was finding it difficult to wrench himself back from what seemed almost another world away. He continued, 'I've been busy with other things. Just haven't had the time. But how did you do it?'

'Walked into that seedy bar near the football ground; took him by surprise. Along with all his sympathisers.'

'You mean, you took them in too?'

'No, no. Just the big cheese.'

Mack, along with all the other things on his mind in the past few weeks, was finding it almost impossible to believe that Charles Hateley was now sitting in a gaol somewhere in Dallas. He was desperate to establish they'd got the right man, that slippery, red-bearded eel in person. 'But how did you know where to go?'

'Rheinischer Hof. Can't be many places by that name in Dallas.'

'How did you know to recognise him, Leroy?'

'You told me, remember? Big old guy with a red beard, surrounded by a string of lousy little woodlice.'

Mack laughed. 'I like your imagery. But listen, forgive my hesitancy. There must be any number of guys in Dallas with red beards.'

Leroy was starting to sound impatient. 'We did a missing persons check. A thorough one, before we went anywhere near the place. And sure enough, there it was, on the list: Charles Hateley; wanted for serious crimes committed in Texas, going back forty odd years.'

There was silence down the phone for a moment before Mack asked, 'Bit of a gamble, wasn't it? He can't be the only guy in Dallas with a red beard. How could you be certain sure he was your man.?'

'You told me, remember? I trusted your judgement. Sure it was a gamble. We called the guy's bluff. He didn't deny it, went clean as a whistle when I confronted him and his confederates with three other officers, all larger than me.'

Mack's legal mind, distracted by the excited noise of the party inside, was trying hard to process accurately the information Leroy was giving him. Not many lawyers in the world would take chances like that, and there could be no room for disastrous error. 'When you got him back to the station, how did you establish the guy you'd arrested was indeed Hateley?'

Brief pause before Leroy came back on the line. 'There was a match, Mack. Remember? That little prayer-book? We already had a template of Hateley's DNA. We asked him politely if he'd be so good as to give us a sample of his sputum. I think that's the word.. As said, he went like a lamb.'

'Sounds water-tight, Leroy. I suppose you have to take chances every now and then. Bluff and chances. That's life. I can't thank you enough, Leroy. Keep him under lock and key. He's slippery. Listen. I'm real busy right now, I won't go into details, but I'm about to undertake the most difficult task that's ever come my way in life.'

Leroy chuckled. 'You mean there're other Redbeards around, Mack? You're a busy man. Good luck, my friend. Don't you worry about Redbeard. He'll sit behind bars twiddling his fingers for as long as it takes to arraign him and put him on the stand to answer for his misdemeanours. That simple.'

'Leroy, you've done amazing work. I'll call you; maybe in a day or two, maybe sometime longer. But you can count on it. I'll call you. It's part of my life's work putting Hateley on the Stand.'

'I get your message, Mack. You done a good job too. And good luck with that undertaking you told me about. Hope she's worth it.' The line went dead.

When Mack reappeared in the dining-hall, basking in the news he'd jut received, and, in addition, vaguely wondering how the Police Chief had guessed he was involved in 'women' matters, the Head, Edward Doublejoy, had already been on his feet to deliver the customary congratulatory speech to those present who'd taken part in the Play Production. All but the two most senior students had by then been ushered back into the general school program by Mrs. Doublejoy, ever vigilant and firm in the belief that a rigid time-table lay at the heart of any well-run school. The adults at last had the place to themselves and were free to enjoy a good dinner. Mack cast a quick, somewhat anxious glance over towards where Adam was sitting, talking now happily with his new-found son, and seeming no longer like an unusual creature in the menagerie, to be handled with care. For the first time since he'd arrived in this heady environment of Hillcrest, he recognised the old Adam Riley, in gestures and expressions, a teacher, relaxed and at home in any situation. He went across and sat down beside him and said quietly, 'They've arrested Hateley.'

As Adam for a moment sat grappling with this news, Mrs. Doublejoy called from across the room, 'Ah, Mack, I thought you were going to miss all the ceremony, you and your mobile phone.' She scolded gently, and added, 'More importantly though, miss the food my culinary husband has prepared for us.'

'I'm really sorry, Margaret. I hate people who break off conversations just to answer a mobile. It's really not my style. Please forgive me. ' He paused a second. 'The only thing I can say in my defence is that it was an important business call, from the police, and I suppose you could say, concerns the school, this very school.'

'Then you must tell us, Mack. But later. You know, with all your important comings and goings, you've always secretly reminded me of one of those puppet manipulators at Punch and Judy shows, those back-room people who hold all the strings.'

'I'm not sure I like being cast as a manipulator, Margaret,.' There was general laughter as Mack paused. 'Aren't they usually villains, those sorts?'

'No, of course not. I mean in the best possible way, bringing everything together for the good in the end. 'Impresario' is more the word, surely.'

Hayden, one of the two remaining Seniors in the room, remarked timidly, 'Like that character in the Play today.'

'That's very observant of you, Hayden,' said Mrs. Doublejoy. 'Well done. Yes, things did seem to come happily together in the end, didn't they?' She threw the remark out to all and sundry. '

'Yes', said Elizabeth, sitting over by Tessa. 'But who is the manipulator, in that case, Hayden?.

The conversation had taken an unusual turn, and the amazing news Mack had been about to announce seemed to have been temporarily forgotten. Silence ensued while everyone sought an answer to Elizabeth's random question. At last the answer came from an unexpected source. 'There was no *one* manipulator in *A Winter's Tale*, unless it be Shakespeare himself.' The remark was delivered starkly and concisely by Georges, the Greek, who'd said nothing much since his arrival at Hillcrest several days ago. 'If you've got to have a 'manipulator', it's got to imply a god; or else someone like God, who's telling the story.'

'Don't let's get on to Religion, Georges,' said Mack flippantly, unable to resist confronting his old friend from the Mensa.

'Quite the opposite. This wonderful 'tale' we watched today involves everybody, not only God but people too, working together to create *the best of all possible worlds*.' He paused a moment. 'It's nothing less than our duty in the new 'Enlightenment'.'

However, it was Ingrid finally who had the last word, as she so often had in those days at the Mensa. 'It certainly *sounds* like religion, Georges. And I always thought you were a denier. A non-believer.'

Georges, eyeing her with an alert and scornful expression, replied enigmatically,. 'Not Religion, Ingrid. It's Existence.'

Nobody knew exactly what Georges' reply meant, and Mr. Doublejoy, beginning to realise his and his wife's agenda for the evening was threatening to become lost in philosophical and theoretical argument, tapped lightly with his spoon on a plate beside him. 'It's such a pleasure for us humble teachers (he indicated his wife) to be, for once, in the company of such learnéd, academic discussion; however, "*at my back I always hear Time's Wingéd chariot hurrying near*" '.There was a murmur of approval at Doublejoy's pertinent reference, and he continued, 'So I think we should bring our discussion down from the lofty heights to the here and now.'

Another murmur of approval, and the speaker looked across to William, sitting alongside Mack and Adam. 'I believe that William, our *raison d'être* for this evening, has a small announcement to make.' There was the trace of a secretive smile on Doublejoy's face as he beckoned William over, to deliver his 'announcement'.

William had meanwhile stood up and casually joined the three women guests sitting together by Margaret Doublejoy. His 'announcement' was brief and happy. 'Ingrid and I,' he placed his hand gently on Ingrid's shoulder, 'have become engaged.' He smiled, 'I think that's the correct expression.'

'Of course it is, William.' Margaret Doublejoy was also on her feet, and they were all applauding delightedly. 'We're so happy for you, William. And, forgive me - I have to say it - perhaps it means we'll have the pleasure of enjoying your fiancée's wonderful company here at Hillcrest for a while longer.'

Another round of smiles and clapping, and William confessing, 'I let her go once but I got a second chance. I won't make the same mistake twice.' A burst of applause, and the two of them looked into each other's face with joy.

In retrospect, and in the wake of the dire ensuing events, Mack stated later that although Adam had seemed to be contributing enthusiastically to all these happy exchanges, an unexpected look of concern had slowly begun to darken his expression during those few minutes that William was making his 'announcement', and Adam's whole involvement had increasingly become mechanical rather than spontaneous. His entire demeanour had changed. Something was disturbing him.

Ingrid was by now replying to Margaret Doublejoy's earlier remark. 'I'd love to, Margaret, but I've not really been trained as a teacher and I don't think my English would allow me to teach your students anything other than German.'

'Then we must place German on our academic schedule,' chimed in Edward Doublejoy. 'We could do with another foreign language, and French is so damnably difficult. We're not bound, as I think you are in Europe, to any rigid academic guidelines, and Hillcrest has a long tradition of innovative courses of study. We play it off the cuff.'

This remark received enthusiastic applause and, as it died down, Ingrid replied gracefully, 'I've already noticed, in the short time I've been here, how eager and grateful - if that's the right word - your students seem to be for their studies.'

'It is indeed the right word, Ingrid' said Doublejoy. We encourage curiosity in our students and leave them a wide choice of courses; there's very little compulsion.'

'I think I understand, Edward. I'm glad to say, I already found it not difficult to establish a mature relationship with some of your Seniors.

They're very grown-up and don't seem stifled by the academics.' She paused a minute. 'But I confess, William and I have hardly had a moment to think what our future plans should be. Unfortunately, I believe I might have to return to Europe before long to look after my ageing mother. Perhaps, now the vacation has started, William and I can travel, and see a bit of your wonderful country. And then of course there's always a wedding to think about.'

Margaret interrupted. 'Get married here, Darling. There's always the Country Club, or even the school campus, to take care of such an event.'

'That's very kind of you. That's at least one hurdle crossed.' She glanced happily at William, 'My fiancé and I can perhaps get down now to making a few plans for the future.'

The party continued and, as is usually the case in such events, the wine continued subtly to flow too. Mack was talking earnestly with Adam about the arrest of Hateley and, of course, even enlisting his help, should matters eventually come to trial. The fact was, Adam obviously would be a more than important witness. Over among the ladies, Tessa and her sister and Ingrid were eagerly pursuing an already firm friendship and on one occasion Tessa crossed the room, took Adam's hand and bent to kiss him on the cheek. Adam couldn't conceal a look of delight, perhaps relief too, as Tessa attempted to seal a new friendship with her old partner, and, express perhaps the willingness to let the past remain in the past.

The lights dimmed suddenly, as Doublejoy, by the turn of a switch, produced an ambiance in the room to accompany the gentle, relaxed conversation among friends. Desert was produced, home-baked Pecan Pie, and an air of well-being settled on the gathering.

All at once, Margaret Doublejoy was on her feet again. 'Before our party concludes, we have yet another short ceremony.' She looked now across the room at Mack, sitting with Adam. 'Isn't that right, Mack?'

Among the replete and contented guests, it was hard to imagine what further ceremonies awaited them. Mack, however, already knew, and had risen, somewhat half-heartedly, certainly nervously, to his feet, as Margaret continued to fix her gaze on him. 'You'd better stand by me over here, Mack. I think I have something in my pocket for you, here in safe-keeping. You might need it shortly.' There was a coaxing smile on her face. 'Let's do things properly.'

She produced from a pocket in her dress a very small velvet-covered box, and as she held it up for all to see, she explained to her guests, 'Mack asked me to take care of something precious for him before he went on stage this evening to perform.' She smiled and paused for a moment. 'Perform so professionally too, I might add.' Gentle applause, even laughter, from everybody, who, by the silence in the room, seemed genuinely surprised by this impromptu ceremony

At that same moment, Mack, the master impresario, on his way across the room to propose marriage to the girl of his dreams, sensed something wasn't right, wasn't in place. However, his own imminent involvement, right there and then, in the ceremony, compelled him to continue, and say nothing. Margaret handed him the little box, and Mack, making a gallant bow and casting a hurried glance across the room, at Tessa, declared,. 'I suppose this terrifying moment comes at some stage to most men in their life, but why should it be so frightening? Let me explain then. Just once in a lifetime a man has to place himself at the mercy of a woman he cannot do without.' He paused and looked across again towards the group of ladies. 'Well, it seems that moment has come for me.'

Loud laughter followed this remark from those assembled, and the ladies looked at one another, apparently perplexed. Meanwhile Mack continued, 'So, I'm compelled to surrender my life momentarily to the mercies of this beautiful, generous, clever, and many other virtues...' He'd taken a step across towards the women while at the same time opening the box and holding up a ring.

Since the moment William had made his own earlier joyous announcement, and Mack had gone across and accepted the ring from Margaret Doublejoy, it was apparent, in retrospect, that nobody had been watching Adam. If they had been, they would have seen the first signs of his very evident distress. His face was contorted and anxiety spilled from his eyes. At the very same moment that Mack made his way with the little box towards the ladies, all those in the room became aware of a noise, a distant humming, the noise as of someone or some creature in increasing distress, and apparently standing on the brink of some disaster, but not daring to peer over the edge. The sound grew now by the second until it became nothing short of a roar, and in the wake of that horrific noise, it was Mack, who, coming first to his senses abruptly changed direction and hurried, not towards the lady of his life, but over to Adam, who was now silently staring and pointing, as if hypnotised, at Margaret Doublejoy, in his direct line of fire. 'That woman! that woman! Get her out of here. She must not be allowed....' The rest was muffled, hidden inside an incomprehensible gasp, and his finger still pointing towards where she'd stood, but moving slowly across in the direction of her husband....'

Mack grasped at once the situation, and, bending down, reached out his arms towards Adam. 'It's not you he's seeing, Margaret, it's someone else. From long ago. His mind's pictures are distorted; it's not the here and now they're portraying, but another time and another place. I remember, it was Charlene who lifted the goblet and chucked in the ruby. Seated just there, in front. Where you are.' He pointed abruptly at Adam. 'I'll never forget that moment, but *he* had to bear the brunt. Look,. For him, it's a replica image.' Adam was now moaning, incoherent words issuing from his mouth 'Stop time, stop the world spinning...but I cannot bear to face this moment...it's happening again...I knew it would.'

Mack reached out and took him in his arms, lifted him from his seat and led him slowly out onto the patio, that place where it had all concluded long ago. A terrible shout arose at that moment from Adam's throat. 'It was *here*, Mack, the very spot; *Help me*....'

Mack sat him onto one of the chairs, and hurried back into the room, where people, still unsure whether to move or what to say, were sitting aghast. He looked at Margaret Doublejoy. 'Margaret, he'll be all right now; it's not you he's remembering....' Momentarily lost for words, he sought to pull himself together, realising only *he* could make sense of this moment.' He flung his arm out towards Adam. 'He died there, you see... out there on the terrace.... He knew this moment was approaching... he predicted it...*one final giant 'wave'*... that's what he said to me; those precise words.'

Margaret said, 'What must we do, Mack?'

'Get him to somewhere else, at all costs away from there. Help me lead him to a bed.'

Margaret crossed the room quickly and the two of them, with the help of Edward Doublejoy, led him gently away from the apartment and out into the night.

It was several minutes before the three of them reappeared. Margaret said to everyone. 'It's all right; he's calmer now. We left him comfortable, in his old room on campus. He seemed to recognise his surroundings.. I'm sure he'll nod off and be all right in the morning.'

She did her best to smile, and her husband got to his feet. 'Right, I think, in the light of these recent events, we should conclude the evening's festivities; postpone them for another day. Thank you all for coming, and I would ask you not to allow the difficulties we've just witnessed to discolour what has been a jubilant end-of-term. Mr. Smith is just unwell, but he'll recover.' He paused. 'We don't, after all, want *our* memories of this happy occasion to be blemished too.'

Mack and Tessa of course were the only ones in the room who could make any sense at all of the sequence of events they'd just witnessed, nor the Head's rather unfortunate, ironic reference to 'memory', and, followed by the others, they soberly left the room and headed for their various places of rest.

Mrs. Doublejoy joined Mack early next morning and they made their way to Adam's quarters. The room was empty, nor was he subsequently to be found anywhere on campus. Mr. Doublejoy later organised a search within the locality of the school without result, and after several days it became apparent Sol/Adam had vanished, and those present the previous evening began to wonder if they would ever set eyes on him again. His disappearance seemed so final and absolute.

(THE END)

Milton Keynes UK
Ingram Content Group UK Ltd.
UKHW021033090524
442331UK00006B/80

Lit

Jesus
teaches

illustrated by Gordon Stowell

Jesus told many stories about how we should help others. One of the best is about the Good Samaritan. "What shall I do?" said someone who was listening to Jesus one day.

"Love God with all your heart, and love your neighbour as yourself," replied Jesus. "But who is my neighbour?" asked the man.

Jesus then told the people a story about a man who was on a journey from Jerusalem to Jericho.

He had to travel through some very dangerous places.

In a lonely spot, up in the rocky hills, he was attacked by cruel thieves.

They hurt him badly and robbed him. He was left lying on the hard ground almost dead.

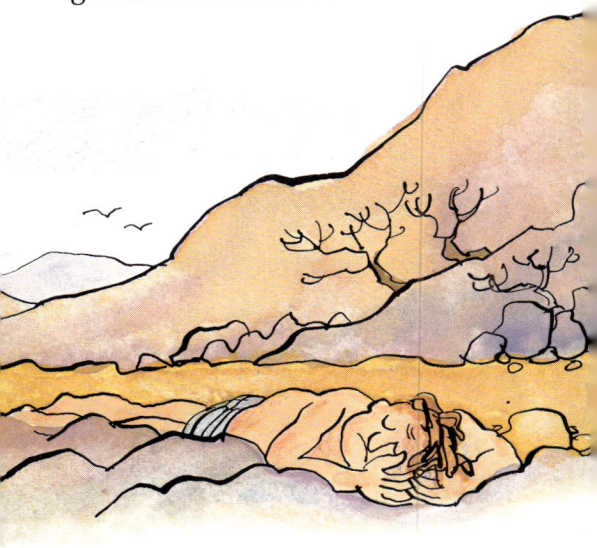

Soon a priest came by, but he did not try to help the man at all. He passed by on the other side of the road.

Then another man came along,
but he passed by as well.
He was not going to help.

Finally a Samaritan man came along. He was a long way from his home town Samaria.

He hurried over to the hurt man. He bathed his wounds. He bandaged him up and put him carefully on his own donkey.

Then he took him along to an inn and looked after him there.

"I have to go now," he told the landlord. "But here is some money for you to look after this man. When I come back I will pay you whatever extra it has cost."

"Who was the good neighbour?" asked Jesus. "Why, the one who looked after the hurt man," came the reply.

"You go and do the same," said Jesus. "Help those who need help, no matter who they are."

The story of the Good Samaritan is in Luke chapter 10, verses 25–37.

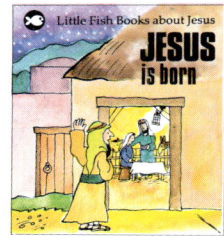
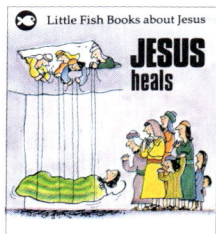
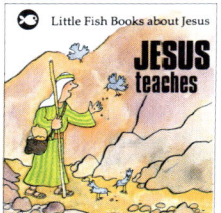
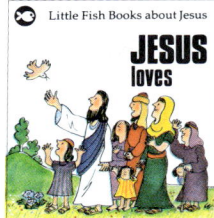
 Little Fish Book